SWORDS
AROUND THE
THRONE

IAN ROSS

HEAD
of ZEUS

First published in the UK in 2015 by Head of Zeus Ltd
This paperback edition first published in 2018 by Head of Zeus Ltd

9 7 5 3 1 2 4 6 8

A CIP catalogue record for this book is available
from the British Library.

ISBN (PB): 9781788542746
ISBN (E): 97811784081157

Typeset by Ben Cracknell Studios, Norwich

Printed and bound in Germany by CPI Books GmbH

Head of Zeus Ltd
First Floor East
5–8 Hardwick Street
London EC1R 4RG

WWW.HEADOFZEUS.COM

*Te uero, Constantine, quantumlibet oderint hostes,
dum perhorrescant. . . Cautior licet sit qui deuinctos
habet uenia perduelles, fortior tamen est qui calcat
iratos.*

But let our enemies hate you as much as they please,
Constantine, provided that they are in terror of you. . .
Certainly to keep one's foes bound by pardon is more
prudent, but it is more courageous to trample them
down in their fury.

Panegyrici Latini VI

*Qui insultaverant deo, iacent, qui templum sanctum
everterant, ruina maiore ceciderunt, qui iustos
excarnificaverunt, caelestibus plagis et cruciatibus
meritis nocentes animas profuderunt.*

They who insulted God are laid low; they who cast
down the holy temple are fallen with greater ruin; and
those who tormented the just have poured out their
evil souls amidst punishments inflicted by Heaven,
and amidst deserved tortures.

Lactantius, *De mortibus persecutorum*
(On the Deaths of the Persecutors)

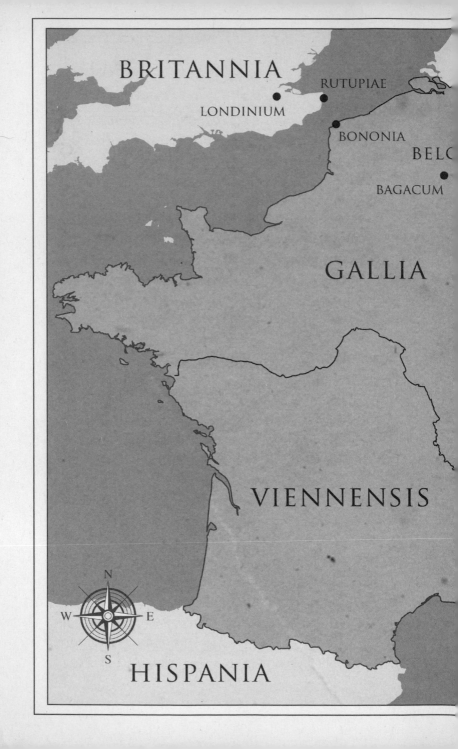

ROMAN GAUL
A.D. 308

FRANKS

BRUCTERI

CA

COLONIA
AGRIPPINA

TREVERIS

ALAMANNI

RAETIA

UGDUNUM

MASSILIA

Sea Gate

Valley
Gate

VALLEY

Temple of
Apollo

Temple of
Artemis

Rome Gate

CULARO

Agora

Theatre

Palace

DOCKS

ARELATE

HARBOUR

MASSILIA

ITALIA

HISTORICAL NOTE

In AD 305, the emperor Diocletian stunned the world by abdicating after a reign of twenty years. He left the Roman Empire ruled by the system he had created, later known as the Tetrarchy: two senior and two junior emperors sharing power between them.

The following year, Constantius, the new senior emperor of the west, died while on campaign in Britain. His troops, in defiance of the protocols of imperial succession, elevated his son Constantine to rule in his place. Galerius, senior emperor of the east, was forced to recognise the usurper, while still supporting his own appointees Flavius Severus and Maximinus Daza.

Only a few months later, in the city of Rome, Maxentius, son of the former emperor Maximian, seized power with the support of the ancient Senate and the Praetorian Guard. His father soon emerged from retirement to rule Italy at his side.

By AD 307, there are six emperors in power, ruling a divided Roman world. Each builds his power base, secures his frontiers and prepares his troops.

All know that the future holds nothing but confrontation.

PROLOGUE

Treveris, April AD *307*

I t was the hour of the beast hunts. Across the oval of bright sand, four long-horned bulls from southern Gaul charged and veered, as a pair of men on horseback and two more on foot lunged with spears and javelins. Above them, the amphitheatre rose in tier upon tier of seats, and the voices and laughter of twenty thousand spectators merged into a low steady drone. The bulls were wounded; the sand was scarred and streaked with red, and the rich stink of animal sweat and fresh blood reached the spectators. But many of them paid only partial attention to what was happening. This was not the main attraction of the day, after all.

For now, men hunted beasts. Soon, beasts would be hunting men.

A little below and to the left of the imperial podium, an unremarkable-looking middle-aged man sat alone in the crowd. He was dressed plainly, and wore no ornament besides the red leather belt that marked him as one of the emperor's functionaries. His bland face showed no expression; his greying brown hair was styled in an ugly and unfashionable bowl cut. For all of his power, and his growing reputation in the imperial offices, Julius Nigrinus, Tribune of Notaries, was still a forgettable figure, and deliberately so.

He had chosen his position well; it was a good place to speak without being heard. But even so, he did not turn to the man beside him as they talked. Both sat casually, as if enthralled by the violent drama of the bull hunt, and to a nearby observer they would not have appeared to be talking at all.

'Was our source forthcoming as usual?' Nigrinus asked.

'Oh, yes,' the other man said, twitching a smile. He had a greasy sheen to his face, and his hair was slickly oiled. His fingers were chunky with cheap rings, and his short cloak was secured with an enamelled brooch portraying a lion mauling a fallen captive. He rubbed his fingers together. The rings glittered. 'He has an expensive mistress to support!'

Nigrinus tightened his lips. This man, Flaccianus, was distasteful to him. So, by the sound of it, was his source in that morning's private meeting of the imperial *consistorium*. Weak men, Nigrinus thought, with their ungovernable vices.

'So? What does he have to report?'

'A *proposal* has come from Rome,' Flaccianus said, rolling the words around in his mouth. His eyes flickered between the bull hunt and Nigrinus's shoulder. 'An offer of marriage, between the sister of the usurper and our own Augustus, Constantine. A marriage alliance, in other words. Us and them against Galerius and his people. West versus east.'

'This is Maximian's daughter, Fausta? She's of marriageable age?'

'Oh, yes. Fourteen or so,' Flaccianus said, in an artfully strangled whisper. 'But the strange thing is that I *did* think our Augustus was already married. . .'

'Did you?' Nigrinus replied, no trace of warmth in his voice. 'Apparently you were mistaken. And *if* you thought such a thing you had best *unthink* it. Such a suggestion could soon become dangerously undiplomatic.'

4

Flaccianus shifted in his seat and let out a slow chuckle. It was unconvincing; Nigrinus could tell that his warning had struck home.

'What of the emperor's opinion?' he said. 'Is it known?'

Flaccianus sucked in his greasy cheeks, then shook his head. 'Our source could report nothing,' he said. 'He's only a *silentiarius*, after all, a mere court usher. . .'

'He takes my money all the same. Next time, tell him I want everything. He'll be well paid.'

'And what do I get out of the arrangement?'

'You are an officer of the *agentes in rebus*,' Nigrinus said blankly. 'Providing information is your job.'

'Yes. But not to you, *brother*.' Flaccianus yawned, long and insolent. 'I don't know who you're working for, do I?' He stood up. 'You must excuse me, I need to piss.'

Nigrinus watched the other man as he bobbed his way down the steps to the lavatories. It galled him having to do business with a man like Flaccianus, but if he wanted inside information, he had to use lateral channels, however distasteful.

Everyone has a flaw, everyone a weakness. Learn their weakness and you might turn them to your purpose. Such had always been Nigrinus's maxim, and it had served him well so far. Flaccianus, for example, had certain sexual tastes which Nigrinus found despicable, but they at least made him a malleable informer.

Down in the arena the last of the bulls was on its knees, blowing bloody froth. The stalls were full of motion now, people shifting from seat to seat, vendors moving between them with baskets of hot nuts and flasks of iced water. High at the rim of the amphitheatre, pump-nozzles emitted hazy gusts of perfume. From somewhere came the sonorous drone of a water organ.

Turning in his seat, Nigrinus gazed up towards the imperial podium. He could just make out the figure of the emperor in the blueish shade beneath the white and gold canopy. The podium was ringed with a cordon of bodyguards, white-uniformed men of the Corps of Protectores. They wore no armour, but carried their swords openly, forbidding anyone to trespass on the sacred imperial precinct. Constantine sat tall and erect on his folding stool, his gold-embroidered robe falling stiffly from his shoulders, his heavy-boned face blank and grave. Already he had perfected the statue-like immobility and calm that people expected of their emperors. Only thirty-three, and already ruler of a quarter of the Roman world.

Nigrinus himself was proud to have played a small part in that success: the operation he had directed in northern Britain two years before had been vital in getting Constantine posted to join his father's field army, who then acclaimed the son on the father's death. An effective operation indeed, although at one point it had looked dangerously close to unravelling: some idiot of a centurion stumbling back across the frontier with stories of treason and conspiracy. Nigrinus had managed to hold that problem down; he had not even been forced to kill the centurion. Such people can have their uses, after all.

Everyone has a flaw, everyone a weakness.

But what, he thought, of the emperor's council, the senior ministers of the consistorium, the military commanders and the eunuchs? All of them had their ambitions, their schemes and alliances. All their secret vices, their closely held treacheries, their closet corruptions. And Nigrinus made it his business to discover as much of what these men concealed as he could. Such knowledge was a tool; it was also a defence.

A sudden brassy surge of trumpets broke into Nigrinus's thoughts, and he turned his attention back to the arena. The dead bulls were being hauled away by gangs of slaves with ropes and chains, while other slaves heaped fresh sand to cover the slick of blood. Meanwhile, on the balcony above the northern gateway, a rotund figure in a blinding white ceremonial toga was commencing an oration. The crowd, hushed momentarily by the trumpets, soon resumed their mumbling. Nigrinus put one finger in his ear and tried to concentrate on what the orator was saying.

'... *O great and heaven-sent Augustus, on this day that we celebrate the birth of Rome, the Eternal City, Mistress of Nations, we praise you for restoring to us the divine peace and prosperity of our lands!*'

Nigrinus snatched a quick glance back at the imperial podium: Constantine still sat stiff and motionless, staring forward. What was he thinking? Was he even listening? Around him his advisors and eunuchs lolled, some of them whispering together.

'*For is it not so that in the days of your father, the deified Constantius, the Kings of the Franks gave oaths that their people would never again trouble the serenity of our empire?*'

A stir ran through the crowd: at the centre of the arena floor a dark opening had appeared. Sand sifted down into the void below. The noise in the stalls died away once more into an expectant hush, broken by a vast collective hiss and yell as the platform was winched up from the arena cellars.

'*And is it not so, most Divine Intelligence, that as soon as the dire news of your father's illness and demise crossed the narrow seas, these same savage men, these men ungovernable by honour, broke their promises of peace and once again bared their savage jaws against our kin?*'

Between twenty or thirty prisoners stood huddled on the platform, Nigrinus guessed; all that remained of the Frankish war parties that had crossed the Rhine the previous winter. They were naked, their bodies pale, starved-looking and covered in bloody welts and bruises. For the last three months they had been kept in the darkness of a dungeon, only to be flung into this blaze of light and noise, this roaring oval of thousands of hateful eyes and mouths.

The voice of the orator was almost drowned by the yelling.

'O greatest of emperors, then you came to our aid, falling like a comet from the western sky and destroying their warlike bands! And now, O great one, allow us to see and admire the terror of justice falling upon those same barbarians!'

From the dark gates in the wall, snarling wolves were being herded out onto the sand by men with whips and tridents, scores of them loping and ranging around the margins of the arena like grey smoke. The prisoners were still clustered on the platform at the centre of the oval: a couple were kneeling, awaiting their fate, while others stood locked in terror, cupping their genitals; Nigrinus noticed that they had been chained together in pairs by the neck.

A cry went up from the crowd: one shackled pair of prisoners had made a stumbling bolt for the wooden barriers that ringed the arena. The nearest wolf, attracted by the movement, leaped towards them. Others followed at once; then the whole pack was in motion. Nigrinus made a sound between his teeth.

As soon as the first two men went down the rest scattered, fleeing clumsily in all directions, hampered by their neck-chains. The wolves loped in amongst them, yelping and frenzied, and the killing became rapid and bloody. Nigrinus saw one beast tear out a man's throat with a single flying lunge; another pair brought a running fugitive to the ground, clawing at his arms and chest. Blood sprayed and spattered on the sand.

Nigrinus could clearly make out the sound of cracking bones and rending flesh. He could smell the hot blood, the reek of offal and faeces, the sickening taint of death in the air. He felt his guts tighten, and glanced away. He had no qualms about the idea of death, mutilation and extreme violence, but still felt an instinctive squeamishness about having to watch it. It was childish, he knew, quite unmanly. He forced himself to raise his eyes and watch, dispassionately, as the men died on the sand. The arena is a stern teacher, he told himself.

There was a presence at his side; he thought it was Flaccianus returning, but instead another man was leaning from the row behind him. A hefty, bearded man in red clothing, wearing many gold ornaments.

'What is the purpose of this, can you tell me?' the man asked in a thick Germanic accent, flinging out a fat hand towards the slaughter.

'King,' Nigrinus said in greeting, making the barest of salutes. Hrocus, King of the Alamannic Bucinobantes, had been hanging around the court of Constantine, and his father before him, for nearly a decade, but was still entitled to a shadow of courtesy. He had, after all, been one of the first to acclaim Constantine as emperor, back in Eboracum.

'These men are warriors!' Hrocus exclaimed, sounding genuinely pained. 'They surrendered in good faith, so I believe. Why does the emperor waste them like this? They would make good soldiers, loyal to him. Instead they are just used as sport – this I do not understand! It is *ridiculous*. . .'

'How many warriors are there in Germania?' Nigrinus asked, leaning back and speaking over his shoulder. 'How many among the Franks, and your own people, and all the other nations beyond? A multitude. And nearly all of them tied by treaty to keep the peace with Rome.'

'Yes? What of it?'

'Making an exhibition of a few prisoners,' Nigrinus went on, summoning a smile, 'not only reassures the citizens of the provinces that the emperor can enforce his demands. It also reminds the barbarians across the river that Rome takes promises very seriously. And that reminder is worth a legion of men.'

Hrocus grunted, clearly not convinced. It must be hard, Nigrinus thought; those men dying down there were very similar to his own people, and spoke almost the same language. But it was true: displays like this worked. Now all the tribes of the Franks had presented their submission; only the Bructeri remained, and they too would be subdued soon enough, this year or the next.

Down on the sand, most of the prisoners were already dead. The last few cowered in a knot to one side. Some were screaming for mercy, but their voices were lost in the vast noise of the baying crowd that surrounded them. The wolves, however, were slinking off to the other side of the arena, apparently tired of their work. One, its muzzle bloodied to its ears, was intently trying to eat the body of its victim; two of the guards tried to drive it away as a wave of boos and angry yells echoed around the stalls.

But soon enough the guards with their whips and jabbing tridents had forced both prisoners and wolves back into motion, and the animals despatched their last few victims with sullen efficiency. One of the final prisoners, dragging himself free from the corpse of his chained partner, made a dash for the arena wall. Nigrinus watched the man approach, then vanish beneath the wooden palings that ringed the oval of sand; the man hurled himself upwards and managed to grasp the top of the fence, but the wolves were already upon him. Then he fell back, out of sight, and a mist of blood sprayed up to spatter over the clean white tunics of the closest spectators.

'Why do they laugh?' Hrocus asked, baffled. The cheers and jeers rang out from the stalls around them.

'Fools will laugh at anything,' Nigrinus told him. Shock will do that too, he thought. He had heard of men laughing in battle as their friends died around them. Some of the spectators were giggling, or cackling like the mad. Relief, perhaps, that it was the barbarians being torn apart by wolves, and not them.

Now the drone and warble of the water organ filled the bowl of the amphitheatre once more. Already the guards were herding the wolves back though the gates, while slaves dragged away the mangled corpses of the dead Franks and shovelled more sand over the trampled morass of blood and viscera that remained. It was time for a new spectacle, before the attention of the crowd wandered.

'Ah!' Hrocus declared, slapping his meaty hands together. 'Now I hope for naked tarts, dancing on platforms!'

But the king was to be disappointed.

Two smaller trapdoors opened in the arena floor, and to another blare of trumpets the platforms rose from the darkness below. Each was mounted with a tall wooden post, and to each post a man was chained by the neck. Twisting in his seat, Nigrinus read the placards fixed to the tops of the posts: 'MEROGAISVS – KING OF THE CHAMAVI', 'ASCARICVS – KING OF THE CHERVSCI'.

The spectators began yelling again, standing in their seats, the men in the lower stalls screaming abuse at the bound captives.

'Now *they* are fools,' Hrocus said, shaking his head sadly. 'I could have told them! I could have said: *Don't attack Rome. . .* Now look at them!'

But the two Frankish chiefs appeared defiant still. One, Ascaricus, hung his head so his hair covered his face, but his lean muscles were hard as he gripped the post behind him. The other Frank, Merogaisus, was a huge man, his yellow hair and beard dirty and matted but his eyes glaring. His body was striped with blood from a recent whipping. As he felt the hatred of the crowd he began shouting back at them, straining at his chains.

'What's he saying?' Nigrinus asked Hrocus.

'He's saying,' the king replied, 'that he wants to be armed. *Give me a weapon, Roman dogs. Let me fight and die like a man. . .*'

Abruptly the noise from the crowd shifted to a cheer and a growing chant. Nigrinus glanced away from the bound captives, and saw two bears emerging from the gates at either end of the arena. They were monstrous beasts, scarred veterans of the Treveris arena, and the crowd knew them well.

'*UL-TOR! UL-TOR!*' the crowd near the southern gate chanted.

'*OMI-CI-DA! OMI-CI-DA!*' those in the northern stalls chanted back.

So it was a contest, Nigrinus realised – which bear would kill his victim first? Already he could see some of the spectators making bets, gauging the odds – was the man-slaying Omicida the fittest champion, or the avenging Ultor?

The first kill came quickly, and those betting on Omicida lost out. The other bear, Ultor, dropped into a loping run; with unnerving speed it closed with the bound victim. Before Ascaricus of the Cherusci could even scream, the bear had reared up, bellowing, and smashed one paw across his chest. The victim was punched back against the post; then the bear lunged forward, throwing its full weight against him. The post gave way, toppling over and dragging the bound man with it – he was dead before he hit the sand, with the bear's massive gouging jaws clamped around his face.

'*UL-TOR! UL-TOR!*' the crowd in the southern stands chanted.

Nigrinus looked back at Hrocus. The king sat with a woeful grimace, his beard in his fist. Another throw of the dice, Nigrinus thought, and it could easily have been Hrocus down there, chained to a post, getting his skull crushed by Ultor the bear.

How strange the turns of fate, Nigrinus thought as he stared in queasy fascination at the scene in the arena. Hrocus was born a king, his father was a king before him. Nigrinus's own father had been born a slave. Now Nigrinus himself was climbing the ladder of imperial offices, his power growing with every passing year, while Hrocus declined and did not even know it. Was it just fate? No, Nigrinus thought. It was more than that. He knew how the game was played, and men like Hrocus did not.

A sudden movement caught his eye – the crowd saw it too, and a gasp and a yell came from the stalls. Merogaisus, the second Frankish chief, had managed to break the fastening of the chain that secured him to the post. Roaring, he was heaving and dragging at the post itself, trying to wrench it from the ground. The bear Omicida idled closer, head swinging, drool glistening around its jaws.

With a straining heave, the Frankish chief ripped the heavy post up out of the ground. He lashed the chain around it, then lifted it above his head and brandished it at the packed tiers of seats all around him.

'And now things become interesting,' Nigrinus said quietly.

The bear Omicida was already closing in. Merogaisus cried out in defiance, hefting the ten-foot baulk of wood and chain like an ironbound club. He swung, and the chain came loose and flailed at the bear's head. The crowd in the stalls was hushed, expectant, many of them on their feet. Nigrinus could see the flicker of bets being laid. Man against beast.

Swinging his lump of wood and iron, Merogaisus had driven the first bear back. But now Ultor had picked up his scent, and come bellowing across the sand to join the attack. Both animals circled the man, keeping back from the lash of the chain and the sweeping reach of the wooden club. Merogaisus was chanting something, or singing; he was holding the beasts off, but his strength would give out before long.

Now the crowd was beginning to shout, some of them urging on the bears, others – unbelievably, it seemed to Nigrinus – switching their support to Merogaisus. Only moments before they had been screaming for his death; now they chanted his name, punching the air in unison. Hrocus was on his feet too, joining in the chant.

Something had to be done, Nigrinus thought. The message of this display was being lost. He could see many in the crowd stretching out their arms towards the imperial podium, begging the emperor's mercy for the man in the arena. Nigrinus smiled grimly: how the fickle populace loved an underdog!

One of the bears – Omicida – reared up suddenly and made a lunge, smashing the club from the Frank's grasp. The crowd let out a vast groan. The other bear, its muzzle still clotted with gore, lurched closer. Merogaisus snatched up the chain and managed to haul the club after him as he backed away. He swung at one bear and caught it across the jaws with the chain; then he jabbed the baulk of wood at the other, driving it back. Cheers and a rhythmic stamping rose from the stalls.

'The emperor!' somebody was shouting. 'The emperor!' Nigrinus turned to the podium. There was Constantine, standing stiffly, his golden robe blazing in the sun, one hand raised. Nigrinus stood up, instinctively raising his hand in salute.

'He will grant him freedom?' Hrocus was asking. 'Constantine will allow the Frank to go free?'

Down on the bloody sand, Merogaisus too had seen the emperor. For a moment he stood motionless, the heavy club raised, the two beasts prowling just beyond his reach. Then, with a shout of rage, he tossed the club aside. Head back, fists raised to the crowd and the emperor alike, he cried out in his own language, a single phrase repeated. Then he ran at the nearest bear with his arms outstretched.

'What did he say?' Nigrinus demanded.

'He said,' Hrocus replied, then raised his voice: '*Roman slaves! Watch how a free man dies!*'

Omicida made one savage bellowing swipe, and the man was down.

Shocked silence filled the amphitheatre, and in that unnatural hush, before the great eruption of angry noise, Nigrinus was sure he could make out the last cries of the dying man as the bears tore into him.

They sounded, he thought, like mocking laughter.

PART ONE

ONE YEAR LATER

CHAPTER I

May AD *308*

The sea was grey as old meat, veined with dirty white foam. Three hours out from harbour, the round-bellied Gallic merchantman *Pegasus* butted across the choppy swell, her deck crowded with legionaries huddled under their rain capes. On the western horizon, the coast of Britain was vanishing into the haze, while three more vessels followed in the wake of the *Pegasus*, carrying the rest of the Third Cohort, Legion VI Victrix across the sea to Gaul.

On deck, beneath the bulge of the leather sail, the briny sting of the sea breeze could not erase the reek of bilge water, vomit and urine rising from the hold. Two of the legionaries stumbled up from their crouch in the scuppers to lean into the breeze, bracing themselves expectantly against the rail.

'Other side!' a heavy voice said. 'Downwind. Unless you want it in your faces!'

One of the soldiers glanced back, too sick to speak; before either could move their centurion had seized them by their capes and hauled them back across the pitch of the deck. Staggering, they plunged against the leeward rail, just in time to blow the meagre contents of their stomachs out over the waves.

A fresh whip of wind spattered rain across the deck – it had been raining constantly, on and off, since the ship had left Rutupiae. Centurion Aurelius Castus planted his feet firmly on the slope of the deck, pushed back the hood of his cape and tipped his broad face into the rain. He felt the wind shift, and the straining cordage overhead wailed. Unlike most of his men, Castus seemed immune to the effects of seasickness. Half of his sixty-strong century had spent the first few hours of the voyage vomiting helplessly over the side. Later, after a brief meal of barley porridge and vinegar wine, it had been the turn of the other half. But Castus felt no discomfort from the motion of the waves: his men, he knew, joked between themselves that he lacked a stomach, or any internal organs. Their centurion had a solid body, to match his solid head.

This was not the first time Castus had been aboard a ship, but most of the soldiers under his command had been recruited in northern Britain, and had never before left the island. For them the ocean was a new and terrible experience. Castus himself was from distant Pannonia, born on the banks of the Danube, and his fifteen years in the army had taken him from the wilds of Caledonia to the delta of the Euphrates. The Ocean, he knew, was a powerful deity, and should be respected. But he also knew that the Gallic Strait in early summer held only a minor risk of storms, whirlpools and sea monsters.

Castus ran a hand across his cropped scalp, and rainwater dripped down his neck. He was young for a centurion, only just over thirty, but he had enlisted young too and his long career in the army had toughened him beyond his years. Squinting into the greyness of the open sea, he tried to make out the green smear of the distant shore. Would they make it to harbour before nightfall? He picked his way aft, swaying between the uprights, stepping carefully around the huddled bodies of his men and the heaps of baggage and stores secured in their rope netting. The captain, a bearded Spaniard from Gades, was perched beside the steersman on the raised stern platform.

'You'll see the Gallic coast soon, centurion,' the captain called as Castus approached. 'Unless this wind picks up, we'll have a nice smooth crossing all the way to Bononia!'

Smooth, Castus thought; a couple of the nearer legionaries glanced up in queasy confusion.

'How much longer?' Castus asked.

'Two hours, perhaps three, if Neptune and Boreas allow. Your men should look to the west – this might be the last they'll see of Britain!'

An ill-omened comment, Castus thought, and several of the men had overheard it. Hands fluttered, making warding signs against evil, and lips spat. Even so, a knot of soldiers rose to their feet and stood at the leeward rail, gazing back at the last trace of green on the western horizon. They raised their hands in salute, crying out to their native gods: to Brigantia Dea, and Mars Cocidius. To Fortuna the Homebringer. Most were leaving behind families, wives and children. They were going to a distant war, in an unknown land. Many of them wept openly.

Castus too stared back at the retreating shore. He had no farewells to make; he was leaving little. For nearly four years Britain, and the old legionary fortress of Eboracum, had been his home. He had served there with the Sixth Legion since his promotion to centurion; he had led men into battle for the first time in that province, known victory and defeat, honour and shame. But he left now with few regrets. The last two years had been quiet, and the legion had spent its time in construction work, renovating and rebuilding the fortress, tearing down the leaking old barracks and erecting new ones, and reconstructing the headquarters building, where the emperor Constantine had first been acclaimed by the troops, on a suitably grand scale.

21

He would miss little of that, Castus thought. His friends in his own cohort were travelling with him, and the only person he was sorry to leave was a woman. Afrodisia was a prostitute, but he had grown fond of her over the years. It had surprised him, when they finally parted, how fond she had grown of him too.

But that was the past. The Third Cohort of the Sixth had been summoned across the sea to Gaul, to join the imperial field army on the Rhine: reinforcements for the coming campaign against the barbarians. Castus relished the prospect. He had feared, at times over these last two years, that life was done with him, that the world had turned and left him to sink into a languorous peace, old age, slow death. But away on the Rhine there was war, and war was his purpose. It was his only trade, and he knew he was good at it.

The *Pegasus* ploughed on across the heaving waves, and Castus gripped the backstay and gazed towards the eastern horizon. With every rise and fall of the swept-up prow the shore of Gaul drew closer. Silently, so none might see, he shaped a prayer to Sol Invictus, the Unconquered Sun. *Let me not return this way too soon.*

Dawn was cold and damp, and in the camp on the hillside above the port of Bononia the men of the Sixth Legion stumbled and cursed among the tent-ropes and fires as they prepared to march. They had come ashore at nightfall, salty-wet and hungry, and had had only a few hours' sleep. To add to their grievances, they had shared the camp with a detachment from the other British legion, II Augusta. The Second had arrived before them, and cunningly positioned their latrine pits upwind of the tent lines of the Sixth.

'Bastard *Secundani*,' said legionary Aelianus. 'And they'll be churning up the road ahead of us, I suppose, all the way to Colonia.' The Second had taken the first march, and had left an hour in advance.

'That or making us eat their dust, if the rain stops,' said legionary Erudianus, sniffing at the sky. 'Smells to me like a dry spell coming on.'

'Quiet!' yelled the optio, Modestus, pacing back up the line of shuffling, red-eyed soldiers. He reached the front of the column and saluted to Castus.

'All present, centurion.'

Castus nodded, turned to the men behind him and raised his stick. His century was leading the cohort that morning, but no word was needed, no order given. Everyone knew they had a stiff march ahead of them: at least twelve days across the flat plains of Belgica, full-step marching all the way, to Colonia Agrippina on the Rhine. They had done more than that coming down from Eboracum to the south coast of Britain, but this was an unfamiliar new country for most of them. Castus let the stick drop, turned and set off. Behind him the column of his own soldiers, then those of his friend Valens and the other centuries beyond them, creaked and stamped into motion. Nearly five hundred men, with pack mules and baggage wagons, army slaves and artillery section, and the straggle of civilian hangers-on that had already attached themselves to the rear of the column before the last files tramped out of Bononia.

Departure had been shambolic, but after a couple of hours on the road the thin grey rain had stopped, the sun had broken over the cloudy horizon, and the usual routine of marching was shaking some order into the ranks. At noon they came up with the rearguard of II Augusta, and passed them as the men of the other legion stopped for their midday meal. Jeering

23

laughter and shouted insults from both sides; there had been bad blood between the Second and Sixth for over a hundred years. The Second were based in the southern province, in Londinium and the coastal forts, and they regarded the Sixth as semi-barbarians from the hairy north. Two years before, the invading Picts had beaten the Sixth Legion in the field and driven them back into their fortifications; the men of the Second still believed that their own detachment had defeated the marauders single-handed and saved the province.

'Centurion, keep your men in line!' Tribune Aurelius Jovianus of the Second was the appointed *praepositus*, commanding both legion detachments. He was supposed to be impartial.

'Of course, dominus,' Castus said, saluting as the tribune rode on by. He swatted at a couple of his men with his stick, and glowered at the soldiers of the Second lined up on the verge until they fell silent.

'Smarten up,' he said in a carrying rumble. 'Double pace – let's show these bastards what soldiers look like!'

His men needed no further encouragement.

Two days, then three days. The roads rolled out before them, spreading their web of gravel and churned mud across the plains of Belgica. Castus did not care for the look of this country: much of it was farmland, wide flat fields of wheat and barley. But much more was untended, waste acres that had not been ploughed for generations, now high with tangled weeds and scrub bushes. It gave the landscape a maudlin, sepulchral look under the heavy grey clouds.

'The tragedy of Gaul,' said the narrow-faced balding soldier marching beside him. Diogenes had been a schoolmaster before he had been recruited into the legion; Castus had recently

24

promoted the rather unmilitary man to *tesserarius*, keeper of the watchwords, which granted him immunity from the more strenuous fatigue duties, and also perhaps excused some of his more unusual comments.

Castus gave a questioning grunt.

'That used to be some of the finest arable land in the western provinces,' Diogenes explained. 'Then, about thirty years ago, in the time of the emperor Probus, barbarians invaded from across the Rhine. By the time the owners had got their peasants and slaves back to the land, they owed too much in tax arrears to afford to farm it. So they let it run to seed, claimed it wasn't theirs.'

'Stupid,' Castus said. 'So everybody loses?'

'Indeed. And if anyone was tempted to try and cultivate it, you can bet that some good neighbour would be only too ready to inform on them to the tax officials. Once again, you see, centurion – the curse of private property!'

Castus had become accustomed to Diogenes' strange views over the years, his *philosophies*. One of these was the idea that private property was the sole cause of the empire's decline; if everything was owned by the emperor, Diogenes believed, all would be equitable. A situation which seemed to Castus very much like army life, which sadly was not a very good example of fairness.

'But if we look just over there,' Diogenes explained, with new enthusiasm, 'we see the future of the Gallic provinces!' He pointed away across the weed-grown scrub to a nearby field in cultivation. Rows of dark figures were at work, bending low over the crop.

'Barbarians!' Diogenes announced. 'Prisoners, taken in war and settled here by the emperor. Probably Franks or Alamanni, I should think. They work the land for free, and send their sons for military service in our armies.'

'And everybody wins?' Castus said, sceptical. Surely the idea of surrendering large areas of Roman land to the barbarians could not be a good one, whoever they were supposedly working for? Was this really the future?

'Perhaps, indeed,' Diogenes went on, in a musing rhetorical tone Castus had learned to recognise, 'those barbarians in the fields are the brothers of those we are now going to fight? Convenient, one might say! No doubt our enemies of tomorrow have done some terrible deed, to deserve the vengeance of empire?'

'*No doubt*,' Castus said in a tone that forbade further rhetoric. Diogenes was a strange sort of soldier, but he had proved himself brave, and tougher than he looked. Even so, there was a limit to how much Castus could take from him, and directly questioning the motives of the emperor and his army was pushing towards that limit fast. There had been enough of that sort of scepticism in Britain two years before, although all knew it was warranted. Diogenes, sensing the limit's approach, wisely fell silent.

The column moved on, and the barbarian labourers stood for a time to watch the soldiers go by, before once more bending to their work.

On the evening of the fifth day, the twin legion detachments reached Bagacum, nexus of the road systems of northern Belgica.

Two hundred years before, in an excess of civic pride, the citizens of Bagacum had erected for their city a forum and basilica to rival anything north of the Alps. But those days of glory had long passed: Frankish raiders had sacked the city two or three times, and the grand forum was now surrounded by ramparts and bastions, a fortified redoubt and military supply depot for the army of the Rhine. The city itself had shrunk from its heyday, and the grid of brick streets had more abandoned than occupied buildings. The descendants of the proud decurions of ancient Bagacum now ran taverns and brothels for the soldiers that passed so frequently through the city. They knew all too well the rough tramping of hobnailed boots along their streets, and the favourite obscene songs of half a dozen different legions.

They also knew what happened when the army detachments came through: the legion's billeting officers had arrived earlier that day, chalking their quotas on the doors of houses. A third of any requisitioned property must be given up for the accommodation of troops. Not surprising, Castus thought, that so many towns in northern Gaul seemed deserted when the army arrived. He had seen the same thing all across the empire.

Not that he was complaining; he had little use for the scruples of civilians. Besides, the legion *mensores* had done well for him: he was billeted with two other centurions in the upper rooms of a grain merchant's house two blocks south-west of the old forum. Good rooms, comfortable beds, and the merchant had even instructed his slaves to feed the *noble soldiers* from his own larder, before departing for his house in the country.

'If only all civilians were so prompt and generous,' Valens said, propping his boots on the dining table, 'a soldier's life would be a lot less arduous!'

'*Arduous*?' Castus said, glancing up with a wry smile. 'You don't know the meaning of the word!' He wiped a hunk of coarse bread around his earthenware bowl, scraping up the last of his meal of chopped olives in fish sauce.

'Oh? All this marching up and down, risking blisters and cramps in the service of the emperor? Is that not arduous?' Valens ran a chicken bone through his teeth, then tossed it over his shoulder and belched. 'Anyway, at least I know how to *spell* arduous.'

The third man at the table, Rogatianus, a dark wiry soldier from north Africa, laughed down his nose. Castus just nodded, still smiling, trying not to blush. When he had first joined the Sixth Legion four years ago, he had been unable to read or write. Since then, in sporadic and entirely secret lessons with Diogenes the former teacher, Castus had picked up the rudiments of literacy. Valens still mocked him about it, slyly, although there was a rough affection in his humour. Not many men in the legion knew, after all.

Since birth, people had taken Castus for stupid. It had started with his own father, then almost every officer he had known and most of his fellow soldiers too. And most civilians assumed soldiers to be little better than brutal animals. It did not worry him unduly. Sometimes it suited him for people to think that way, to expect little of him beyond strength and loyalty. His appearance suggested it: the heavy torso, with the blunt, broken features and thick neck that had given him, in successive units, the inevitable nickname 'Knucklehead'. But all the same, just occasionally, his lack of learning needled him. His ignorance of so much in the world, beyond the narrow regulated margins of army life. He had hoped that learning his letters might broaden his mind, but the stuff Diogenes tried to get him to read just baffled him. In fact, it had often occurred to Castus that if Diogenes had been such a good teacher, he would never have had to join the army. . .

'Centurion!' A shout up the stairs, then a hammering of studded boots on boards, and a soldier pushed past the slaves and into the room. He was one of Castus's century, legionary Aelianus.

'No enlisted men!' Valens called, flourishing a chicken leg at the soldier. 'This drinking and dining club is officers only!'

'Centurion,' Aelianus gasped, breathing hard, 'message from optio Modestus – there's trouble; you have to come quickly.'

'What's happened?' Castus said, sobering at once. He pushed aside his bowl and picked up his centurion's stick.

'Men from the Second Legion,' the soldier said, already halfway back down the stairs with Castus at his heels. 'They pushed their way into a bar over in our part of town – there's a lot of them. . . some of ours are down already. . .'

Behind him, Castus heard Valens and Rogatianus jumping up to follow him. Their steps thundered on the stairs, then they were all spilling out into the street and marching quickly towards the forum. By the time they reached the corner they could hear the sounds of fighting. Bellows of rage, screams, the thud and crash of breaking wood, the grating clatter of studded boots on stone paving.

Castus held himself back from running. Already he could feel the energy of combat rising in him, the heavy beat of his blood. He tried to slow himself, calm himself: he needed a clear head. It was his duty to stifle the trouble, whatever it might be, but his sympathies were with his men. Five days of forced marching had put a lot of strain on them, and the presence of the rival legionaries of the Second only stoked the tension higher.

Up the street there were running figures, some of them his own men. Others formed a gang around a gate in the wall; as Castus approached, two men shoved their way out and into the street, throwing punches at anyone who tried to bar their way.

'Let them through,' Castus said, in his drill-field bark. A few of the men at the gateway noticed him and straightened up, saluting. One of them was Modestus, the optio, and Castus caught him by the shoulder and dragged him close, fixing him with a level stare. Modestus had been a drunk and a shirker once, but if he had over-indulged earlier tonight, the fighting and riotous confusion had cleared his head. Castus nodded curtly at him.

'Hold this gate,' he said. 'Don't allow anybody else in. Anybody wants to leave, let them.'

'Yes, centurion!' he heard Modestus say as he strode through the gateway. Valens and Rogatianus were somewhere behind him, with a knot of other men from the Sixth, but he didn't have time to check now. He could only hope there were enough of them to back him up.

A narrow paved yard, wooden balconies on two sides, rooms above and below. For a moment it looked as though blood was pooled on the cobbles – then Castus saw the shards of broken pottery sprayed across the yard and realised it was wine from a shattered amphora. There were men on the ground, others gathered around them, and at the far end of the yard, indistinct in the dusk shadow, a brawling melee.

Castus noticed the graffiti scratched on the wall by the steps. He squinted, deciphering it: 'EPPIA SUCKS THE BEST', 'ANTHIOCA HAS A FINE ARSE', 'I SHAT HERE'. The place was a brothel, amongst other things.

Lowering his brow, jutting his jaw, he marched on across the yard, crushing broken pottery underfoot. Movement from above him, and he stepped aside smartly as another heavy amphora came toppling over the balcony and exploded across the cobbles. Screams of laughter, quickly cut short – Rogatianus was already storming up the stairs with three men behind him. Was this really a fight, Castus wondered, or were they just destroying the place?

'Centurions!' men were shouting – his own or theirs he could not tell – 'Centurions, get out!' Bodies collided with him and he shoved them aside.

30

He grabbed a man by the tunic, hauled him off his feet and flung him back towards the gate. A figure barged against him, bloody-mouthed, shouting. Not one of his own.

'Cocksucker!' the man screamed, and swung a wild punch. Castus leaned out of the man's reach, then jabbed the heel of his palm against his breastbone, knocking him back. The man reeled; one swift blow to the jaw and he dropped cold.

Castus strode on across the yard into the surge of bodies around the far door. Diogenes was at his side, and Flaccus the standard-bearer.

'Stay close at my flank,' he said. 'The rest of you keep in behind.'

He glanced back and saw Valens casually headbutt a soldier of the Second Legion. The man fell sprawling, and Valens grinned and shrugged.

There was another man on the ground near the door, ringed by bodies. In the spill of firelight Castus recognised one of his own soldiers. Unconscious, blood all over his face. One of his tent-mates kneeling beside him, screaming.

'They've killed him, centurion! The bastards have murdered him!'

Castus leaned over the fallen man. Cut scalp, shallow but bleeding heavily.

'He's not dead. You three, get him back to his billet. Go!'

Flaccus and Diogenes had cleared the other men from the entrance to the lower room. The heavy door was half-shut, with something wedged behind it, a bench or table. Castus took a step back, drew up his shoulders and then kicked at the boards. Sound of shattering wood from inside.

'After me!' he said. 'If anyone resists, drop them.'

Over the wreck of splintered timber he pushed his way inside, four men at his back. A single glance took in the scene: the

31

low brick-vaulted room fogged with smoke, bodies wrestling in the glow of the fire, other men cheering, yelling; a woman standing on a table in a ripped gown, shrieking with laughter. Stink of burnt food, sour wine, vomit and blood.

With his stick thrust forward Castus forged his way into the mass of men. He grabbed at them, heaving them back towards the door as he pushed between them. The noise of the fight rang under the low ceiling – his own shouts were lost in it. He reached up, seized the shrieking woman around the waist and hoisted her to the floor, then leaped onto the table where she had been standing, bending his head beneath the low brick arch.

'Enough!' he shouted into the clamour. 'That's enough!'

But now he could see over the heads of the mob into the depths of the room. He saw the man pinned to the floor between benches – another of his own men, a young recruit named Speratus – with three or four soldiers grouped around him, kicking him and stamping on his body. He saw, at the rear of the chamber, another table with men seated on it, watching the fight with expressions of drunken glee, like spectators at a gladiator bout.

His own men were hanging back now, falling away towards the door, and only the gang of Second Legion men were left, with their prisoner, Speratus, trapped between them. Looking at the fallen man, Castus remembered how his father would beat him that way, stamping on him as he lay prone.

Something crashed beside his head: a flung jug shattering against the bricks. Shards sprayed his ear. Down off the table in one bound, he shoved two men aside and grappled a third, dragging them away from Speratus. Somewhere behind him were Valens and Flaccus, but just for a moment he was surrounded by hostile bodies. Someone swung a fist and he blocked it; from the corner of his eye he saw the flash of a drawn blade. He was standing astride the fallen man, shielding him with his body.

'What's this?' cried one of the men at the table, surging to his feet. 'Who the bloody fuck are you?' Castus saw the centurion's stick, the scarred and weathered face of a veteran. He pulled himself upright.

'Aurelius Castus,' he said. 'Centurion. Third Cohort, Sixth Legion. You?'

The other man strode up to him, standing so close that Castus could smell his breath, his rank wine-sweat. He was a hand's breadth shorter, but almost as heavily built.

'Satrius Urbicus,' the man said with a sneer in his voice. 'Centurion. First Cohort, Second Legion. Now tell me you've come to apologise.'

Castus held his stare, said nothing. The blood was beating in his head, and the cuts on his ear throbbed. Urbicus edged closer, his scarred upper lip twisted back from his teeth.

'My men came here for a quiet drink. Your savages attacked them,' Urbicus said. 'So you owe us an apology.'

'I think not.' Castus spoke in a breath. All his life he had deferred to his superiors, and Urbicus was clearly senior to him. When he glanced down he saw the injured man, Speratus, lying at his feet, his face a pulp of blood, one eye swollen shut.

'You trying to argue with me, young man?'

The blow was sudden, a slashing upper-cut – Castus flinched, blinking, as the stick smacked against his skull.

'You should learn to respect your elders, I'd say.'

A heartbeat's pause, too brief to think or balance the odds. Then Castus drove his fist up into the centurion's chest, throwing the full power of his arm behind it. Urbicus let out a tight gasp. He was caught off guard, fighting for balance. His feet skated on spilled wine and he went down hard. Castus followed him, dropping to one knee, and drove two hard accurate punches into the other man's neck. He drew back his fist to punch again, but his arm was seized – somebody else was wrestling his chest, pulling him back. He fought against them, but he could hear the other shouts now, and sense the swirl of the mob as it parted.

Urbicus was trying to get up, but his own men had him pinned. Castus realised that Valens and Flaccus were gripping him; Diogenes had his arm tightly clasped.

'Leave it!' Valens was hissing in his ear. 'The tribune's here with troops – Infernal gods, leave it!'

Numbed, breathing hard, Castus let them drag him upright and across the room to a bench. He could make out the noise from the courtyard now, the voice of the tribune Jovianus as he called for order. Armed men were in the room: Frisiavone auxiliaries, armed with staves. Sitting on the bench, legs spread, he let out a great gasping sigh and felt the red heat of anger rushing from his body. Hollowing remorse rushed in.

Thin rain misted the paved plaza of the forum. Grey morning, sore heads, and the incense smoke from the sacrificial altar sickening men's stomachs. The cohorts were drawn up in two facing lines, the men of the Sixth on one side and those of the Second on the other. On both sides bruised faces, raw scars. Between them, the praepositus Jovianus intoned the words into the thin smoke.

'*Sacred Concordia, Sacred Disciplina, hear our prayer and accept our sacrifice. In your name we cast aside our strife. In your name we bind ourselves in true brotherhood.*'

Four elders of the Bagacum curia stood with covered heads, acting as officiating priests for the ceremony. They mumbled the prayer between them, looking far from pleased. The altar was a rough, temporary thing, a stone with a painted dedication, but money would be deducted from the funeral funds of both cohorts to pay for a stonecutter to make a proper inscription. Money would be deducted, too, to pay for the damage caused by the night's affray.

The punishments should have been much greater, Castus knew. Two men from his own century were invalided with broken limbs, and many of the others had sprains and bruises. The cohort as a whole was down four fighting men, and the Second Legion looked to have suffered similarly. There should have been floggings at the very least for what had happened. Brawling in public with a fellow officer could have cost Castus his rank, even his life – he had risked all that for a moment's rage, and the thought sickened him. But Jovianus had a duty to get his detachments to the army muster; he had lost men and he had lost time, and could not afford to lose more of either.

'Soldiers,' he cried, turning from the smoking altar. 'Last night you disgraced the honour of your legions. The emperor has summoned you to join his campaign against the barbarians. Instead, you have turned your anger upon each other. What use does the emperor have for men who cannot control themselves? Men without discipline? Such men are not soldiers, but savages.'

He paced down the lines, tapping the ground before him with his staff. A small man with a well-groomed appearance, but his authority was palpable and his anger unfeigned. He halted at the centre of the line. To one side of him Castus stood at attention, hands clasped at his belt. To the other, Urbicus of the Second Legion held the same stance.

'We have made a sacrifice,' Jovianus called out, 'to the divine spirits of Concordia and Disciplina, the presiding goddesses of the parade ground. May they restore to us the true spirit of soldiers! May they restore the brotherhood of the legions, and allow you to redeem your courage in the purity of battle!'

He gestured with his stick, and Castus took four long steps forward. Urbicus marched out to meet him. Castus could still feel the smart of his cut ear, the bruise on his temple, but he was glad to see that the other man showed more obvious marks of violence.

'Clasp hands in good faith,' Jovianus ordered.

Castus took a breath, then stuck out his hand. Urbicus grasped it. A squeeze of hard bone and muscle.

'Let all strife end,' Jovianus called out, 'and the order of the legions prevail!'

The two centurions stepped close, shoulder against shoulder, and embraced.

In his wounded ear, Castus heard the older man's breathing hiss.

'If I meet you on the battlefield, you're a dead man.'

CHAPTER II

On the evening of the twelfth day after leaving the coast, the men of the marching detachments came in sight of the walls of Colonia Agrippina, the great fortress city on the banks of the Rhine. The massive drum towers of the fortifications, with their decorative brickwork glowing in the low sun, were a welcome sight. The troops had marched hard since leaving Bagacum, making up for the day they had lost, but Jovianus led them away to the north of the city and on down the river another three miles to the camp ground of the field army. It was almost dark by the time the weary legionaries of VI Victrix raised their tents in the lines allotted to them.

For Castus, the end of the march was a relief. The tensions and resentment left by the riot at Bagacum had not eased, and his mood had been black for days afterwards. No matter that he was provoked, that Urbicus had struck first, no matter that he was defending his men. He had lost control of himself; he had been goaded, and had given in to blind rage – the same goading, the same rage had caused him to attack his father once. Castus had believed he had murdered the old man, and fled to join the legions. Now, with a similar uncontrolled outburst, he had almost undone all that his career in the army had given him. Some of his men had tried to thank him for coming to their aid, or to congratulate him, and he had snarled them into silence. He was not proud of his actions. He had been careful to avoid centurion Urbicus of the Second Legion too.

But the following dawn brought a sight to gladden the heart. Bright sun, a breeze driving off the last of the river mist that rose from the damp turf, and, all around, the field army of the emperor mustered for a new campaign. Thousands of leather tents in regular rows, horse lines and entrenchments, the shout of the sentries, the call of the trumpets from the command enclosure. Here, Castus knew, was the antidote to his foul mood. Here, and in the warfare to come.

By mid-morning the troops were assembled on the broad, level field beyond the camp ground. The British detachments had been the last to arrive at the muster, and joined similar detachments from each of the Rhine legions: I Minervia and XXX Ulpia Victrix, VIII Augusta and XXII Primigenia, I Martia and I Flavia Gallicana. Together they fielded almost five thousand heavy infantry, brigaded together with the irregular *numeri* of *auxilia*: the Batavi and Mattiaci, Frisiavones and Menapii, the Tungrian and Nervian archers. With the cavalry troopers of Equites Promoti, Mauri, Dalmati and Primo Sagittarii, the army mustered over ten thousand strong.

In the breeze the draco banners streamed against the clean-washed sky. From his position in the ranks with his men, Castus gazed along the lines of brightly painted shields, the glinting and glimmering of mail and scale armour, burnished helmets, honed spearheads. Trumpets rang out the imperial salute, and the assembled troops began throwing up their arms and cheering in acclamation. Castus cheered with them, feeling the lingering remorse and anxiety punching out of him with every breath.

'*Imperator Augustus! Imperator Augustus! Imperator Augustus!*'

The emperor rode onto the muster ground at the head of his

mounted bodyguard of Comites and Equites Scutarii, followed by his senior officers and the officials of the imperial household. Castus had not seen Constantine for nearly two years, ever since the strange and intoxicating days in Eboracum when the emperor had first been acclaimed by the troops after his father's death. Back then, it had been hard to think of him as more than the tribune he had been. Now, Castus thought, Constantine looked in every way an emperor.

He rode slowly, on a powerful grey warhorse. His cuirass was gilded, glowing in the sun, and his purple cloak was woven with gold. A soldier rode behind him carrying his helmet, gold set with gemstones and decked with peacock-feather plumes. Constantine sat stiff in the saddle, barely moving his head to acknowledge the cheers as he rode between the ranks of his troops. His face looked flushed, raw-boned, his eyes deep-set.

Castus stared at the emperor as he passed, almost willing him to turn and see him there in the ranks. He remembered a previous meeting, back in the basilica of the headquarters in Eboracum. Constantine had recognised him then; would he know him again? Impossible, surely. But, even knowing all that he did about the murky background to the imperial accession, Castus was struck with a sense of awe. Emperors, he had been taught to believe, were like gods on earth. And Constantine had certainly come to appear like a god.

The imperial party reached the tribunal at the heart of the muster ground. Castus peered over the heads of his men, but could see little of the rituals that followed. Smoke rose from the altars, together with sounds of discordant trumpeting to deter evil spirits as the pig, sheep and bull were sacrificed to the gods of Rome. The omens were proclaimed as favourable, and then the standards were carried forward to the altar, to be anointed with the blood of the victims.

As he watched, craning his neck, Castus picked out another figure among the imperial party. A very large man, powerfully built, but ageing. He stood to one side, bare-headed, with a white and gold cloak drawn around him. His features were heavy, and he wore a thick dark beard, greying around the jowls. Castus had never seen him before, but he appeared somehow familiar. He noticed the way that the men around him, even the high officials, appeared to defer to him, or perhaps draw back from him slightly. A nimbus of stern authority surrounded him.

Now the emperor's voice rolled out across the muster ground. The breeze stole away the words, but the troops did not need to hear them – they would learn soon enough what was expected of them. When the address was done the cheering commenced once more, and the last cries were still ringing across the churned turf as the imperial party mounted up and rode back towards the comforts of the city.

'Two days from now,' the tribune Jovianus announced, 'our emperor will complete the bridge of boats across the Rhine and lead his field army against the Bructeri, the last of the Frankish tribes to remain in defiance of Rome. The intention is not only to punish them for daring to raid our provinces but to demonstrate the power of Roman arms to strike deeply into their lands, and break their power utterly.'

Twelve men sat before him on folding stools; others stood at the rear of the tent: centurions, and some of the commanders of the auxilia units. Castus was glad to see there was no sign of Urbicus or the other Second Legion men. Jovianus was standing, his staff clasped behind his back. He looked well bathed, his hair freshly dressed, and he wore a clean white tunic embellished with silver.

'The barbarians will not be surprised at our coming,' he went on. 'They have expected Roman vengeance for over a year now, and their scouts are watching from the eastern bank of the river. They will already have seen the preparations for the bridge of boats, and will be assembling to resist us and ambush our vanguard troops as they cross. But what *will* surprise them is the speed and strength of our attack – they are always accustomed to flee at the first onslaught, and take shelter in their tangled forests, but, like a bolt of lightning, we will outpace them and destroy them!'

The tribune paused to allow his audience to digest what he had said. He clearly had aspirations, Castus reflected, to higher command – his style of speech suggested it. Through the open tent-flap came the late-afternoon sun and the sounds of camp life: men laughing as they gathered wood or cleaned weapons and equipment; lowing cattle; the distant neighing of horses from the cavalry lines. The familiar scent of the cooking fires too. Castus stared at the leather wall of the tent, as if he might be able to see through it. His empty stomach grunted and roiled.

'To secure the bridgehead, therefore,' Jovianus went on, 'five hundred men of the Sixth Victrix and First Flavia Gallicana Legions, together with detachments of the Batavi and Mattiaci auxilia, will cross the river in small boats tomorrow night, three miles downstream. You will then make your way back southwards to the bridging area, and drive off any enemy force that you meet.'

A stir of muffled comments passed between the assembled officers. Castus saw the scepticism in their faces. They were veteran soldiers, and knew all too well the hazards of a river crossing, a march and an assault by night. Jovianus twitched his jaw, waiting for silence, then broke in, raising his voice slightly.

'The task will not be easy! Absolute discipline must be observed. The crossing must be accomplished in total silence, to avoid alerting the barbarian scouts to our stratagem. Once on the far bank of the river, the boat parties must assemble, maintain formation, and reach the enemy positions before dawn. Keep the river directly to your right and you will not stray. The night should be clear, so you will have the stars to guide you.'

'*And the moon to guide the Frankish scouts to us,*' Valens whispered. Jovianus paused a moment, as if daring anyone else to comment, then went on.

'Your men will be lightly equipped, without armour, to move fast and silently. In order to sow confusion and terror among the barbarians, each century will move as a separate unit. In this way, you will attack the enemy at many points simultaneously, and make them believe that the entire Roman army has beset them. When all enemy forces have been routed from the far side of the river, you will signal using trumpets, then the engineers will complete the construction of the bridge and the army will commence crossing at first light.'

Jovianus squared his shoulders, rocked back on his heels and inhaled through his nose, obviously very pleased with the plan. As if, Castus thought, he had devised it himself. Perhaps he had?

'Remember!' the tribune declared. 'The success of our assault depends on you, and your men. Our emperor is depending on you. Do not give the barbarians a chance to escape your swords, or to maintain their position on the river. Strike fast, with discipline and accuracy, like true Roman soldiers, and with the aid of the gods you will prevail!'

The river appeared peaceful that evening, the broad expanse of water like burnished iron in the last of the sun. Like a well-forged sword blade, Castus thought as he watched the surface swirled and patterned by the deep, muscular currents beneath. The far bank was hazy, trees and thick undergrowth, no sign of human life at all. And in the distance wooded hills ranged across the horizon, smoky green and purple in the coming dusk.

'How wide, do you reckon?'

'Over two stades,' Valens said. 'Maybe near three. You could swim it, but I wouldn't recommend it. That current's slow, but it's strong.'

They were on the riverbank, a meadow of long grass running down to the trees and high thick reeds at the water's edge. Valens bent to rub at the ears of his dog. He had found the lean grey creature in Bagacum and it had followed him from the town and all along the route of the march. Castus was wary of it: the animal looked mangy and half-wild, and he distrusted dogs.

Out in the middle of the river, a hulk of floating timber cruised slowly downstream – an entire tree, it looked like, mostly submerged, rotted black. Not something to run into at night, Castus thought, in a small boat.

'What do you know about the Bructeri?' he asked. Valens had served in one of the Rhine legions before his promotion. His friend squatted beside his dog, chewing on an apple and squinting across at the barbarian shore.

'They're Franks,' he said. 'Most Franks live further downstream, in the marshes and the plains, but the Bructeri live in the hills and river valleys. Fiercest of them all, so I've heard. Their priests can work magic. They sacrifice their prisoners to dark gods, eat some of them. . . Keen archers, and they use poison on their arrows. . .'

Castus glanced at him. It was often impossible to know whether Valens was joking or not. 'We'll find out about that soon enough,' he said quietly.

To his right, along the riverbank, Castus could see the muddy scar of the bridge-building operation. Engineers from the Eighth and Twenty-Second Legions had already driven tall wooden pilings into the bank and the shallows, and a mass of heavy flat-bottomed barges was drawn up along the shore and the slope that descended to the water. More barges would be moored upstream, and when the moment came they would be floated down with the current, each anchored and firmly secured as it arrived in position, then the timber trestles for the roadway laid across them. Castus had heard that the entire operation could be completed in half a day. He hoped he would be around to see it.

There was artillery there too, each heavy ballista mounted on a platform and aimed across the river at the point the bridge would reach on the far shore. Were there really barbarian scouts across there now? Was that silent and placid-looking woodland teeming with hostile warriors, just waiting to attack the first men across the bridge? Strange to think so. Nobody in the Roman camp had seen anything moving on the far side of the river at all.

A flight of geese flew slowly across the surface of the water, silently, vanishing into the dusk.

'Who was the older man at the parade this morning?' Castus asked. 'Standing with the emperor and his party. He had a beard, red face.'

'You don't know?' Valens said with a sideways smile. He took a big bite of his apple, chewed and swallowed.

'No, I don't.'

'That, my remarkably solid-headed friend, is the man whose image you saluted for thirteen years!'

Castus blinked slowly, then looked back at the river. Of the four emperors who had ruled the Roman world when he had first become a soldier, he had seen three in the flesh: Diocletian and Galerius on the Danube and the Persian campaign, and Constantius in Britain. Only one was a stranger to him.

'That was Maximian?'

'Indeed it was. Marcus Aurelius Valerius Maximianus, the *Man like Hercules*, formerly supreme Augustus of the western empire. Nowadays father-in-law of our own supreme Augustus, Constantine.'

'How did you know?'

'He was commander-in-chief when I served with the First Minervia,' Valens said with a shrug. 'Still, it took me a while to recognise him. He looks so. . . *old* now. But it must take it out of a man, being driven away by your own son, having to go begging for shelter from your son-in-law. . .' His friend had a crafty look, Castus thought. Some knowledge he wanted to share.

'Tell me about it.'

'His son is Maxentius, the usurper who's seized Rome,' Valens said. 'So Maxentius calls the old man out of retirement to help him run things – plus there's an army advancing on the city, and he hopes having his father at his side'll swing the enemy troops to his cause. It worked well enough – Maxentius saw off two expeditions against him, first by Flavius Severus and then by Galerius, and got his sister wedded to Constantine in a marriage pact.'

For a moment Valens paused, listening to the quiet sounds of the river in the reeds. It felt grubby, even vaguely disloyal, Castus thought, to be discussing the affairs of emperors like this, but he wanted to know more.

'Anyway,' Valens went on in a lower voice, 'it didn't take long before father and son fell out about who was the top dog in Rome. Old Maximian thought he should be senior, but the

Praetorians and the senate had acclaimed Maxentius first, so when his father tried to depose the son, they supported their man instead. There was a *most* undignified scene, a public quarrel, and Maximian had to run for his life.'

'And he came back here?'

Valens nodded slowly. 'Can you credit that? This is the man who used to rule half the world, reduced to a fugitive, running for favours from his daughter's husband. He expected, I suppose, that a lot of Constantine's older officials would owe him their loyalty. He's still a powerful man, in Gaul at least.'

Castus said nothing. Part of him believed that such things were none of his concern. Another part recognised that anyone could see the danger in this situation.

'And what's his role here now? Maximian's, I mean.'

'Esteemed former Augustus? Imperial advisor-in-chief? Glorious father-in-law? Who knows?' Valens stood upright and brushed the grass from his tunic. 'I reckon Constantine wants to keep the old man close because he doesn't trust what he might do otherwise. Praise him, honour him, and *watch him as you watch a snake.*'

Castus stiffened, as if something had brushed the nape of his neck, and for a moment he feared a presentiment, some evil prophecy creeping from the gathering darkness. He shrugged it off. It was a memory; that was all: two years ago, in Britain, he had strayed dangerously close to the intrigues of empire. Since then his life, and his loyalties, had been simple.

'Don't worry, brother,' Valens said. He tossed the apple core out into the water. 'These matters are not for the likes of us. Tomorrow night we cross the river and face the barbarians – like the tribune said, the purity of the battle is our business!'

The dog whined, and Valens scrubbed his fingers under its jaw; then the two men turned back towards the camp.

CHAPTER III

Awarm night, the still air damp and greasy, and the men were sweating by the time they reached the boats. They wore no body armour, only helmets and their rust-brown tunics, and their shields were fitted with leather marching-covers to hide the bright emblems. Their swordbelts, javelins and spears were wrapped with rags to muffle the clink and scrape of metal. Even so, as they slumped down on the riverbank after their four-mile march in the darkness, the noise was clear and unmistakeable. Five hundred soldiers, Castus thought to himself, are incapable of moving silently.

The river was screened by mist, the water invisible, and there was something uncanny and forbidding in the pressure of the air. Despite the warmth, Castus could hear the teeth of some of the younger recruits tapping together. They were right to be nervous. The river before them was like a living presence, a black god, freighted with slow doom. And on the far side, somewhere in that motionless darkness, was the enemy.

'Don't worry,' he said to the young soldier beside him, 'it's only a boat trip and a walk in the woods.' He sensed the man's nod.

Now the mist shifted, and the boats came into view, scores of them nestled together like rafts amid the reeds. Castus remembered his orders: fifteen men should board each boat. He would lead the first party, Modestus the second, the standard-bearer Flaccus would go in the third boat and Diogenes in the fourth. There would be a steersman and a pilot – local people who knew the river and its currents – to guide them across. They had practised boarding, but what had been a simple operation on dry ground beside the tent lines now seemed a daunting prospect. Castus had imagined that the boats would be bigger, like the barges used in the pontoon bridge, or the cutters used by the river flotillas. He tried to conceal his shock as he made out the shapes of the craft that awaited them in the reeds: slender canoes, only a few feet wide, each made of a hollowed log. He felt his skin chill; surely it was the wildest folly to trust his life and the lives of his men to these flimsy sticks, out on the wide, deep expanse of the great river?

Quelling his nerves, he motioned his men to their feet and led them down through the reeds. Watery mud rose around his boots, and when he breathed he felt the mist filling his lungs, the scent of rotting vegetation and the heavy drag of the river in the air.

At the bows of the nearest boat was a small figure – a boy of about thirteen, straggle-haired and almost naked, squatting over the water. The boy gestured down the length of the boat. 'Quickly! Quickly!' Was this the pilot?

Castus climbed in over the stern, and felt the narrow boards pitch and rock beneath him. As he moved forward he noticed a second figure, waist deep in the shallows among the reeds. An old man this time, the boy's father perhaps. He spoke with a strong Germanic accent. 'Get aboard, dominus. Fast and quiet!'

Muffled noise from the riverbank, men's boots sliding in the mud, shields and spears clattering together, voices cursing and hissing. Bent double, stepping high over the thin rowing benches, Castus scrambled along the length of the boat and lowered himself to sit behind the boy at the bows. Other men were boarding behind him: the narrow log canoe rolled precariously, water slopping along the low sides. Shields bumped; boots scraped. Somebody let out a sharp gasp.

'Quiet!' Castus whispered into the hissing of half a dozen men.

As soon as all were aboard and seated, the old man leaped up onto the stern, grabbed a pole and began heaving the laden boat out from the bank. The mist thinned and parted briefly, and when Castus looked to his left he could see dozens of other boats, each packed with men, shoving out from the reeds and into the current of the river. He saw a nearby canoe ghosting out silently from the shore, paddles beginning to dip and splash. Above the huddled figures and the row of blank-faced oval shields rose the bristle of spearpoints and javelins, strange in the misty dark. In the prow, Valens's rangy grey dog sat up erect, its muzzle raised.

Valens, his face pale beneath his hood, lifted his javelin in salute, and Castus caught his whispered words clearly across the water. '*Good hunting!*'

Now they felt the motion of the river beneath them, the heavy stir of the water turning the shallow craft. The boy at the bows was muttering, then holding up a twist of leaves and scattering them on the water. A prayer to the spirit of the river, to carry them safely across. A hushed word to the men behind him, a collective movement, and the paddles began to strike down at the surface of the water.

The mist closed around them once more, and they were alone.

Up above, Castus could make out a few stars bright through the haze, but the moon was lost behind cloud. The black water was very close – he could touch the surface with his hand –

and, with every dip of the paddles, spray spattered back over the sides of the boat. The men were so quiet it seemed as if all were holding their breath; the river defied sound, seemed almost to defy life. With a shudder of unease, Castus thought of the stories of the afterworld, the black river and the silent boat that carried the souls of the dead across to Hades. He had never believed in such things – there was nothing after death but emptiness and darkness, unknowing sleep for eternity. . . The thought did nothing to reassure him.

A sudden cry came across the water, impossibly loud and sharp. The men tensed, and the boat rocked wildly. An owl, somebody said, and a muffled ripple of laughter passed through them, quickly hushed. Once more the paddles rose and fell.

For all the warmth of the night, it felt cold out on the river. A chill breath came up from the water, through the boards of the boat, and they all felt it. Castus stared hard into the bank of mist ahead, straining his eyes to try and make out the shape of the far bank. But there was nothing – just water and night and the hanging mist only faintly illuminated by the stars.

Then the boy made a sound between his teeth, fanning with his hand. He was gazing down into the depths of the water ahead.

'What is it?' Castus whispered. The paddles fell silent; the boat swung with the current.

The boy called out something to the old man with the steering oar at the stern. Castus heard the man exhale as he heaved the oar against the flow of the current, and the canoe swung again. Some of the men began to shift at their benches, and the boat rolled, water slapping at the sides.

'Stay still!' Castus hissed, gripping the sides in fear of being pitched out into the river.

Suddenly a scream came from somewhere out in the darkness; no bird call this time, but a man in agony. Then another cry, and the sound of a body hitting the water. All along the boat men tensed and hunched. Castus could make out another sound, a staccato lisping hiss that seemed to rise from the surface of the water.

The arrow appeared suddenly, punching into the side of the boat only inches from his hand. Another skimmed past his head.

'Shields up!' he cried, forgetting caution now. 'Those with paddles, heads down and keep working!'

The zip and hiss of arrows all around them, in the air and cutting the surface of the water. A man in the centre of the boat screamed as he was hit; he lurched up, then toppled sideways into the water. Another arrow slammed into Castus's shield.

'Quiet!' the boy said from the bows. 'They shoot at noise! Cannot see!'

But the men in the boat were panicking now, half of them trying to crouch down inside, the rest trying to lift their shields against the invisible stinging arrows. With the paddles neglected, the boat swung round into the current, then gave a lurch and a thud.

'Sandbank!' the old man called from the stern. 'Everyone move back. . .'

Another cry as another arrow found its mark. With one fluid motion, the boy at the bows stood up and dived, arcing into the black water and vanishing with barely a splash. The whole boat tipped as the soldiers scrambled to one side, then yawed back the other way, but it was too late to right it. Castus felt the flood of cold river water soaking his knees, then the rolling lurch as the water rushed in over the side and the boat capsized.

Head first he plunged into the river, and the blackness rushed up and punched the breath out of him. For a moment there was only a strange muffled silence. He was aware of his own heartbeat pressing in his ears, a curious gulping sensation in his throat, and he felt the weight of his body, the heaviness of his limbs. He opened his mouth and felt the black torrent fill his lungs.

Sudden panic – his churning feet grated against mud and shingle, and he came surging up out of the river. He gasped air, and the noise burst around him. He was in shallow water, only waist deep, and as he blinked the muddy flood from his eyes he could make out, just for a fleeting moment, the shape of trees away to his left.

'Come on!' he shouted, and the words caught in his throat, almost gagging him. He choked, spat water. 'After me – this way!'

Thrashing through the water, feeling the slow pressure of the current, he stumbled towards the bank. He lifted his shield and held it in front of him; the broken stub of the arrow shaft still jutted from it. Water streamed down his body, and the river caught and dragged at his limbs as he tried to run.

A few more steps and he tripped, falling into water only knee-deep. Up again, breath heaving, he kicked the last few yards out of the river and onto hard muddy sand. Down on one knee, he crouched behind his shield and drew the sword from his scabbard. His javelin was gone; his cape was gone. Around him he could hear other men crashing up out of the shallows, calling to each other.

Figures moving to the left – he turned his shield to face them, rising to a fighting crouch with his sword levelled.

'*Jupiter!*' he called into the darkness. The watchword.

'*Preserver of Rome!*' the cry came back. Modestus and his men. Castus whispered a swift and silent prayer of thanks.

The optio dropped to one knee beside him – he was still dry, Castus noticed, and all of his boat's company seemed to be with him.

'Get your men up to the treeline and form a perimeter,' he said. 'I'll round up mine and send them to join you.'

Modestus saluted quickly, then gave the order.

The others from Castus's boat were dragging themselves ashore now, some with arrow wounds, some missing shields or weapons. Castus ranged between them, pulling them to their feet if they flagged, shoving them towards Modestus's strengthening perimeter of shields. He counted them off – there were ten, and two incapacitated by wounds. He had lost three in the river; of the old man and the boy there was no sign.

'*Jupiter!*' came the call from the trees, then the reply, '*Preserver of Rome!*'

Hefting his shield in its soaked leather cover, Castus jogged up the slope of muddy river beach to the crumbling earth bank and the line of trees that overhung it. The mist was thicker here, but he found Modestus and took command from him. The newcomers arrived: Diogenes and his boat party.

'We hit a capsized boat out in the mid-stream somewhere,' Diogenes said, breathing hard. 'There's no sign of Flaccus or his company.'

No sign of the enemy either, Castus thought. He was staring into the murk of the trees but there was no flicker of movement there. The enemy scouts had used them as target practice while they had been out on the river, but they had melted back into the forest as soon as the first men had come ashore.

Think, Castus told himself. The land ahead seemed vast, full of threat, his own men so few in number, so alone.

'There's no time to wait for Flaccus,' he said. 'We need to start moving upriver. With any luck we'll meet up with others

53

as we go. Flaccus and his men can follow as best they can.'
Unless they're all sucking mud at the bottom of the Rhine...

Of the two wounded soldiers, Florus and Themiso, one had been shot through both legs and the other had an arrow in the shoulder. The first would have to be carried: to leave a man alone on this wilderness riverbank with barbarian scouts prowling about was to consign him to death, or perhaps something worse. Castus lowered himself down beside the second casualty, who sat wincing with his back to a tree.

'Is it poisoned, centurion?' the man asked between his teeth. Most of the men had heard the same rumours.

'If you're alive enough to ask, I'd say not.' Castus probed at the wound with his fingertips, and Themiso bit back a cry. 'Barbed head,' he said, and then turned to the soldier beside him. 'We'll need to leave it in there, until there's light enough to cut it out. Break the shaft close to the wound and bind his arm so he doesn't move it.'

The soldier nodded, and Castus moved back up the riverbank, mentally cursing Jovianus, or whoever else had devised this particular stratagem. Between the trees the mist coiled and writhed, forming shapes in the scant light that dispersed before his eyes. Now and again the moon ran clear of the clouds and cast a strange dead radiance through the leaves overhead.

'Find Erudianus and send him up here.'

'I'm here, centurion.'

The legionary materialised from the shadows, slim and silent. Erudianus was a recent recruit, only twenty but with the creased and leathery face of a peasant patriarch. He also had an unnaturally well-developed sense of smell. He claimed to be able to scent changes in the weather, among other things, but more importantly he could certainly pick out the smell of either enemy scouts or fellow Romans.

'Walk just ahead of me,' Castus told him. 'If you. . . *smell* anybody, let me know quick.'

Erudianus nodded briefly, then slung his shield on his back and set off at once, stooped low like a tracker hound. Castus followed in his wake, swinging his arm for the rest of the surviving men to form up after him.

The woods were thick along the riverbank, and there seemed no clearer ground inland either. Low branches whipped and grabbed overhead, brambles and thorny undergrowth caught at the legs of the men as they marched, and sometimes they had to detour around impassable barriers of tangled vegetation, ramparts of nettles and fallen wood. The only paths ran across their route, formed by men or animals moving down to the water. Erudianus was a skilled guide: he had been a shepherd before joining the legion, and his night vision was almost as keen as his sense of smell. But behind him Castus could hear the other men crashing and stumbling on the sticks and rotted logs underfoot, colliding with each other, cursing in the dark.

For an hour or more they struggled onwards, trying to keep the river close to their right. Every few hundred paces Castus called a halt, to let the column re-form and to listen into the silence and the shadows. Moonlight moved between the barred trees, and sometimes he thought he saw movement out on the flanks – animals perhaps, or enemy scouts tracking them as they moved. The shapes of trees, thick-grown with ivy, loomed up like armed sentinels from the darkness. Glancing behind him, he picked out Polaris, the North Star, clear between the trees – at least they were going the right way. It seemed incredible that the several hundred men from the other boats could have been swallowed up so utterly.

'Men ahead,' said Erudianus, crouching. Castus almost stumbled into him. He motioned for the column behind him to pause. A few heartbeats, and he could hear them himself: low voices, bodies rustling through the trees. He tightened his grip on his sword, and raised himself with his back to a tree. They were making too much noise to be barbarians.

'*Jupiter!*' he called, low and clear.

'*Preserver of Rome!*' the cry came back a moment later.

In the darkness the two groups met. Twenty men of Legion I Flavia Gallicana; they had lost their comrades and their leaders during the river crossing. Castus could sense their fear, and knew they were at the edge of surrendering to panic.

'Fall in at the rear of the column,' he told them quietly. 'Modestus: take charge of them.' The men waited gratefully as the rest of the century filed past. Now Castus had more than sixty men at his back, but still no firm idea of where he was leading them.

'You know what I think, centurion?' Diogenes said. Castus turned, hushing. The former teacher had moved up the column to walk behind him.

'*What?*'

'I think this land had been abandoned for many years. Perhaps generations. The Bructeri have withdrawn from the river completely and let it run wild. Their scouts and warbands know the trails through it, but nobody lives here. As a defence, I suppose. A defence against *us*.'

'And you're going to tell me this is. . . what? The tragedy of Germania?'

'Oh, no, there's plenty more land to the north and east,' Diogenes said, not at all perturbed. 'Germania is practically infinite!'

'How pleased I am to hear that,' Castus said.

'Centurion!' Erudianus hissed. He had stopped again, crouching low. 'More men coming!'

56

Ahead of them the trees thinned out, leaving an area of open ground, high grass and bushes indistinct in the dappled moonlight. Castus shuffled forward on his knees, his shield slung on his back, until he could shelter behind a knot of saplings and squint into the darkness. He heard the voices almost as soon as he stopped moving – they were coming quickly. A lot of men too, several score of them, moving through the trees to the left and approaching his position. He snapped his fingers behind him, gesturing urgently for Diogenes to bring some support. The noise of his own soldiers moving up through the undergrowth was achingly loud.

Now he could make out the voices: the approaching men were calling to each other, hushed but distinct. Not in Latin either. The moon glinted on a speartip, on the oval of a shield.

'Form around me,' Castus hissed over his shoulder. He slung the shield from his back and readied it. The approaching men were moving into the open now, forging through the long grass. If he remained still they might not notice him. . . but they would surely hear the soldiers behind him shuffling through the bushes.

His breath was tight; his chest ached. He stood up, shield raised.

'*Jupiter!*' he shouted, the sound of his voice seeming to boom in the silent dark.

The figures in the grass froze, stunned for a moment. Then some of them swung their shields towards him, other hefted spears. Voices called back, Germanic.

Well, he told himself, this is what we came here for.

'After me – *charge*!'

He lunged up out of the trees, shield up and sword levelled. Behind him he heard the eruption of branches and bushes as his men piled after him. Three running strides and the first of the figures loomed up ahead; he crashed against the man, shield to shield, and knocked him down. Screams from his left, bellows of rage.

'*Preserver of Rome!*' somebody was shouting in a Germanic accent. Castus swung around, blood beating fast. The man he had toppled had vanished into the shadows, and all around him was flickering confused motion, figures running and crying out. He paused suddenly.

'Hold back!' he shouted. He could see the men ahead of him more clearly now. Twin feather plumes on their helmets. Mouths open, shouting back the watchword.

'Identify yourselves!'

'Numerus Mattiacorum,' someone called back.

Castus raised his sword high, calling out in his parade-ground voice. 'Hold back! Weapons down! They're on our side!'

Germanic auxilia, he realised. His blood slowed as he saw the two sides pause and step away from each other, his own men backing warily towards the trees. On the far side of the clearing somebody screamed, blades thudded against shields.

'Juno's tits, didn't I tell you to stop! They're. . .'

But something was wrong. There were other figures weaving through the shadowed grass, not auxilia. The fighting was real now, and men were dying. Arrows flicked and hissed in the air.

'Shields up! To the right!'

Now the auxilia too had seen the attackers – they turned with Castus's men, calling out their own war cries. The enemy was streaming all around them in the darkness, seeming to materialise out of the surrounding woods. Castus saw one dashing closer – he took a long step, swung low with his sword, and felt the blade bite.

Behind him he heard the clatter of shield rims as his men formed their fighting line. Keeping his own shield up, he backed towards them. *Keep together*, he told himself. *Got to keep them together. . .*

A man fell behind him, tangling his legs, and Castus almost tripped. Two dark shapes reared up from the grass, spears feinting and darting. Castus parried the first spearhead, the ring of iron loud in the dark. The second he caught on his shield. A step closer, a shove, and he was between the attackers. He thrust left, under his shield rim, and felt the blade drive home. The man screamed and fell back, but the second man had whirled his spear and stabbed again. Castus heaved his body back and felt the speartip slash the air across his chest. A wheeling overarm cut brought his blade down across the attacker's shoulder – a crack of bone and flesh, and the man went down.

All around him, fighting in darkness, wild cries, spears jabbing and cutting. There were men on the ground, some dead and others thrashing wounded in the grass. Castus glanced behind him and saw his own shield wall waver and break apart. An arrow struck his helmet and clattered away. The grass crackled and rushed with the noise of running men. Somewhere a dog was barking madly.

For a moment, panic took him. In the darkness he could barely distinguish friend from foe. His own men were dying, and his senses reeled with the realisation of disaster. Where had the enemy come from? They must have been tracking the other group, the auxilia, and struck when they saw the confused confrontation. It did not matter now.

'*Sol Invictus!*' he cried out, planting his feet firmly. A man ran at him and he cut him down with a single slashing blow. He sensed movement behind him and spun around, but his shield caught in the grass – a bare-chested figure raised his arm for a killing blow. Castus released his grip on the shield, tried to swing his sword around to block the strike – too slow, too slow. A whirr in the air and a chop, and a Roman javelin spitted the man through the torso from shoulder to ribs.

'*Jupiter! Jupiter!*' The cries came from the far side of the clearing, and for a few moments Castus could make no sense of them. The dog was still barking. Then he heard his own men yelling the watchword back, and saw the tide of the confused fighting shift. Roman voices now, and a line of advancing shields.

'Aurelius Castus, that you?'

Valens came striding through the grass, the dog still capering around him with bared teeth. Behind him, his men had herded the enemy forward into the clearing; between the legionaries and the Mattiaci auxilia, the barbarians were trapped.

Castus threw his arm around his friend. 'Thought I'd lost you back in the river!'

'Not me – I float like a cork. Nice to see you made a start without us, though.'

Castus shoved Valens away, laughing with relief.

Side by side they moved across the clearing, shields up and swords ready. Others fell into line beside them: Modestus grinning savagely from the darkness; Diogenes with a dark smear of blood on his face. Within a few heartbeats most of the fighting was done, but the butchery continued. The ground was black and wet underfoot, the grass choked with fallen bodies. By the time Castus and Valens reached the far trees the last of their attackers had either died or fled.

It seemed only moments since he had crouched in the bushes with Erudianus, but when Castus glanced up he saw the eastern sky lightening over the treetops. Birds screeched and cried out of the pre-dawn shadows.

'The riverbank's about fifty paces that way,' Valens said, jerking a thumb over his shoulder. Now it was lighter Castus could make out the mud and blood on his face. 'We should be able to make out the boat bridge on the other side. Trouble is, we've lost our hornblower. Where's yours?'

Castus glanced around, then remembered that his own century's hornblower had been in the boat with Flaccus. Where were all the other detachments? Surely they had not all been lost in the crossing?

'Modestus, lend me your cloak,' he said, 'then follow me.'

Passing quickly through the long grass, he pushed his way back into the undergrowth and between the trees. It was almost light enough to see clearly now, although the sun was not yet up. Kicking his way through the tangled scrub, not caring about the noise any more, Castus reached the bank of the river. Mist still covered the far bank, and he cursed under his breath.

He thought of the batteries of artillery over there, the heavy ballista bolts aimed at precisely the point he was standing now. The energy of battle was still in him, driving him onwards.

'Cut me a long pole,' he said to the men behind him. They gladly shrank back into the cover of the trees, thrashing about, breaking sticks.

Heaving himself up onto the mossy bole of a fallen tree, Castus gazed out across the water into the slow roll of mist. He considered shouting, but didn't trust the men on the far bank to distinguish his voice. The artillerymen had been known to loose off shots at anything that moved or called from the barbarian shore.

One of the legionaries passed him up a cut stick, ten feet or so long. Castus looped the cloak over the top of it, tied it securely, then raised it over his head.

Come on, you bastards. Open your eyes!

Waterbirds cackled and splashed down in the river. The mist rolled steadily by.

A distant call from out of the mist – recognition, or a challenge?

'*Jupiter!*' Castus shouted. '*Jupiter*, by the arse of Mars! *Preserver of Rome!*'

The cloak flapped over his head, beating the mist.

Then the noise of a trumpet call from the far shore. One trumpet, then more.

Cheering drifted across the water.

Castus let his arms drop.

CHAPTER IV

For the first day after crossing the river, the army crawled through a wilderness abandoned by man. Trees grew thick and wild, shagged with ivy and moss, and the ground between was lost to vaulting banks of brambles and fortresses of fern. The cavalry scouts and light-armed auxilia went ahead of the column, picking out a route, and the army marched behind them along overgrown droving trails criss-crossed by narrow footpaths, with forest massed all around them.

After the exploits of their detachment in the riverbank fight, the Sixth Legion had been assigned to the rear of the marching column. There were no baggage wagons with the army: all the supplies and even the artillery were loaded onto mules, and the animals left a rich fester of trampled dung all over the track behind them. Through hot dappled light and plunging shade, the column marched deeper into the barbarian wilderness. In places Castus could make out the shapes of ruined buildings, roofless and overgrown. He remembered what Diogenes had suggested on the riverbank. Surely it was true, he thought. The Bructeri had withdrawn their habitations for many miles from the Rhine.

But there were at least traces of human presence. They passed through clearings with the remains of fires, and in some of them the embers still glowed and smoked. Later in the day

63

the soldiers saw bodies tumbled into the undergrowth beside the trail where the cavalry scouts had cut them down: bearded men in rough woollen tunics and breeches, some with a cloak shrouding them, others left exposed. The men of the Sixth glanced at them dispassionately as they marched by. These were the men that had attacked them on the riverbank, and sniped at them from the darkness. They owed them no respect – let the wild beasts of the forests take their dead flesh.

The soldiers made camp that night in clear ground, cutting timber to make a rough breastwork around their position, and the next morning in the cool grey of dawn they marched on once more. Now Castus and his men began to see signs of settled life: small fields stitched into the folds of the hills; the remains of plundered cattle byres. They crossed a small river, the banks rutted and boggy from the passage of the men and mules ahead of them, and climbed up through dense and tangled forest onto a high grassy ridge. From there, the men at the rear of the column could see the trails of black smoke rising from the horizon.

'Is it true what they say, centurion? asked Aelianus. They had paused on the ridge in the hot sun to rest and drink water. 'Do those trees stretch all the way to the frozen ocean at the top of the world?'

Castus stared out over the winding valley of the river, the hills and the plains beyond. A landscape of treetops, green shading into distant blue and grey.

'With any luck we won't have to find out,' he said. 'I've seen quite enough trees to last me a lifetime.'

'You shouldn't disrespect trees,' came a voice from his left. Erudianus, the tracker, tipped his head back and directed a jet from his waterskin into his open mouth. He swallowed, then nodded away into the forested distance. 'Trees are all different,' he said. 'They have quite different scents. The smell of an oak – like that one there – is completely different to a larch like those down the slope. And those pines up there on the hillside opposite. . .' He paused, closing his eyes and breathing in, as if he was inhaling the choicest perfume.

They marched on along the ridge, and the sun shone down on the column of men, blazing off their armour, their polished helmets and the ranked tips of their spears. Almost like a triumphal procession, Castus thought. Was it just a ritual, then, this attack on the Bructeri? A show of power, to overawe the barbarians?

He remembered what Valens had told him three nights before as they had looked across the river, and apprehension itched at him. The Bructeri were the last of the Franks still under arms, and with them subdued there would be no further threat from the peoples across the Rhine. Then, with his rear and flank secured, the emperor would be free to direct his army against the new enemy: an enemy that came from the south, within the empire. Civil war was coming, of that Castus had no doubt. Roman against Roman, legion against legion. It was a type of war that Castus had never known, the sort of fighting that would make this foray into Germania look like a rabbit hunt. The thought of it roused his blood, but it chilled him to consider the cost.

And even if this expedition was a parade, or a rabbit hunt, the fighting here was real, the killing too. By midday the troops saw the first wounded men coming back down the line of march. First came walking men, hobbling on crutches or groping along in linked groups led by slaves. Then came others carried on stretchers, or on the backs of mules. The men of the Sixth moved off the trail each time to let them past; most were silent, a few called words of encouragement to men they knew.

Soon afterwards, as the trail began to descend from the ridge, the first groups of prisoners were herded back down the column. A few at first, then they came in their scores, roped together at the neck and driven by slaves, destined to be slaves themselves. All of them were women and children, or older people. Not a man of fighting age among them. Castus watched one group of them as he stood in the shade of a spreading tree, drinking water. The captives were dressed in rough tunics of red or yellow wool. A lot of them had yellow hair, and the women wore it in braids down their backs. They passed with heads down, many of them weeping, but as Castus watched, one young woman raised her head and glared back at him, her eyes bright blue in the sunlight, her face taut with sorrowing hatred.

'Not surprising their menfolk don't let themselves be taken,' Diogenes commented. 'The last lot of Franks that surrendered to us got used as wolf-bait in the arena!'

'They look like my people,' Castus said. He watched the woman as she moved away, but she did not glance back at him again.

The trail dropped further, then rose onto a last ridge before winding into a wide river valley. All along the valley the smoke trails were rising, and in places Castus could make out the roofs of the thatched houses as the fire took them. This was surely the heartland of the Bructeri, the place they had thought safe from Roman arms. He had to remind himself that Bructeri warbands had raided freely across the Rhine for years. The savagery they had brought to the Roman province was being repaid to them now.

The soldiers moved down into the valley, following wider dirt roads between fields of standing corn and clusters of ransacked huts. At one point a cow stood in the middle of the path and would not move, and the troops streamed around it; no doubt it would be butchered later. Bodies were piled in the ditches, the blood bright in the sun.

Smoke from the cooking fires hung low over the encampment that evening. Around every fire clouds of insects shimmered, and the men sat eating in weary silence, swatting at them occasionally. They had brought no tents, and would be spreading their bedrolls for the second night on open ground, but the air was warm and the long march had tired them. Sentries paced the perimeter wall of staked and heaped timber, and beyond them the forests grew hazy in the lowering light.

Castus sat a little way from the fire, out of the smoke, polishing the spots of tarnish from his helmet with a damp rag and ashes from the firepit. His muscles ached as he sat, but it was a welcome ache, a familiar one. Tomorrow the Sixth Legion would move up to the head of the column and lead the advance further along the valley to the north-east. There would be fighting ahead, and after two days of trailing the rest of the army the men were ready for it. Now and then he would remember the face of the barbarian woman, the captive who had stared at him, and the hatred in her eyes. But he had lived with war for most of his life; people always suffered, he told himself. It was the way of things. The will of the gods.

He went on with his polishing. Even on campaign, he kept the highest standards, and expected his men to do the same. The slightest spot of rust weakened a sword or a helmet; the slightest worn patch of leather weakened a boot or a belt. A soldier should make sure that his tools would not fail him when he needed them. He was glad of these practical things, which distracted him from other thoughts.

Distorted in the curve of polished metal he saw the figure of a man behind him.

'Centurion Aurelius Castus,' the voice said. 'I haven't forgotten you.'

For a moment Castus did not turn – he had recognised the man from his reflection. Looking up slowly at his own men around the fire, Castus silenced them with his glance. Only then did he turn, slowly, without obvious concern.

'I haven't forgotten that tap you gave me in Bagacum either,' Urbicus said. The centurion was standing just out of reach, a couple of his soldiers from the Second Legion flanking him, but he was close enough to draw the men at the fire to their feet. He glared at Castus, his twisted mouth curling into a smile. 'One of these days I'm going to give you a tap back,' he said to him. 'And I'll make sure you feel it. May be the last such tap you'll need.'

Modestus had moved up beside Castus; he reached across and laid a hand on his arm, but Castus did not need it. There was no way he was rising to the challenge. Not here.

Urbicus laughed, a dry bitter creaking sound from the back of his throat. Over his shoulder Castus watched him, saying nothing. The two men from the Second Legion were looking sure of themselves, chests out – but there were half a dozen of the Sixth around the fire. They were bluffing.

'Well, I'll be seeing you, then,' Urbicus said, and began backing away. He mimed a thought striking him. 'I hear they call you Knucklehead,' he said.

Castus felt his shoulders rise and tighten. Modestus kept the grip on his arm.

'Perhaps, one day,' the other centurion went on, 'I'll get to weigh that skull of yours, see how dense it really is, eh?' He made a gesture with his cupped hand, as if he were weighing a sack in his palm. Then he barked a laugh and strutted away between the fires and the groups of other, oblivious men, his own soldiers grinning in easy triumph as they trailed after him.

Modestus spat on the ground where the centurion had been standing, and punched his fist up with his thumb jutting between his fingers.

'May Hades break his arse,' he said.

Three hours into the march the next day, they met the first of the barricades. A great barrier of fallen trees, rising higher than a man and blocking the neck of the valley. From a distance it could have looked natural – just windblown timber. Closer, and the ripe yellow scars of fresh-cut wood were clear to see, and the way the limbs of the trees had been artfully meshed together. The light infantry of the auxilia had already clambered across the barricade by the time the legionary vanguard arrived; they would create a perimeter on the far side, but for the rest of the army, the cavalry and the baggage mules to pass, the obstruction would need to be cleared.

Without the tree cover the morning sun was hot and bright. Stripped to his waist, sweat tiding down his back and dripping into his eyes, Castus worked with the rest of his men, swinging an axe at the mesh of timber. Most of the others had also shed their tunics; each man was surrounded by a flickering nimbus of insects, drawn to the sweat and the hot blood. The noise of the axes and picks was constant, metal biting wood, chopping and clawing. As each axe-scarred length of trunk was cut free other men wrestled it up between them, carrying it and hurling it off the path. The rest of the army was drawn up along the trail behind them in close defensive formation, alert for ambush from either flank.

'This is labour for slaves!' Flaccus cried, wiping a hairy forearm across his brow. 'Why don't they get them to do this?' The standard-bearer and his boat's company had reappeared early on the morning of the river crossing, to much mocking comment, after a night wandering lost in the forest.

'Army slaves got it easy,' said Speratus. His broken nose gave him a brutally wicked squint. 'They just have to clean our boots and cook our dinners – not toil like this!'

'Shut up and get cutting,' Castus told them. He heaved the axe back, and then swung it down into a shower of wood splinters. They had been an hour at this work already, and the barricade was only halfway cleared. When he glanced over his shoulder he saw Jovianus the tribune standing with a group of other officers, calmly surveying the work. He clenched a curse between his teeth.

One of the men further up the pile let out a cry and tumbled backwards. Castus paused for a moment – it looked as if the man had missed his footing and fallen, but he was writhing as he lay, plucking at something in his side. A snipping sound in the air and a thud; then Castus saw the arrow shaft jutting from the timber.

'Shields!' he yelled, throwing down his axe. 'Arrow attack! Get behind your shields!'

The shields, armour and weapons had been stacked a few paces back on the trail – now most of the men made a rapid dash to retrieve them. Some stood paralysed, gripping their axes, and others leaped down among the fallen trees, trying to shelter.

'Where are the piquets?' Modestus cried. 'Where are the fucking auxilia?'

Another man screamed and fell, spinning on his heels and toppling from the barricade with an arrow in his chest. More

70

arrows were arcing down into the stacked shields, driving the men back as they scrambled for them.

Castus crouched low, dragging his shield towards him and lifting it. He scanned the wooded slopes to either side – a movement caught his eye, and he spotted the archer stepping out of cover to shoot. His reaching fingers found the shaft of a javelin, but by the time he had raised it the man was gone.

Sounds of fighting from the slopes: the auxilia on guard duty up the trail had finally noticed the attack and doubled back to drive off the archers. From the arrow-struck barricade the men of the Sixth saw running figures on the higher slopes, and heard the distant yell and cry of combat. But it was clear that most of the attackers had fled.

'Centurion!' Aelianus called. Castus jogged over to where the man was kneeling. Speratus lay beside him, an arrow in his thigh. Not a mortal wound, unless it had cut an artery, but Speratus was twisted with pain, delirious, his face swelling and turning dark red. As Castus – and the others who had gathered around – watched, Speratus's body convulsed; his mouth champed and frothed. Aelianus had been holding the wounded man, but now he released him and backed away in horror.

'Poison,' somebody said quietly.

Before long, Speratus lay silent, blue-lipped, his body still twisted and racked. Castus eased down his shoulders, and a long-held shudder ran through him.

'Four of you, bury him and the others, as deep as you can,' he said. 'The rest, get back to work.'

There were more barricades further along the valley, but rather than try and cut through them the troops made long slow detours, scaling up the valley sides through the trees, dragging

71

the protesting mules behind them. The column split apart, spreading into three ragged single files, snaking up and down the slopes, scrambling along narrow rocky dirt paths. It was late afternoon before they closed around the next village.

'We're flanking,' Castus told his men, as they gathered around him on the slope in the dapple of light. Some eased themselves down to squat in the bracken, braced on their propped spears. 'That means we move as quick and quiet as we can down this hillside and across the stream in the valley down there. That bit of yellow you can see beyond the stream is a field of barley – we follow the ditch around the rear of the field and wait there until we hear the trumpets of the main column attacking from over there. Then we go in, through the field and into the town.'

It was all they needed to know. It was all Castus knew himself; the orders had been passed down from Jovianus, and beyond him from the army commanders. There were other small units moving up on similar duties around the perimeter of the settlement; this time, the enemy would not be allowed to run.

The soldiers drank water, then began the descent. The slope was steep, and they felt their way down with reaching spears, clasping at the trees to either side. Already the sun was low in the sky, the long summer day slipping towards evening. From the lower slopes, the men could see the huts and fences below them, the orderly patchwork of fields, the animal pens and the cattle byres. Smoke rose slowly from several of the huts. Smoke of cooking fires and hearths. Soon, Castus thought, there would be far more smoke than that.

Scrambling down the last descent, the century formed a double column and splashed across the stream. Crouched low, they followed the shallow ditch up the rear of the barley field.

Once Castus drew level with the largest house at the edge of the settlement he motioned his men to halt. They dropped down gladly, settling themselves along the trench where the wall of barley would screen them from any sentinels in the village.

Castus sat on the baked lip of the ditch, his heels in muddy water. He took a chunk of spiced sausage from his haversack and pared off a slice, then chewed patiently. It could take a while for the main column to move up along the valley. The sun was still hot, and he took off his helmet to cool his sweating head.

'Centurion,' said Diogenes, dropping down to sit beside him, 'may I ask you something?'

Castus just looked at him and grunted, still chewing. The sausage was very tough.

'Do you ever experience fear, before going into combat?'

Castus chewed a bit more, then swallowed hard. The chunk of sausage jerked its way down his throat. 'Of course,' he said. 'Only madmen and liars say otherwise.'

'Then you are afraid of death?' Diogenes asked, as if this were some novel philosophical concept. They were both speaking quietly, barely above a mumble.

'Never said that,' Castus replied. 'What's death? The ground opens up and down you go, and you know nothing about it afterwards.' Although, he thought, he would not care to die as Speratus had earlier that day, frothing and writhing.

'But you say you're afraid? Of what, if not death?'

Castus thought for a moment. It was something he had never properly considered. 'Wounding,' he said at last. 'Being crippled. When it comes to swords and spears, there's plenty of sharp iron all around you. Anyone can get a hamstring cut, or lose a hand or an eye. Even a simple wound can fester, then you lose a limb. And then what?'

'And then. . . what?'

'If you've served your sixteen years you can get an honourable discharge with pay, land and tax exemptions, otherwise you're out of the army with the bare minimum.' He failed to suppress a twitch of superstitious dread. His father had ended his army career like that – fifteen years in the legion, then he lost half his left hand in a skirmish on the Danube frontier and could no longer grip a shield. The army had no use for cripples. The bitterness of that had poisoned his father's mind, and he had passed that poison on to Castus himself, in kicks and blows and savage words.

Diogenes sat silently for a while, digesting. From the village a rooster crowed, loud and raucous. Birds were wheeling about the sky.

'I was afraid during the fight on the riverbank,' Castus said quietly. He wanted nobody else to hear. 'During it, not before. I thought I'd led the men into something that was going to get them all killed.'

'Fear of shame, then?'

'I suppose so,' Castus said. Shame, he thought, was the worst punishment of all.

The sound of the trumpets was sudden and clear, riding across from the direction of the valley. Immediately afterwards came the echo of a massed war cry as the legions stormed into the western end of the settlement. Castus was already up on his feet, lacing his helmet straps beneath his chin, the rest of the men quickly rising behind him as he swung his shield to the front and strode into the swaying wall of barley.

They moved with a steady crackling step, breasting through the barley with their shields, trampling loose stalks beneath their boots as the pollen dust rose around them. Every man had spear or javelin readied, eyes fixed on the edge of the village. There was a brief noise of clacking chickens from behind the huts, but the only other sound was the rush and swish of the massed stalks parting before the advancing troops. Off on their right flank Castus could see other units also moving, scrambling along culverts and across meadows, closing around the village from all directions. He was braced for the first cries from between the huts, the first arrows or javelins slicing down from the clear sky.

'After me!' he shouted as he neared the edge of the field, and broke into a run, kicking through the last of the crop. Behind him his men sprang forward, erupting into a broken roar.

There was another ditch at the field edge, then an earth bank up to a fence of close-woven wattles. Castus leaped across the ditch in a stride, his boots grinding the loose soil from the bank; then he slammed his sword into the wattles of the fence. The dry weave of sticks burst apart, and he heaved his shield against the breach until it was wide enough to pass through.

Inside the broken fence, the smell hit him first; then he felt his boots slide beneath him and managed to catch himself clumsily before he fell sprawling. Wet puddled manure underfoot, and a great muddy sow staring at him from the corner of the sty. Two more men crashed through the fence behind him, then gasped in disgust.

'Through here,' Castus yelled over his shoulder. He crossed the pigsty, stamping through liquid shit, and kicked at the gate. The flimsy boards shattered, and he charged through the gap.

Silence. The village was as placid as it had appeared from the hillside. A few chickens still squabbled in panic around the open hut doors. But there was no sign of the inhabitants. Castus glanced up, and saw the smoke still rising peacefully from the hut roof. He looked to his left, and saw the vanguard troops of the main column moving between the huts, kicking doors, finding nobody. Behind him his men were piling through the gate of the sty, several streaked and spattered with filth – they had slipped and fallen as they had broken through the fence.

Fearing ambush, Castus moved around the wall of the hut, motioning for his men to follow. His ears were primed for the sound of a bow, his senses for the thwack of an arrow into a mud wall, or into flesh. His breath came in bursts. He raised his right forearm to wipe his face, and the mail grated against his brow – he had forgotten he was wearing armour.

The hut was a forge. As he reached the wide front doors, Castus glanced in at the straw and the big iron anvil, the tools still laid out ready for use. He edged inside, into the dim familiar stink of metal, charcoal and soot. Memories of his youth rose in him for a moment. The forge fire was still hot, the embers glowing orange in their nest of grey-white ash.

'They've even left their dinner here,' Aelianus said. On a low table just inside the hut door there were chunks of black bread and hard white cheese, with a platter of honey cakes. Aelianus picked up a cake, smiled and raised it to his mouth.

Castus swatted it out of his hand, and it dropped into the dust.

'Remember Speratus?' he said savagely. Aelianus's face paled, and his throat rose and fell as he swallowed back bile.

As he left the hut there were already troops moving in columns though the central cleared space in the village. The sky was smudged with smoke, and the smell of burning thatch soured the air. A sudden cheer went up from the soldiers, and they turned to face back down the road. Castus moved up to join them, still wary. From the direction of the main valley road a mounted cavalcade was cantering between the enclosure fences and into the village. At the head, the unmistakeable figure in the gleaming gilded cuirass and purple cape. Castus stiffened to attention, then threw up his arm in salute as the emperor and his retinue

76

rode past. Constantine's face was set hard, reddened and furious. And then they were gone, and dust fogged the air in their wake.

It was only moments later that the men gathered around the huts heard the shouting from the far village boundary. Castus glanced around, and saw Erudianus with his head raised, scenting the air.

'Trouble,' the tracker said.

'Lead me,' Castus ordered, then waved for the rest to follow as Erudianus set off at a jog.

The air was still full of fine dust, but as he ran Castus could hear the sounds of fighting: a yell, a ring of iron and a thud of blade against shield. He doubled the fence between two huts, and saw the knot of men gathered along the far boundary of the compound. Bodies sprawled in the dirt: enemy warriors. Whatever skirmish had just erupted seemed over already. He slowed to a stride. A dog was barking and whining.

'They were hiding in the ditch!' a soldier exclaimed. A man from another legion; Castus did not recognise him. 'Tried to burst out and get to the emperor and his people!' The man's mouth was grinning slackly, stupidly. 'But our men got them! Yes, we did – and only that one centurion down!'

'Who?' Castus demanded, and then broke into a run again before the man could blurt out his guesses. Already he could see the cluster of soldiers surrounding the fallen man; their dark blue shields had the winged Victory emblem of the Sixth Legion. The lean grey dog sat to one side, its head down on its outstretched paws.

Before he could reach them, Rogatianus was holding him back, a palm on his chest. 'I'm sorry, brother,' he said. 'Nothing you can do for him now.'

Castus shoved him aside. He strode the last few paces, hauled the men back from the fallen figure and dropped to his knees.

Valens turned his head, wincing with the effort, and Castus could see the pain in his eyes. His friend's mouth was bloody, and there was a slow red lake forming in the dirt below him. He was not wearing his mail shirt, and half of his tunic was soaked with gore.

'Got them,' Valens said weakly, and stretched his mouth in a wry grin. 'Reckon we got them all!'

Castus took his hand and clenched it tight. He tried to speak, but there was a knot of iron twisting in his throat, and he knew Valens would hear nothing now.

The ground opens up, he thought, *and down you go.*

CHAPTER V

The roaring echoed through the mutilated forest, between the trees and across the hacked stumps and the muddy green-scummed floodwater. It started as a low humming, then built rapidly into a bellow of massed voices before cresting with a shout. A moment of silence, then the hollow drumming rattle of spears against shields reverberated from behind the barricades. And then the great cry went up once more.

Castus remembered the noise the Picts had made, the hissing and howling they had raised before their attack on the hilltop redoubt, years ago in the far north of Britain. This war cry of the Bructeri was similar, but more unnerving in its volume and its barely leashed aggression. Many of the men in the Roman battle line were clearly feeling its effects; they stood with wide eyes and clenched teeth, gripping their shields and the shafts of their weapons. Some of the younger men were visibly trembling.

'They should save their breath for fighting,' Castus called out as another roar came from the enemy lines. 'They'll need it soon enough.'

A few of the men laughed, if nervously, though Castus was in no mood for humour. The death of his friend was a stone in his heart, and he felt primed with a violent need for revenge. Even so, for all his desire for battle it was clear that there would be no combat soon. The Bructeri had constructed a formidable fortification, and were not about to sally out of it and fight in the open. And any force trying to attack them would take severe casualties. All the Roman troops could do was shelter behind their shields and try not to lose their nerve as that terrifying noise rose from the forest opposite them.

It was even worse that they could barely see their enemy; only the tips of their wickedly barbed spears showed above the rampart of fallen trees the Bructeri had constructed on the far side of the shallow valley. The stream had been dammed or diverted in some way, and the waters had swelled to flood the valley floor, transforming it into a wide morass of muddy pools studded with the stumps of the hacked-down trees. Many of the tree stumps had been sharpened into stakes; in the sunlight the water appeared placid, shimmering with tiny insects, but many more such stakes were surely concealed beneath the surface, ready to impale the legs or groin of anyone attempting to wade across.

The distance over the valley and the swollen stream was not too great – Castus reckoned that a man could cover it on dry ground in two score running paces. But as soon as anyone left the cover of the trees on the Roman side they would be in range of the slingshot and arrows from the men behind the barricade, even as the water and sharpened stumps slowed any charge to a stumbling crawl. And after that, a scramble up a muddy slope into a storm of javelins, then a climb across a head-high breastwork of creaking timber. And only then would they get to face the enemy. Against those obstacles, any advance would be a slaughter yard. A prospect to chill the blood.

But that was not the plan, Castus reminded himself. The legionaries in the centre were just a blocking force, drawing the attention of the enemy while the cavalry and light troops forded the stream further to the west before attacking on the flank. Only when the cavalry attack had gone in would the legions advance. But they had been nearly an hour waiting in stoic passivity, and there had been no word from the flanking column at all.

Every time he closed his eyes, Castus saw Valens lying in the dust. The town where he had died was only two miles to the south; the scouts had reported the Bructeri position an hour after his death. The day had already been sinking into evening by then, but the soldiers had clamoured to advance at once, shouting down their tribunes when they had given the order to make camp for the night, even raising angry voices to the emperor himself as he had ridden among them. But the order was justified: the troops had been exhausted, and they had a hard fight ahead of them. Besides, the Bructeri clearly were not going anywhere.

That night the town had burned, flooding the camp of the Roman army with hot orange light and filling the sky with sparks and smoke. It was a fitting send-off for Valens, Castus thought as he stood at the camp boundary watching the fires. His friend's funeral pyre had been built of beams and hut-posts ripped from the town, stacked high, with his linen-wrapped body placed on top, the centurion's stick laid on his breast. Many of the men of Valens's century had wept openly as the pyre burned. Castus did not weep. Valens had been his closest friend since he had joined the legion back in Britain, and even if he once had reason to distrust the man, he had since forgiven him. Certainly Valens had saved his life that night on the riverbank. But all he felt was a cold desolate anger, and a sense of shame that he had not been there to help his friend in the fight. When the smoke smarted in his eyes he just blinked it away, staring into the twisting flames.

The army camped under arms, every man lying beside his shield and weapons, with a double sentry guard. Few of them slept, and in the dew-damp ash-grey dawn they rose and assembled in battle formation for their march to meet the enemy.

And there they were, Castus thought, impregnable behind their barricades. He had not had a good look before at the warriors of the Bructeri, but now as he watched he saw several of them climbing up onto their own wooden rampart to gesture and yell abuse or challenges at the Roman lines. They were tall men, muscular, some stripped to the waist and others dressed in woollen tunics. All were bearded, their long yellow hair drawn up and tied at the top of their heads, and they carried round shields painted in bold patterns of red, white and black.

Besides the barbed spears and javelins, many of them were armed with long, powerful-looking bows. The Romans were assembled in their cohorts just beyond effective archery range, but now and again one of the warriors leaped up on the barricade, flexed his arms and shot an arrow arcing over the swampy water. Most fell short, but when an arrow came down through the trees, shivering the leaves and bark overhead, the soldiers recoiled, cowering behind their shields in the fear that the slightest scratch or nip from one of those terrible missiles could bring a rapid and hideous death.

Castus had no idea whether the arrows were poisoned or not, but the fear was eating through his men, and their lust for battle of the evening before was rapidly draining away.

He looked to his right along the lines, and saw Rogatianus standing before his men, shield up, almost daring the distant archers to take a shot at him. On the far side of Rogatianus's men were the big red shields of Legion XXX Ulpia Victrix. To Castus's left was the old century of Valens, now commanded by his optio Macrinus. And beyond them, Castus could see the serried sky-blue shields of Legion II Augusta, with centurion Urbicus prominent in the front rank.

Urbicus glanced around, as if he sensed Castus's gaze upon him. He raised his hand in a mocking salute, his top lip drawn back from his teeth, then made a weighing gesture with his open palm. Castus lifted his sword in reply. *If I meet you on the battlefield. . .*

'Centurion!' a voice cried, and Castus looked back to see a runner pushing his way between the armoured bodies of the men in the battle line. 'Tribune Jovianus sends his greetings and requests to speak to you!' the man declared, pointing back through the trees.

Castus nodded, directed a last glare across the water at the enemy barricade, then followed the runner back through the lines, calling out to Modestus to take over. He stamped his way over the bracken and trampled ferns behind the last ranks, and by the time he found Jovianus most of the other centurions of the detachment had already joined the tribune. Urbicus was there too, standing to one side with his arms folded across his chest.

'I'll make this brief,' Jovianus said, to a growl of assent. 'The flanking attack by the cavalry and auxilia has been held up – the stream further down was wider and deeper than expected, and they've had to march further west and south to find a crossing. Therefore, the legions must advance against the enemy position.'

'Against that?' said Rogatianus, flinging his hand in the direction of the barricade. 'Dominus, we'll be cut to pieces!'

'That matters little,' the tribune declared. 'We are soldiers, and we have our orders. . . I will lead the advance myself, and the centuries of the Sixth and Second Legions will be the vanguard.'

As he spoke, Castus could see the twitch of the tribune's jaw. The man was trying not to let his fear show. He had never thought much of Jovianus, but at least he was brave, or attempting to be.

By the time he returned to the front ranks of his men, the news of the impending attack had already spread among them. They muttered, many of them bunching closer together and crouching tighter behind their shields as if they wanted to root themselves to the ground.

'Men of the British legions!' Jovianus cried, striding out into the mud-scarred clearing before the battle lines. 'Now is your chance to redeem your reputation as soldiers! Now, before the eyes of the emperor himself, you can display the true courageous virtue of Roman warriors!'

That was a mistake, Castus thought. At the mention of the emperor half of the men had turned to look back, craning their heads to stare through the trees. The barbarians on the other side of the flooded valley must have heard it too. They sent up a massed yell of defiance, then started beating their weapons and shields against the timbers of their barricade.

'Soldiers, face to the front!' Jovianus cried, his voice cracking. He swept his cloak back from his sword arm, hefted his shield. 'After me – ad-*vance*!'

A shiver ran along the lines, a few knots of men edging forward. Castus stepped out from the ranks of his men, swinging the flat of his blade against the nearest shields. *Unconquered Sun, protect me now. . . Your light between us and evil. . .*

'Come on, then!' he said. 'Or are you going to let me and the tribune fight this battle on our own?'

The line shuddered again, the men keeping themselves covered. Only a few of them began to shuffle forward, one step at a time. Castus felt cold sweat breaking all over his body. He had trained these men himself – would they really disgrace him now? Or, he thought as he turned again to face across the swamp, was the disgrace his own? He felt the fear racking him, threatening to buckle his body. His men could read that, as clearly as they could hear the fear in the tribune's voice when he had addressed them. . .

Only madmen and liars say they are not afraid.

Yells from his left, and Castus glanced around to see Jovianus sprawled on his back. He thought the tribune had slipped in the mud, then saw the blood welling from between the cheek guards of his helmet. On the enemy barricade, a lone bare-chested slinger gave a shout of triumph, raising his fist above his head before dropping back out of sight. A party of soldiers rushed out from the Roman lines to raise their shields over the fallen tribune.

'Slingshot hit him in the mouth,' Flaccus said, wincing as he gripped the standard with white knuckles. 'Reckon that's the end of his career as a public speaker.'

From the enemy barricades the great roaring battle cry went up again. But now the Roman horns were blowing the general advance, a discordant brassy braying. Castus saw Rogatianus and his men beginning to push forward towards the swampy water.

A little to the left, a fallen tree lay partially submerged, black with rot and old moss, but the jutting craggy branches offered some cover.

'This way,' Castus called quickly, gesturing to Flaccus, then scrambled down the slope towards the tree. When he turned he saw the standard-bearer coming after him, a loose array of men following. His boots slid in mud, then he was in water up to his knees. Already arrows were pocking the surface ahead of him, some of them smacking into the wet timber of the tree. Castus recoiled as a slingstone exploded off the trunk beside him, scattering flakes of bark. To his right, Rogatianus and his men were wading out into the flood, surging the water into dark brown froth, but their advance was already slowing under the rain of missiles.

Shouts from behind him, a trumpet cry and the sound of horses; Castus crouched beside the fallen tree and looked back, and the blood froze in his body.

Three riders, coming at the gallop down through the troop lines. Two wore the white cloaks of the Corps of Protectores, but the lead rider blazed in purple and gold.

'Men of the Sixth Legion!' the emperor cried as his champing horse circled before the trees. 'Remember Eboracum! You were first to acclaim me then – who will follow me now?'

Without waiting for an answer, Constantine spurred his mount forward towards the water, the two bodyguards galloping after him. For a moment the troops were motionless, stunned, their faces blanched above their shields.

'The emperor!' Castus yelled, shoving himself away from the tree. 'Protect the emperor!'

Water lashed and sprayed around the horses, brilliant in the sunlight. One of the Protectores went down at once, straight over his horse's head as the animal stumbled and fell. Castus grabbed the standard-bearer and hauled him up beside him.

'Wedge formation!' he shouted, the words tearing his throat. 'Form on me!'

Shield high above the water, he began to force his way out into the stream. Behind him men stumbled and staggered, bunching into a tight knot of shields. The water felt thick as oil, the bed soft sucking mud grabbing at their boots, and all around them was the whip and whine of arrows and slingshot.

The second bodyguard was down, his horse rearing back with an arrow in its breast and spilling the rider from the saddle. The animal tumbled, thrashing its hooves, and the surface of the water shattered into fountains of spray.

Castus kept his head low, concentrating only on pushing forward into the stream. The light was hot around him, and the muddy water dragged at the links of his mail – he was thigh deep, now waist deep, half swimming as he drove himself onward. Beneath his breath he muttered a constant prayer. When he risked a glance above the shield rim he saw Constantine, his big white horse foaming, poised in midstream with his sword raised towards the enemy and his stretched face crying defiant rage.

Then the horse shuddered, tried to rear and collapsed upon its haunches in the flood. Its chest was streaming with blood where it had run against one of the submerged stakes. Castus could hear the wild rage in the voices of his men, the fear-dispelling anger. Something caught at his ankles and he toppled forward, plunging face first into the water; a fist gripped the back of his mail and hauled him to his feet, and he surged forward again.

Constantine was down, arrows flickering around him as he tried to roll from the saddle of the dying horse. Brown water seethed, turning dark red with blood. Two arrows struck Castus's shield in quick succession, and a slingstone cracked off his helmet, but he could feel the ground getting firmer beneath him, the slope of the bed rising.

Four more thrashing strides and he was beside the emperor, raising his shield above his head as the arrows lashed around them. Other men – his own men – slammed up around him.

'*Testudo!*' he could hear himself shouting, and the word was almost lost in the noise of the water and the frantic screams of the dying horse. Two men were knocked down by a flailing hoof, but the rest stayed firm. Shields rattled together into a ragged screen above the fallen man.

'Modestus, Firmus,' Castus ordered, 'pull the emperor loose and carry him. We retreat to the bank.'

'No, no,' Constantine shouted. '*Advance!*' His face was grey with pain and shock, his teeth clamped hard as the two soldiers dragged him from under the fallen horse.

'Dominus! We need to pull back!' Castus glanced down at the emperor, but even as he spoke he knew there was no turning now. Constantine seized Castus by the belt, hauling on it to drag himself free of the horse. His gilded cuirass streamed with blood and muddy scum.

Castus lowered his shield and peered over the rim; the enemy barricade was only a score of paces away, the enemy beginning to scramble across it and spill down the bank towards the stricken emperor. But there was another sound now, a regular snap and hiss from the forest behind and the air above. As he stared, Castus saw a warrior on the barricade transfixed by a ballista bolt. Arrows were falling among the advancing Bructeri. Roman archers had moved up to support the attack, and artillery too.

Over to the left, beyond Rogatianus's men still trapped in midstream, Castus saw a solid wedge of legionaries forcing their way across the flood. At their head was Tribune Jovianus, his face a mask of blood as he screamed through broken teeth. With the defenders distracted by the emperor's charge, the men at the barricade had thinned at that point – Jovianus was already halfway to the far bank, and the men behind him moved with a fierce discipline.

Dragging Modestus close, Castus yelled into his ear. 'Take two men and get the emperor to safety. Cover him with your shields – don't let him move forward again! Do it, whatever he says!'

Modestus nodded, slack-jawed but resolute, and Castus shoved him away.

'Wedge!' he called, striding forward again through the shallows. 'Wedge formation – follow behind me!'

His men meshed behind him, pressing forward for the bank. Every step dragged a weight of soaked clothing and armour, the mud trawling off them as they moved. But they were together, shields locked and spears levelled, every man screaming his own hoarse cry as they stumbled up out of the water onto the bank.

Castus looked to his right, and saw Flaccus fall with an arrow in his face. He saw Diogenes snatch the standard from the bloodied water and raise it high.

He looked to his left and saw Jovianus and his men hurling themselves at the barricade, the bristle of spears raised against them, bare-chested men pelting slingshot and loosing arrows from a sword's length away.

Up the slope, skidding and sliding on the wet earth and bloody grass. Something nicked his thigh, and pain lanced up into his hips as he saw the flung javelin skittering away. A body fell against him – Aelianus, dead eyes turned skywards – and he shoved it aside with his sword arm. Stumbling, he dropped to one knee and saw that his shield was fletched with half a dozen arrows; two of the vicious barbed heads had punched through the wood.

Over to the left the attack was faltering, men falling, others spilling back down towards the water. Through a fog of pain Castus watched the last of the soldiers scrambling up onto the barricade. He watched Jovianus shouldering his way between two Bructeri warriors, cutting and stabbing low on the brink of the fortification. He watched the spears dart out and cut at the tribune's legs, a swinging club knock him down. Then they were on him, dragging him across the mesh of timber, stabbing him in the face and body with savage triumph.

Move, got to move. . . Castus dared not look back to see how many of his own men still lived. The pain rushed in waves through his whole body, and his right leg was streaming red. When he raised his hand an arrow skimmed across the back of it, slicing the skin, and for a moment he saw his own blood misting the air.

Roaring, he forced himself upright. His shield was heavy as lead in his left hand, his right hand a bright fist of agony as he gripped his sword. Ahead of him rose the enemy wall, but he spilled left, along the line of the timber barricade, running crablike to keep his shield partly covering his body.

Three men had grappled Jovianus's corpse between them; one was still stabbing the fallen man in the face, plunging his knife as though he was breaking ice with a pick. The other two were trying to wrestle the body back over the barricade, but the armoured torso was caught between the meshed branches.

Castus took three more running strides, then hurled away his arrow-stuck shield and leaped. His reaching left hand grabbed at the spiked branches of the barricade and he hauled himself up. Timber groaned and shifted beneath his weight. *Gods, if I slip and fall now I'm done. . .* But he moved with the surety of a condemned man, all terror and pain gone and only fighting rage driving him. One slashing blow, and a yellow-bearded face burst red and vanished. Three more heaving lunges and he could stand upright, braced on the tangled mass of fallen trees.

The two men trying to drag the tribune's body had already slithered back. The knifeman was still intent on his mutilation; Castus chopped down and his blade half severed the man's head. He pulled, and for a moment terror gripped him as he felt the sword jammed tight in the dead man's spine. An arrow punched into his shoulder, almost knocking him off his feet; his armour and the padding beneath stopped the impact, but the arrow remained stuck there, trapped in the links of his mail. A javelin cut the air beside his face. Then the sword came free, and Castus was crouching above the ripped corpse of Jovianus, staring down into a howling mass of enemy warriors.

Shouts behind him. An unearthly calm possessed him, an absolute sense of focus, slowing time. He had known this before in battle. The hollow at the heart of fear. He glanced back and saw Rogatianus powering up the slope at a run, his dark face open in a yell and his men formed up behind him.

'*Victrix! VIC-TRIX!*'

Castus remembered Valens as he lay dying. Blood on his teeth as he tried to smile. What had happened to that rangy grey dog he had befriended? Had anyone even looked for it after the funeral? He glanced down at the ruined mess of Jovianus's face.

Then the howl of combat was all around him, and he felt his legs shaking as the barricade shuddered beneath a rush of armoured men. *A clean death*, he thought. *A fighting death. Without shame.*

Grinning, he turned to face the enemy, then hurled himself down into the glittering array of their blades.

CHAPTER VI

Scented quiet, the air moving slowly on cool marble, stirring the long drapes.

Before him were the tallest doors he had ever seen. Inlaid wood set with bronze, three or four times the height of a man. Without turning his head he lifted the sword from his scabbard and held it out. Unseen hands bore it away. Somewhere, very distant, he could hear a speaking voice, slow and sonorous, echoing slightly.

With the faintest squeal of oiled bronze the doors parted and opened. He stood still for a moment, braced. His leg still ached. Then he breathed in and marched slowly forward over the threshold.

An immensity of light above him. High arched windows spilled sun, but the lower depths of the vast chamber still appeared dim, the polychrome mosaics of the floor vague as the bottom of a deep pool through still water. A purple drape shifted gently in the low stir of air as he advanced with measured step, then halted again.

He was barely aware of the figures standing to either flank, the silent men in their heavily embroidered mantles, the guards with silvered spears.

'Aurelius Castus, centurion of the Sixth Legion,' a voice announced.

'You may proceed,' another said, more quietly.

The drapes parted as he approached, and he felt himself sinking in stature even as the space rose above him. Across the polished floor was the stepped dais, a tall apse rising behind it, blazing with light. Suspended between the glare and the deep shadow, a single seated figure in purple and gold. Castus dropped his eyes at once, concentrating on taking the right number of steps forward. When he came to a halt once more, the cry of acclamation went up from the assembly, and he joined his voice to theirs.

'Constantine Augustus! The gods preserve you for us! Your salvation is our salvation! In truth we speak! On our oath we speak!'

For what seemed a long time there was only breathless silence. It had been months, maybe years, since Castus had felt so utterly alone. He thought of his men, of Diogenes and Modestus, Rogatianus and the other few survivors of that desperate foray across the river valley three months before. He had left them at Colonia Agrippina, only the day after he received the imperial summons. He remembered them cheering him, drinking with him before his departure. Would he ever see them again? He thought back to the days of the campaign against the Bructeri, the long marches after that battle in the valley, the burning towns and the columns of slaves. The enemy had put up no further fight, but it had been hard, wearying toil all the same, a tedium of sweat and blisters, dirt and badly healed wounds, of realising the loss of men he had not known had fallen. All that was behind him now. The life of the legion was behind him, perhaps for good. The simple life he had always known, and loved.

'Aurelius Castus.' The voice was high and lisping, as if it came from the dead air. 'As it has come to our notice that

93

you have performed with valour upon the field of battle, and upheld with great courage and loyalty your military vows, it is the desire of the Divine Wisdom that you be received into the body of the Protectores of the Sacred Bodyguard. Approach the altar and make sacrifice.'

Four steps, and the low altar was before him, the images of the gods lit by a twisting flame. A grave-faced attendant stood beside it with a gold platter; Castus kissed his fingers and touched them to his brow, then took a pinch of incense and sprinkled it onto the flame, trying not to cough as the fumes rose.

'Now recite the oath.'

Tight-chested, he drew a long breath. For a moment he feared his voice was gone; to speak into that vast hush was surely an act of madness. The honour being conferred upon him seemed a vast weight – most men were not elevated to the Protectores until they had served twenty years or more. It was a distinguished position: the Protectores were an elite corps, the closest bodyguards of the emperor, all of them individually selected. Castus felt the pressure of an immense expectation upon him, but he found the words, the phrases of the terrible vow he had been taught. He raised his hand, and heard his voice reciting them.

'I swear to Jupiter Optimus Maximus, to Sol Invictus, to all the immortal gods and goddesses of Rome, and to the emperor himself, that I shall be loyal to the Emperor Flavius Valerius Aurelius Constantinus Augustus, his children, household, and descendants throughout my life, both in word, deed, and thought, holding as friends those they hold as friends and considering those as enemies whom they judge to be enemies.

'I shall not be sparing of my body or my soul or my life, but as Protector of the Sacred Bodyguard I will face every peril in the emperor's service in accordance with this vow. If

I should recognise or hear spoken, plotted, or done anything contrary to this, I will report it and be an enemy of the person speaking, plotting, or doing harm to the emperor or his family. Whomsoever they judge to be enemies, or who imperils them or their safety by arms or by civil war, I shall not cease to hunt him down by land and by sea with iron in hand.

'If I should do anything contrary to this oath or fail to do what I have sworn, I impose a curse upon myself encompassing the destruction and total extinction of my body, soul, life, children, and my entire family, so neither earth nor sea may receive their bodies nor bear fruit for them.'

A brief pause, then the same voice spoke again. 'You may approach the Presence.'

They had given him soft-soled shoes that pinched his toes, and he walked without the familiar grate and stamp of hobnails. He kept his gaze on the floor ahead of him, then ascended carefully the first two steps of the dais.

'Kneel, and perform the Adoration of the Purple.'

Castus eased himself down on one knee on the cold stone. Before him was the hem of the imperial robe, spread upon the marble floor of the dais. He stooped forward, and took hold of the heavy cloth. His fingers felt clumsy, the scar on the back of his right hand still raw and livid. He lifted the hem of the purple robe to his mouth and lightly kissed it, then let it drop.

'You may receive the codicil.'

Still kneeling, Castus raised his hands with palms spread. He was aware of the whisper of bodies moving quietly around him, and then his hands were draped with a strip of white linen embroidered in gold. He lifted his veiled hands towards the seated emperor, and felt something placed upon them. When he lowered his hands, a thin roll of vellum sealed in purple wax lay upon the linen strip. His letter of appointment.

'Aurelius Castus.' It was a shock to hear that voice again. He remembered it well, that same hard flat tone. The last time he had heard that voice, it had been screaming at him from the bloody spume of the flooded valley as the arrows whined around them. Did the emperor remember that Castus had ordered his men to retreat? If he had, that lapse had been forgiven now.

'We accept you into our Corps of Protectores, with the rank of *ducenarius*,' the emperor said. 'May the gods give you strength in our service.'

Castus was still staring at the letter in his palms, but he could tell that the emperor had barely moved as he spoke. Not a trace of emotion in the words.

'Stand,' the lisping man said quietly, 'make your salute, and retreat.'

Moving carefully, clasping the rolled codicil, Castus raised himself from the steps and took ten paces backwards, never once glancing up or turning himself from the emperor. Then he lifted his hand in salute.

'*Constantine Augustus!*' he said, and his words rang back at him. '*The gods preserve you for us! Your salvation is our salvation!*' In the echoes of that sound the whole vast chamber seemed to stir into life, men moving to either side of him as the purple drapes descended once more.

Castus felt the tension break inside him. He was trembling, and the sealed imperial letter in his fist was growing damp with sweat. He was a Protector now, one of the elite guardians of the emperor himself. The swords around the throne. And nothing in his life would be the same again.

PART TWO

CHAPTER VII

January AD *309*

'You know what they're calling you now, don't you?'
Nigrinus gave a thin smile and shook his head.

'The Flycatcher,' Flaccianus told him, smirking. 'I overheard them, but wasn't sure what they meant at first – it had to be you, though.'

'I can think of worse names.'

'Seems you're getting quite a reputation for yourself these days.'

'What is a man without a reputation?' Nigrinus said, shrugging. With a slim gold pin he speared one of the pickled olives from the dish on the table between them. 'They find what I do undignified, is that it? *The eagle does not catch flies.*'

Outside the sealed room, the night was cold and the wind skittish, rattling at the shudders and moaning in the deep courtyard. It was late, and the sprawling imperial palace was mostly closed and darkened in sleep. Only in this minor wing of the School of Notaries was there light and subtle speech.

'It's more probably that thing you do with your mouth, when you're thinking,' Flaccianus said. He thinned his lips, then opened and closed his mouth, like a fish.

Nigrinus gave a sour grimace. He lifted the olive to his mouth. 'Well, if my brothers in the imperial offices suspect I am merely catching flies. . .' he said thoughtfully, before chewing and swallowing, 'then it only makes them more careless, and my task more interesting.'

'But isn't that what you want?' Flaccianus said. His fingers flexed and closed with a rattle of cheap rings. 'To catch them, I mean?'

'If they are doing wrong, it is my sworn duty as notary of the emperor to prevent them. Didn't you take the same oath, when you joined the *agentes in rebus*?'

Flaccianus was laughing silently, his glistening cheeks bulging and contracting in the glow from the single lamp. 'Everyone takes the oath,' he said. 'Not everyone follows that particular clause so avidly.' He helped himself to an olive, his fingers dabbling in the dish of oil. Nigrinus tightened his lips in disgust, then put down the pin and pushed the dish away from him.

'What's the news from the consistorium meeting?' he said, turning to the stack of documents that Flaccianus had brought him, wax tablets and scrolls piled on the tabletop in the lamplight.

'Mainly talk of the conference at Carnuntum,' Flaccianus told him. He had noticed Nigrinus abandoning the olives, and drew the dish over to his side of the table. 'It's definite that Licinius has been proclaimed as the new western Augustus. Our Constantine has been officially demoted to Caesar, although nobody expects us to pay any attention. And Maxentius is officially declared a usurper and enemy of the people. Who is Licinius anyway?'

'Old military friend of Galerius,' Nigrinus said, running his fingers over the documents. As an *agens in rebus*, an imperial courier, Flaccianus was permitted to examine the mail, but forbidden to tamper with it in any way. Nigrinus, however, had managed to lean on him. He had a remit to investigate the communications of the household of the former Augustus

Maximian, and identify any potentially treasonous dealings with the usurper Maxentius in Rome. A delicate task, and necessarily conducted in secrecy.

The orders came from his own chief, Aurelius Zeno, the *primicerius notariorum*. But it could also be a dangerous task, if the surveillance were discovered. Which was why Nigrinus had seen fit to widen his remit and investigate all communications between the palace and Italy, including those of Aurelius Zeno. . . One could never be too careful about these things, after all.

He selected a tablet, and with a practised flick of the gold pin he lifted the seal without breaking the wax impression. Only the emperor's officials were permitted to use the imperial despatch service, and most of them used it for their own private correspondence as well. A tolerated abuse, and a useful one.

'What of Maximian?' he asked. Constantine's difficult father-in-law had also attended the conference on the Danube. Its ostensible purpose: to restore the harmony of the empire. Real purpose, Nigrinus thought: a blatant bid by Maximian to have his own power restored.

'Apparently he left empty-handed,' Flaccianus said, idly sifting through a few of the documents. Nigrinus batted his fingers away. Flaccianus pursed his lips in assumed pique. 'He did make a last bid to tempt Diocletian out of retirement.'

'He did?' Nigrinus looked up from the rather boring love letter he was scanning. 'And?'

'Diocletian said. . .' Flaccianus began, and then chuckled. Not a pleasant sound. 'He said. . . *If you could see the size of the cabbages I've grown with my own hand at my villa at Spalatum, you wouldn't ask such stupid things of me!*'

Nigrinus smiled, despite himself, and had to look away. Diocletian had always been the intelligence behind the partnership of emperors. Maximian was all bluster and rage, good at leading men but impulsive, boorish and often rash. Nigrinus was glad that Diocletian had kept himself out of these current turmoils. He had always regarded the old senior emperor as an admirable figure, a titan in a world of comparative dwarfs. Let him remain with his cabbages. Heroes should know when their day is done.

'So Maximian is coming back here to us,' Flaccianus said, 'to rejoin his household-in-exile.'

'To rejoin his loving son-in-law and devoted daughter, you mean. Such is the line to take. Meanwhile, we must assume that the breach with his son remains officially irreparable.'

Nigrinus snapped open another of the tablets. More dull stuff, something about villa renovations. He tried to force himself to concentrate, but would far rather do this alone. Any amount of code might be concealed in such mundane material – although anyone genuinely planning treason would be unlikely to communicate it via the imperial post; all he could hope for were the ripples of conspiracy, the shadow of a plot. He was sure that such a conspiracy must exist; if it did not, it was his job to create it.

'According to this,' he said, studying the tablet, 'the wife of Gregorius, *comes rei militaris*, claims that her husband had a dream in which he fell into a vat of purple dye.'

Flaccianus sucked in breath. 'That might give a man ideas above his station!' he said. 'Very dangerous things, dreams.'

'Yes, people should really try not to have them,' Nigrinus said vaguely, his eyes flickering over the text on the tablet. 'Or, if they must, they should try not to tell their wives about them. . . What of matters in Rome?'

'There are food riots,' Flaccianus said. 'Maxentius sent in the Praetorians to put them down, which the plebs loved, of

102

course. They're beginning to regret their choice of usurper.'

'He had no alternative, as long as Domitius Alexander holds Africa. He can choke off the grain supply whenever he wants.'

Domitius Alexander was another problem. The former governor-in-chief of the African provinces, apparently a feeble old man, had allowed himself to be proclaimed emperor by the provincials and the garrison. *Just what the world needs now*, Nigrinus thought: *another emperor. . .* So Alexander was an enemy of Maxentius, who believed that he should control Africa, and needed the grain. But was he yet an ally of Constantine? Nigrinus reminded himself that he should research links between those at Constantine's court and the supporters of the African usurper.

'Apparently Maxentius has also thrown out the high priest of the Christians,' Flaccianus said. 'He officially ended the persecution in Italy, declared their religion legitimate, allowed them to appoint a chief priest, but then they immediately fell to fighting among themselves. Seems that now we're not persecuting them, they're busily persecuting each other – one half reckons the other half surrendered their faith for a quiet life, or something. So Maxentius banished their man and installed his opponent. He'll have no peace with them!'

'Indeed not,' Nigrinus said. He felt a laugh gathering in his chest and suppressed it. 'Anything that vexes our enemies is a boon.' But Constantine also favoured the Christians – would they cause such turmoil in his domains too?

There was nothing of interest in the documents, or nothing that his tired eyes could decipher. A shame: he always thought he would pick out the telling word or phrase, the key to the lock of treason. And with treason there came possibility. . .

'If you are the Flycatcher,' Flaccianus said as he gathered the documents back into his satchel, 'what does that make me? One of the flies? Or am I a spider, perhaps, who helps you construct your webs?'

He was smiling, unctuous. Nigrinus said nothing – he needed no help constructing his webs. And a man like Flaccianus was strictly expendable anyway, he and all those others like him, weak and venal men, liars to their oath.

'You do rather well by me,' he said. 'As I rise, you too shall rise. One hand, as they say, washes another. . . And for someone with such tastes as yours, I'd say I have proved remarkably open-handed to you.'

'Tastes?' Flaccianus said, and stretched his mouth in a yawn. Nigrinus looked away. 'Oh, that. . . Why, that's no cause for shame. I'm a man; my blood is red. Anyway, the deified emperor Tiberius is said to have enjoyed much the same sort of thing.'

Nigrinus fought down an expression of disgust. Surely, he thought, Flaccianus did not train infants to swim around him as he bathed and suck at his genitals, as that most depraved old emperor was said to have done? That was in the biography by Suetonius, he reflected. Such a quaint old style too, the Latin of two hundred years past. Emperors could never get away with such gross perversions now: the solemn mantle of state weighed too heavily upon them. The awesome burden of power. Or did they merely lack imagination these days? And perhaps such enormous gravitas made them brittle too. . .

'There is an anecdote about the emperor Domitian,' he said in a musing tone, still thinking about the biographies of Suetonius. 'He enjoyed catching flies too. But apparently the black tyrant claimed that the lot of emperors is never happy. Nobody ever believes in conspiracies against them until the conspirators are successful, which tends to leave the emperor dead.'

'An interesting conundrum – for the likes of you. After all, treasonable action is seldom called treason by posterity, if it succeeds.'

'Exactly,' Nigrinus said with a tight smile. Very occasionally Flaccianus surprised him with his acuity. He leaned back on the end of the couch, steepling his narrow fingers. 'So, to profitably uncover a conspiracy, one must first wait for the seeds of treason to bear fruit. The more fruit, the better the crop when harvest comes.'

'But if you wait too long. . .'

'Then the treason is out in the open, and you have no secrets left to reveal.'

'And then you have to decide which way to jump. . .'

Flaccianus's smile died as he took in the full implications of what he had just said. He shuddered slightly, and glanced towards the shuttered window as if feeling a draught. But Nigrinus was nodding, slow and cold.

'Let's not get ahead of ourselves,' he said quietly. 'Just follow my orders, in all things, and matters will be well.'

Flaccianus stood up, gathered his satchel and wrapped the dark cloak around his shoulders. The lamp guttered.

'Oh, and take those olives with you. I don't want them any more.'

CHAPTER VIII

S now had fallen in the night. Castus could feel it tightening the air as he rode out with the hunting party before dawn; the frozen crust muffled the sounds of the horses' hooves as they moved through the empty streets, skirting the forum, down to the river gate. Ice groaned and cracked beneath the arches of the stone bridge, and first light revealed a snow-blown landscape of white and grey as the hunters climbed into the hill country to the north-west of Treveris.

By the time it was full daylight the party had reached the boundary of the imperial hunting reserve. A score of riders, with as many men on foot accompanying them, and as they neared the villa lodge at the edge of the reserve they could hear the whine and yowl of the dogs kennelled there. An hour later they were spread out across open country, and the day was bright and cold around them, every sound crisp-edged.

They had given him the largest horse in the stable, and it bore his weight well, but even after five months of training on the practice ground to the east of the palace Castus was still not a comfortable rider. He sat heavily in the saddle, his thighs clasping the horse's flanks, chilled fingers gripping the reins. His nose was numb, and every time he inhaled he could feel the ice at the back of his throat; he had known worse on the Danube frontier, but being up on a horse seemed to make the cold sting more sharply.

The small group of Protectores rode in single file, a perimeter cordon flanking the main party of hunters around the emperor. When he glanced to his right Castus could see them, a dozen riders with hunting spears, swathed in brown mantles as they rode along the margin of the woodland. The bodyguards were supposed to remain in sight of the emperor at all times, but keep a distance, out of earshot. The hunting party included the former emperor Maximian, newly returned from the imperial conference on the Danube, and whatever matters of state might be discussed there were not to be overheard. Castus was glad of that: he had no wish to be a party to such things anyway. The trees beyond the hunters were black, and flocks of birds wheeled above the bare branches, routed out by the plunging dogs. Like the field after a battle, Castus thought.

'What are we supposed to be guarding against anyway, out here?' he called, his lips barely moving above the bunched folds of his cloak.

'Brigands!' replied Brinno, riding behind him. 'Bandits and robbers!'

Sallustius was laughing from up ahead. 'More likely the importuning provincials,' he called back, 'wanting to disturb the emperor's leisure with their pleas!'

They drew together, slowing their horses; the imperial party had paused at the edge of the wood, perhaps debating the direction of their chase.

'We'd be better off surrounding some of that lot over there,' said Victor, the last of the four men. He nodded towards the emperor and his companions, and the string of other riders and men on foot that trailed behind them, kicking up the snow. 'They're much more of a threat, I'd say. Civilians! Too many eunuchs as well – why bring eunuchs on a hunting expedition?'

'To massage their tired thighs, no doubt,' Sallustius said, compressing his squashed face into a deep grimace. He dropped from the saddle to the ground, and stood flexing his legs. 'Or somebody might be struck by a profound thought, and need it copied down before it fades. . .'

'Why are there so many eunuchs at court anyway?' Brinno asked. 'Eunuchs and Christian priests. And women!'

One of Constantine's first acts as emperor had been to lift the prohibition on Christianity in his domains; now he seemed even to favour them, and several of their priests were indeed residing at the palace. But they were quiet, studious-seeming men, not the crazed cannibal degenerates Castus had been led to expect. About the eunuchs he was less sure.

Sallustius was grinning. 'Seems strange to you, eh, my young barbarian friend?' he said to Brinno. 'The ways of the civilised world! Eunuchs make good courtiers,' he went on. 'They're loathed by most men, and owe everything to the emperor. They're ambitious, but they lack the balls to aspire to the highest offices. If you see what I mean. . .'

Brinno just shrugged, gazing with mute incomprehension towards the imperial party. Castus could not help but sympathise with the young man's disdain.

He had assumed, when he first came to the palace, that the other members of the Corps of Protectores would be men like himself, former centurions, veterans of the legions. Many of them were, but he soon discovered that many others were not.

There were fifty Protectores quartered in the palace at Treveris. Of those in Castus's section, Sallustius was a former decurion of the guard cavalry, a bow-legged man in his forties, with thinning hair and a wry squashed face; he reminded

Castus of his old friend Valens. Then there was Victor, barely out of his teens, the son of a wealthy landowner from western Gaul who had purchased his commission in the Corps; he made up for his youth and inexperience with vigour, going out every morning at dawn to ride circuits on the equestrian field, and practise the showy individual sword drills his father had taught him.

Brinno, meanwhile, was the son of a war chief of the Salian Franks. He had been captured in battle ten years before, when he was only sixteen, and held as a hostage at Treveris until his father's loyalty was assured. A lean and rangy young man, he wore his yellow hair much longer than any Roman, and had a downy growth of beard on his chin. He seemed to Castus very much like the warriors of the Bructeri he had been fighting only a few months before.

It had been strange, at first, living and serving beside such men, but Castus had quickly grown accustomed to their company, and they had accepted him with ease. The Protectores were not like a regular military unit, but there was a keen sense of pride and discipline amongst them even so. He could respect that at least.

'Do you know,' Sallustius said, as he squatted in the frozen grass, 'how they make eunuchs?'

'Make them?' Castus said. He sensed this might be another of Sallustius's strange anecdotes. Brinno at least appeared curious.

'There are three ways,' Sallustius said, raising a finger. His breath made a thin fog as he spoke. 'First, the dissolving method. This is done to boys before they reach manhood. The boy is placed in a bath of very hot water, and his ball sack is squeezed and gently crushed, until his balls dissolve. . .'

'Not possible!' Brinno said, with a look of horror.

'True! Next, the cutting method, for older youths. The

youth is made to sit on a bench with a hole in it, and his balls are pulled down through the hole. . .'

Castus shifted in the saddle; he noticed Brinno and Victor doing the same.

'. . . then two cuts are made in the ball sack with a sharp blade, and the balls pulled out and twisted together. The youth is left sitting there like that, and when the balls turn blue they can be safely nipped off with a pair of pliers.'

'People do that?' Brinno said. 'It's allowed?' He shook his head and gazed off into the snowy distance with an expression of appalled disbelief.

'No, it's illegal. But mainly it's done in Armenia and Persia, places like that,' Sallustius said, getting up from the grass. 'The eunuchs are brought into the empire as slaves. Though some desperate Roman parents do it to their children, pretending it was an accident, in the hope they'll rise to greater things.'

He swung himself back up into the saddle; over to the right, the hunting party was moving again, on along the margin of the woods.

'You said there were three ways?' Castus said. He caught Sallustius's wink.

'Oh, yes,' the older man replied. He rode up alongside Brinno. 'The third method is to place the victim upon a trestle and jerk him up and down. It's usually done in winter, in severe cold. The motion feels like riding a horse, you see. . . Eventually the balls go numb and just drop off, and the victim doesn't feel a thing. . . Sometimes, riding a real horse can have the same effect. . .'

'Bastard!' Brinno said, grinning as he blushed.

It was a few hours after daybreak when the hunting party paused to eat. They had already covered miles of woodland and hill country, and the local huntsmen that accompanied the party had brought in a few rabbits and a couple of small deer they had caught with the dogs. But there had been neither sign nor scent of the boar, their intended prey. The hunting nets had yet to be rigged, and the horsemen had not yet had a chance to try their spears.

In a clearing between the trees the slaves cleared the ground of snow, rolled out matting and stretched a canopy overhead, then piled straw bolsters to make a three-sided dining couch. They hung clay charcoal burners in the trees all around, to warm the frigid air, and then the emperor and his hunting companions reclined upon the couches, eating freshly roasted rabbit and venison while the dogs yapped and snarled over the bloody scraps in the snow nearby.

Castus stood at a discreet distance with the other Protectores. His stomach growled – he had eaten nothing that day except half a raw onion before leaving Treveris. He tried to clear his mind of everything but the task appointed to him, but still his eyes kept drifting back to the party sprawled on the dining couches beneath the canopy. Being in close proximity to the emperor and his advisors was usual for him now, but Castus had never been able to lose the unnerving sense of awe and discomfort he felt. He watched the diners on the couches, knowing that they were some of the most powerful men in the world. And yet they *were* just men: Constantine himself, red-faced and open-mouthed as he related some anecdote or called for more wine. At his right hand Maximian, greasy-fingered as he brought the steaming meat to his lips. To most of humanity these figures were as remote and austere as the gods. More powerful than gods, in a way, for their authority was immediately felt, immediately enforced here on earth. What would it be like, Castus thought, to sit among them, to share their meal and their easy laughing talk? He dared not even imagine.

Instead he scanned the others gathered around the imperial party, all at a distance, some attending to the horses while the rest just waited for the emperor's pleasure. The huntsmen were dressed in patched green clothing and sheepskin capes. Castus had noticed that several of them carried a bow mounted on a stock – they reminded him of the weapons used by the Picts, but Sallustius had said these crossbows were common hunting tools in Gaul. . .

His eyes stopped, drawn to a single figure, a single face.

'Who's that man there?' he asked in a tight-lipped whisper. 'Standing with the group between the saplings. Hair like a bowl.'

'Him?' Sallustius replied quietly. He shrugged. 'One of the notaries, I think. The short man he's talking to is Zeno, their primicerius. He must be here assisting his chief. Don't know his name, though.'

Castus nodded, but his mind was racing back through the years. Back in Britain, he had known this man. A slow heat stirred through his blood: a memory of anger. Julius Nigrinus, that was the name, and the man had conspired to start an uprising among the Picts that had killed all of Castus's men and almost killed Castus himself.

Yes, he remembered clearly now. And here the man was again, at the margins of the emperor's inner circle of power. As Castus stared at him, the man looked around. Just for a moment, their eyes met and a slight flicker passed across the face of the notary. Something close to recognition, but not quite.

Then a slave brought bread and cheese for the Protectores, with warm spiced wine, and when Castus looked back again the notary was gone.

'You know the story about the old emperor Diocletian,' Sallustius said, 'when he was a tribune here in Gaul?' They had ridden for another mile or two beyond the glade where the emperor had breakfasted. Castus shook his head.

'They say he was passing through just this area when he met an old woman. One of these old witch women, I suppose, with the power to see the future. . .'

Castus noticed Victor quickly making a sign against evil. 'Anyway,' Sallustius went on, 'the old woman accused him of being stingy – he always kept a tight purse, old Diocletian, so they say – and he told her that he'd be more generous when he was emperor.'

'Ha!' said Castus, smiling and nodding.

'No. . . that's not the funny bit,' Sallustius said with a frown, and hooked one leg casually over his saddle horn. 'The woman told him that he'd only become emperor once he'd killed *the Boar*. . . So from then on Diocletian went out hunting every chance he got – slaughtered a hecatomb of boars everywhere from here to Armenia. But he still wasn't emperor. . .'

'These old women are all liars!' Victor broke in. From the corner of his eye Castus saw a flock of crows rise from the treetops of the wood to his right. He drew in the reins and turned his head, listening.

'*Anyway*, by this time Diocletian was chief of the Protectores of the emperor Carus. But Carus died in Persia and his son was murdered on the way home. And it so happened that the Praetorian Prefect, who was next in line for the throne, was called *Boar*. . .'

Three short blasts of the hunting horns, and frenzied barking from the dogs deeper in the trees. The horsemen away to the right broke into sudden motion.

'There they go!' Victor shouted, but Castus was already

dragging his horse's head around and kicking with his heels, and then all four Protectores were riding at the gallop across the snowy flank of the hill towards the line of the forest. The emperor and his party had vanished.

Into the wood the horses plunged. Castus ducked his head to avoid a low branch thickly pelted with snow; ice showered over him and spilled down his back. Beneath the trees it was dim as twilight, and he stayed low and clung tight to the saddle, trusting the animal to forge its way through. There were other riders around him now, and men running on foot, shouldering their hunting crossbows – they shouted at first, but then fell silent as they approached the sounds of the conflict.

Dogs were howling, whining – runners, Castus saw as he drew nearer. They were hanging back from the boar and keeping it at bay, while the other dogs, the mastiffs, had closed in to attack. One already lay wounded, its rear leg ripped, while two more circled and pounced. The clearing was wide, carpeted with a black mulch of dead leaves dusted with snow. Nets hung from the trees all around; the boar was trapped as the hunters closed in.

Sallustius seized Castus's bridle, dragging the big horse to a halt. 'Stay back,' he said. Castus pulled the reins tight and the horse circled, pawing the dirt. He could make out the others now: the emperor and the other mounted men surrounding the trapped boar, some dismounting, spears in hand. The huntsmen with the crossbows formed a loose cordon around them.

The boar was a monster, waist-high at the shoulder, with long ridged tusks and a thick black hide covered in welts and scars. It dashed in a tight circle, tossing the attack dogs away from it, letting out a low groaning bellow. Its flanks were streaked with gore: its own, or the dogs', Castus could not tell.

'A beauty!' Sallustius said, dropping from his horse and

114

dragging its head down. Castus remained in the saddle, his own horse blowing a fog of breath in the tight air. The footmen were whistling, trying to call back the mastiffs; one dog slunk back, wounded, but the other had fixed its jaws in the boar's hide and was clinging on, claws raking the scarred black flank of the beast. As Castus watched, the boar seemed to shrug and lunge, swinging one great tusk, and the mastiff was jolted loose. Another lunge, and the dog lay in the dirt with its throat pumping blood.

Now the hunters closed in, their big spears held low. All of them were dressed alike in brown mantles, and for a moment Castus could not make out which of them was the emperor. He saw Maximian to one side, his massive bulk and beard marking him out, then another man rode in close on horseback, raising a javelin. Castus recognised him too: Priscus, the emperor's young legal advisor.

The boar remained still, only lifting its snout as the rider approached. Priscus swung back in the saddle, then hurled the javelin; it was barely out of his hand when the boar charged. The javelin went wide, the horse reared, and Priscus was tumbling from the saddle, the rushing boar almost upon him. Crossbows snapped – one dart jabbed into the animal's shoulder. Priscus was on the ground, lying flat and face down with his arms across his head. The boar kicked at him, butted him with its snout, but could not get at him with its tusks.

Castus had been so diverted by the scene that he had not noticed the shouts around him, the men crying out to Priscus to stay on the ground, keep himself covered. Now the shouts changed to cheers: Constantine, the emperor himself, was closing in on foot to tackle the boar in person.

A clever bit of theatre perhaps, Castus thought. But Priscus could still be badly hurt. Constantine edged closer, gripping the levelled spear in both hands, his legs firmly braced like a wrestler in the ring. Castus saw the emperor's face, raw and red from the cold, his heavy jaw set hard, eyes fixed on his prey. The boar turned its head, snout twitching, then swung to face the new threat. All around the clearing, the shouts and cheers died to breathless silence. For a few long heartbeats hunter and animal faced each other, and then with a keening squeal the boar charged.

At that moment Castus's horse jinked and pulled at the reins, distracting him. As he glanced back up he saw movement away to his left, figures edging between the trees around the upper slope of the clearing. They were huntsmen, stubble-bearded and dressed in sheepskin mantles, but one of them had a crossbow raised and aimed directly at Constantine. Nobody else was looking; all eyes were on the emperor and the boar. Castus blinked, a cry caught in his throat, and then the man loosed his bolt.

It darted straight and true across the clearing, but at that instant Constantine lunged forward and planted the heavy point of his spear deep into the shoulder of the charging boar, the beast driving up onto the blade until its flesh met the twin lugs at the top of the spearshaft. The crossbow bolt flicked past, just behind the emperor's head, and buried itself in the flank of Priscus's horse.

Castus hauled the reins and kicked at his own horse, and the animal's bound almost threw him out of the saddle. Up in the trees he could see the bowman struggling to reload. He swept the sword from his scabbard, crying out a warning to those behind him. Only a few onlookers had seen what had happened; the rest were still intent on the emperor as he forced the dying boar down at his feet.

Ice sprayed up as Castus urged his horse on through the bushes at the gallop. Frozen branches crackled and whipped, and plumes of snow cascaded from the trees. The second huntsman glanced back at him, then canted his arm with a javelin in his hand.

Stooping low, his thighs tight to the saddle leather, Castus saw the arc of the weapon as the man threw. He waited a heartbeat, then tugged the reins. The big horse jolted to one side, and the flung javelin darted past. Castus looked up and saw the huntsman reaching for his second javelin. Too late; the man's face emptied in fear, but in two long strides the horse had closed with him. Castus levelled his *spatha* downwards like a lance, and the tip of the blade drove into the man's chest. He dropped his arm with the weight of the body, then dragged the sword free and galloped on.

Trees all around him now. The man with the crossbow had his weapon loaded and raised. He loosed, and Castus had only a moment to crouch over the horse's neck before he felt the bolt cutting the air above his head.

The bowman threw his weapon aside and turned to run, making for a long snow-covered bank rising from the clearing.

'Grab him!' somebody shouted. 'Get him alive!' The men in the clearing had seen what was happening now. Another horse came crashing between the bushes on the far side of the slope: Brinno, sword in hand, galloping to cut off the huntsman's escape.

Castus shook his head as shards of ice flickered against his face. The fleeing man was just ahead of him, his sheepskin cape swinging behind him as he ran. More shouts from either side, other figures closing in, but Castus was closest and gaining fast on the fugitive.

The running man reached the snow and hurled himself up the slope, but the heavy horse came ploughing through the frozen undergrowth behind him. Castus dropped his sword and dragged back hard on the reins; leaning from the saddle, he seized the fugitive's trailing cape with one outstretched arm. The man screamed as Castus dragged him off his feet. Then blood sprayed up against the horse's flank.

A black bolt jutted from the side of the man's neck. His body fell limp, almost dragging Castus from the saddle. Castus released his grip on the cape and the man dropped. When he looked up, he saw one of the hunting party, a fleshy bald-headed man in a blue tunic and brown mantle, quickly handing the crossbow back to the huntsman beside him.

'I had him!' Castus yelled, breathing hard. 'I had him – alive!'

'He threatened our emperor, and I. . . acted on instinct,' the man in blue said. His voice was unbroken – a eunuch.

Castus twisted the reins and backed the horse away. Behind him in the clearing the last saga of the hunt was being played out, the boar blowing bloody spume as it died, the victorious emperor raising his killing spear to the applause of his retinue.

Observed by only a few, the corpse of the fallen man lay twisted beneath the sheepskin cape. The snow around the body was spattered pink, then reddened and soaked into black as the blood welled from the body.

CHAPTER IX

Night had fallen by the time the hunting party returned to Treveris. Nothing had been said about the attempt to murder the emperor – the matter was best forgotten, it seemed. An unfortunate accident, and at worst the act of a madman. But Castus could not forget the look on the man's face as he threw aside the crossbow and turned to run; neither could he forget the speed with which the eunuch in the blue tunic had shot the fugitive down. If the man's bolt had not struck the horse, nobody but Castus himself would have seen it. If it had struck the emperor, or even passed close enough to distract him, the boar would have knocked him down with ease. And if the emperor fell, who would step into his place? Even to think like that ran ice through Castus's veins.

Tired after their labours, the emperor and his guests soon departed to their beds, but Castus and Brinno were on sentry duty that night and it was nearly midnight by the time they returned to their quarters in the precinct of the Protectores. Castus was climbing the steps to his room when he heard the slave in the atrium below asking for him.

'You want me in particular?' he called over the balcony.

'Aurelius Castus and Flavius Brinno,' the slave replied.

'What's it about?'

'I cannot say, dominus. I was just ordered to find you and bring you. . .'

The night was achingly cold, and both men wrapped themselves in their cloaks again before following the slave. Outside, across courtyards empty in stark moonlight, they were led down darkened passages, deeper into the labyrinths of the palace.

In a side chamber of the hall of notaries, gloomy and thick with the smoke of oil lamps, the slave left them. There were two men waiting there. The first, lounging on the corner couch with a smirk on his face, Castus did not recognise. The second, perched stiffly on a folding stool, was a thin man with reddened eyes and a clump of ugly bowl-cut hair, dressed all in grey. Castus did not try to hide his disdain.

'Forgive us for summoning you at this unusual hour,' the thin man said. His voice was sharp and bitter as a knife blade. 'Some business is best conducted while others sleep. I am Julius Nigrinus, Tribune of Notaries, and my associate Flaccianus here is an officer of the agentes in rebus. I believe I know one of you already.'

'We've met,' Castus said. His jaw cracked as he yawned.

'I shan't keep you long. Earlier today, as you know, an attempt was made on the life of our beloved Augustus Constantine.' Nigrinus paused, and Castus noticed him wetting his lips with his tongue. 'I have been ordered to conduct an inquiry into the matter, and discover who was responsible for this treasonous act.'

'The men who tried it are already dead,' Brinno said, his Germanic accent giving the words a harsh clip.

'Indeed. Your comrade here saw to one of them, and as for the other. . . Very convenient, would you not say, that both died before they could be questioned? Convenient for those who paid them, and planned this outrage. . .'

'I killed the first man because he was trying to kill me,' Castus said. 'I had the second one – if that eunuch hadn't shot him he'd be alive now.' He was trying to guard his anger, but the memory of all that this notary had done in Britain four years before felt fresh in his mind. The men who had died for his schemes.

'Ah, yes, the eunuch,' Nigrinus said quietly. 'His name is Gorgonius. He is the steward of the former emperor Maximian's household. Have you met him before, perhaps?'

'Never.' Castus could see the man at the back of the room, Flaccianus, smirking to himself again. Remain calm, he told himself.

'Because it's strange, is it not, that the two of you were so quick to go in pursuit of the men? Perhaps with the second you were merely holding him, so this eunuch Gorgonius could get a clear shot?'

'What are you suggesting?' Brinno said, raising his voice. He looked as though he wanted to leap across the room and attack the notary.

Nigrinus spread his palms in a placatory gesture, but his eyes remained cold, filled with subtle menace. How much power, Castus wondered, did this man really have?

'It has come to my attention,' Nigrinus went on, apparently unmoved by Brinno's display of anger, 'that there may be a traitor within the Corps of Protectores.'

'Not possible!' Brinno hissed. Castus remained silent. He remembered all too well this game of insinuations, of crafty threats and bargains.

'Shocking, but true. This person is apparently working in collaboration with agents of a rival power. Perhaps of Maxentius in Rome. Perhaps. . . somebody else.'

'And you think one of us is this traitor?' Brinno's eyes were wide with fury.

Nigrinus merely smiled. 'Let us say, some might have reason to suspect so. However, I know that you, Flavius Brinno, are the son of a Frankish chieftain. You owe everything to the emperor Constantine, you are formidably devoted to him, so I hear. As for you. . .' He turned to Castus. 'We have, as you remind me, had dealings with each other before. You seem to me a very. . . *dependable* person.'

Expendable, he means, Castus thought. His back teeth were clamped tight.

'You saved the life of the emperor back in Germania, and he selected you personally for his guard. You seem unlikely to forget such a thing. There are many duplicitous people around us. However, I rather think you. . . lack the guile for duplicity, shall we say.'

Castus knew very well what he was saying. Let him think that. Many others had thought the same way. The idea that these two men, and perhaps others like them, had been observing him for all these months, studying and assessing how he might be used, made his skin crawl and his scalp contract. But he managed to smile. He refused to be outmanoeuvred by this man again.

'Loyalty can never be taken for granted,' Nigrinus went on. 'It must be demonstrated. Conspicuously demonstrated. So if you wish to be considered loyal, you would do well to be vigilant. Watch your comrades carefully, pay attention to anything they may say or do. I would remind you that in cases of potential treason, all immunity from questioning is withdrawn. That includes questioning by torture. . .'

'You want us to spy for you?' Castus said heavily. He shrugged off the crude implied threat.

'Such a weighty term,' Nigrinus said casually. 'All I require is that you remember the vow you took when you were made Protectores.'

'I have no need to be reminded of my vow, especially not by you.' *And I will do nothing to help you*, he thought.

122

Nigrinus stared at him for a moment, then smiled as he exhaled through his nose. 'Of course not,' he said. 'We are, all of us, servants of the Sacred Augustus. Let all of our efforts be directed towards his continuing majesty, eh?'

* * *

> '. . .Then Romulus, wolf-nursed, proudly clad
> In the she-wolf's tawny pelt, shall further the race,
> And bestow upon the Romans his own name.
> To them I give no bounds of time or power,
> But empire without end. . .'

The voice came from behind the tall bronze-studded doors of the emperor's private office, his *tablinum*. A child's voice, a boy speaking clearly enough for his words to carry through the close-woven latticed panels of the door and across the painted atrium to the point where Castus was standing on guard duty. Castus himself knew the lines well: Virgil, the same verses that the former teacher Diogenes had made him copy time after time during his writing lessons.

Sounds like you've been getting the same kind of lessons, lad, he thought.

He shifted his weight gently from foot to foot, while keeping his posture completely immobile. Castus had spent uncountable hours standing on guard, back when he was a legionary, and he could remain like this all day if required and think nothing of it. He had no spear or shield, no helmet, no armour to weigh his shoulders. Only his sword, belted high at his side.

The floor of the atrium was polished marble, grey and white tiles. On the walls, gods in armour battled giant men with serpents for legs, casting them down into the sea or into pits in the earth. Castus frowned slightly as he gazed at the painted figure: had the painter intended the god to look so much like Constantine? And, now he came to notice it, was the largest of the serpent-legged giants, a red-faced, bearded figure, supposed to resemble so closely the emperor's father-in-law Maximian?

Castus blinked the thoughts away, letting the images on the walls drift out of focus. A wandering mind could conjure dangerous fantasies, after all.

> '. . . Even Juno, my queen,
> Dread tormentor of land, sky and sea,
> Will yield to better judgement, and with me,
> Protect and bless the Romans, masters of the world. . .'

The imperial palace was a place of long silences and distant echoing voices. Even now, after seven months, Castus still found it unsettling. At its heart was the great basilica, the imperial audience hall, and all around it spread a complex of gardens and porticos, offices and barracks, with the private apartments of the emperor and his household beyond. The complex had expanded over the years, consuming and incorporating whole blocks of housing; now it took up almost a quarter of the space inside the walls of the city of Treveris.

Constantine liked to conduct business while marching from one part of the palace to another, and his progress along the wide corridors and porticos was always attended by a vast array of secretaries and petitioners, officials both military and civilian, slaves and eunuchs, with Castus and a few other Protectores keeping a close and wary eye upon them all.

There were grander events as well. Already Castus had attended several formal banquets, standing stiffly to one side of the hall while the emperor and his guests drank and ate. On the emperor's birthday in February, and the birthday of his deified father in March, and on the festivals of the Cerialia and Tubilustrium, Castus had taken his place behind the imperial dais, dressed in his embroidered white uniform, his silvered helmet and his red belts, carrying the black oval shield with the golden emblem of the Protectores. He had marched with his fellow bodyguards through the streets of the city in the great ceremonial processions, every man's spear wreathed in laurel.

But the emperor, for all his daily appearances, was still a remote and unknowable figure. An awesome figure – and that, Castus thought, was how it should be. Sometimes, as he barked out instructions to his staff, or when leaving some hall of state, Constantine would glance in his direction, but Castus always kept his expression entirely blank. And if the emperor recognised him at all, he never showed it openly.

A shadow fell across the tiled floor, jolting Castus from his thoughts. He glanced around to see a man enter the atrium from the portico. The newcomer was small, almost puny, with a dry shrunken face, but his tunic and cloak were well cut and embroidered, and his round cap and gold-clasped belt proclaimed his membership of the imperial offices.

'I need to speak to the emperor at once,' he declared.

Castus looked at him, impassive. The man took a step towards the doors of the tablinum; Castus stepped forward too, blocking his way.

'I told you, I need to speak to the emperor. It's very important!'

The man appeared nervous, jumpy. His thin top lip quivered as he spoke, and Castus could see his tongue darting inside his mouth.

'No,' Castus said. He stood with feet braced, thumbs hooked in his belt.

Angling his body left and right, the man made a show of looking around Castus at the sealed doors. His nostrils flared. He took a quick step, and Castus blocked him again. There was only the breadth of two palms between them.

'Listen,' the man hissed, weaving his hands and then knitting his fingers. 'I have information. . . for the ears of the Augustus alone! Vital information, concerning the wellbeing of our Sacred Dominus. . . I can make it worth your while to admit me.'

He was already reaching for his belt pouch. Castus hardened his jaw, placed one hand on the hilt of his sword and leaned in close to the man's face.

'I said no.'

'Oh, yes, you have your duty, don't you!' The man's whisper was harsh, echoing. 'Easy for you, I suppose, with your big stupid face. . . I'm telling you the emperor is in danger!'

Castus blinked, uncomfortably reminded of that midnight meeting with the notary back in February. Nearly two months had passed since then, and he had heard nothing more of Nigrinus or his secretive investigations. Could this be a test? He was careful now not to let his interest show.

'If you want to see him,' he said, slowly and heavily, 'you must speak to the Master of Admissions, who will give you an appointment. If he feels it justified.'

'The Master of Admissions! And how do I know that he isn't one of the plotters? In fact, how do I know that *you* aren't? What's your name?'

Castus glowered, breathing slowly into the man's face, saying nothing.

'Well. . . well, you can't force me to leave. I shall wait!'

The man retreated to a carved wooden bench beneath the painting of the battling gods and giants. Castus shrugged. How had the man even got into this part of the palace anyway?

A few moments passed, and then came the sound of footsteps from behind the doors. Castus stepped aside as the bronze rings turned and the doors swung open. First two slaves stepped over the threshold, holding the doors, and then a small boy walked calmly out into the atrium, followed by an old man, his tutor. The boy was about six years old, curly-haired and smartly dressed in an embroidered dark blue tunic and breeches; he had something of his father's face, but softened by youth and milder blood.

Flavius Crispus was Constantine's son, by his concubine. Castus knew of the lady too – the domina Julia Minervina was a Greek woman, and she had been with Constantine for over ten years; Sallustius had told him that the emperor still loved her and doted on the child. Since the emperor's marriage to Maximian's daughter, Minervina had lived in a house just outside the palace compound, with a covered passage and door leading to the emperor's own apartments. Already Castus felt he knew more than enough about that.

Looking at the boy now, Castus had a sudden recollection of another child: the son of Cunomagla of the Picts. What would that boy be doing now? At least, Castus thought, he would never have to recite Virgil to his father.

But Crispus walked with a proud step; presumably his father had been pleased. The boy passed through the atrium and out into the portico, slaves all around and his tutor following behind, and the doors of the tablinum swung closed after him. Castus moved to stand in front of the doors, but the small man had already leaped to his feet and darted out after the boy and his party.

The man's words lingered in Castus's mind, unsettling him. There was no action he could take, but even so it was his duty to report what had happened. And not, he thought, to Nigrinus either, or his odious assistant. He waited another half an hour, the time lagging. His leg muscles were beginning to ache slightly, and he reminded himself that he had been a much younger man when he had stood sentry watch as a legionary.

Finally he heard steps from the portico, and Brinno entered the atrium. The young barbarian gave a casual salute, and then slapped Castus lightly on the shoulder.

'Greetings, brother!' he whispered. 'Is he still in there?'

'Yes, but I need to go and see the chief,' Castus told him, speaking from the corner of his mouth. 'Can you take the door until I get back?'

Brinno nodded, falling easily into a guard posture.

'There's a man roaming about trying to get in there – I've sent him away once but he might come back.'

'Don't worry about him,' Brinno said, and lowered his brow.

Afternoon sun threw stripes between the pillars of the colonnade. Castus paced quickly through the light and shade, around the curve of the portico and through the vestibule, saluting the two fellow Protectores who stood sentry there, into the central court. It was quite possible, he knew, that the small man had been a mere fantasist, seeking attention or preferment from the emperor for some concocted tale. But something about the man's nervous desperation had seemed genuine – he had feared more than just rejection. Perhaps he had even feared for his life? Castus had always been good at reading character from the signs that others inadvertently revealed, but in this case he could not trust his judgement.

Hierocles, Primicerius of Protectores, was a stern and humourless man, once a senior centurion but now carrying rather more fat than muscle, and Castus suspected that his mask of rigid discipline concealed the fear of a faint heart. He found the primericerius in the archive room of his offices, and stood at attention before him as he narrated briefly what had happened in the Atrium of the Giants.

'Did you take the name of this man, his position?' Hierocles asked. He had barely glanced up from the codex in his lap.

'No, dominus!'

The primicerius appeared to consider the matter for a moment. 'No matter, then,' he said. 'I shall pass your information to the relevant officials, and they will investigate. No doubt this man will be traced and questioned appropriately. You may return to your station.'

'Yes, dominus!'

Castus turned crisply and paced from the room. Out in the portico of the central court again he rubbed a knuckle across his scalp. He had expected no great reaction from his chief, but even so Hierocles' apparent disinterest was startling. Perhaps, he thought, people frequently brought him this sort of allegation? Perhaps he had been stupid to give it any credence at all?

Heavy with disquiet, Castus retraced his steps through the vestibule and around the curved portico. To his left, between the pillars, the semi-circular garden was green in the spring sunlight, a statue of Triton rising from the pool at its heart, but Castus felt his mood darkening

There was a fountain between the pillars, water gushing from a lead pipe in the mouth of a stone dolphin, and Castus paused to dip his head and take several thirsty gulps. He straightened up, eyes closed, and stretched his back until he felt the cartilage in his neck crack.

'Ah,' a voice said sharply. 'Just what I'm looking for!'

Castus turned quickly, blinking at the figure standing in one of the bands of light between the pillars.

He seemed to have come from nowhere. Of indeterminate age,

compactly built like an athlete or a dancer, he was neatly dressed and wore a silver collar. His face had the bland smoothness of a child but his eyes were sharp with wry intelligence. Another eunuch, Castus realised, and thought of Sallustius's tales of the warm bath, the bench and the pliers. The man bowed slightly, as if remembering his position.

'What do you want?' Castus said curtly.

'I want a man!' the eunuch declared. 'Seems I've found one. Follow me, please.'

'I'm on duty. I don't have time to help you. . .'

'A whisper of time is all I need, dominus. Come – come, you won't be missed, and it would oblige my mistress greatly.'

He had already set off around the portico, turning to gesture briskly over his shoulder. His slippers made no sound on the mosaic floor – felt-soled, Castus guessed. He frowned, irritated, and rubbed the back of his neck; he was not accustomed to taking instructions from slaves, even ones wearing silver collars. After his meeting with the nervous man in the atrium he felt wary. But he was curious too, and nothing in the eunuch's manner suggested danger. A swift glance back around the portico – nobody in sight – then he straightened his shoulders and marched after the eunuch as he slipped away though an open doorway.

'This had better be quick,' he said, but the eunuch gave no sign of hearing him. He led Castus through another courtyard, half in shadow, down a paved alleyway between high brick walls, through another door and then along a narrow passage whose ceiling rose into gloom. There was a scent in the air, something soft that Castus did not recognise. He realised that they were entering the part of the palace called the Domus Faustae, the apartments set aside for the emperor's wife and her retinue.

He had seen the *nobilissima femina* Valeria Maxima Fausta several times, at public ceremonies. Sometimes too she passed, hedged about with slaves and eunuchs, through the halls of the palace in her stiffly embroidered *tunica* and mantle, wearing half a city's ransom in gemstones and pearls. She was very young, and her face still had the rounded softness of childhood, but her eyes were large and dark and her mouth plumply petulant. She had come from Rome with her father about eighteen months before, bringing a train of noble Roman ladies to form her household, and gave the strong impression that she disliked Treveris greatly, and everywhere north of the Alps too. Castus felt for her – as the daughter of one emperor, wife of a second and sister of a third, the girl surely had little say in the direction of her life. He had overheard some of the senior men of the court laughing sourly about her – the 'gilded piglet', they called her – and had pretended not to hear.

The corridor made a sharp turn, then the eunuch led Castus out into a courtyard surrounded by colonnades and set with flowering bushes in large painted urns. There he stepped aside, and made a sweeping gesture towards Castus, like a merchant showing off his latest wares.

'Oh, yes,' a woman said. 'He'll do very well.'

Castus stood still, rocking back on his heels, and hooked his thumbs into his belt as he took in the scene. For a moment it seemed there were flowers everywhere. Then it seemed there were women everywhere. The flowers were heaped in profusion on the tiled floor, and strung between the pillars of the colonnades. There were three couches set in the shade, and on each a woman reclined; the other figures around them were slaves, plainly dressed.

'Bring him over here, Serapion,' one of the reclining women said. Her round face was heavily whitened, and she wore a tunica and gown of rose-pink. All three women wore their hair elaborately curled and waved, the waves gathering into glistening plaits coiled above the nape of the neck: the imperial style. They were ladies of Fausta's household, Castus realised.

'Step forward, please, into the light,' the eunuch Serapion told him.

'What is this?' Castus growled at him from the corner of his mouth.

'It will only take a moment, dominus. . . The dominae wish to, ah. . . compare their wreaths. . .'

'They wish *what*. . .?'

'The eunuch hasn't told him!' the second woman declared, laughing. She was slim, small-featured and languid, dressed in a patterned green *stola*. Leaning back on the couch, she lifted her wine cup for a slave to refill it. 'We're making flower wreaths to present to our emperor Constantine Augustus at the Floralia,' she said, addressing a point just above Castus's head. 'We need to know which looks best on a man, that's all.'

'Wreaths,' Castus said. He winged his shoulder slightly.

The eunuch leaned close. 'If I might hazard a comment, dominus,' he said, 'you do somewhat resemble our Sacred Augustus. More heavily built, of course, and facially. . . well. But I think you too are from Illyricum, yes?'

'Pannonia,' Castus said, speaking only to the eunuch. 'But this is none of my concern. You could use a slave. . .'

'A slave!' Serapion exclaimed. 'Surely not – to have a slave stand in for our emperor would be close to sacrilege. . . But, ah—' he lowered his voice, leaning closer still '—please, just humour the noble dominae. It will take but a moment, and would, ah. . . greatly help matters here. . .'

Already the maids were bringing the first floral wreath, the ladies on the couches sitting up to admire the effect. Castus stood straight, his jaw tightening and heat flushing his face and neck. The humiliation twisted his gut, and he was on the verge of turning and marching back the way he had come. But these were ladies of the imperial household, intimates of the emperor's wife – was he somehow required to obey their bizarre commands? Was this part of his duty, to be exhibited like this, made fun of like this? Even the slave maids were trying not to smile.

'No, no, not that one, Plautiana. He looks like a garlanded ox being led to the sacrificial altar! Try the one with the roses and marigolds. . .'

Castus had little experience of the ways of aristocrats; those few that served with the army did not associate with the common soldiers or centurions. He had seen them from a distance, in the retinues of the emperors on campaign, but their ways were alien to him and he felt no great connection to them.

Neither had he very much experience of the ways of women. His mother had died when he was born, and his father had only the harshest of things to say about her. But since childhood Castus had associated women with kindness; his father would often beat him so hard that he could barely stand, and throw him out of the house for some supposed failing, and it was always the women of the neighbourhood who would take pity on him and tend to his wounds, protecting him until his father's rage had abated.

Since joining the legions he had known few women, and with the exception of two – the Pictish chieftainess Cunomagla, and Marcellina the envoy's daughter in Britain – all of them had been prostitutes. There was a brothel in the city frequented by the palace staff, and Castus had been there a few times in recent months with Brinno and Sallustius, but he had formed no bond with any of the women there. In his heart he still felt tied to Afrodisia, his girl in Eboracum, although he knew he would never see her again. Floralia, he remembered, was a festival observed particularly by prostitutes. . .

But none of those working women resembled the trio on the couches before him now, with their sheen of luxurious living, their pearls and jewellery, their sly mocking smiles and laughter. These women resembled none he had ever met; they were more like fabulous birds from a wall painting.

'Yes, now that one. . . Crescentilla, I really think that one looks quite special!'

Soft blooms pressed his forehead, and Castus felt petals itching down the back of his neck, sticking to the sweat. The smell of the flowers was sickening. A muscle was twitching in his cheek, and he tried to ease the aching grimace from his jaws. Hot shame rose through him, a keen sense of disgrace. Then anger – what did these women know of the world? What did they know of the violence and slaughter that allowed them to sit here in such amused ease: the burning villages out on the frontier, the men crippled in battles of which they had never even heard?

One of the laughing women, the lady in pink, glanced up and caught the look on his face. Her expression shifted and her fingers went to her throat as her laughter died.

'Now,' said her languid friend, oblivious, 'I really think we should try the peonies again, I thought that one was quite beautiful. . .'

Castus blinked, trying to appear more agreeable. This would soon be over, after all. Sallustius, he was sure, would have enjoyed the experience much more. He stared towards the rear of the courtyard, then dropped his eyes and found the third woman, who had remained silent, looking back at him.

She was younger than the other two, with an olive complexion, glossy black hair and deeply hooded dark eyes. She wore a simple yellow tunica and shawl, and sipped wine from a blue glass goblet in a gold lattice holder. Her face was a narrow blade. Castus stared at her, and she held his gaze.

'Oh, very well, Plautiana, the white roses, if you insist. Now, we have only to choose the best of the three – what do you think, Sabina?'

The woman in yellow said nothing for a moment, but only smiled slowly, swirling the wine in her blue glass.

'Which one do you like best?' she said, addressing Castus directly. The other two women appeared briefly startled.

'Me, domina?' Castus said, his voice thick in his throat.

'Yes. You're a man. Which do you prefer?' She gestured to the wreaths piled on the floor between the potted shrubs.

'Oh, yes!' her friend exclaimed, grinning. 'We should know what a man thinks, a man of action, like our emperor. . .'

Castus exhaled slowly, frowning as he stared at the flowers. Show me three swords, he thought, and I'd pick the best, no problem. Three javelins, even three horses. But not this. Was this some trick, some further humiliation? He had no idea what he was supposed to say.

'I don't know.'

'Oh, he doesn't know!' the woman in green said behind her hand. 'Perhaps we should have made a wreath of. . . oh, raw onions and boot leather, or something?'

'I am a soldier,' Castus said heavily, slowly. 'This isn't what I do.'

Something in his words stilled the mirth of the two ladies. The woman in yellow regarded him over her goblet. She narrowed her eyes, and seemed to nod just slightly as she smiled.

'I believe we're done here,' the eunuch said, with undisguised relief.

* * *

135

Brinno gave him a wry glance as he marched back into the Atrium of the Giants and took up his position before the doors of the tablinum.

'Did that man I mentioned come back?' Castus whispered. His voice was still stiff with annoyance.

'No,' Brinno said. He leaned a little towards Castus, flaring his nostrils.

'Brother, are you wearing perfume?'

'No, I'm not.'

'There's a. . . Wait.' The young Frank raised his hand and brushed lightly at Castus's shoulder. A couple of stray petals fluttered to the mosaic floor. Brinno gave a quizzical half-smile.

'Don't ask.'

Brinno raised an eyebrow, then pondered for a moment. 'This is a place of many perils,' he said under his breath, nodding gravely.

Sound of footsteps from inside the tablinum, and both Protectores straightened abruptly as the doors swung back. The slave doormen stepped aside, and a figure in a heavy purple robe stepped over the threshold. Castus gazed straight ahead at the painted gods and giants on the far wall.

The emperor paused. There was the sound of a light sniff, then another. Then Constantine cleared his throat and walked on, trailed by his slaves and secretaries.

Releasing his breath, Castus fell into step with Brinno as they followed the imperial party out into the fresh air of the portico.

CHAPTER X

They found the dead man between the pilings of the bridge foundations, his body almost submerged in the muddy water. Castus stood on the riverbank and watched as a group of legionaries, stripped to their tunics to work on the bridge, waded in and hauled the corpse free.

The body turned as they dragged it clear of the heavy wooden baulks, and the blanched face rose to the surface. Castus felt his throat tighten. The dead man's thin lips were drawn back from the teeth, but even without the nervous gestures and the gold-clasped belt he was easy to recognise. The soldiers towed the body to the bank and heaved it up onto the mud, then wiped their hands and stamped back up onto the bridge scaffolding to get on with their work.

It was only an hour after dawn, and the vast cavalcade of the imperial retinue was pulling out of Colonia Agrippina. The day before, the emperor had made his ceremonial inspection of the new bridge, performing sacrifice and taking the auspices. All the omens had been good for the new construction. But this, Castus thought, could be nothing but a very poor omen indeed. He touched his brow with his thumb between his fingers, a warding sign against evil.

Luckily for the emperor and his engineers, there were few people around to see the corpse pulled from the river. The emperor's party had already set off along the road southwards, and the main street of the city was still flowing with carts and carriages, horses and marching men. Even the eyes of the gods were elsewhere this morning.

Gazing out over the slow grey flood of the Rhine, Castus could see the cleared ground on the far bank, and the first scaffolding and brick heaps of the new fortress that would soon rise there, a bridgehead fortification on the barbarian shore. The bridge itself was creeping steadily out from the bank: huge coffer-dams had been constructed, and men in barges were lowering stones and cement down to form the foundations for the bridge piers. Further out, in midstream, more barges were moored with cranes and tackle to lift massive timber pilings and drive them down into the riverbed. The bridge itself would be a permanent structure, with heavy wooden arches firmly bedded on nearly twenty solid stone and concrete piers. Now even the mighty Rhine would pass beneath the yoke of Rome, and no barbarian would dare oppose the will of Constantine – or so the orators had proclaimed during the ceremony the day before.

'He must have gone for a walk along the bridge supports last night and fallen in,' Sallustius said, nudging the waterlogged corpse with the toe of his boot. 'Probably drunk after the ceremony. Wonder who he was?'

'He didn't fall off the bridge,' Castus said. 'Look at where they found him – on the upstream side. He must have gone in further up and floated down here.'

Sallustius made an appraising face. 'A neat deduction. Although it doesn't help matters, does it? Far easier to account for a dead drunk. . .'

Castus turned away from the river and made his way up the slope with the bow-legged former cavalryman walking by

138

his side. Nearly a month had passed since he had last seen the nervous little man in the Atrium of the Giants; there had been no further sign of him, nor any word from Hierocles about whatever plot he might have been trying to report. But now here he was, dead in the Rhine as the imperial party left town. Presumably the centurion of the detachment of Legion XXII Primigenia working on the bridge would attend to the body, or the curator of Colonia Agrippina would. Either way, the emperor would be long gone by the time the man's identity was revealed, whoever he was.

'Perhaps he dived off the bridge?' Sallustius said, glancing back. 'Or how about swimming? He could have had a few drinks and decided to go for a night swim in the river.'

'Wearing his cloak?'

Sallustius pondered this. 'They brew their beer strong in Colonia, brother!'

They skirted the heaps of bridging timber, cut stone and rubble piled on the riverbank, and returned to their horses. Mounting, they rode back between the wooden barracks of the engineer detachment, through the river gate of the city and up the slope between the temples and the curia to the main street. The ground before the pillared façade of the forum precinct was rutted and strewn with flower heads and petals, trampled into the mud where the dignitaries of the town had gathered at first light to pour their praises upon their departing emperor. Castus and Sallustius had been seconded to the office of the Master of Dispositions, who had posted them at the rear of the convoy. Castus did not mind, although it meant he missed the *adventus* ceremonies when the imperial retinue arrived at each new settlement along the road. Then again, he considered, once you've seen one group of town councillors roaring themselves hoarse and throwing flowers in the air, you had pretty much seen them all.

Again Castus's mind circled back to the dead man. It was possible, he told himself, that the death had been an accident. There were several thousand people travelling with the retinue, the population of a large town, and it was surely not impossible that one of them might suffer such an end. But his instincts told him otherwise. Fate sent a prickle up his spine: the man had died by violence.

He wondered if he should report it to Hierocles, but the chief of the Protectores was not easy to find with the retinue on the road. Besides, he had told only Hierocles about his previous meeting with the man. Again that prickle of apprehension, more insistent now. Hierocles had been a member of the hunting party back in February, when the killers had made an attempt on the emperor's life. A traitor among the Protectores, Nigrinus had told him. Was it possible, Castus thought, that his own chief could be the guilty man? He fought down the notion; he had no proof, and if it were true then such knowledge could be lethal. . .

The carts and carriages were still streaming along the main street towards the south gate, wheels hissing in the mud. It had rained in the night, a heavy summer shower, and the thoroughfares of Colonia had been churned to a sucking morass by wheels and hooves and marching feet. As he nudged his horse back into the shelter of a temple wall to let the column past, Castus noticed the opulence of several of the passing carriages, the women's faces at the slatted windows.

'What are they doing here?' he asked.

Sallustius reined in his horse beside Castus. 'Didn't you know?' he said, twisting his squashed face into a smirk. 'The nobilissima femina Fausta and her household joined the retinue last night. They'll be with us for the next few days up the river, all the way to Confluentes.'

'Why? Isn't it dangerous here for them?'

'But that's the point!' Sallustius said, cuffing Castus on the shoulder. 'What could better demonstrate the sublime security of the empire, and the complete subjugation of the barbarians, than the emperor's wife and her ladies parading up the bank of the fearsome Rhine? Let the Franks and Alamanni glower from their forests – Rome is untouchable, and the emperor supreme! Didn't you even *listen* to that panegyric yesterday?'

'My concentration slipped after a while,' Castus said ruefully. Even so, it was, he admitted, quite a bold display. The Rhine frontier had been a military zone for generations, ever since the barbarians had first poured across the river in the days of the emperor Valerian. But there was little real danger now, he supposed – not with the Frankish and Alamannic chiefs defeated and under treaty, and thousands of armed men surrounding the imperial party. Since the campaign the previous summer the Germanic tribes had been quiet.

Even as he considered this, Castus was scanning the passing carriages for one particular face, not even sure if he would recognise her now. Unlikely she would be wearing the same yellow dress.

'Who are they,' he asked, 'these women?'

'Fausta's ladies?' Sallustius said with a dismissive air. 'They're the wives of officials in Rome, most of them. Sent up here with Maximian's daughter to remind her what proper civilised company looks like. Not that she cares much about that, by the look of her. To act as hostages too, of course, against the good behaviour of their husbands and families. Although that leaves most of them a little uncomfortable these days, since Maxentius fell out with his father. They've rather ended up in the enemy camp.'

'Maxentius isn't our enemy yet,' Castus said quietly.

Sallustius snorted down his nose. 'Can't have two cocks in the barnyard,' he said. 'Why ask about the women anyway? Fancy one of them, do you?'

'No,' Castus said, too quickly, and glanced away. 'I've never spoken to them!'

'Wouldn't be surprised if you did,' Sallustius went on in a worldly tone. 'There are some peaches among them. And they're no Vestals either, brother – I hear quite a few stories going around the palace. What do you expect? Stuck up here, far from their husbands. Those eunuchs they've got surrounding them can't massage that itch away. Oh, make no mistake, they might be the daughters of senators, but between their legs they're as hot as any Lupanar whore. . . And I speak from experience, brother.'

Castus gave him a sidelong look. Sallustius made much of his comprehensive, near-universal experience with women, but in this case at least his claim seemed doubtful. But what did Castus know – perhaps these things happened?

The last of the carriages had slipped past now, and the street was filled with the slow-moving train of ox carts and marching soldiers that formed the tail of the column. Castus sat and watched from his horse as the rearguard tramped by, then turned to follow them. Outside the southern gate of the city the road was a mire of mud and dung, and within a mile the rain started falling again. But the image of the dead man in the river would not fade.

For days the imperial retinue crawled southwards, along the narrow road that followed the western bank of the Rhine. Three miles it stretched, from the vanguard cavalry to the marching troops that brought up the rear. Over three thousand people, Castus thought to himself as he picked his way in the opposite direction along the verge of the road. Nearly two thousand horses; more than two hundred carts, carriages and wagons. The gods knew how many oxen. He had seen whole armies move with less. They were three days south of Colonia Agrippina now, and every town and fort and military settlement they passed was left stripped behind them, storehouses empty, nothing to show for the glory of hosting the emperor and his retinue but a vast amount of dung.

'You're going the wrong way!' a wit called out to him from the marching ranks of the rearguard.

'Forgot something, did you?'

Castus smiled tightly and urged his horse onward. An hour before, he had been summoned to speak to the Master of Dispositions, Nicomachus Cassianus: a consignment of despatches had been mislaid at Rigomagus and Cassianus badly needed them delivered to him at the next station, Antunnacum, by nightfall.

Six miles back to Rigomagus, twelve from there on to Antunnacum. Castus wished that Sallustius had been chosen for the task instead – he was still not comfortable in the saddle and he felt the rigours of many days' riding in every bone and muscle. His rump was sore and his thighs ached, but he pushed himself onward, thinking only of whatever sort of bath he might be able to get when the day was done.

The river here passed between steep slopes, the trees rising on the far bank dense and green up to the crest of the valley. The road followed a narrow strip of level ground that traced the curves of the river, climbing in places to cut across a wide bend before descending again to the waterside. Now and again as he rode Castus glanced to his right, across the grey expanse of water at the stacked forests of the eastern bank. Had there been anyone in those trees, watching the progress of the emperor and his retinue? Was there anybody still there now, watching him?

It was late afternoon by the time he arrived back at Rigomagus, and after the turmoil of the imperial visit the town seemed to have slumped into an exhausted torpor. Castus was directed to an upper room of the *praetorium*, where a man sat lounging on a couch with his boots propped on a low table, eating walnuts.

'Hope you're not looking for dinner,' he said as Castus entered. 'Unless you like nuts, that is.'

Castus stood solidly in the doorway. He knew the man at once: the hair curled with thick grease, the rings on his fingers and the smug half-smile. Flaccianus was clearly pretending not to recognise him, but Castus was tired and hungry, and in no mood for games. 'I'm here on the orders of Nicomachus Cassianus, *magister dispositionum*,' he announced, 'to collect a package of imperial despatches and take them to Antunnacum.'

Flaccianus stirred slightly, but did not rise. 'I have the despatches,' he said. 'As a courier of the agentes in rebus, I have responsibility for them. No need to worry – I'll leave tomorrow morning and give them to your man Cassianus myself when I get to Antunnacum.'

Castus took a few strides across the floor, pushing back his cape to show the patches on his tunic and the sword at his side.

'As a Protector of the Sacred Bodyguard,' he growled, 'I outrank you. The despatches now, and I'll be on my way.'

The agent slid his boots off the table. He shot a glance towards the far end of the room, where a pair of slaves were working at a desk, compiling accounts. Swift oily apprehension slid across his face; he hid it quickly, but Castus had noticed the nervous flicker of the man's eyes. An image came to him of the dead man in the river at Colonia, and he had the unnerving intuition that this man had been somehow connected to that death.

'Do I need to tell you again?' he said slowly.

With a sigh Flaccianus got to his feet, brushing the residue of the walnuts from his hands. The heavy rings on his fingers clicked together.

'Wait here,' he said, then made for the far end of the room. Castus stamped after him, and the agent paused and glanced back with a baffled smile.

'I'm not waiting anywhere,' Castus told him.

The agent went to a doorway; he tried to shut the door after him but Castus trapped it with his foot and pushed his way through. The chamber beyond was small, and the light fell dimly through a latticed window high in the wall beneath the eaves. Flaccianus was already shuffling together the tablets and scroll tubes that lay on the central table. He turned quickly, but Castus closed the distance between them in one long stride, forcing the agent back against the table as he brought the edge of his heavy broadsword up to the man's throat.

'What are you *doing*?' Flaccianus managed to gasp. His face drained of colour, and his mouth stretched into a terrified grimace.

'Next time a senior officer gives you an order,' Castus said quietly, holding the honed blade against the agent's windpipe, 'don't think about making excuses.'

'You wouldn't dare harm me!'

'Want to find out?' Castus tugged slightly at the blade, and Flaccianus let out a tight hiss as the edge nicked his skin. Then Castus stepped back, reversing the sword and slamming it back into his scabbard.

Flaccianus dodged quickly around the table, scrabbling for the documents. Castus could see that many of them had been opened and read. After stuffing the documents back into the leather despatch bag and tying the seal, Flaccianus shoved it across the table towards Castus.

'I apologise if I seemed. . . disrespectful,' he said with a tight smile, trying to regain his composure. 'Please forgive me. In fact I have some information for you. From Nigrinus.' Even with the table between them he still seemed nervous.

'What information?'

'Ah, well,' Flaccianus said. He was clearly relishing the reversal of power. 'Very soon,' he said, 'our emperor Constantine will be departing on a journey to Britain. You won't be accompanying him. . .'

Castus made no comment. His hand idled on his sword hilt. Flaccianus noticed, and his fingers went to his throat, where a tiny spot of blood still showed against his pallid skin. 'It's been decided,' he went on quickly, 'that it would suit the dignity of the former emperor Maximian for a small personal guard of Protectores to be attached to his household during the absence of the imperial retinue, and quite possibly also after their return. You'll be one of them.'

Castus shrugged, digesting the news without expression.

'So you see,' the agent said, 'you'll be ideally placed to observe the activities of Maximian's retinue. . . and report any suspicions you might have!'

'Tell your master,' Castus growled, picking up the leather despatch bag, 'that he can find another spy.'

He turned to leave, but at the door he paused, as if a thought had just occurred to him.

'That dead man at Colonia,' he said. 'You know anything about how he died?'

The bead of blood on the agent's throat jogged slightly. He took a moment before he could answer.

'Nothing at all,' he said, with a bland smile.

But he did. Castus was certain of it.

CHAPTER XI

The sun was low to the west, and the road along the riverbank was in deep shadow. Across the water, the forested eastern shore glowed gold and green in the last of the light. Castus rode heavily, the bag of despatches slung over his saddle horn, but the horse seemed to sense the end of the day's journey and kept up a smart pace. They passed around a tight bend of the river, where the road was clasped between the water and the trees; Castus's senses had grown so dulled by the motion of riding and the slow quiet of the evening that he would have missed the carriage completely had a shout not drawn his attention.

'Glory to the gods! I prayed to Lady Isis to send us deliverance, and it has arrived!'

For a moment he thought it was a woman calling out. He reined in his horse and drew closer, one hand going instinctively to his sword hilt.

It was not a woman, but neither was it a man. As the figure came towards him Castus saw the silver collar winking in the shadow, the unnaturally smooth face. Serapion, they had called him, he remembered.

'We have a broken axletree, it seems,' the eunuch said, clasping his hands before him. If he recognised Castus, he did not show it. 'We thought it might be spliced, but the repairs will take some time. The commander of the rearguard was supposed to send riders to help us, but there's been nobody. . . I see by those patches on your cloak and tunic that you are a Protector, however. . .'

Castus glanced at the carriage. It was small, a closed box of lattice-sided wood mounted high on a wagon chassis. The front nearside wheel was off, the axle propped on timbers. The draught horses had been released from their traces and stood cropping the verge, while three slaves sat by the fallen wheel, one of them chewing on a stem of grass while the other two tried to light a fire.

'I can't help you,' Castus said. 'I'm carrying despatches, and they need to be in Antunnacum before nightfall.' He looked up at the sky; already the first stars were showing.

'How far is it from here?' called a voice from inside the carriage. A curtain screened the interior.

'Two or three miles. I'll send someone back to you when I get there.'

Castus tugged on the reins and nudged the horse into motion.

'Wait,' the voice called, commanding.

Castus turned, saddle leather creaking beneath him. The curtain was drawn aside, the door of the carriage opened and a woman stepped down from inside.

'If it's only two miles I'll come with you,' she said. 'Anything's better than spending a night on a wet riverbank with only slaves and a eunuch for company.'

Castus knew her at once, but it was a few moments before he saw the slightest flicker of recognition on the woman's face, swiftly dispelled. She wore deep red instead of the yellow gown, with a shawl of fine white wool draped around her shoulders and drawn up over her hair.

'Domina Sabina,' the eunuch was saying, 'the road, as you see, is very muddy, and soon it will be dark. I really think. . .'

Castus was looking at her shoes: soft red leather openwork, not much good for walking long distance. The woman caught his eye and gave him a cool smile.

'I'm sure the noble Protector would allow me to perch on his horse,' she said.

'Domina, really, riding is no fit activity for women!'

'I only need cling to the saddle – we won't be performing any equestrian exercises, I assure you. Cinna and Petrus can bring the brass trunk with my overnight things. Xanthe can bring my wicker case, the round one. You can wait here with the carriage, Serapion. Protect it from thieves in the night. . .'

Castus sighed heavily, and drummed his fingers on the saddle horn. He was very tempted to put spurs to his horse and ride on before anyone could try and stop him. The woman, Sabina, was already marshalling her slaves and having them pack the trunk and basket. With a low groan he slipped from the saddle and dropped to the ground, feeling the cramps racking his leg muscles. It would be good to walk for a while anyway, he told himself, although he would have preferred it to be his own decision. He took the saddlebag and slung it over his shoulder – he was not letting that out of his sight.

'What a big horse,' Sabina said, walking carefully across the wet mud as Castus waited holding the bridle.

'I'm a big man.'

'No doubt,' she said lightly. The two slaves lifted her between them onto the saddle, where she sat with her legs to one side, gripping the leather saddle horn. Without further delay Castus gave a tug on the reins and set off, the horse walking after him and the slaves lagging along the road behind with the luggage. The eunuch, the other slave and the remaining maidservant gathered around the crippled coach, gazing in apprehension across the river as the evening darkened into night.

There were no other travellers on the road, and for a while they walked in silence, on around the next bend in the river until the carriage was out of sight behind them. The only sounds were the steady beat of the horse's hooves in the mud, the jingle of the bridle and the occasional cry of a waterbird. The Rhine took on a grey-blue sheen in the evening light, the smooth flow appearing almost motionless as the forests on the far bank dropped into shadow.

'How menacing it looks,' Sabina said, twisting in the saddle to gaze across the river at the trees. 'I was imagining all sorts of barbarians emerging from it – you can almost see figures moving in there if you stare hard enough. Franks, I suppose.'

'Alamanni, domina, this far south,' Castus told her. He was in no mood for talking, and marched steadily ahead of the horse.

'Oh, yes, Alamanni. Like that king, Hrocus, who hangs around the court. Quite a sad figure, don't you think? All his people have deserted him and gone back to Germania – they said he was becoming too Roman. . .'

Castus made no reply. It felt good to walk again, even with the mud working up over his boots and leg wrappings. They had drawn some way ahead of the slaves with the luggage, who were making a slow journey of it.

'Not much of a conversationalist, are you?' she said, a while later.

'I wasn't aware you needed me to entertain you, domina.'

He heard her laugh quietly to herself. 'Oh, I see,' she said. 'You're thinking of that little game with the flower wreaths, before Floralia. I should apologise. I'm sorry. Crescentilla and Plautiana are not as bad as they seem. I'm probably not either. We weren't laughing at you. Why would we?'

'I don't know, domina.'

'Well, perhaps you're right. We do get so bored, you know, out here in the provinces, and boredom makes one callous. In Rome we are quite different people – better people, I'm sure.'

'You miss Rome?' Castus said. He still had little desire to engage with the conversation, but he liked the sound of the woman's voice. Nobody of her class had ever really addressed him before – it was quite fascinating, he had to admit.

'Oh, of course I miss Rome. Wouldn't you?'

'I don't know, domina. I've never been there.'

'I was born there,' she said. 'Although my family are from Madaurus in Numidia originally, and Phrygia on my mother's side. . . What's your name anyway?' she asked abruptly.

'Aurelius Castus, domina.'

'Easy to remember, I suppose. And you don't have to keep calling me that either. You're a Protector of the Sacred Bodyguard, aren't you? Not so far beneath me, socially speaking.'

Castus shrugged. The social status of the Protectores was largely a matter of convenience, and although he had earned more in the last year than he had done in all his time as a legionary, he still did not feel particularly exalted.

'What should I call you then?'

He glanced back, and saw her look of amusement.

'Valeria Domitia Sabina. *Clarissima*,' she said.

'That's enough names for anybody.'

'You should meet my father,' she said, still smiling. 'He's a senator, you know. *Clarissimus* Lucius Valerius Domitius Honoratus Latronianus. My family have been *clarissimi* for four generations. My great-grandfather served as Praetorian Prefect to the emperor Severus Alexander.'

Was that a good thing? Castus could not remember whether Severus Alexander had been deified, or his memory damned.

'And your husband?' he said. There was a slight pause.

'My husband, Maecius Flavianus,' she said in a noticeably stiffer tone, 'is in Africa, serving as *rationalis summarum Numidiae*.'

'What's that?' Castus felt no need to conceal his ignorance of imperial titles.

'It means he controls the imperial finances in Numidia. Only of course at the moment he's serving under Domitius Alexander, who's a relation of mine, actually, a cousin on my mother's side, I think. Which makes things difficult, because Maxentius in Rome calls Alexander a rebel and a usurper. . .'

'Are you related to Maxentius too?' Castus could not help smiling as he asked.

'Him? Certainly not! His father was a common soldier before he became emperor, and his mother was some Syrian nobody. . .' Her words trailed off as she realised her mistake. Much the same could be said of Constantine, after all. 'Meaning no disrespect, of course,' she added.

Castus raised one shoulder in a half-shrug, and for a while they walked on in silence.

'You have children?' he asked. He wanted her to carry on talking; while her words tried his patience, the tone of them captivated him: the slightly rough deepness under the gloss of her voice.

'No children,' she said, and he heard the stiffness returning, that cold bitter edge. 'My husband has little interest in such things; he is often far away, and when he returns he. . . keeps alternative company. As do I.'

Castus recalled what Sallustius had told him about the ways of the ladies in Fausta's household. He made no comment. Behind them the two slaves laboured through the mud with the heavy trunk; one was a youth, with a broad flat face and a pug nose, the other almost an old man. The girl hurried after them with the basket. Night was drawing in, and the river seemed a less peaceful place now.

'Help me down off this horse, would you,' Sabina said. 'Riding's a lot less comfortable than it looks, and I'd rather walk. Good shoes can be bought.'

Drawing the horse to a halt, Castus stepped up beside her; she reached down and grasped his shoulders, and he took her by the waist and lifted her from the saddle. For a moment he held her in his arms, and her perfume was all around him, a dark sweet musk that reminded him of the markets of Antioch.

'Thank you,' she said, drawing her shawl tighter around her shoulders.

They walked on along the road, Sabina stepping carefully in the mud with her hems of her gown lifted while Castus led the horse.

'Will you be returning to Rome soon?' he asked her.

'May the gods grant that I do,' she said quietly. She had moved closer to him as they walked, and her voice had dropped to a whisper against the hush of the night. 'But it is as the emperor decrees. And with Maxentius controlling Rome it seems unlikely, unless Constantine divorces his wife or sends her away. . .' Castus caught the pale flicker of her fingers as she made a warding sign against bad luck. 'He might – he spends all his time with his concubine and seldom sees the nobilissima femina at all.'

Castus nodded, uncomfortable. This woman, he reminded himself, knew things about the inner life of the court that he did not.

'But I do miss Rome so much,' Sabina went on. 'If you've never seen it you could not comprehend. . . There are houses there the size of small towns, temples and basilicas entirely

154

covered in marble and gold. It's the mother of cities, the centre of the world.'

'So I've heard.'

He looked at her then. Her shadowed profile was outlined against the radiance of the river, and he saw the proud elegance of her face, the curve of her lip, the line of her nose. He felt an urge to reach out and touch her, to turn her face to his. But then he became aware of himself, and felt heavy and coarse beside her. He knew that he must smell strongly of stale sweat, horse, the dust and mud of the road. Even to feel attracted to her felt shameful. He remembered seeing the woman and her friends in the courtyard and thinking that they resembled members of some other species.

'Don't you miss your own home?' she asked him.

'My home's the army,' he told her. *And, yes*, he thought, *I do miss it.*

She staggered and let out a cry as her foot slipped beneath her, and grabbed at his arm to steady herself. Her slender hand gripped his biceps, and he smelled the wave of perfume again, intoxicating in the darkness.

'That's Antunnacum up ahead,' he told her, conscious of the thickness of his voice. 'See those lights along the valley there? The imperial camp.'

'Oh, yes,' she said, with almost a note of disappointment. 'We should be there in no time.'

A movement from the shadows at the side of the road, and Castus halted suddenly. He had been staring at the distant glow of the encampment, and for a moment he could see nothing of the shapes that seemed to gather from the surrounding darkness. He cursed under his breath as he reached for the hilt of his sword: the woman's presence had distracted him, and he had let his attention slip.

There were men all around them, closing in on both sides. Sabina drew a quick breath, stepping closer to Castus, both hands clasping his arm. He could feel her involuntary shudder as he eased the sword smoothly from his scabbard.

'Who's there?' he said, low and steady. The horse blew and nuzzled at his shoulder.

'Identify yourselves,' came a voice in response. Latin, but Castus kept his guard up.

'Aurelius Castus, Ducenarius of the Protectores of the Sacred Bodyguard.'

He could make out their forms more clearly now. Eight men, wearing military cloaks, several with shields and spears. One of them uncovered a lantern, and for a moment the wavering light flared brightly, throwing wheeling shadows across the road.

'Aurelius Castus?' the voice replied. 'We meet again then, eh?'

Something in the tone was familiar; an ugly memory surfaced in Castus's mind. The lantern had dazzled him for a moment, but when he blinked and squinted the features of the man before him were clear. He wore the uniform and insignia of a centurion in the Praetorian Cohorts, but the scarred face and sour grimace were the same. The last time Castus had seen them, he had been staring across a battle line.

'Oh, yes,' Satrius Urbicus said. 'You weren't the only one who got promotion after that fight back in Germania. And I still haven't forgotten you, either. Who's your lady friend?'

Sabina had stepped quickly away from Castus as soon as the lantern appeared. She pulled the hem of her shawl across her face, but her shoulders were tight with anger. Castus heard a couple of the Praetorians laughing quietly in the darkness.

'You address me as *dominus*,' he said in a growl. He was still holding his naked sword. 'And the lady is none of your concern.'

Urbicus hissed between his teeth, stepping closer. It seemed that his men advanced a step too. Castus had already used his sword in anger once that day; if he did it again now, men would die. He flicked his gaze between them, judging distances. There were too many; he could take down three, maybe four, but if they all set upon him at once he would have no chance. And he had the woman to consider. . .

'I'm travelling on imperial duty,' he said, in as calm and clear a tone as he could muster, though he spoke through his teeth and his jaw was locked. 'Let us through.'

The centurion was close enough that Castus could smell the damp wool of his cloak. 'Seems to me, *dominus*,' Urbicus said, 'that this might be an ideal opportunity for you and me to settle a few things. A dark road, no bystanders or witnesses. . . And my optio here's taken a fancy to your sweet little friend.'

The soldier with the lantern grinned, showing crooked teeth.

Sabina stepped forward quickly, drawing herself up and throwing the shawl back from her face. The lamplight gleamed off her gold jewellery. 'You heard what the Protector said,' she declared, loud enough for them all to hear. 'I am a lady of the imperial household – step aside and let us pass!'

In her voice was the unmistakeable note of privilege, of authority. Castus saw a ripple pass through the squad of Praetorians as they recognised the truth of her words. Behind him he could hear the slaves approaching, the two men with the trunk and the maid. He smiled, slipping the sword into his scabbard. Urbicus took a step back, and another. Then the rest of his men retreated, and the road was clear.

'I'll be looking out for you, Aurelius Castus,' the centurion said quietly. 'Next time, maybe we'll meet on the battlefield. . .' He made that same weighing gesture with his cupped palm. Castus spat air between his teeth, then tugged at the horse's bridle and walked on, the others following him through the open cordon of Praetorians and down the road.

Silence for a time, all of them eager not to appear to be hurrying. Castus saw Sabina touch her face with a trembling hand.

'What a charming character,' she said after a while. Her voice was taut, but she managed to sound calm. 'Friend of yours?'

'I brushed up against him once or twice,' Castus replied. Now that the moment had passed he felt the rage hot inside him, the shaming sense of powerlessness. He knew that he should thank her, but could not find the words.

Another hundred paces, and they entered the spill of torchlight. The walls of the town were before them, with the horse lines and pavilions of the retinue set up all around it.

'Well,' Sabina said, turning to him. 'Thank you for escorting me.' She paused a moment, her arms across her chest, her eyes holding his gaze. The slaves were gathered behind her, shuffling with the baggage. Castus could only nod curtly.

'I hope we'll meet again soon,' she said. And then she turned and walked away.

Castus hefted the bag of despatches on to his shoulder. He thought of the cold bath that awaited him. 'I hope so too,' he said quietly.

CHAPTER XII

'Constantine Augustus! The gods preserve you for us! Your salvation is our salvation!'

The collective salute died away in echoes as the eight Protectores advanced and dropped to their knees on the cold marble. On the far side of the audience chamber of the emperor's private apartments, Constantine was seated beside Maximian on a low dais. To one side stood Probinus, the Praetorian Prefect. To the other side stood a heavy-fleshed eunuch with a shaven head; the same eunuch Castus had seen in the hunting party back in February – the one who had shot and killed the man that had tried to murder Constantine.

'Rise, and stand before your emperor,' Probinus said.

They stood, eyes to the floor, while the two men on the dais inspected them. Castus barely heard the voice of the Praetorian Prefect telling them what he already knew: all eight would be attached to the household of former emperor Marcus Aurelius Valerius Maximianus, father of the nobilissima femina Fausta, until such time as the Sacred Presence once again required their services. Several of the men stirred, breathing deeply as they absorbed the news. Aside from Brinno, Castus had told none of the others what he had heard.

A chair squeaked on marble, and slow heavy steps approached them.

'So these are the men who will defend me with their lives?' A deep voice, loud and rough-edged. 'Look up! Let me see you!'

The man before them was aged around sixty, his face reddened and swollen above a black beard twisted with grey. This was the man, Castus thought, who had ruled the world beside Diocletian for two decades. The man whose image he had saluted when he had first joined the legions.

Maximian, the *Man like Hercules*.

The former emperor paced before them, moving down the line of Protectores and inspecting each man.

'My former colleague Diocletian,' he said, 'used to favour ceremony and protocol. All this Persian-style bowing and prostration. My son-in-law thinks the same way. I do not – I prefer to look men in the eye, get the measure of them. . . No, I don't have time for courtliness or etiquette. Politics neither. I left all that to Diocletian too. Now I defer to my son-in-law Constantine, of course. . .' He made a half-turn, and sketched a bow towards the back of the room. Constantine remained seated on his chair upon the dais, unmoving, expressionless.

'So, I am merely your commander,' Maximian went on, pacing slowly. 'But remember, all of you, that I was your emperor for twenty years! I still expect discipline from you. Proper soldierly conduct! Don't forget that.'

He paused before Brinno, drawing himself up to stare at the young man.

'You Frankish, boy?' he demanded.

'Yes, dominus. My father is Baudulfus, war chief of the northriver Salii.'

'Salii, eh? I remember them. Fought against them myself! Maybe I crossed blades with your father, eh?'

Brinno swallowed heavily, nodding. Maximian moved on.

'How about you, soldier? What's your name?'

'Aurelius Castus, dominus!'

'Aha, yes, I've heard of you. You're the one that pulled my son-in-law out of that river in Germania!'

Castus glanced quickly towards the emperor. Constantine shifted slightly on his chair, but said nothing.

'Yes, dominus!'

'Good man. . . good. Tell you, though, you'd have had a harder job trying that with me. Eh? Eh! Carrying a bit more weight these days!' Maximian slapped a palm against his meaty chest. He took another step, then quickly turned back to Castus again.

'What do you think, soldier – you're a big man, could you take me on, hm?'

Castus tried to keep his face blank. He felt the attention of the whole room upon him. Maximian was right in front of him; Castus saw the small eyes, the pouched cheeks, the network of broken veins dark red around his nostrils. He smelled the wine on the man's breath.

'I'm sure I wouldn't like to try, dominus.'

'Ha! That's right!' Maximian declared with a grin. 'Nobody takes me on. Fucked if they did, ha ha!'

He paced back towards the dais, hands clasped behind him. Halfway back to his chair he stopped again and flung out a stubby finger.

'Least I'm not as fat as him!' he said, pointing at the eunuch with the shaven head. 'That's Gorgonius, my *castrensis*, the steward of my household. If you have any trouble with my staff or slaves, you go to him, understood?'

'Yes, dominus!' the men said in unison.

Surely now they would be dismissed, Castus thought. But why did Constantine keep the old emperor so close to him like this? He remembered what Valens had told him once, the year before.

161

Honour him, and watch him as you watch a snake. Maybe that was all it was. But perhaps, Castus wondered, there was more to it? Nobody else, after all, would dare talk to Constantine like that, or talk about him in the emperor's own presence. Castus knew all too well the solitary burden of authority; he had never forgotten the words his old centurion had told him once. *The bronze mask of command*. Perhaps Constantine enjoyed having the old man to spar with him, drink with him and treat him like a human being, not a god, and to tell him truths that others were too cowed or obedient to dream of uttering?

Maximian was stamping heavily back up the steps to the dais, but a ripple ran through the room, an almost imperceptible shift of attention. Castus saw the old emperor pause, saw Constantine straighten in his chair. The men beside him shuffled, drawing themselves up more smartly.

'The nobilissima femina Valeria Maxima Fausta,' the slave at the door intoned.

A scent in the air at first, rose-water and saffron. Then the hiss of silk on marble, and the emperor's wife and her ladies approached the dais. Castus kept his eyes on the far wall, where a pair of painted peacocks stood beneath an arch of flowering trees.

'Daughter!' Maximian exclaimed, stepping down from the dais. From the corner of his eye Castus saw him embrace Fausta and kiss her heavily. Then Constantine descended to the floor, and she accepted his rather stiffer embrace. Angling his gaze, Castus saw the slave maids and the eunuchs, and behind them the women in their brightly patterned gowns. It took him a moment to pick Sabina out, and when he did he saw that she was looking right back at him. She blushed quickly and turned her face away.

'These are the men whom your husband has ordered to protect me,' Maximian said to his daughter. 'And you as well, if

162

your lord husband is obliged to leave you here while he attends to his duties abroad. . .'

Castus tried not to react to the words. The trip to Britain was not a military expedition; ordinarily, there would be no reason for Fausta not to accompany her husband. Was he travelling with his concubine and her son instead?

Wordlessly, Fausta moved along the line of Protectores just as her father had done. Each man kept his eyes fixed on the back wall, never daring to glance at her. When she reached Castus she seemed to linger for a moment. Gathering his nerves, he dropped his gaze to meet hers.

The emperor's wife was a short girl, almost plump, aged sixteen or seventeen. She wore a tunica and mantle of richest purple and blue, woven and embroidered with silver. Pearls were roped in her hair, thick necklaces of amber and gold around her neck. Her eyes were deeply lidded and protruded slightly, giving her a languid look, but her round face wore an expression of sour displeasure. Castus remembered feeling sorry for her. Perhaps he had been wrong. Perhaps the girl was just spoilt, or even stupid. But he knew too well that appearances could deceive.

A moment passed, two heartbeats, and then Fausta moved on, turning from the line of Protectores and briefly bowing to her husband. Then she moved towards the door, her entourage of ladies, eunuchs and slaves swirling in her wake. The tension seemed to flow from the room after her.

'Women!' Maximian exclaimed with hefty relief, then clapped his hands. A brief stir of amusement ran through the audience chamber.

'Protectores,' the Praetorian Prefect called. 'You are dismissed!'

* * *

Three steps to the left, boots scuffing dust, and he dodged the sweeping blow.

His opponent leaped in fast with a backhand cut, and Castus caught it on his shield and turned it. Two more wild blows; he parried the first and dodged the second, still circling. The sun moved around him; now it was hot on his bare back. He stepped quickly forward, shield raised, then swung a low cut beneath the rim. Weapons clashed and grated. The response came fast: two heavy hammering blows that he only just blocked with his shield. Wicker cracked, and he felt the jolt up his arm.

Sweat ran into his eyes. He was thirty-two years old, and age was against him. His opponent was six years younger and a hand's breadth taller; he had speed and he had a longer reach. But he had not been trained to use his shield as a weapon. Castus had: he waited, taking the blows, soaking up the attack until his opponent made too quick a lunge, then he struck. Throwing his weight into the hollow of his shield he surged forward, battering his opponent off balance. A swing to the right, and he hooked the rim of his shield around that of his opponent and twisted hard. A cry as the shield turned, opening his adversary's unprotected left flank, then Castus jabbed hard and felt the blow meet flesh.

'Ha!' he said, leaping back. 'Killed you!'

Brinno let out a shout of frustration and flung his shield down. They were using wooden practice swords, but there was a bloody red graze on his side where the splintered tip of Castus's weapon had jabbed into him. If it had been a real sword with some weight behind it, it would have stabbed deep into his bowels.

'A filthy trick!' Brinno said, grinning against the pain.

'A *Roman* trick,' Castus told him. He dropped his own battered wicker shield onto the packed dirt of the training courtyard, then flipped his wooden sword up and caught it by the blade. He gave a nod to the boy waiting in the portico, who ran over with a skin of water.

Both men were stripped to boots and breeches, and in the close summer heat their scarred bodies poured with sweat. Castus raised the waterskin, tipping back his head and filling his mouth with the cool liquid. He let the water pour over his shoulders and chest, then tossed the skin to Brinno.

The young Frank took two long swallows, then swilled his mouth and spat in the dust. 'This time,' he said, throwing the waterskin back to the slave boy, 'we fight without shields, yes? And I think I will beat you!'

Castus rolled his shoulders, smiling, then the two men faced off, both dropping instinctively into a fighting crouch. They circled, their shadows pooled beneath them. Castus knew his disadvantage now: Brinno had grown up duelling like this, back in his own county, but the legions fought only with shield in hand. The younger man had a wiry agility too, and this sort of fighting suited him well. To match it Castus had only his quick reactions, and the brutal strength of his blows. With the wooden sword held level, he kept his left hand low as he circled, curled into a fist against his thigh, as if he were still gripping a shield. Brinno's left arm was up and reaching wide, a counterbalance to the wild swinging attacks he favoured.

Slowly they shuffled, scuffing dust, each waiting for the moment to strike. Over Brinno's shoulder, Castus saw a figure watching him from in the shade at the end of the wooden portico. Silver winked from the figure's throat, and Castus recognised the eunuch, Serapion. A flicker of apprehension crossed his mind.

Brinno leaped, swinging a fast overarm strike, and Castus blocked it at the last moment. The clash of the wooden swords

165

was loud, and for a few heartbeats the two men were locked together, pushing against each other, the wooden blades grating in their fists. Brinno tried to reach out with his free hand and grab Castus by the neck, and Castus punched his arm away and then spun on his heel to break the contact. Brinno's lashing blow clipped his shoulder as he turned, but then he was circling again. Pain bloomed up his arm; both of them would wear bruises tomorrow.

Sparring with Brinno was often a dangerous activity; the young Frank was keen to win, and tended to work himself into a fighting frenzy heedless of restraint. Now he made another wild cut, which Castus only just parried before it cracked his skull. He swiped his blade down, catching another blow before it met his shin, and managed a lunging stab that sent Brinno dancing back out of his reach. Breath hammered at the back of his throat.

But along with his ferocity, the young barbarian was also very easy to read. There was no economy to his movement, and after a few moments Castus found he could judge the direction of his next blow quite easily. Brinno's narrow face contorted, his eyes bulged, and he let out high shouts and grunts. Castus kept to his fighting stance, stayed silent and moved only when necessary.

Two more blows, then Castus cut high and his blade clipped Brinno's shoulder. Enraged, the Frank leaped forward behind a swinging overhand strike; Castus blocked him, then punched his left arm up and under Brinno's reaching right. With his cupped hand he grasped the bunched muscle of the young warrior's neck, shoving him backwards. A sweeping kick, and he knocked Brinno's legs from under him. The Frank went down hard on his back, and Castus dropped to one knee, straddling his body, sword angled at his throat.

'Roman bastard!' Brinno yelled. 'You fight like some common gladiator!' But he was laughing again as he scrambled to his feet. 'In my father's country, these tricks would not be allowed!'

'Then I'm glad we're in a civilised part of the world,' Castus said, breathing hard. With his wooden sword under his arm, he walked heavily to the wooden railing of the portico. Stooping, he dashed his face and torso with water from the trough.

'We fight again?' Brinno said, stalking up and down swinging his sword.

'That's enough for today,' Castus said. He grabbed a rough tunic from the railing and used it to swab his face. 'I'm for the baths. I need a cold plunge and rub down.'

'You just know I'd win in the end, old man!' Brinno declared as he tossed his sword to the slave boy. 'Youth beats age, every time.'

'You don't have the stamina for it,' Castus growled. He threw the tunic aside and walked along the portico. Serapion was still there, apparently waiting for him.

'You play hard in the Protectores,' the eunuch said.

'It's no game,' Castus told him. 'You can lose your edge, standing around in a palace all day.' He extended the wooden sword, hilt first, towards Serapion. 'You want to try?'

'Hmm, thank you, but I think not,' the eunuch said with a tense smile.

'Let me know if you change your mind. I've trained softer-looking men than you.'

Castus put the sword down, placed his hands on the portico railing and leaned forward, feeling the burn in his bunched shoulder muscles. The ache of combat lingered these days as it never had in his youth. Brinno's jibes about his age had not been far off the mark.

'In fact,' Serapion said, 'I'm here with a request.'

Castus straightened up. He waited for the eunuch to go on. From the corner of his eye he could see Brinno still pacing in the courtyard, pretending not to notice the conversation at the portico railing.

'The request comes from the domina Valeria Domitia Sabina,' Serapion said. 'She wishes to make an. . . excursion tonight, a rather particular excursion, and has asked that you accompany her.'

'A what?' Castus said. He wiped a forearm across his brow.

'I. . . cannot say anything more now,' the eunuch went on. He was clearly embarrassed, or nervous. 'But the domina Sabina asks that you meet her outside the stable gate of the palace, at the beginning of the second watch tonight. Dress plainly, she said, and come alone.'

Castus stared at him for a few moments, feeling the doubt massing in his mind. The promise too, and the impossibility. 'Why don't you go with her?' he asked.

'I'm afraid it's nothing that would suit me,' Serapion replied, looking far from comfortable. 'Besides. . . the domina rather suggested that she might need. . . *protecting*?'

Castus grunted, then rubbed a knuckle across his scalp. 'How do I know this isn't some ruse of yours?'

Serapion widened his eyes. 'I assure you it's not,' he said. 'But the domina told me, if you asked, that I was to give you this.' He reached into the sleeve of his tunic and drew out a slip of white muslin, passing it to Castus.

Even as he took the cloth, Castus could smell her scent upon it. Rich and dark: he recognised it at once. Quickly he balled the cloth into his fist and thrust it under his belt.

'You may return it to her tonight,' Serapion said, then turned and walked swiftly back into the shadows of the building behind him.

'What was that?' Brinno asked as Castus returned along the portico.

'Nothing,' Castus said. 'Nothing at all.'

Several times that afternoon and evening Castus resolved to forget the whole thing; it was some trick to mock him, or a mistake. But the goad of curiosity drove him. With the emperor and most of his court away on the expedition to Britain, the chambers of the palace felt unnaturally quiet and empty. Only the occasional slave appeared, sweeping the summer dust from the porticos and mopping the mosaic pavements in the great echoing audience halls.

Castus was on duty for the first watch that night, but it was an easy matter to slip away from the precincts of the Protectores after the sentries changed. The two men standing at the courtyard gate just gave him a knowing smile and a nod when he called out the watchword, assuming he was making a private visit to one of the city brothels. He wore his old buff-brown military cloak, with a plain red tunic and round cap; his baldric he had shortened so that his sword hung high on his left, where it would be concealed by the cloak; Serapion's instructions had not specified that he was to come to the meeting armed, but he felt unprepared without a weapon. As he paced down the paved alleyway that led to the stable gate, Castus fought down a rising wave of apprehension. He was not sure what he expected of the night ahead, and felt uncomfortably as if he had slipped into a dream from which he might awake suddenly, disorientated.

CHAPTER XIII

The night was warm, the air clammy on his skin. Just outside the arched portal of the stable gate, a covered two-wheeled carriage stood in the shadow of the palace wall. Light flared as he approached, and Castus saw the carriage driver lift a burning torch above his head. His hand moved beneath his cloak, fingers closing around the hilt of his sword.

'I thought you'd abandoned me,' she said, drawing the curtain aside from the carriage door.

Castus shaded his eyes from the torchlight. 'I came as soon as I could.' He passed her the slip of perfumed cloth that Serapion had given him, then clambered in beside her. He had not travelled in a carriage before; the chassis rocked beneath his weight and he was thrown immediately off balance, almost falling onto Sabina. He caught himself on the doorpost and lowered himself down to sit beside her on the bench seat. It was narrow; their bodies were pressed close together. Sabina too was plainly dressed tonight, Castus noticed, in a simple dark stola and shawl.

She called to the driver and pulled the curtain across, and at once the vehicle lurched into motion. Castus twisted to glance back through the latticed rear window, and saw the arch of the stable gate vanish into the night.

'Now maybe you can tell me where we're going?' Castus said. He was crushed into the corner of the seat, trying to preserve at least some distance from the woman beside him, although she appeared not to mind the proximity.

'Not just yet,' she said quietly, and he sensed her smile in the dark. The carriage wheels jolted over the paving of the street. 'This is one advantage of living in the provinces,' Sabina said. 'In Rome only Vestal Virgins are allowed to travel by carriage. Everyone else must use a litter. . . But for our purposes this is far more convenient.'

Castus was not sure. The carriage swung from side to side as it moved, pitching him against Sabina, and his sword was digging into his side. He lifted the swinging curtain and saw the dark porticos that lined the streets of the city flashing past. The carriage swung around a corner, passing a fountain carved in the shape of a lion's head.

'Are you easily scared?" Sabina asked, almost whispering. Castus had to lean closer to hear her above the noise of the wheels.

'Depends. Of what?'

'Oh, of the dark. Of spirits, perhaps. The world of the dead.'

'Isn't everyone scared of that?'

'Maybe. You seem to me less easily frightened than most men. Serapion, for example, would not accompany me tonight.'

'Serapion's a eunuch.'

'Indeed,' she said. The carriage made another turn, and Castus saw that they were passing the big grain warehouses down by the river. 'We're taking a rather circuitous route,' Sabina told him.

They slowed as they approached the small gate that led out through the wall to the river meadows. Torchlight on the cobbles outside, and the voices of soldiers. Castus kept quiet, barely breathing; wherever this strange journey was leading, he did not want anyone identifying him. But the driver spoke only briefly to the soldiers at the gate, then Castus heard the flick of his goad and the jingle of the horse trappings, and the carriage was moving again, down the slope through the gate and out of the city. A damp warm breeze swept in beneath the curtain, and the scent of the river mingled with Sabina's perfume.

Another wide turn, but the darkness outside was total and Castus had lost his bearings. Close beside him he could feel Sabina tensing, her body drawing tight with nerves. They were moving along a narrow dirt track now.

'Whatever happens tonight,' she said, 'you must promise to do exactly what I say. Will you do that?'

'Domina, how can I promise when I don't know what we're doing?'

'Are you afraid of doing things that are wrong? Things that are illegal?'

Castus shoved himself back from her. 'What sort of things?' he said warily. 'I would do nothing dishonourable. . . not through choice anyway.'

The carriage slowed suddenly, then came to a halt.

'Quiet now,' Sabina said. 'I'll tell you everything soon enough.'

After the cool breeze of motion the night seemed even warmer. Castus helped Sabina down from the carriage, then he turned and drew a sharp breath. All around him in the moonlight, stretching away into darkness, broken shapes rose up from the tangled grass. Some were the size of houses, others mere slabs of masonry.

'This is the old necropolis,' he said. As his eyes grew accustomed to the darkness he could make out gaping empty doorways, the shapes of mouldings, statues and portrait busts mossy and weathered into indistinction.

Sabina was already leading him away from the carriage, along a path roughly traced between the tombs. There were torches moving in the near distance, little points of weaving light, and Sabina seemed to be heading in their direction. Castus paced after her, feeling the dread crawling up his spine. The vast tangled necropolis seemed to breathe a foul black air. He could almost taste it in his mouth, and feel the cold touch of the dead upon his skin.

'You *are* frightened, aren't you?' Sabina said, drawing close to him. She placed her palm upon his chest, as if to steady his heart.

'And you're not?' he asked her.

She laughed quietly. 'Of course I am. That's why you're here.'

They moved slowly, stepping over fallen stones in the grass. The tombs made fantastical shapes in the moonlight: some rose into tall spires or pyramids, while others were built low and square like houses, their faces thick with crumbling stucco. Every city had its necropolis outside the gates, but this one was older and grander than most. The tombs must be hundreds of years old, Castus guessed; some still had the great slabs blocking the doors, but most had been stripped a long time ago. Everywhere Castus saw faces: the empty eyes of the dead staring back at him from oblivion. He kept his hand on the hilt of his sword; not, he thought, that a sword would do much good against a ghost or a demon. But not all the eyes in the darkness were dead stone: there were animals moving in the undergrowth, and perhaps men too. Cemeteries had long been haunts of brigands and thieves.

Sabina paused at the corner of one large structure. She pulled her shawl tightly around her shoulders. Castus leaned against the wall beside her. 'So,' he said, trying to keep the nervous irritation from his voice. 'Tell me what we're doing here.'

'There's a sorcerer. . .' she told him. Castus shoved himself away from the wall in sudden anger.

'Gods below!' he hissed. 'Is that what this is about? Black magic in a necropolis?'

'Listen. . . Listen to me. You don't need to worry – I only needed a companion to see me to the place where the ceremony will be conducted. . .'

'Ceremony?' Castus said. The practice of magic was strictly illegal, and punishable by a grisly execution; it was well known that Constantine hated it above all things. 'What is this? Summoning spirits to curse your enemies? Bringing back the dead?'

'Only divination,' Sabina said quickly, pressing herself back against the wall. She had been nervous already, but Castus realised that his anger was scaring her more.

'Tell me.'

'His name is Astrampsychus,' she said. 'He's a Babylonian, they say, an expert reader of the future. One of the most powerful.'

'Oh, yes?' Castus said. He had been to Babylonia, and had met no fortune tellers there.

'The ceremony has to be a secret, for obvious reasons, but many people are going. Highly placed people. Who wouldn't welcome the chance to know the future? I thought about disguising myself, but only those who share the secret will see me, so. . .'

'And why does it have to happen in a necropolis?'

'Don't you know?' she asked, and he saw her eyes widen in the darkness as she drew closer. 'The presence of the dead makes the magic stronger!'

For a moment she stared at him, smiling, then leaned towards him and kissed him lightly on the mouth. 'You can wait outside if you prefer,' she whispered.

They found the tomb quickly enough; it was one of the largest, and would have been a grand edifice once. The stone and stucco around the black portal of the doorway was shaped to resemble pillars and a pediment, and there was a miniature courtyard before the door with an ivy-grown wall around it. As they approached they could see dark figures, cloaked and cowled, moving around the doorway and disappearing inside: others drawn by the illicit promise of magical divination.

Sabina left him in the overgrown courtyard, with only a silent touch on the shoulder before she stepped through the portal. There were long stones in the trampled grass, and Castus was about to sit on one when he realised that it was a sarcophagus. Probably dragged from inside the tomb, he thought, and shuddered.

Now that he was alone his senses became a lot sharper. He moved back into the shadows as a couple more people came stumbling between the tombs and passed in through the open portal. He could hear a low echoing murmur of voices from inside now. How many people had come to witness this ceremony? Out in the wilds of the necropolis an owl cried.

Time passed. Castus stilled his mind and forced himself to calm, remembering the long watches he had spent on night sentry duty. This was no different, he thought, in a way. . .

Then, with a quick prickling of nerves, he made out the strange roaring noise coming from inside the open tomb. Like the sound of wind rushing through trees; but the night was still and motionless. The roaring rose and fell, from a low hum to a high whine. Castus was on his feet, sword partially drawn, staring at the black mouth of the tomb: the sound was coming from within it. Then he heard the voices.

The first voice he could not make out: a sort of rapid cackling chant. The second voice rose above it, above even the continued hum and whine.

'*BARBARITHA CHENUMBRA ABRAXAS ABRAHAT!*
O Chthonic gods! O Dis Pater! O Mother Hecate!
BARHARRANGES AOIA MARAAROTH AMARZA!
Holders of the keys to Hades! Gods and Daemons of the Underworld! Spirits of the Untimely Dead! Rouse yourselves for me, bring yourselves to me! *THOOTH PHOKENTAZEPHU BARBARITHU ABRAHAT!* Demons who lie here! Spirits who reside here! I adjure you to aid this divination – Rouse yourselves! Bring yourselves. . .!'

Castus felt the sweat burning on his brow, but his heart was ice. He had drawn his sword and held it ready, as if to strike at anything emerging from the black mouth of the tomb. Panic beat in his chest – he wanted to run, needed to escape this foul place. *It's just a man*, he told himself. *Just a man, just some words.*

The strange chant ended, with a dull dying echo, and the roaring noise fell away into silence. For a few heartbeats there was no sound, and then Castus heard other voices speaking, hushed but carrying. A pungent smell was coming from the tomb, like burning hair and incense.

Fighting down his nerves, Castus edged closer to the open door. At first he could see only blackness, then he made out the faint glow of lamps from deep inside. There were steps leading down from the doorway into a sunken chamber. The light and the voices must be coming from another, deeper, chamber beyond. Once again the roaring noise started, rising and falling. Castus slid his sword back into its scabbard, pulled his cloak over it, and began picking his way slowly down the steps.

Close black warmth engulfed him, and he stumbled from the fourth step onto the dusty floor. A moment, crouched in breathless silence. His eyes adjusted to the glow from the inner room, and he saw he was in a low chamber, arched alcoves on all sides. The walls were painted with figures and scenes: he made out the shape of a winged lion, a leaping dolphin. At the far end of the room was a low doorway with a heavy stone lintel, and he crept slowly towards it. The light wavered, and his shadow twisted and leaped behind him.

Now he could make out the speaking voices more clearly: one, high and cracked, was asking questions, and a few moments later a deeper and more sonorous voice seemed to be answering them.

As he neared the doorway, Castus noticed a gap in the wall to his left; the bricks of one of the arched alcoves had been knocked through to make an opening into the next chamber. Stooping, he thrust his head into the alcove and peered through.

The chamber beyond was much larger, twice the size of the entrance room. Scattered lamps burned from niches in the walls, and by their dim smoky glow Castus made out a crowd of figures almost filling the room. There were both men and women, some sitting on the floor and others standing around the walls. Surely twenty or thirty of them, but in the flicker of shadow it was hard to be sure. Castus picked out Sabina at once, sitting against the wall at the far side of the room, her face turned as she listened. He followed her gaze across the clustered heads and bodies to the far end of the chamber.

Between two heavy square pillars, a fire burned in a low tripod set on an altar. The man behind the altar, the speaker with the sonorous voice, was robed all in white. Linen bound his skull, and a white mask shaped like a dog's head with staring black eyeholes covered his face. Behind him, a squat youth held a length of wood with holes bored in it; as Castus watched, the youth whirled the wood around his head on a cord; the weird rushing roar filled the chamber again.

The figure in the white mask – Astrampsychus himself, Castus assumed – stooped forward over the altar fire, raising his hands as he inhaling the fumes. There was a dead cockerel on the altar, its blood staining the stone and its feathers scattered around the fire. Now Castus could make out a second assistant, no doubt the man with the cackling voice, stepping carefully through the throng of spectators. He saw coins change hands, the glint of gold. The magician reared back from the smoking tripod, swaying on his feet.

'The spirits bring good tidings,' he intoned. 'The child is yours, and will glorify your name. . .'

A ripple passed through the crowd, several people reaching out to a man near the front to congratulate him.

The assistant came creeping back towards the altar, holding what looked to Castus like a stack of broken pottery pieces. One of his legs was crooked, and he limped heavily. He placed the shards upon the altar, and the magician selected one without looking at it. The assistant picked up the shard and read from it in his cracked voice.

'O Great Astrampsychus of Cunaxa: *Will my son gain admittance to the Corps of Notaries this year?*'

Castus could see what was happening now: those in the crowd who wished to ask a question wrote it upon a shard of pottery and passed it to the assistant with the crooked leg, along with a coin. The magician, after standing for a moment with his eerie mask gazing out over the crowd, began muttering his incantations.

'*CHAOR CHTHOR CHARABARAX IAO!* Wake demons, wake spirits! Bring me truths, I adjure you. . .'

The assistant tossed a bundle of herbs and feathers onto the fire, and Astrampsychus stooped again into the smoke. The youth whirled his roarer, and the noise boomed out between the pillars.

'You have placed your faith in unworthy men!' the magician cried, reeling back from the smoke. 'You have wasted your riches. False promises bring no reward. . .'

A groan went up from the crowd, and Castus saw a matronly-looking woman hunch her shoulders and cover her face. Now that he had grown used to the dull glow in the chamber, he could better distinguish the people in the crowd. Most looked quite wealthy, for all their drab costumes. He was certain he recognised several from the palace, but could not name them. Then, as he scanned the back of the room, he saw the round bald head and bulky shoulders of the eunuch Gorgonius, Maximian's steward.

The assistant was holding another shard of pottery now, tilting it to read the scratched words by the light of a lamp. His mouth fell open. Astrampsychus, jolted momentarily from his trance, snapped his fingers at the man.

'Next question!' he hissed.

'I. . . I don't know. . .' the little man stuttered. The blank white dog-mask turned in his direction. 'O Great Astrampsychus of Cunaxa,' the assistant read in his cracked and wavering voice, 'the question is: *Who will be our next emperor?*'

A collective gasp filled the room. Castus flicked his eyes to the crowd and saw the ripple of shock, people shuffling and edging back towards the door, others glancing at those beside them in suspicion. To ask any question about the fate of emperors was outright treason.

Castus pressed his shoulder into the alcove, turning his body so that he could watch the crowd without the light from the altar fire dazzling his eyes. He had seen enough of Astrampsychus and his rituals: the reaction of the people filling the room was of greater interest to him now. A hush had fallen, and the lamps seemed to flare up and burn a little brighter. At the back of the room, the eunuch Gorgonius had not moved.

179

The roaring noise again, and the crackle of the altar fire. The stink of burning filled the shadows.

'I see letters forming in the smoke!' the magician intoned.

Castus saw the crowd move forward again. In the lamplight he saw faces raised, mouths open in anticipation. He saw Sabina craning to see over the people in front, her eyes gleaming. Then his gaze fell on another figure, near the first row: a woman, with a deep hood covering her face.

'I see. . . M. . .'

More gasps, and what sounded like a stifled giggle. Somewhere near the back, a woman was quietly sobbing.

'I see. . . A. . .'

This time there were loud cries. Several people in the crowd were scrambling to their feet, hands raised as if to catch the treasonous words in the air.

'I see. . . X. . .'

'Enough!' a man shouted, surging up and shoving his way through the throng. Castus thought he might be one of the Praetorian tribunes from the palace. Screaming women pushed themselves away from him. The man had a sword in his hand. 'Enough! This is treason!'

Damp air rushed suddenly through the chamber, and the lamp flames twisted and died. Utter blackness: Castus scraped his head on the alcove as he dragged himself backwards. The noise of screaming echoed beneath the low ceiling, and already there were figures bursting through the doorway from the inner chamber, rushing in panic towards the steps that led from the tomb.

Reaching blindly along the wall, Castus found the edge of the door and hauled himself around it. A body slammed against him and he punched it aside. Two more, trying to push him back, and he barged between them with arms outstretched. He thought he had memorised the layout of the larger chamber, but now all was darkness and for a moment he was lost in the tumult, bodies shoving him from both sides, a wild confusion of sweat and echoing screams.

He reached the far wall, and heard her voice to his left. His hand caught her shoulder and he pulled her close; she fought against him, panicking.

'It's me,' he said, wrapping his arms around her. 'It's me. Stay close behind me and we'll get out of here.'

Somebody sprawled against his legs and he almost tripped; there were cries from the darkness, and he heard the rasp of a blade striking stone. Sabina was pressed against his back now, clasping his shoulders, and he pushed himself forward into the struggling mass that surged towards the door.

The night air was like a tonic, and they ran between the broken tombs feeling the oppressive weight of darkness sloughing off them. Sabina was still trembling, but gulping back laughter. She came to a halt, bracing herself against a crumbling wall.

'Praise be to Isis! Praise be to Isis!' She grinned, hands raised to the sky. 'I thought I would die in there. . . Thank you. . .' She stepped towards Castus and embraced him, pressing herself against his chest. 'Thank you for coming back for me.'

'Did you get to ask your question?'

'Yes!' she said, raising her head. 'It was one of the first he answered. I asked what the fate of my husband would be, and he said. . .' She pursed her lips, remembering. 'He said: *All will be given to those who are worthy; all will be taken from those who are not.* What could that mean, do you think?'

'I think it means the Great Astrampsychus is a very clever man,' he said. He was all too aware of her body close against

181

his, her arms still lightly draped over his shoulders. 'Plenty of wealthy people in that room. Plenty of gold coins too. I'd bet that if we went back there now we'd find Astrampsychus and his mates crawling about on their hands and knees, collecting up a good sum off the floor.'

'Do you think?' Sabina said, and looked mildly offended for a moment. Then she laughed again and swatted lightly at his shoulder. 'How unexpectedly cynical of you!'

'I also think it means we should find the carriage and get back to the palace as soon as we can, before anyone notices we're gone.'

They took the straight way back to the city, out through the fringe of the necropolis and onto the main road that led towards the Mogontiacum gate. In the back of the carriage Castus sat with Sabina clasped to his side; it was all too soon that the wheels slowed beneath them, he heard the driver calling out, and he leaned from the carriage to see the massive buttressed towers and double arched portals of the gateway looming in the torchlight. He spoke to the sentries himself: he was past caring whether any of them identified him now, and they would be seeing plenty of travellers that night far more exalted than he.

On the paved streets of the city the carriage jolted and rolled. A short ride, a turning, and they were drawing to a halt outside the stable gate of the palace once more. Castus made to get out, but Sabina clasped his arm. The faint light of a torch showed through the gap in the carriage curtain. She looked at him for a moment.

'You're very ugly, aren't you?' she said.

'And this is why you choose to trust me?'

'You have kind eyes,' she said. 'Sometimes.'

Then her arms were around him, her lips pressed against his, and the carriage creaked and swayed as he embraced her.

* * *

It was past midnight as he stepped back through the gateway to the precinct of the Protectores. The watch had just changed, and Victor was standing guard.

'Have you heard the news?' the young man said. Castus could hear the sour disappointment in his voice. He shook his head.

'The emperor's coming back early from Britain,' Victor went on. 'And Maximian's leaving the palace. Which means we're going with him. . . to somewhere called the Villa Herculis, wherever that is.'

Castus knew of the place: it was a few miles up the river. He thanked Victor for the information and walked on towards his chamber. Perhaps it was best to get out of the Sacred Palace, he thought. He had grown used to it over the last year, but it felt hazardous all the same. Would this Villa Herculis be any better?

Back in his chamber he threw himself down on the bed. Sabina's scent was still lingering in the folds of his cloak and tunic, and he stood up again and stripped them off. Sweat ran down his back. For a few heartbeats he stood in the gloom, remembering keenly the sensation of her body pressed against him, her mouth. . .

But then another thought came to him: M. . . A. . . X. . . Was the name supposed to be Maxentius? Or was it Maximian? Somebody in that subterranean room had known the answer, he was sure. The same person who had paid to ask the question. The same person, perhaps, who had rushed up to stop it when only the first three letters of the name had been uttered. Castus thought back to the faces in the crowd, trying to place them. The eunuch, Gorgonius, Maximian's steward: what had become of him?

Pointless to try and work it all out. The whole strange scene was lost to mystery and confusion. Castus felt his mind growing foggy with weariness, the images of the night turning into a smoky whirl of distorted sensations. He needed to sleep, but he had just eased himself down onto the bed again and closed his eyes when a recollection jolted him awake.

The figure he had seen at the front of the gathering, the woman with the hood. In the brief instant before the lamps had gone out, as the man with the sword had pushed through the crowd, she had turned her head and he had seen her face. Had he recognised her at the time? If so, the sudden confusion that followed had driven it from his mind.

But now, abruptly, he was sure: the woman in the hood had been the nobilissima femina Fausta, the emperor's wife.

CHAPTER XIV

'Only twice in her life,' Maximian declared, pushing himself up from the couch, 'is a woman is of any worth. . . Once on the night of her wedding, when you take her virginity. And again on the day of her funeral, when you get rid of her!'

Polite laughter from the dinner guests, the former emperor's intimates and officials gathered on the couches around him.

'Oh, very good, dominus!' said the eunuch Gorgonius. Scorpianus, one of the Praetorian tribunes, rubbed his big blue chin. He had a smile pasted to his face.

'I remember one occasion during the campaign in Mauretania against the Quinquegentiani – you remember it, Scorpianus: you were there!'

Scorpianus inclined his head and made a self-deprecatory gesture.

'Anyway,' Maximian went on, 'we'd surrounded one of their strongholds in the mountains; walls looked as old as Troy. . . We had the son of their chief, a boy of about nine or ten, and we brought him up before the gate and threatened to kill him if they didn't surrender. So then the boy's mother, fine-looking woman in a barbaric sort of way, stands up on the wall in sight of the whole army and pulls up her robe. . . shows off everything! And do you know what she said? *Do you think this body is too old to make more sons?*'

Maximian tipped back his head and laughed, then banged his cup down on the table. 'Well, we took the fort in the end. Executed her and the boy, and everyone else in the place too! Or did we sell the boy. . .? Scorpianus?'

'I don't recall, dominus,' the tribune said with a grimace.

'A marvellous story,' Gorgonius said, with an air that suggested he would prefer to move on to a different subject. But his master was not finished yet.

'What do you think, Constantine?' Maximian said. 'Wasn't there some female chief among the Picts, up there in Britain? What did you do with her?'

Standing on duty at the door of the dining room, Castus suppressed a jolt of concern at the words. He had heard nothing these last four years about Cunomagla, the formidable chieftainess who had, so briefly, shared his bed. Had the emperor learned more about her during his recent visit to Britain?

Constantine was reclining in solitude on the couch facing his father-in-law. He took his time replying. He had drunk as much as Maximian, but held it better. 'I think I recall something of the sort,' he said at last. 'She ran away, I believe, to some cave in the mountains, and was never seen again. I expect she died. . .'

Castus exhaled slowly in relief. Clearly the emperor knew no more than he did.

But now Maximian was heaving himself up from the couch, calling for Constantine to join him. The other men around the table promptly stood as well, and fell in behind the emperor and his father-in-law as they moved for the door. Behind them, the slaves closed around the circular table, removing the debris of dinner and helping themselves to the scraps left on the dishes.

Maximian walked beside Constantine, throwing one hefty arm around the emperor's shoulders. As they passed him, Castus heard them talking quietly together; he waited for the entourage to pass through into the reception chamber, then followed behind them at a discreet distance. Beyond the reception chamber was the broad front portico of the villa, lined with tall arched windows with brass grilles that let in a cool whisper of night air. Castus saw Constantine nodding gravely, Maximian swaying as he spoke, no doubt pressing his advice on the great matters of state. The others dropped back, lingering around the tall inlaid doors of the reception chamber, and let the two men walk on alone down the portico, through the pools of light spilled by the lamps across the marble floor.

Maximian and his household had been in residence at the Villa Herculis for over a month now, but in all that time the old former emperor had never uttered the slightest disloyalty. He railed against his disrespectful children, his wife – who had remained in Rome with Maxentius – his former colleague Diocletian, and the fickle Roman people, who had so soon neglected his grandeur. Even against the gods. But never a word against Constantine. Maximian had nothing but praise for him.

The emperor had been keeping himself deliberately aloof from his father-in-law since his return from Britain, and this appearance at the villa was a rare event. Castus knew why the emperor had at last decided to visit: the news that Licinius, the rival emperor based on the Danube, had invaded Italy, seized Istria from Maxentius and besieged Aquileia had circulated quickly. Perhaps, he thought as he followed the two men along the portico from the dining hall, Constantine had finally decided to listen to the old man's advice.

It was later that night, as he returned towards his room, that Castus saw the figure sitting alone at the end of the rear portico.

He paced closer at once, suspicious, but only as he opened his mouth to call out a challenge did he recognise the plainly dressed man with a cup of wine in his hand. Castus was momentarily shocked; he had believed that Constantine had retired to his own chambers an hour before.

'Dominus,' he said quickly, bowing, and began to kneel.

Constantine raised a finger, dismissing the gesture. 'No need for that,' he said curtly. 'We are not in the palace now.' His voice was hoarse. 'Approach.'

Castus moved closer, just three paces, then halted and fell into a parade rest posture. His breath was caught in his throat: he hoped the emperor did not require him to sit down, join him in a drink, perhaps. . .

'Tell me, soldier,' the emperor said. 'Do you believe that the gods send us signs, messages? Do they guide us to the right path, or do they leave us to choose our own way. . .?'

The directness of the question caught Castus unprepared.

'I don't know, dominus,' he said. He tried to stop himself frowning, but could not determine what answer the emperor wanted to hear. Or even if he wanted an answer at all. For a moment Constantine sat musing.

'I am waiting for a sign,' he said. 'I have waited a long time now, and nothing is clear. So what do I do, eh? The cause of war must be just, would you agree?'

'Of course, dominus.' Castus hoped the emperor was not expecting a more insightful answer.

'Then is it just to declare war against my brother? My brother-*in-law*, I should say. . . Or should I aid him against Licinius? I find that I receive contrary advice, mainly from fools and flatterers, and nothing that feels like a clear sign.' He looked up suddenly, staring at Castus with a piercing eye. 'So what should I do?' he said.

Castus shifted his stance, uncomfortable. 'Seems to me, dominus,' he said, slowing his words, 'that it's like the story of the fox and the lions.'

Constantine stared, and for a moment Castus feared he was offended – was it sacrilege to compare the affairs of emperors to a children's parable? But perhaps Constantine had never been told the story when he was a boy? He gestured for Castus to continue.

'Well, dominus,' Castus said, trying not to let his nerves mangle the words, 'the story asks who would win in a fight between a fox and two lions. The lions are proud and strong, but the fox is cunning. . . The fox speaks slyly to the lions, asking which is stronger, and the lions start boasting and then fall to fighting. Of course, the stronger lion wins, but he's so weakened by the battle that the fox can defeat him with a single blow.'

It would not, Castus thought as he spoke, be the strategy he favoured himself: for him it was always the bold frontal attack and the gods could decide the consequences. For a long moment the emperor said nothing, staring with a fierce frown. Perhaps he thought the same? But then he barked a laugh. 'Yes, I like that,' he said. He stood up, throwing the cup out into the darkness of the garden, and gathered his cloak around him. As he passed, he clapped a hand on Castus's shoulder. 'The sophists say that if a man wants peace he should prepare for war. So if I want war, perhaps I should feign peace, hmm?'

Castus nodded, tense with discomfort. Then the emperor turned and moved away down the portico towards his chambers. Castus even heard him singing to himself.

It was two days later that the women invaded. As the carriages approached along the road from the river, the birds rose and shrieked around the eaves, as if in warning. For over a month the Villa Herculis had been a male domain, only Maximian and his staff of secretaries and eunuchs, his slaves and his bodyguards in residence. But now his daughter Fausta was to pay her father an official visit.

Since the night at the necropolis Castus had barely seen Sabina, and had not once had an opportunity to speak with her. He was not accustomed to frustrated desire; always before in life he had sought women when he needed them, and found them easily enough. Afrodisia in Britain he had cared for deeply, even perhaps loved in a way, but she had been a prostitute. Marcellina the envoy's daughter had been the only woman to tempt him to greater feeling, and she was far beyond his hopes.

With Sabina it was different, and for the first time he had experienced the racking torment of longing. She had used him, he thought, and it pained him that he felt unable to erase her from his mind.

When Fausta and her entourage arrived at the villa, Maximian was waiting on the front steps to receive her. His eight Protectores flanked him, and the courtyard and the road beyond were lined with the slaves of his household, crying out salutations. Fausta descended from her carriage, bowed her head and stood before Maximian, reciting the customary greeting.

'In the name of Juno, Isis and Minerva and all the gods I salute you, Father. If you are well I am well. May my presence here bring good fortune upon your house.'

Maximian stiffly descended the steps and kissed his daughter, then turned without another word and walked back inside.

'Here they come,' Sallustius muttered from the side of his mouth. 'A torrent of hairdressers. A cascade of eunuchs. . .'

But Castus could only stare at the carriages drawn up in the courtyard. The ladies descended one by one, first Plautiana

190

and then Crescentilla, then several others he did not know. Finally he saw Sabina, a veil partly covering her face. With the other Protectores he stood at attention as the ladies filed up the steps to the rear portico of the villa. Only as she passed him did Sabina glance up, lifting the veil for a moment. She met his eyes, and seemed to mouth something to him, but he could not catch the words.

Serapion found him later that afternoon. Castus was in the stone-lined changing rooms of the baths, dressing after a lukewarm soak: Fausta and her retinue had used the suite earlier, and there was little heated water remaining. He pulled his tunic over his head, and when he looked up the eunuch was standing in the doorway that led to the courtyard. A gust of cool air seemed to follow Serapion as he entered the room.

'You have a habit of appearing at unexpected moments,' Castus said. 'Is it deliberate?'

Serapion gave a short, cold smile. He stood a few paces from Castus, gazing into the far corner of the room as he spoke. 'I have a message from my mistress,' he said. 'She will see you tonight, if you so choose. Do you know the garden house by the riverbank, with the fountain court?'

Castus just nodded. He knew the place well enough. His blood was flowing quickly, but the sweat was cold on his brow.

'There is a bedchamber at the end of the corridor of the dancers. Go there at the start of the second watch. Do not be late – she is tired and cannot wait long.'

Serapion looked at him directly for the first time, and Castus found it hard to read his expression. Was it amusement in his eyes, or contempt? Then some other thought passed across his face, and the eunuch turned sharply and stalked from the room.

The rest of the day passed in a torment of anticipation. When evening came Castus was pacing the mosaic floors of the main audience hall, glancing repeatedly at the tall water clock that stood beside the main doors. A fascinating mechanism – he had not seen its like before – but he cursed it for the slow regular drip of its hours. Night had fallen by the time he was relieved, and he returned to his chamber to change into the dull red tunic and cloak he had worn on his last meeting with Sabina. He felt uncomfortable with the idea of disguise, and creeping about in the shadows like a spy or a thief did not appeal to him. But it seemed necessary. He picked up his sword, then thought for a moment and laid it aside. Surely that would not be required. . . but he strapped a military dagger to his waist belt, as a reassurance.

Leaving the villa by a side door at the back of the wing used by the Protectores, he doubled around the building and dropped down into the garden terraces. The night felt thick and humid. Mist had moved up from the river, beading his cloak with moisture. When he looked back at the villa the lamps along the front portico shone though a haze, and he heard the sound of laughter coming from one of the guest suites, quickly muffled by the mist. As Castus paced along the upper garden walk he expected the greyness ahead to form into the shapes of figures.

But the gardens were abandoned to the night. He skirted the long ornamental pool, a gulf of blackness in the mist, passed through a pillared gazebo and down the steps, and then saw the garden house before him with the ground beyond dropping into the dark emptiness of the river. It was a small building, intended for accommodating guests, or the associates of guests, not sufficiently exalted to stay in the main villa. A simple quadrangle of rooms surrounded a courtyard where a dry fountain stood above a cracked stone basin. Castus

192

stepped through the narrow entrance gate, then through the open vestibule into the courtyard.

A single lamp burned in a niche beside one of the doors. Were it not for that, the whole house would have seemed deserted. Crossing the courtyard in ten long careful strides, Castus reached the open door. Another lamp just inside illuminated the end of the corridor: painted girls danced and somersaulted along the length of the wall and away into darkness. At the far end, almost invisible in the shadow, a single door stood partly open. Castus could already smell her scent lingering in the air.

He wanted to call out, speak her name, but the stillness of the night and the empty building around him seemed to forbid all sound. He paced silently along the corridor, running his fingertips over the painted dancers, until he reached the door.

'Sabina?' he managed to whisper. The word came out as a hoarse croak. He lifted his hand and edged the door open.

Complete darkness inside, or so it seemed at first. Castus felt the prickle of nerves running up his spine. Her scent again, fresh and strong. Then he made out the bed set against the far wall, and the motion in the darkness as she rolled from beneath the covers.

'Come here,' she said. He stepped into the room and pushed the door closed behind him. His senses reeled: the awareness of danger, of trespass, eclipsed by the surge of desire. He shed his cloak at the threshold; he unbuckled his belt and it fell to the floor. Pulling off his tunic, he crossed the room, into the field of her warmth. There was a shuttered window high above the bed, but enough grey light seeped between the panels of the shutters for him to make out her pale form as she pushed back the covers. Then her arms were around him, drawing him down onto the bed, and there was nothing in his mind but the feel of her body, the taste of her lips and her skin.

Her thighs were parted, and he eased his body down onto her. He could hear her breathing, loud and rapid. She seemed nervous. For the first time since he had entered the room a knot of alarm twisted at the back of his skull. Sabina had never seemed nervous before, not even in the necropolis. He raised himself on one arm and looked down at her, seeing only the curves of her body in the faint light. He laid a palm on her breast: it was full and round. As he blinked he could almost make out the shape of her face changing from the image in his mind to something else.

'Gods below, what is this?' he said from the back of his throat.

He reared up onto his knees, stretching an arm to grab at the shutters. One heave, and the catch burst; the shutters swung open and the grey misty light fell over the bed. The girl beneath him let out a cry and rolled, covering her face. But Castus had already seen that it was not Sabina in the bed with him.

Ice filled his veins, and his heart slammed against the top of his chest. He was gripping the girl by her arm, turning her, hardly believing what he had seen.

'Don't hurt me,' she whispered, with a sob in her voice. 'Please. . . this wasn't what I wanted. I didn't do this. . . they made me. . .'

Up off the bed in one bound, Castus staggered immediately and fell to the floor. His breeches were still tangled around his knees, and he hauled them up. Gasping breath, he pulled on his tunic and cloak, then snatched up his belt and dagger from the floor. When he glanced back he saw only the bunched covers, and the shape of the girl hiding beneath them.

There was a figure in the passageway as he threw open the door. The shadow darted across the painted frieze of dancers, but Castus moved faster. One lunging grab, and he had the fugitive by the arm, spinning him and slamming him against the wall. The big knife was already bared in his fist.

'If you kill me now,' Serapion said in a choked gasp, 'others will know of it.'

Castus shoved harder against him, his forearm pressed into the eunuch's throat and the dagger pricking the skin beneath his jaw. 'Who will know?' he hissed. 'Who arranged this?'

'I cannot say,' Serapion whispered. In the glow from the lamp at the end of the corridor his face was sheened with sweat. Castus jolted him by the throat. How had he allowed himself to be so stupid? Desire had blinded him – he had been led by the nose. Or maybe not the nose. . . Despairing anger burned through him.

'Who was that girl in the bed?' he demanded, although in his heart he already knew the truth.

Serapion twisted his mouth into a smile. 'You really couldn't tell?' He almost sounded genuinely perplexed. Animal passion was surely alien to him, Castus realised. 'I told you,' the eunuch said, 'that my mistress was waiting for you. . .'

'That was not Sabina.'

'The domina Valeria Domitia Sabina is not my mistress,' Serapion said. Castus almost admired his calm self-control. 'I serve another. I serve the nobilissima femina Fausta, wife of our Augustus.'

The shock of his words wrenched through Castus's body. He wanted to ram the knife hilt-deep in the eunuch's throat, but a sickening dread was stealing his anger, stealing his killing resolve.

'Where's Sabina now?'

'Oh, she left in a closed carriage, shortly after noon. She was safely back in Treveris long ago.'

Castus remembered the words she had mouthed to him on the steps: had she tried to warn him? But then she must have known. She must have been aware of what would happen. . .

'Believe me,' the eunuch said, 'this was not my plan, not my intention. I am a slave, and I must do what I am ordered. . .'

'So people keep telling me. Why should I let you live?'

Serapion took a moment to answer. His eyes flickered towards the far end of the corridor. 'There are three men in the courtyard outside,' he said, quietly and clearly. 'They will try to kill you as you leave. If you run, you might evade them.'

Castus slackened his grip slightly; the eunuch sagged against the wall, breathing deeply. 'Why warn me?' Castus asked him.

'You think I'm just a eunuch?' Serapion said bitterly. 'You think I'm a clay figure, a homunculus? I am just as human as you, and perhaps you can help me if I help you. We are both slaves in this affair. Perhaps I think you deserve a chance.'

Pushing Serapion back against the wall, Castus stepped away from him.

'Don't try to follow me,' he said.

Outside the air was as thick and still as before, but the night seemed darker. Castus lingered in the doorway, trying to blink the after-image of the lamp glow from his eyes. There was no other way from the building, unless he went back into the bedchamber and tried to force his way out through the window, and that would certainly make enough noise to summon trouble.

He took a breath, then exhaled slowly, feeling the strength mass in his limbs. Drawing up his cloak, he wrapped it around his left arm. In his right hand he held the dagger in a low grip. A slight sound from outside, a shuffle of feet on paving, and Castus threw himself through the door.

Two running strides took him to the fountain, and he turned at bay. There were three of them, just as the eunuch had said:

two held shortswords, and the third carried a club that looked like an axe handle. Plainly dressed, but they knew how to use their weapons. Soldiers, Castus guessed; perhaps Praetorians.

He was still disorientated, stunned by the shock of what had happened in the bedchamber. His heart was beating fast, and he willed himself to calm.

The swordsmen moved to either side of him, while the clubman advanced head on with his weapon raised. Crouched, the dagger drawn back in his fist, Castus knew that he could not wait for them to make the first strike: once the first moved, the others would be on him. He considered making a dash for the gate, or perhaps the wall – he could fight with his back to something, at least. But then they would just surround him and use the longer reach of their weapons. . . His only chance was to keep moving, close the distance and tackle them individually. Three heartbeats, three rapid breaths, then he jumped up onto the stone rim of the fountain basin.

His attackers came on at a rush. Castus leaped to the left, flinging out his wrapped arm as the swordsman drove a stab at him. The blade passed through the folds of the cloak, and Castus felt the burn of a gash along his forearm before he dragged the sword aside. The momentum of his leap carried him crashing against the man, his dagger already striking up and out. The man screamed, his legs giving beneath him as the dagger blade slashed through his tunic and dug into his shoulder.

Castus fell with him, the trapped sword dragging his arm and pulling him off balance; then the axe handle came down. The blow struck the arch of his back, and he felt the blast of it in his ribs and lungs but he did not buckle. He rolled, ripping the cloak free of his neck. He needed to get back on his feet; the second swordsman was already above him, blade drawn back to strike.

Rage gripped Castus: he refused to die like this. A wheeling kick, and his boot caught the swordsman behind the leg and tripped him. Up on one knee, the dagger raised, Castus glanced around for the other two attackers. The wounded man was over by the fountain, clutching his shoulder; his friend with the club was circling for a clear strike. Castus twisted himself upright, feeling the blood running hot down his arm. Still no sense of clarity or coordination; he was driven only by a blind desire to survive. The second swordsman had recovered his balance now.

They came fast, and together. First the clubman, striking out with his weapon levelled at Castus's face. The man with the sword dodged in from the right. Castus ducked the club, stepped in at a crouch and came up hard beneath the man's reaching arm. One upward blow and the dagger stabbed through the man's armpit; Castus twisted his grip and felt the blade enter his heart. The clubman gasped, coughing blood as Castus spun the body and hurled it towards the man with the sword. The club clattered to the ground as the swordsman dodged out of the way of the toppling corpse.

Snatching up the club, Castus switched the dagger to his left hand. His palm was wet and slippery with blood. He could see the wounded man by the fountain creeping to his feet, sword still in hand. The third attacker was still unhurt, bouncing on his toes as he circled with his blade low and level. Castus swung the club in wide sweeps, but the man refused to give ground.

One more wide swing, then Castus suddenly hurled the club into the swordsman's face and darted in after it. He grabbed the man's right wrist, dragging his arm out; the dagger almost slipped from his bloody grip, but he raised it high and then punched down twice with his left hand, driving it into the man's exposed shoulder and then into his neck. Something moved fast behind him: the third attacker closing in, and he tensed himself for the killing blow between his shoulder blades; then a scream, and another body sprawled across the paving of the courtyard.

Castus turned. The third man lay dead at his feet, and Brinno stood over him, stripped to the waist, a bloody blade in his hand.

'I'm sure you could have handled all three, brother,' Brinno said. 'But watching you was making me nervous.'

Castus sank down, braced against his knees and fighting for breath. Pain racked his body from his chest to his groin. He rode out a wave of nausea, then straightened and seized Brinno by the shoulder. 'Why are you here?'

'I followed you,' Brinno said. 'I saw you talking to that eunuch in the baths and knew you were doing something. . . I don't know. I'm sorry, brother – I doubted your loyalty. . .'

'Well, thanks anyway,' Castus said. He turned to look around at the courtyard: three dead men, blood spattered on the paving.

'What were you doing in there?' Brinno asked with a cold frown.

Castus just shook his head. 'I have no way of explaining,' he said. 'But you've got to help me get rid of these bodies. . .'

'No need for that,' another voice said. Serapion stood in the lamplight at the open doorway. 'The dead will be disposed of. You need to leave now, though.'

'I told you not to follow me,' Castus said through his teeth. Despite his warning, the eunuch was still his enemy.

'There's something I forgot to mention,' Serapion said, stepping out over one of the bodies. 'If I were found unharmed, it might look suspicious. As if I somehow helped you to escape.'

'True enough.' Castus glanced at Brinno, who shrugged.

'Do what you must, then,' the eunuch said.

'If you insist,' Castus told him.

He stepped up to Serapion, and with one swinging blow he slammed his fist into the side of the eunuch's head.

PART THREE

CHAPTER XV

From the window, Julius Nigrinus watched the horseman crossing the courtyard below. It was night, and summer rain spattered the paving stones and gushed in torrents from the eaves overhead. Closing the shutters, he turned from the window and seated himself beside the brazier. The small room was already uncomfortably warm, but the coals served to dry the air; Nigrinus felt the damp badly. He was tense with anticipation, but he needed to compose himself; he made it a rule never to let his emotions become visible to others. By the time Flaccianus had stamped up the steps from the courtyard and growled his way past the slaves in the antechamber, Nigrinus was perfectly calm, his face blanked, waiting.

Flaccianus threw off his wet cloak, making sure he spattered the notary as he did so. He dumped the leather bag on to the low table.

'There you go,' he said. 'You've got it till dawn. Hope it's worth the effort I put in.'

'I hope you were not too inconvenienced,' Nigrinus replied, forcing himself to take a few slow breaths before reaching for the bag and breaking the seal. Flaccianus stared at him with a sour expression, then slumped down in the facing chair. Nigrinus had ordered him to ride ahead of the normal post schedule, in order to bring him the bag of despatches with enough time to look through it before it was due for delivery. It was risky, but Nigrinus had a suspicion – more of an intuition than he would care to admit – that this time his investigations would bear fruit. The gods knew he needed it; seven months of probing into the imperial communications networks had given him only hints and shadows, suggestions of a conspiracy at work but nothing tangible, nothing that he could use as evidence, nothing sufficient even to bring a suspect to torture and see what he might confess. . . And Nigrinus knew that the patience of his chief, Aurelius Zeno, was running short. If he failed to find something soon, he would be assigned to other duties, and all the power and influence he had worked so hard to build would be stripped from him. Besides, his subordinates were getting restless.

'How much longer are we going to be doing this?' Flaccianus said. The rain had dampened his hair, and it flopped over his brow in an oily slick. 'All this time you've had me sneaking about, putting myself in peril, and what d'you have to show for it?'

'Patience,' Nigrinus said. He was running quickly through the documents spread on the table, sorting them, starting to lever open seals. He was so agitated it was hard to stop his hands from shaking. Surely it was somewhere here. . .

Flaccianus made a wet sound with his lips. The heat in the room was making him sweat. 'All right for you to ask for patience,' he said. 'You promised me rewards from all this!'

Nigrinus glanced up, hardening his expression. He had taken to paying Flaccianus from his own funds, for expenses, but clearly the man wanted more. They all wanted more in the end.

'You never even paid me back for that thing in Colonia!'

'What *thing*?'

'Gods!' Flaccianus flung up his hands in derision. 'You've

forgotten it already! I kill a man in cold blood, on your orders, and it means nothing to you?'

'Ah, yes, that,' Nigrinus said, stooping again to his work. He remembered now: one of the clerks in the financial offices had found information about a supposed plot against the emperor. He had known too little to be useful, no names or real evidence, but enough to alert the plotters and put them on their guard. Nigrinus had tried to buy the man off, but he had wanted to take it further, in the hope of greater compensation no doubt. In the end Nigrinus had ordered Flaccianus to make the man disappear. A regrettable necessity, for the higher good. It meant nothing to him now.

'Do you know how hard it is,' Flaccianus said, 'to strangle a man and make it look like he drowned? Do you?'

'You didn't have to get your own hands dirty,' Nigrinus said. He glanced up. 'Do you still have that man you employed for the business? The big idiot?'

'Glaucus? Yes, I do. And he's not cheap either.'

'Pay him what you need to. We might need him again.'

Flaccianus sighed and subsided onto the couch, and Nigrinus directed his full attention to the documents. His eyes smarted as he flicked his gaze over close-written scrawls, stylus on wax tablet or sooty ink on wood or papyrus. Nothing. There was nothing. He dragged scrolls from tubes, slipped his pin under wax seals, ran his reddening eyes down columns of figures, lists, brief communiqués, endlessly boring family news. . .

'I hear Maximian's going south,' Flaccianus said. 'What's that all about? I though the old man was safely buried in the Villa Herculis?'

'Change of plan,' Nigrinus told him, not looking up. 'Maximian goes to Arelate, supposedly as a private citizen, but there's a field force going with him to watch the western

Alpine passes. The former Augustus is supposed to be rallying the provincials to Constantine's cause, in case his son decides to invade. He's still very popular down there. . .'

He became aware that he was breathing hard, and his hands were sweating. He let the last document, an administrative report from the office of the Prefect of the Grain Supply in Rome, slip from his fingers. Something had escaped him – somehow in all these millions of words and figures some vital scrap of information had eluded his eye. And now he was left with nothing. He felt the black weight of defeat in his gut.

'You know,' Flaccianus said with a crafty smile, 'it's often occurred to me that I could do well for myself if I let certain people know what you've been up to recently.'

'What do you mean by that?' Nigrinus's voice was hoarse, the words clipped hard. He stared across the table at the agent, who remained smiling.

'Oh, you know,' Flaccianus said. 'Just an idle thought. . .'

'Then let it stay idle. Such thoughts are ill conceived.' He tried to control himself, and not let the churning sense of despair that possessed him show in his manner or expression. But he felt as though the air was slowly being sucked from the room. Think, he needed to think. . . He needed cool, calm reflection. . .

With a sharp gesture he shoved the lamp away from him. Flaccianus raised an eyebrow.

'Is that it?' the agent said. He shrugged, and reached for a tablet lying beside the lamp. His gesture drew Nigrinus's eye.

'Wait,' Nigrinus told him.

Hardly daring to breathe, he dipped his head and angled his gaze over the tablet beside the lamp, fearing that all he had seen was a trick of the light. He picked up the tablet, slowly and carefully, and held it close.

There. Sure enough, the angled lamplight picked out the

traces of something beneath the wax, showing where the stylus had dug deep. Nigrinus felt a glow of victory rising through him. He smiled; he wanted to laugh. Flaccianus too was bending closer, frowning, quizzical.

'There's writing on the wood, under the wax,' Nigrinus breathed.

'You think? But how can you read it without destroying the message on top?'

'Precisely. . .' The message itself was almost laughably dull, a simple list of crop yields for various estates in Italy over the last year. He should almost have guessed – nobody would be sending such banal stuff by the imperial post. . . But doubtless the list concealed a code, and whoever was expecting the message would recognise if it did not arrive intact.

He held the tablet up to the lamp flame, watching the wax begin to soften and sweat. If there was some way to make the wax transparent. . . But already the writing was beginning to blur.

'Pass me the ink, and a fresh sheet of papyrus,' he said. He carried the tablet to the window, and held it in the damp draught through the shutters until the wax had hardened again. Then he went back to the table and dipped a soft rag in the pot of ink. Slowly, very carefully, he wiped the inky rag over the surface of the tablet. Flaccianus was watching him, wide eyed.

A moment for the ink to dry a little, then Nigrinus laid the papyrus sheet over the tablet and rubbed his thumb over the back. He exhaled. Sweat was prickling along his hairline. He took one edge of the papyrus and lifted it gently, peeling the sheet from the tablet. When he looked at it, there was a near-perfect reverse print of the writing. Good enough to copy onto new wax, with every mark and flourish preserved, when the original was destroyed.

Holding the tablet close over the lamp flame, Nigrinus watched the wax begin to melt and run. He was being so careful not to scorch the wood that he did not notice as runnels of hot wax coursed over his fingertips. A few heartbeats, and it was done. He seized a scraper and ran it over the face of the tablet, scouring away the oily residue of the wax to expose the wood. Only then did he focus his eyes on the three short lines of writing that the wax had concealed.

He drew a sharp breath, and his brow turned cold.

'What is it?' Flaccianus whispered.

Nigrinus placed the tablet face down on the table.

'It seems the game has changed,' he said. He was still digesting the importance of what he had read.

Flaccianus sat back; clearly he knew Nigrinus too well to expect an explanation. 'Well,' he said, and gestured at the tablet. 'I'm impressed.'

'I don't need you to be impressed. I need you to do what I tell you. We have to go south, and soon.'

'With Maximian, to Arelate?'

Nigrinus nodded quickly.

'I hope you know what you're doing,' Flaccianus said as he got up to leave.

'Of course I know what I'm doing,' Nigrinus said. 'Just pray that nobody else does.'

CHAPTER XVI

'Now this is more like living,' Sallustius said, wiping his mouth and taking another draught of wine. 'I feel like the rat who fell into the cooking pot: *I have eaten, I have drunk, and now I am ready to die!*'

On the broad outdoor terrace of a tavern overlooking the river, the four Protectores lay reclining around a low stone table, shaded from the sun by a trellis hung with intertwining vines. On the table were earthenware dishes of thick beef and olive stew, hunks of fresh bread and a large jug of rich dark wine. It was, Castus had to admit, pretty close to the good life. But Sallustius could not help reminding them of it.

'Look at that,' he cried, flinging an arm towards the river. 'That's the Rhodanus, flowing south towards the Mediterranean. We're out of the northern lands now, brothers. We're heading into the heart of the civilised world!'

'Will he continue like this all the way to Arelate?' Brinno asked. The young Frank tipped back his head and let the sunlight bathe his face. If he missed the colder climes of his homeland, he was not showing it. Over the eighteen days of their journey southwards, the weather had changed only gradually. Only the day before, the skies had been grey, but here, at Lugdunum, they had emerged into the full glory of a southern summer.

But the weather was not the main reason for Castus's relief at leaving the north. Ever since that strange, violent scene at the garden house of the Villa Herculis, he had felt like a condemned man. Although he could barely believe it, there had been no repercussions. It was as if the night and the mist had eclipsed utterly what had happened. Even so, Castus had dreaded daily the summons to punishment. Surely he could not have escaped? He had killed men, probably Praetorians, and worse – so much worse that the thought woke him regularly in a cold, delirious sweat of terror – he had laid his hands upon the body of the emperor's wife. . . more than that, in fact. However much he tried to erase the memory from his mind, he could not. Whoever had planned that encounter knew his name, knew how to find him and knew what he had done. Impossible that he should be allowed to go free.

And yet here he was, still alive, accompanying the former emperor Maximian southwards to his new home at Arelate. Castus did not bother himself with the reasons behind the move – it was enough for him to be away from the villa, far away from Treveris, the emperor, and the emperor's wife.

The worst thing about that night, now, was the sourness that remained between himself and Brinno. He had given the young barbarian a suitable story, a suitable lie – an assignation with the wife of a palace official, killers hired by the cuckolded husband – and Brinno had pretended to believe him. But it was clear to Castus that his friend no longer entirely trusted him. Sometimes he caught Brinno watching him with the flicker of a frown, and that pained him even more than the lie.

As he wiped a chunk of bread around the rim of his dish, mopping up the last of the rich meat sauce, Castus wondered if he should have told Brinno the truth from the first. But taking anyone into his secret could be dangerous. Besides, he had no wish to confess his own stupidity.

He lay back on the cushioned couch. Victor was helping himself to more stew, while Sallustius rattled dice in his empty cup. Behind them, across the low wall of the tavern garden, the ground dropped towards the river. The city of Lugdunum spread along the slopes of the valley and across the hilltop, its grid of tile-roofed houses looking placid in the midday sunlight. But between those roofs the streets were in turmoil; Maximian's household had been accompanied on their trek south by a field force made up of detachments from the Rhine army: four thousand legionaries and support troops under the command of the tribune Gaudentius, appointed *dux* to guard the western Alpine passes against any invasion from Italy. The troops would be leaving them at Vienne and marching south-east to Cularo; from Vienne onwards Maximian's military retinue would consist only of the cohort of Praetorians detached to support him, and by the eight Protectores of his bodyguard.

Castus's gaze wandered, and a movement from the far side of the terrace caught his eye. A young man had entered through the gate from the street, a slave in a plain tunic, passing into the tavern. It took Castus only a moment for the memory to leap into focus: the broad, youthful face, the pug nose. Cinna, was he called, or Petrus? One of Sabina's personal slaves.

Startled, Castus remained staring at the door of the tavern until the young slave emerged once more, carrying an amphora of wine. He had seen and heard nothing of Domitia Sabina since the incident at the Villa Herculis; he wanted nothing more to do with her. And yet the memory of her stalked him.

'You're leaving just when the game's getting started?' Sallustius said as Castus rolled to his feet. He shook the dice again and dashed them onto the stone table.

'Doesn't want to get beaten!' Victor said.

'Got to use the pot,' Castus told them. The slave with the amphora had left again by the street gate, and Castus forced himself to walk slowly and casually back towards the tavern door. Only when he reached the shade of the portico did he glance back – Brinno was shaking the cup, engrossed in the game. Castus made a quick step to his left, then dodged out through the gate into the street.

There was no sign of the slave, but the narrow lane to the right led uphill into a warren of packed houses. Castus moved quickly in the other direction, and when he reached the next turning he saw the young man walking downhill, towards the river, with the amphora cradled in his arms. Keeping him in sight, Castus unpinned the gold brooch at his shoulder and reversed his cloak, then pinned it again with the patches that identified his rank concealed on the inside. Head down, walking fast, he set off after the slave.

He did not have far to go. Around the next corner the street opened into a small square, and Castus saw carriages drawn up in the shade of a temple wall opposite. The slave – Cinna, or Petrus – approached one of them. Castus only had time to step back into the open doorway of a shop before the carriage door opened and Sabina climbed down into the street.

She appeared unchanged, and her travelling dress was almost identical to what she had been wearing that evening on the banks of the Rhine. Only now, as he stared at her, did Castus realise how much the thought of her had come to obsess him over these last months. He realised too what had drawn him here: anger, a fierce desire for the truth, but yearning too. Peering from the shop doorway, while the shopkeeper ducked and weaved at his elbow, Castus watched Sabina speaking briefly to the carriage driver. Then she set off along the street, stepping carefully across the worn cobbles with four slaves following after her, one carrying the amphora while another held a red linen parasol over her head.

She would not be going far, Castus knew. He had learned enough about the ladies of the aristocracy to realise that they seldom went any distance on foot, if they could help it. He shrugged off the shopkeeper and marched quickly across the square, past the carriages, after Sabina. A crowd filled the mouth of the street, and he shoved between them. He did not care about trying to conceal himself himself now.

The street was narrow, running between the high walls of public buildings, and Sabina and her party had almost reached the far end before Castus outpaced them. He turned, confronting her. Immediately, all four of the slaves gathered close around their mistress.

Light fell through the parasol, dyeing Sabina's face, but Castus could see that she was blushing. A shawl of ivory silk draped her head, and she raised the hem to cover her mouth. For a few heartbeats they faced each other in silence while the traffic of the street moved around them.

'Domina,' Castus said, and took a step forward. One of the slaves, a thick-set older man, immediately moved to block him.

'It's quite all right, Phlegon,' Sabina said calmly, dropping the shawl and looking at Castus. She had regained her composure now. 'I do not believe the Protector wishes me harm.'

There was an open gateway in the wall to their left, leading into a courtyard at the rear of one of the public buildings. Sabina made the slightest of gestures towards it. Castus nodded curtly, and walked ahead of her. The slaves followed, and then gathered around the gateway after they had passed through.

Sabina tugged the shawl back over her head; after that first challenging stare she would not look directly at him. Castus stood in the sunlight, pushing his cloak back and hooking his thumbs into his belt. The courtyard was small, deserted, with the curved brick wall of an apse filling half of it.

'Why are you here?' Castus said. His voice sounded rough, demanding, but he did not care.

'We arrived this morning,' Sabina said, nervously fingering the amber beads of her necklace. 'Fausta and all her household. We're to join Maximian at Arelate. He requested that his daughter keep him company, and the emperor had no complaint. . .'

Castus felt a leaden weight plummet in his gut. Everything that he had been so glad to escape had somehow followed him. . . He stood with teeth clenched, saying nothing, waiting for her to speak.

'I never knew,' Sabina said abruptly, stumbling on the words. 'I never knew they would try and kill you. . . I'm sorry.'

'Then what *did* you know, domina?'

She stepped closer, and then leaned back against the wall of the apse. Castus could see that she was struggling to maintain an appearance of dignified calm, but her hands were shaking and she clasped them at her waist.

'Do you realise the pressures that are placed upon us?' she said. 'Upon women, and women of the imperial household especially? We are not *free*, no matter how we might appear.'

If you're not free, he thought, *I don't know who is.* But he said nothing.

'There are people – people in the palace,' she went on, 'around the emperor and around Maximian – who will use anything, no matter how private, for their advantage. These people prey on tenderness, on human emotion. Certain of those people made demands on me. They knew that I had. . . *feelings* for you. . . I don't know how. And they ordered me to obey their commands. . .'

214

'What people? Don't talk in riddles with me.'

Sabina threw up her hands, exasperated. She glanced quickly around the courtyard. Castus became aware of that familiar scent, and it evoked powerful memories.

'How can I explain?' she said, dropping her voice. 'Do you really not know what happened?' There was anger in her voice now, genuine bitterness.

'No, I don't know. Explain it to me.'

'Really? You don't know that the emperor neglects his wife, and has done since their wedding? You don't know that Constantine still loves his concubine Minervina – claims *she* is his true wife – and spends his nights with her? You don't know that he barely ever goes to Fausta's bed, and when he does he makes sure he's so drunk he can hardly act? That even when he can, he's careful never to spill his seed inside her. . .?'

'That's enough!' Castus cried, strangling the words in his throat. He could feel his face burning with the shame of what he had heard. But Sabina was truly angry now, the furious words spilling from her.

'Oh, of course you know! But you look away; you don't see or recognise it. Like everyone! But me – I have to know. I hear what Fausta says. I have to listen to her tears and her miserable threats. . . And all the time they fear, she and her father, that Constantine will divorce her, send them both back to Rome to beg for mercy from Maxentius. And without a child, the divorce would be easy. Now do you see?'

Castus did see. He had guessed something of it before, but it seemed too incredible, too obscene to be believed.

'They needed a man,' Sabina went on, slow and deliberate now. 'They needed somebody to. . . to impregnate her. The time was right; they'd checked that. Because if Fausta was pregnant Constantine would have to claim the child as his own – how could he not? And then Maximian's place would be secure. Why, Constantine might even elevate him to joint Augustus!'

'You're telling me that Maximian planned it? Her *own father*?'

'Oh, Maximian didn't prostitute his daughter, or not knowingly. . . But there are those around him whose task it is to *divine his unspoken desires*, and act upon them. They approached me. I have family in Rome – you must understand. My father, all our ancestral property. They only needed to hint at how my fortunes might fall if I did not do as they ordered. But I tried to warn you – that morning at the villa, I tried. And if I'd known they planned your death as well. . .'

'Then what?' Castus asked. He did not truly want to know; he suspected she would have done the same. The guilty can always find excuses for such things.

But Sabina gave him no answer. She dropped her head, pulling the edge of her shawl across her face once more. Was she actually crying? Castus could not tell.

'And now what?' he said. 'These people just forget what happened, now their plan's failed?'

'We can hope so,' she said quietly. 'It would be too hard to explain if they acted against you, or against me. After all, neither of us is likely to confess our part in it. Their master Maximian would not have been told. And as for Fausta herself. . .'

For a moment Castus remembered the girl in the bed. The fear in her eyes. Pity clasped his heart.

'We've been used, all of us,' Sabina said quietly.

From the street outside came the raucous yells of a party of legionaries, swaggering towards one of the wine shops on the river quay. Castus envied them enormously. A desolate sense of despair ached through him.

Sabina raised her head to look at him, and he saw the gleam of tears in her eyes. He was suddenly aware of her beauty, and he had the urge to reach out to her, take her in his arms. Was that what she expected?

'So,' she said. 'Now I've explained myself. I don't expect you to forgive me my part in this. But it's a shame. . . I did genuinely like you.'

'Why?'

'Can't you tell? I exist in a cage. It's made of gold, but the locks are real. Family, duty, constraint. All my class live like this, the women especially. I look at you and I see a free man. Do you even understand how attractive that is?'

Castus had no answer for her. She tugged the shawl back over her face, and by the time she glanced up again the courtyard was empty and he was gone.

All along the riverside, barges were moored at the stone wharfs, and slaves laboured at the ropes of tall wooden cranes. Sacks of grain, barrels and stacked amphorae covered the dockside. Supplies for the field army that was to march for Cularo and the Alpine passes. Between the wharfs and the wooden porticos of the shops and taverns, the street was crowded, soldiers and citizens mingled together as they watched the slaves at their work.

Castus had walked down to the river without thinking, and now he moved through the throng barely aware of any of it. With his reversed cloak covering his tunic and belt and hiding the torque he wore at his neck there was nothing to identify his rank. Nobody moved aside for him; nobody saluted. A party of soldiers shoved against him as they reeled from a wine shop, but he did not notice. Sabina's words, and the full realisation of his danger and his shame, had driven everything else from his mind.

He would have given anything to be allowed to join the legions again. To forget all this, all the dignity of his rank and position, and to become a common soldier once more. But he was not free, whatever Sabina might imagine. His commission had come from the emperor, and could not be surrendered. The oath he had taken when he had joined the Protectores bound him for life. But where was his duty now? His nerves were deadened, his senses dulled. Even revenge was denied to him; he knew very well that the first attempt to track down the men who had conspired against him would result in his immediate death. He was no better than a slave, and far closer to an unearned punishment.

He turned into a wide street running down from the hilltop to the river, intending to make his way back to the house that had been allotted as his billet. Stone colonnades ran along both sides, but the street was lined with stationary wagons. Heavy vehicles, Castus noticed, with solid wooden wheels, for transporting military supplies. He would have passed them without interest, but something else caught his eye and roused him from his numbed trance.

There were soldiers all around the wagons, watching the street carefully, but these were not men of the legions. Beneath their plain ochre-brown cloaks Castus could make out the glint of silvered scale armour: they were Praetorians, fully armed with spears and shields, swords by their sides. As he watched, Castus saw slaves carrying hefty ironbound chests from the gateway of a large building and heaving them onto the wagons. There were six of the vehicles, most of them almost fully loaded.

'What's in the boxes?' he asked one of the guards as he stepped between the nearest two wagons.

The Praetorian turned to him and blinked with slow contempt. 'Not yours to know, brother,' he said.

Castus squared his shoulders, contemplating whether to throw aside his cloak and reveal the insignia of his rank. As he did so, a figure moved up behind him and he turned quickly, his hand instinctively going to his sword hilt.

'Easy now,' the man said. 'There's nothing for you to see here. . . *dominus*.' Urbicus's scarred mouth twisted as he smiled. 'This is business for the Praetorians,' he said. 'Why don't you run off and find that high-born female of yours, eh? I hear she's in town. . .'

Anger flared in Castus's head, and his neck tightened. He eased his hand away from his sword, his fists clenching; he could see that Urbicus was trying to provoke him, and several of his men were watching now. *Step away*, he told himself. *Just turn and walk away.*

But already the other Praetorians were closing in, trapping Castus between the two stationary wagons. Surely, he thought, they would not try anything here, in broad daylight in a public street? The look of cold determination in Urbicus's eyes told him otherwise.

'Those were some of my men you put down,' the centurion said, 'back there at the villa. Reckon that's three deaths you owe me now.'

Urbicus was only two steps away, rolling his shoulders beneath his cloak. Castus felt the energy of violence roaring through his blood. The other man was shorter, but stocky and heavily muscled. And he was wearing armour. . . Castus watched him, breathing slowly, waiting for him to move. Some of the men between the carts had turned their backs, raising their shields to screen the confrontation from the crowd passing in the street only a few paces away.

Urbicus lunged forward suddenly, reaching for the broad-bladed dagger hanging from his belt. He was fast, but Castus was faster; whipping out his arm, he seized the centurion's wrist, trapping his hand over the dagger hilt. His other arm was up, elbow out, ramming against Urbicus's throat and knocking him back against the cart behind him.

The two men collided, grunting breath, and the timbers of the wagon groaned beneath their weight. From the corner of his eye Castus saw the Praetorians to either side take a step forward. He saw the centurion's bared teeth close to his face, felt the flex of muscle and the sour hiss of the man's breath as he tried to wrestle his hand free. At any moment the first blows would fall on his exposed back, the first spear stab between his shoulder blades. . .

A cry came from over by the gateway, and a jostle of movement. The knot of Praetorians broke apart. Castus shoved himself back, releasing Urbicus and taking two long steps away from him. Now he could see what was happening: two of the slaves loading the chests onto the wagon had lost their grip, and the load had slipped from between their hands and crashed to the muddy cobbles. The wood fractured as the iron restraining bands burst apart. Silver spilled bright in the dirt.

After a brief shocked pause, the crowd surged across the street, many of them dropping to their knees to scrabble at the cobbles.

Urbicus glanced around, squinting, then shoved himself past Castus. 'We're not finished yet, you and me,' he said over his shoulder, then strode towards the wagon.

Coins were scattered in the mud, freshly minted and bearing the profile of the emperor Constantine. At once Urbicus and his Praetorians closed in, kicking and striking at the crowd to drive them back before locking their spears in a barrier around the shattered chest of silver. Castus was pacing backwards across the street, keeping clear of the confusion, watching everything.

Another figure came striding from the gateway, hedged with guards. Castus knew him at once: Scorpianus, the burly Praetorian tribune with the big blue chin, who had often joined Maximian at dinner. He called to Urbicus, and the centurion saluted smartly. With a jolt of realisation, Castus remembered the night on the road beside the Rhine. Urbicus had seen him with Sabina. And now Urbicus reported to Scorpianus. What had Sabina told him? *They knew that I had feelings for you. I don't know how. . .* Urbicus and Scorpianus, he thought. And above them – who? He felt a chill of clarity: the outlines of the plot laid against him were easier to make out now.

Castus counted the wagons again as he backed away across the street, trying to work out how many chests each carried. The big building was surely the imperial mint, second only to Treveris in all of Gaul: the place must have been almost emptied. And if the Praetorians were guarding it, all that coin and bullion was surely not going to Cularo with the field army.

The tribune stood beside the broken chest, legs spread wide and fists on hips, glaring at the crowd as it shrank away from Urbicus and his men. At his feet, slaves scraped up the gush of silver and poured it into sacks, making sure to find and retrieve every last solitary coin from the dirt.

The following morning, the great convoy moved out of Lugdunum; a day later, at Vienne, it divided. The field army troops led by the dux, Gaudentius, marched eastwards towards the mountains, while a smaller but more diverse retinue continued along the river road to the south. Maximian travelled with his own household and that of his daughter, a column of carriages and carts raising the dust, with the marching Praetorians and their heavy-laden wagons bringing up the rear.

After the slow ten-day journey down the banks of the green Rhodanus, Maximian and his cavalcade appeared before the crumbling walls of the ancient city of Arelate. His arrival, Castus guessed, had been announced well in advance: the city councillors, prominent citizens, the priests of all the cults and the chief members of all the municipal *collegia* lined the road before the single remaining gateway, crying out joyous salutes and acclamations to their former Augustus.

Maximian and his household rode in through the gates, and behind them, flanked on all sides by marching Praetorians and horsemen, rolled the six heavy wagons with all the coin and bullion from the imperial mint of Lugdunum. The cries of the city notables went on until the last wagon had passed, as if they were greeting one of the gods descended from the heavens to grace their city.

CHAPTER XVII

Closing one eye, Castus squinted along the shaft of the arrow, trying to keep the head aimed straight at the target on the far side of the meadow. His right biceps ached as he kept the powerful bow at full draw. He exhaled slowly, trying not to let his aim waver, and then released the arrow. The fletching grazed his wrist as it flew. Veering in the air, the arrow skimmed the top of the straw target bale and arced away into the long grass at the far side. Castus could already hear Brinno's disbelieving laughter.

'I don't understand it!' the younger man cried. 'You're a terrible horseman, and now I find you're an even worse archer!'

Castus frowned at the bow in his left fist. None of his arrows had so far struck the target; somehow he just could not make them fly the way he wanted. Brinno had hit the centre of the target with almost every arrow he had shot.

'It's strange,' Brinno went on, still grinning. 'With a sword and shield you're like a fortress. You can throw a javelin fair enough. But give you a bow and you're like a child! I don't know what sort of soldiers they make where you come from.'

They picked up their swordbelts and put them on. Castus was glad that some of the warmth had returned to their friendship since their arrival in the south. Perhaps, he thought, Brinno had decided to trust him after all. The shadows were already long across the meadow, and the noise of the crickets was a steady pulse. Slaves were poking through the long grass, collecting Castus's spent arrows.

Pinning the brooch to secure his cloak, Castus walked across to the far side of the meadow, where the grass sloped down to the edge of the river. The water looked an almost luminous blue-green at this hour, the river curving slowly away to the south, beneath the blackened pontoons of the floating bridge, to lap the stone quays and old wooden pilings of the city. There were figures moving on the far riverbank, and Castus levelled his palm against the low sun to watch them. Soldiers; a lot of soldiers.

Seeing them brought a stab of nostalgia. Envy too – only that morning news had arrived that the Franks had once more broken their treaties and raided across the Rhine, trying to burn the bridge at Colonia Agrippina. Constantine was about to lead his army against them, and Castus dearly wished that he could be there with them.

But the soldiers across the river were not with Constantine either.

'Who are they?' Brinno asked, coming to join him.

Castus stared, trying to pick out the emblems on their shields, or to make some estimate of their numbers. 'Must be the troops from Spain,' he said. 'I heard Sallustius mention them yesterday.'

'Maybe going to join the field army at Cularo?' Brinno suggested. There was a note of uncertainty in his voice. 'Could be Gaudentius and his men are going back north, to support the emperor on the Rhine, and these are going to replace them. Strange they should stop here, though. . .'

'They're billeted in the old warehouses over there. Looks like three or four thousand men.'

Brinno whistled between his teeth. The slaves had finished

collecting the arrows, and were waiting by the path. Beyond them to the south, the old walls of Arelate were glowing in the evening sun.

It had once been a great city, the oldest in Gaul, though never, Castus suspected, as great as its inhabitants liked to claim. But the place had a tired air, a sense of long privilege and dignified repose. In all its history it had never been attacked by a hostile foe; those three-hundred-year-old walls were sagging and neglected, entirely collapsed or built over in some places, the ramparts and walkways grown with grass in others. Maximian and his entourage had taken up residence in a complex of buildings that stretched along the river, once used by the governors of Narbonese Gaul a century before.

They had only been in Arelate a few days, but already Castus was feeling uncomfortably constrained. There was something in the air here, a gathering threat that he did not like to try and identify clearly. The sense of stagnation and quiet in the city felt deceptive. Seeing the troops assembling across the river, Castus was struck by a sudden intuition, something he felt he had known for a long time but had not wanted to consider directly.

'What's on your mind, brother?' Brinno asked.

Castus shrugged, unwilling to try and answer but not wanting to concoct some plausible lie. He had told Brinno enough of those already. He knew that his friend's question was not asked lightly. The sound of the crickets rose again into the silence between them.

Brinno turned suddenly, clasping Castus by the shoulder. 'I am not a fool!' he declared. His Frankish accent made the words sound harsh. 'Something troubles you. . . Something troubles you for many days now!'

Castus squinted and looked away, unwilling to shape his thoughts into speech.

'Heh!' Brinno exclaimed, shaking him roughly. 'We're not women, always gabbling about things. But if there's something you need to say. . . You can trust me, brother.'

'I'm sorry I couldn't speak of it before,' Castus said. It was hard to utter the words; he felt them in his mouth, clumsy and sour. 'I don't know what to believe, but. . . yes, I think something's wrong.'

'Tell me,' Brinno urged.

Castus glanced back over his shoulder; the slaves were far away, waiting for them at the far side of the meadow. Nobody could hear them.

'Back in Lugdunum,' he began, 'I saw Praetorians loading the silver from the imperial mint onto carts. Those same carts they brought down here.'

Brinno nodded, knotting his brows.

'At the time I wasn't sure why, but those troops over there. . .' He gestured across the river. 'You're right, it's strange they've come so far south. If they were marching to Cularo there would be no need.'

'Perhaps they come to pay respect to Maximian?'

'Perhaps. Those Spanish legions served with him in the Mauretanian war ten years ago. Once of them was formed by Maximian himself. But I was thinking. . . that amount of silver would buy the loyalty of a lot of men.'

Brinno stepped back with a hiss of amazement. 'Brother, what are you thinking?' he said.

'I'm thinking that somebody here wants to use the coin from the mint to pay the Spanish troops. To bribe them. Not just them either – look how much Maximian's been spending since he got here. Games and shows every night. Banquets in the palace. He's buying the provincials, the governors and the city councillors. You know he asked Constantine to let

Fausta and her household come south with him?'

'He asked for that? Why? He hates having women around him!'

'Perhaps so they can't be used as hostages?' Castus felt a nervous energy running through him. He had been suppressing these thoughts for so long, it was a heady sensation to put them into words. But he was afraid too, as if by speaking about these things he was giving them substance.

'But it can't be true,' Brinno whispered. 'Even if those men over there were bought, there's only three or four thousand of them. . . Not enough to stand up to the Rhine legions! But then. . .' He thought for a moment. 'If the Rhine army is tied up with this new campaign against my treacherous bastard brethren in Germania, perhaps they might be enough to try something. . .'

Castus nodded. 'Maximian was being very friendly to Gaudentius, the commander of the force that went to Cularo. They were always at dinner together, them and that Praetorian tribune, Scorpianus. And Gaudentius left us *after* Lugdunum. . .'

'And another four thousand men with him,' Brinno said quietly. He was gazing across the river. From the far bank came the distant sound of laughter.

'Plenty more in Italy too, with Maxentius. If the mountain passes were held for him, he could cross without difficulty.'

Brinno rubbed his palms across his face. He looked jittery, as if he wanted to attack something. 'So. . . who do we trust? I don't know, brother. . .'

'I feel likewise,' Castus said. He had never liked subterfuge and politics. Even considering these things seemed to leave a stain upon his honour. He took a last glance across the river at the assembling troops, then turned back to follow the slaves in the direction of the city.

The path climbed the slope to the road. Ranks of tall dark cypresses threw their long shadows across the gravel, and to either side, beyond the trees, were scattered huts and sheds between cultivated plots and tiny orchards. All this land had once been a northern suburb of Arelate, but as the city had shrunk back inside its old walls so the ruined buildings had become overgrown, populated only by squatters and the poor.

Castus and Brinno walked in silence, with the slaves going on ahead of them. A cool evening breeze came from the river. As the battered arch that marked the northern boundary of the city came into view, Castus heard the rattle of wheels on gravel behind him, and moved off the road. A two-wheeled mule cart was approaching, with a heavy ox wagon and several riders following behind. The cart had a wicker roof over it, and the two men inside were lost in its shade. Travellers from the north were not uncommon, and Castus paid them no attention until Brinno nudged his arm.

'I know that man,' he said, his voice tight.

Standing on the verge in the shade of the cypresses, they waited until the cart had drawn level with them. The driver dragged on the reins and the mules came to a halt. Both the vehicle and its passengers were covered in grey dust, and it took Castus a moment to recognise the man who sat beside the driver.

'A good evening to you both,' Nigrinus said. He was blinking, his eyes reddened from the dust. He shook at the mantle that covered him like a blanket, and grey plumes rose around him. 'I had hoped to meet you in Arelate, but it seems some helpful god has directed that our paths cross even sooner. . .'

Behind the cart the ox wagon had also heaved to a stop. Castus saw that one of the riders following behind it was the imperial agent, Flaccianus. Brinno was staring at the man in the cart in hostile silence.

'What do you want here?' Castus said. 'You're supposed to be in Treveris, with the emperor.'

'Ah, yes, but matters have called me south.' Nigrinus gave a thin smile, and his face under its mask of dust appeared ghoulish. 'Perhaps,' he said, 'at some point soon, we might speak together? I'm sure you must have learned a great deal during your time with the former Augustus?'

'Nothing that need concern you,' Castus said. He had hoped to have no more dealings with the notary, or his repulsive assistant.

Nigrinus's smile did not slip. 'Well,' he said, with a few last dabs at his dusty mantle. 'I'm sure there will be plenty of time for you to think about that!'

He made a curt stabbing gesture, and the driver flicked the reins. The mules heaved forward again, and Castus and Brinno stood aside as the cart, the wagon and the riders moved past them towards the outlying buildings of the city. Flaccianus, the last rider, glanced back as he passed with an expression of knowing disdain.

Brinno spat in the dust after them.

It was past midnight when Castus was woken suddenly by the sound of a cry from the courtyard, a slamming door and voices from the room downstairs. He lay on his bed for a moment, disorientated; he felt he had not been properly sleeping, but the memory of a dream was still vivid in his mind: Sabina, an underground room, terror in the darkness and a man with the face of a white dog. . .

He heard another shout, and his mind returned to clear focus. With one roll he was up off the bed, dragging on his tunic and snatching up his swordbelt as he moved for the door. Stepping out onto the wooden balcony, he leaned over the railing and looked down into the large chamber below.

The scene was lit by two flickering oil lamps. Sallustius had come in from the night dragging a thin man behind him. Victor was there too, both of them with drawn swords. Castus took the stairs in four leaps and went to join them.

As Castus reached them, Sallustius flung his prisoner against the central table, then wrestled him down onto a bench. The man was ragged and unshaven, dressed in a tunic almost black with mud and old stains. His face was swollen and bruised on one side, and his lips were flecked with blood. Sallustius held his sword at the man's throat.

'Please, domini. . . Please forgive me if I've wronged you!' the man cried. 'I told you what I was doing! This is a mistake, an error. Please, there's no need for violence!' Tears were running down his bruised face, and he was cringing on the bench, clasping his arms around his chest.

Castus went to the table and poured himself a cup of water from the jug. He took two long swallows, then dashed the rest of the water in the man's face.

'Shut up,' he said.

The man fell silent at once, swaying on the bench with his mouth open in shock.

'What happened?' Castus asked. Brinno was coming down the stairs now, blinking sleepily.

'We caught him on the rear portico,' Sallustius said, 'coming up from the river towards Maximian's apartments. Victor challenged him and he ran – but unfortunately for him I was at the other end of the portico, and he ran right into my fist. . .'

'He had this,' Victor said, and threw a short dagger in an ornate scabbard down on the table. 'That's no weapon for a beggar like you!' he sneered at the prisoner. 'You were planning to get into the apartments and murder somebody. *Eh?*' he added, smacking the cringing man across the top of his skull.

'Domini, please, I told you,' the man said. 'I was paid to deliver it to the eunuch Gorgonius. That's all – I can show you the gold piece they gave me to do it!'

'Who paid you?' Castus demanded.

'I don't know, dominus! I'm a poor man – I don't know the imperial officers! A soldier, I think. . . A fine man, such as yourselves. . .'

Castus looked at the dagger on the table. The hilt was silver, although a little tarnished, but the scabbard had a gold-plated framework. He picked it up and drew the blade. Clean and sharp.

'Could be a message hidden in the scabbard?' Sallustius said.

Castus had been thinking the same. If the weapon was for Gorgonius, and came from a soldier, it could be a communication from the troops across the river. He stared down the throat of the scabbard, but there was no folded slip of papyrus hidden inside it. He sheathed the dagger and placed it back on the table again.

'What do we do with him?' Brinno asked, sitting on a bench with his elbows on his knees. He stretched his mouth in a long yawn.

'There are notaries and *quaestionarii* with Maximian's staff,' Sallustius said. 'We can deliver him to them in the morning. And *they*, my friend,' he told the man, 'will soon use their hooks and irons to drag the truth from you!'

The man had started gasping and shaking again. Castus looked back at the dagger. Something about it was not right. He picked it up again, turning it in his hands, rubbing at the scabbard with his thumb. One side looked fine, but on the other was a line of crude stitching. Inside the flashy framework, the leather of the sheath was just thin rawhide, poorly sewn together.

Drawing the blade again, he slid the tip beneath the brass lug that held the scabbard frame together and twisted hard. Sallustius and Victor were peering at him, perplexed. The rivet broke without much effort, and then it was a simple task to lever open the framework and cut the stitches along the tube of the rawhide sheath.

'What is it?' Brinno asked, looking more awake now.

Castus unrolled the tube and flattened it on the table as Sallustius gazed over his shoulder. There were letters painted in black ink on what had been the inside of the sheath. Castus leaned closer, his mouth moving as he carefully read them aloud.

'I don't understand it,' he said, frowning in disappointment. Had he read it wrong? His knowledge of letters was still not too good – the terrible weight of his ignorance pressed on his mind. '*Calvikal Sepihn*? What does it mean?'

For a moment he remembered the strange incantations that the sorcerer in the necropolis of Treveris had intoned. A slight flicker of superstitious dread ran through him. Sallustius had snatched up the message and was peering at it in the light of the lamp. His lips moved for a moment, then suddenly his face cleared and he laughed.

'It's a date and time!' he said. 'The second part anyway. The first must be either a name or a place. Look. . .' He took a wax tablet and pen and began tracing the letters, then turned it so Castus could see. For a moment it still did not make sense.

CALV.VI.KAL.SEP.II.HN.

Then Sallustius placed his thumb over the first four letters, and Castus saw the rest jump into recognisable shape.

'The sixth day before the kalends of September, at the second hour of the night,' he said. 'That's tomorrow night.'

'Must be an arranged meeting,' Victor said, leaning closer. Even the man on the bench had ceased trembling and was looking interested. 'But who, or where, is *Calv?*'

Castus took the message back from Sallustius. He had known already what he would have to do, although the thought filled him with angry foreboding.

'Leave this to me,' he said.

Julius Nigrinus had initially appeared annoyed to be disturbed in his chambers in the dead of night – if not, Castus thought, all that surprised. The lamp had already been burning when he had arrived. Now, with the message before him, the notary seemed his usual devious self.

'*Calvisiana,*' he said, looking up from the message with a knowing smile. 'It's a villa, a few miles south-east of Ucetia. A day's ride from here. If you can get out of the city tomorrow without attracting attention you'll easily be there by the appointed time.'

'Then what?' Castus said. He was standing before the table in the small dimly lit anteroom of the notary's bedchamber.

'And then,' Nigrinus said, casting the message aside and rubbing at his eyes, 'you can observe, and if possible apprehend, whoever is attending this meeting – this no-doubt *treasonous* meeting!'

He stood up, pulling a rough homespun blanket around his shoulders. The night was not cold, but the notary was almost shivering as he paced a few steps to the wall and back. 'Take only men you can trust – your Frankish friend and the two others in your section. Tell nobody else of this – nobody! I'll order four of the agentes in rebus to accompany you, plus a few other armed men in case they're needed. You must act in the name of the emperor, no matter what the rank or station of these conspirators might be. . .'

'You're quite sure this is a conspiracy, then?' Castus asked. The notary's nervous excitement was making him wary. Or *was* it excitement? He had the strong sense that there was more going on here than he was being told. But that was a familiar sensation.

'Why else would a military officer hire a common beggar to carry a concealed message to Maximian's chief eunuch? Don't worry, I've been observing things for a long time. I've known of the Villa Calvisiana for a while too – it's been mentioned in correspondence.'

'I see,' Castus said. He could well imagine this cold-blooded man sitting up late into the night, reading other people's mail. The odium he felt for Julius Nigrinus had not diminished at all over the years, he found. Being forced into such close company with the man filled him with a clenched rage all the harder to endure the more he tried to suppress it.

'Best go and prepare yourself,' the notary said. 'And remember – tell absolutely nobody about this.'

Castus nodded once, then turned to go. At the door he paused.

'Do you never sleep?' he asked.

'Night suits me,' Nigrinus replied. 'Daylight hurts my eyes, you know. In ten years' time I will doubtless be completely blind.' He gave a couple of long slow blinks. 'And so,' he said, 'I must ensure that all my work is done before then. But it is a hard, slow business, soldier. Harder than you will ever know.'

For once, Castus did not doubt him.

CHAPTER XVIII

Clouds covered the moon, and shadow filled the narrow valley. The twelve men picking their way along the track slowed and then paused, disorientated in the total blackness. Castus could sense the river moving to his left, flowing in its deep channel between boulders and shingle banks. He could smell the wild herbs growing between the trees and thick scrub on the upper slopes of the valley. He recalled the last time he had led a party of men through a darkened wilderness, the summer before after the crossing of the Rhine. But that had been different – this was no barbarian frontier, but the heartland of Roman Gaul, and he could fear no sudden onrush of savage enemies from the night. But still he felt the stir of apprehension up his spine.

Then the clouds shifted and moonlight flooded the valley once more, seeming almost unnaturally bright. Castus looked back and saw the massive arches of the great aqueduct that crossed the valley behind them. It looked ghostly, unreal in the midst of this empty forest.

'We should see the place soon,' Flaccianus whispered. 'Just around the next bend in the river.'

Castus had not realised that the man was so close behind him. If he despised Nigrinus, he hated the greasy agens in rebus even more. Flaccianus's hired bodyguard was no better, a hulking flat-faced ex-wrestler named Glaucus, who said nothing and followed his master around like a loyal mastiff. Hunching his heavy shoulders, Castus moved off once more down the track. They had left the horses beneath the arch of the aqueduct, in the care of a couple of slaves; the villa was a mile upriver, but they could approach more quietly on foot, and if they got separated in the dark the aqueduct made a good rendezvous. Even so, without the horses their scanty numbers were even more obvious. Not for the first time, Castus had serious misgivings about the planning of the night's mission.

He had talked little with Flaccianus or the other three agentes in rebus during the journey from Arles. They had left the city in the slumbering quiet of mid-afternoon and ridden hard across the flat open countryside, moving northwards parallel to the river until they reached the great spur of rough wooded country that concealed the valley and the villa within it. They paused there in a grove until after nightfall, then moved up the valley once more. Five slaves had accompanied them, and Glaucus the bodyguard; it hardly seemed enough to tackle and capture a group of highly placed plotters, who probably included military men. But there was nobody else they could trust for the job. Besides, Castus had been the one to find the message hidden in the dagger scabbard, and he felt a sense of responsibility for what had to be done. He remembered the words of his oath. *I shall not cease to hunt him down by land and by sea with iron in hand. . .*

The valley curved, wrapping around the narrowing trench of the river, and now the great aqueduct was hidden behind them. Up ahead, Castus could see a low wall through the trees, and an arched gateway. He motioned to the men following him, and together they moved up to the wall and crouched in the long grass. All of them were wearing dark clothes, with no ornaments that might catch the light.

'Once we get inside the walls,' Flaccianus said, 'we should split up. The Protectores should circle individually around the sides of the villa, while the agents and I move in close and try and observe what's happening. . .'

'Why does this small man give us orders?' Brinno hissed from the darkness.

'I don't like the sound of it,' Castus said. 'I've had about enough of skulking about in the dark for one night already.'

'Oh, really? And what do you *noble Protectores* suggest instead?' Flaccianus said in an acid voice. 'Rushing in through the front doors, waving your swords about?'

'He's right,' Sallustius said quietly. 'We need to circle the perimeter, stop anyone getting away.'

Castus exhaled slowly, leaning back against the rough stone wall. 'Whatever we're doing, we need to do it fast,' he said, 'and work together.'

'Ah, good!' Flaccianus said. 'What a splendid idea – so, *as I said*, we split up and take individual positions. . .'

'We stay together in pairs,' Castus broke in. 'Me and Brinno go round to the left of the villa, Sallustius and Victor to the right, along the river. You and your agents creep in close and find out what's happening inside. As soon as you have them in sight, whistle twice and we'll get in there. The slaves stay here and hold the gateway.'

He looked around quickly at the gathered men: a few heads nodded in the moonlight; the rest stayed silent; Flaccianus just shrugged. Castus took that for agreement.

'Let's go,' he said.

* * *

Inside the wall of the estate they moved through an orchard, the close-planted trees giving them good cover right up to the bank and ditch that screened the villa buildings. Lying on the bank, Castus peered out between the trunks of a row of poplars and saw the back of the tile-roofed house, the squat columns of a brick rear portico and the low whitewashed half-domes of a bath-house. There were lamps burning inside – Castus could make out the faint glow thrown between the pillars of the portico – but otherwise there were no signs that anyone else was there. The villa was not a lavish place, by the look of it, more a hunting lodge combined with a farm. That was some relief at least. Perhaps nine armed men would be enough to surround it effectively.

From the low scrub and fields on the far side of the villa came the steady, constant chirruping of insects in the darkness. No sign of anyone on watch; or, if they were, they were well concealed.

'I don't like this,' Castus said quietly. 'Why are there no guards? All too open. . . like they're waiting for us.'

'Afraid of the dark?' Flaccianus said with a sly grin. 'We're out in the middle of nowhere – why would they need guards?'

Biting back an answer, Castus slid his sword from its scabbard. He wished he had brought a shorter weapon. His broad-bladed infantry spatha was a formidable tool in a pitched battle, but awkward for the sort of work the night promised. He noticed that Flaccianus and the other agents had armed themselves with short ring-pommelled swords, which looked far handier.

'Remember,' he whispered harshly, 'two whistles – right?'

'That's right,' Flaccianus said. 'And remember to come when I call!' He ran forward at a crouch with the other agents and Glaucus behind him. Sallustius and Victor had already moved off to the right, towards the riverbank. Castus motioned to

Brinno, and the two of them scrambled up the bank and jogged towards the left-hand corner of the villa.

He was tensed for the barking of dogs, but only the rhythmic pulsing sound of the insects disturbed the quiet of the night. Halting, he dropped to a crouch with his back against the wall of the villa. Brinno ran up and crouched beside him.

Senses alert, his body primed, Castus listened intently. He almost thought he could hear the sound of voices from somewhere inside the building: men speaking quietly. Tapping Brinno on the shoulder, he moved forward again, following the wall until he reached the corner of the building. To his left was what looked like a stable block; ahead of him, steps led up to the garden terrace at the front of the villa.

'Somebody moving out there,' Brinno whispered, and nodded towards the trees beyond the stables. 'They see us, I think.'

Tensed, Castus tried not to imagine the whip of arrows from the darkness. He and Brinno would make easy targets against the whitewashed wall. His senses were screaming at him to pull back, get out of this. But he was committed to it now.

Two whistles from the far side of the building. Castus and Brinno were up and running immediately, doubling the corner and leaping up the steps to the terrace.

Trees and hedges in moonlight, the grey rectangle of a dry ornamental pool, and the ranked pillars of the front portico above them. A scream came from the darkness beyond, and suddenly the night was full of men running at them from both directions.

'It's a trap – get out!' Victor's voice cried out from the far side of the terrace. Men on the portico, spilling from the house; others closing in from the garden.

Brinno grabbed his arm, trying to pull him back, but Castus shook him off. In his mind's eye he saw the villa mapped out, the terrace and the riverbank. He had no idea who was attacking them, but this was a battleground now. This was tactics.

'Straight on,' he shouted, 'after me, though the middle of them!'

He ran, hoping Brinno was behind him: whoever their attackers were, they wanted to keep the four Protectores apart, cut them off individually. Castus needed to link up with Sallustius and Victor.

The men coming from the house had expected him to flee, expected to pursue him, but instead Castus charged straight at them. At them and *through them*. . . He wheeled his blade and slashed at the first man, who dodged too late. The blade slid across the man's shoulder and bit the back of his neck, and he was down and screaming. No time to finish him; Castus knew he only needed to put his opponents out of the fight. Running, he sidestepped to slam against another figure coming from the shadows. The man flung up his arm, and Castus noticed his ring-pommelled sword before he chopped his legs from under him.

Brinno raced past, bellowing, and shouldered down one of the attackers coming from the garden. Castus saw his blade rise and then stab down. Then he was weaving between bodies, striking out. The darkness was on his side now; his attackers were confused, fearful. He slashed, and felt a brief shock up his blade.

'My hand!' a man screamed. 'Fuck! He's cut off my hand!'

They were falling away from him, and he was through. At the far wall of the terrace he paused and turned, looking for Brinno. The Frank was right behind him, bodies scattered on the dark turf in his wake, and above, in the flare of light across the portico, Flaccianus and his big bodyguard stared back at him, yelling to the others to press the attack.

No time to think. Castus scrambled up onto the wall and across in a single movement. A longer drop on the far side as the ground sloped down to the riverbank; he fell into tangled undergrowth and thick grass, lost his footing and rolled. His cloak caught on something and he ripped it free of his neck. A crash as Brinno came down beside him, but before the men on the terrace could reach the wall they were both on their feet, dragging each other as they stumbled along the riverbank in the direction of the aqueduct.

Victor almost collided with them. 'Sallustius is down,' he gasped, and there was panic in his voice. 'The others – we were betrayed! That bastard Flaccianus and his men. . .'

'I know,' Castus said. 'Save your breath and run.'

There was pursuit now; men dashing towards the higher ground at the edge of the river slope, aiming to cut them off. Castus could not guess their numbers; he had seen ten or more back in the garden, but there could be twice as many. Who were they? Just Flaccianus and his fellow agents, or were there others? It surely mattered, but Castus had no time to think about that. The deception was clear to him: the fake message in the scabbard, the interview with Nigrinus. . . all of it designed to draw them out here to this isolated place and pick them off one by one.

They were no fighters anyway, and there was fortune in that. Castus could hardly believe that he and Brinno had somehow woven their way out of the ambush apparently unharmed. The thought gave him a sense of unreality, as if he were running in a dream. Their pursuers had lost time getting back around the side of the villa, and the three Protectores had a good head start on them. Up the dry slope, stamping through the thorny brush, Castus saw the estate wall and the gate before him. His breath was coming in aching heaves – he had not had to run like this in many months.

The two slaves had bolted from the gateway. Castus and Brinno hurled themselves through, but Victor turned and raised his sword towards the pursuers.

'You go,' he shouted, his voice high and cracking, 'I'll hold them off here!'

'Don't be an idiot,' Castus said, grabbing the young man by the shoulder. 'We *run*. . .'

He pulled Victor after him, through the grass and bushes and onto the track beside the river. He was still holding his sword; without breaking step, he slammed it back into his scabbard and held it as he ran. Noise of breath, of boots stamping the dry grit of the trackway. Castus could feel his lungs burning, and a stitch was twisting into his flank, but the three of them were still together, still ahead of the pursuit.

Around the bend in the river, the aqueduct rose before them. Light flared beneath one of the great arches, throwing the shadows of men and horses over the stonework.

'Heh! They're ahead of us!' Brinno cried. He turned as he ran, then halted on the track. Dust scuffed up pale in the moonlight. 'Ahead and behind.'

Victor was doubled over, braced on his knees and drinking air. From the direction of the villa came the shouts of the pursuers as they ran, answered now by the echoing yells of the men beneath the arch. Castus heard one voice raised above the rest: Flaccianus.

'Throw down your weapons! You're cut off! Surrender!'

He could hear Victor sobbing as he retched. To his right, he could make out the thin grey scar of a path climbing the valley side between the trees.

'There,' he said, but Brinno had already seen it. Castus took Victor by the arm, pulling him upright and leading him after the Frank.

The path rose steeply almost at once, and they were stumbling upwards, grabbing at branches and spurs of rock. When the leaves closed over them they were fighting their way through total darkness, reaching blindly for handholds. Dry thorny scrub snatched and grabbed at them. Their boots scuffed and kicked at the dry stony soil; Castus half fell, the ground grating out from under him, and he ripped skin from his palms as he dragged himself to his feet. Above him, Brinno toiled upwards without pause, grunting as he breathed. The path turned, doubled back, and the trees broke in places to spill moonlight over them as they looped around outcrops of pitted grey rock jutting from the valley sides. Somewhere below them the pursuers were climbing too, calling out to each other, crashing and scrambling in the dark.

At another turn of the path Castus paused, sucking down great lungfuls of air. His head was reeling. 'What happened to Sallustius?' he said, gasping the words. 'Was he wounded or dead?'

'He fell. . .' Victor said, coming up behind him. 'I don't know if he was hit. He said to run and. . . and I ran. I'm sorry. . .' The shame was in his voice. Shame and fear.

'No time for that now.' Brinno had clambered up the next incline and was waving down to them; Castus could just make out his gesture against the sky.

Up the last twist of the path, the trees fell away and they stood on an open summit with the aqueduct stretching across the valley before them, massive and pale, as if it were made of moonlight. Castus had not realised they had climbed so far. The slope rose again ahead of them, but it was thick forest now, holm oak and thorns, impassable. He could not see where the path had gone.

'We need to cross there,' Brinno said, pointing at the aqueduct. Along the crest of the uppermost tier of arches,

243

above the water channel, there was a narrow walkway of flat stone slabs. Castus looked at it: a thin grey ribbon stretching across a vast gulf of air. He felt his heart clench in his chest.

'No,' he said.

But Brinno was already pushing his way between the dry bushes towards the end of the aqueduct.

'Come on – if we get across there we're on the far ridge! We'll be well ahead of them. . .'

'No,' Castus said again. 'I'm not going across that.' But Victor was coming up the path behind him; he needed to follow Brinno or move aside. Trying to swallow down the tightness in his throat, Castus moved off after Brinno, down into the hollow where the upper arches and water channel of the aqueduct met the hillside. His calf muscles were burning, but a wild dizzying fear was rising in him.

'I can't do it,' he called. 'I don't like heights.'

'It's nothing,' Brinno called back. 'Look – it's ten feet across on the top. We can run over it easily! Just don't look down. . .'

Now they were in the hollow, and Castus saw the huge masonry of the aqueduct rising out of the scrub and grass. The big rough stone blocks looked reassuringly solid – it was only when he glanced to his left and saw that stone walkway stretching out like a tightrope into the night that his blood froze.

Brinno had already clambered up onto the top of the water channel. He reached down and heaved Castus after him, and Victor scrambled up behind them.

'Now,' Brinno said. 'We run.'

He set off at once, jogging easily along the walkway with his cloak pulled up around his left arm. Castus started after him; only a few paces, and the trees fell away to either side. He stepped out into the sky.

There was a breeze coming across the high ridges and he felt it at once pushing at him. Fixing his gaze on Brinno's receding figure, he concentrated on putting one foot in front of the other, keeping moving. He thought of Victor coming across behind him; he could not stop or slow down now. But the stone path along the crest of the aqueduct, which had looked so straight and level, seemed to have a subtle curve and chamfer: every few steps Castus found himself veering towards one side or the other, his breath getting tighter and tighter.

He glanced desperately to his left, and saw the gulf yawning beneath him. The drop must be close to two hundred feet. He could just make out the thin vein of the river in the moonlight far below him. Then a bolt of stark terror went through him so fierce his legs almost buckled. Something whirled close to his head and he flinched: it was just a dry leaf carried on the breeze, but he ducked to let it blow past him and then found he could not straighten up.

Forcing himself onward in a half-crouch, he moved out onto the central span of the aqueduct. Behind him he could hear the shouts of the pursuers as they boiled up out of the forest. The drop to either side of the stone walkway seemed all-consuming; Castus felt it sucking him over the brink. Again and again he had to close his eyes, then open them again as his senses whirled, convinced that he had slipped off the path and was falling through the empty black air. Again and again he found himself still perched on the veering ledge, precariously balanced above the emptiness.

May the gods get me out of this, he prayed. *Sol Invictus, light against evil, guide in darkness. . . Jupiter, lord of thunder and rain, Isis, Queen of Heaven, I vow sacrifice to you. . . carry me safely from this place. . .*

When he looked up he saw the walkway open before him: Brinno had already reached the far end and vanished into the dark trees. Glancing back, Castus saw Victor standing alone with his sword in his hand, facing back towards the valley slope and the pursuing men.

'Victor!' he managed to shout. 'Don't stop! Keep moving!'

'No – you go!' the young man called back. He looked firm and steady, his head high. 'You go and I'll hold them here – they won't get past me!'

'That's madness – come on! Just move!'

'No! I shouldn't have left Sallustius behind – I shouldn't have tried to save myself. I failed, brother. Now I have to pay my debt!'

Already the first of the pursuers were climbing up onto the far end of the aqueduct, edging out along the stone walkway. Victor stood braced, in a fighting stance, waiting to meet them. Castus knew that there was nothing he could do to save him, short of grabbing him and pulling him away by force. There was only room for one man to fight effectively on the narrow ledge.

This was Victor's moment, Castus realised. All his training, all his elaborate sword drills, had led to this. The enemy were closing on him now, cautious, weapons ready.

Castus forced himself to turn away and push onwards towards the far slope. He heard Victor's high scream of a battle cry. Then something else: the clink of metal against stone, and a familiar snipping whine in the air.

Archers. They had archers.

'Victor, *move*!'

Even as the yell left his throat he saw the young man jolt and stagger, clutching at the arrow in his hip. As Castus watched, Victor's leg gave beneath him. He flung his sword wildly upward, but his balance was gone. Breathless, Castus saw the young man topple sideways. Victor made no sound as he fell, his body seeming to fold and then spin like a leaf as it vanished into the depths of the valley.

'Don't shoot! Idiots! Don't shoot – take them alive!'

It was Flaccianus shouting. Castus had dropped to lie face down on the walkway. The stone still felt warm beneath him from the heat of the day's sun. Raising his head, he could see the men beginning to edge out once more along the aqueduct, coming slowly but surely towards him.

Had Brinno got clear by now? At least that would be a victory. If Brinno could carry word of what had happened to the north, to Constantine, their enemies would pay with their lives. Nigrinus would die. But Brinno needed time.

Castus could taste blood in his mouth. As he raised himself to kneel, and then to stand, he felt a new strength in his limbs. The drop to either side no longer dragged at him, no longer sucked his courage or his nerve. He took two steps forward, braced his legs and drew his sword.

'Come on then!' he cried. 'Come on, you goat-fuckers!'

His opponents slowed as they approached, bunching together on the narrow walkway. Castus recognised the man in the lead: one of the agents who had accompanied them from Arelate, a man named Delphius. His face was a blanched mask of terror. Behind him were two others armed with spears.

Castus waited until they were only a few strides away from him, then he launched himself forward. He closed the distance quickly, yelling, stamping ahead with his right foot in a lunging blow. Delphius gave a strangled cry, thrashing with his shortsword to try and parry. Castus feigned a high cut, then swung his blade in a wheeling arc and sliced up behind Delphius's knee. He pulled the blade, and the man screamed as his hamstring parted. Throwing out his arms, Delphius tried to keep his balance, but his body buckled and he pitched sideways over the stone brink.

The falling man let out a harrowing shriek, but Castus was already pressing his attack against the spearmen. The wind whined all around him.

One blow, and he hacked through the first man's spearhead, leaving him with a splintered stave. The second man darted in, and Castus knocked his weapon aside. The two attackers were crowding each other now, shrinking close to keep back from the edges of the walkway.

Another feint to the left, flicking his sword at the face of the man with the broken spear, then Castus took a long step forward and stabbed out with his arm straight. The man gasped, trying to fend off the blow, lost his footing and fell back sprawling on the stone slabs. The second made another weak lunge with his spear, and Castus dodged it, seized the shaft of the weapon in his left hand and pulled.

Stumbling, the second man tripped over the sprawling body of the first, letting go of his spear and grabbing wildly for a handhold to stop himself tumbling over the edge. Castus flipped the spear in his left hand and threw it – bad aim, but it made the man flinch and slip. He spilled off the side, fingers scrabbling, but managed to cling on before he fell.

The first man had crawled to his hands and knees now: Castus booted him in the ribs, then drove his sword through the back of his neck. He heard the crunch of bone as the man died, then without looking down he knelt and heaved the body over the side. Striding forward, Castus flicked his blade at the man clinging to the far side of the ledge. The man's desperate pleading cries cut off suddenly, and he was gone.

Three down: how many more were there?

From the edge of his vision Castus caught movement below him and glanced over the side of the precipice. There were narrow ledges running along the sides of the next tier down, outside the span of the arches, and Castus could see men edging their way carefully along, clinging to the stones. Trying to get behind him, he realised. For a moment he wondered whether he could somehow swing himself down onto the lower tier, but the drop was twelve feet or more and the ledge only wide enough for a single man to stand pressed against the wall. Besides, the brief glance downwards made his guts roil and his head spin. He straightened up again quickly.

Shouts from behind him now. Castus looked back over his shoulder, and saw more men emerging from the dark scrub at the far end of the aqueduct. A stab of painful dismay: how long had they been there? Had they caught Brinno before he could get clear? They were moving out onto the stone walkway now, the man in the lead carrying a trident over his shoulder and swinging a weighted net, like a gladiator.

But the enemy were closing in again from the other direction too, and the man in the lead was the giant bodyguard, Glaucus. He strode along the summit with a heavy wooden club in his fist, as if he were walking down a city street and not perched two hundred feet above a dark valley.

Castus backed up, shuffling, keeping his eyes on the ex-wrestler. Blood was spattered over the stone ledge where the three men had died, but Glaucus paid no attention to it. He began swinging the club, wide swipes in the air. Castus waited, staying braced in his crouch with his sword levelled. He knew that the bodyguard could fight; no point trying to distract him with feinting attacks.

The gap between them narrowed. Castus risked another glance backwards and saw the net-man closing in, slow and cautious, with others coming up behind him. He was right out in the middle of the aqueduct's span now, directly above the river.

'Lay down your weapon!' The shout came from the air, or so it seemed, but it was Flaccianus again. 'Lay down your weapon and surrender – you won't be harmed!'

'Balls!' Castus shouted. He found himself laughing suddenly. 'You want this sword, you can come and get it!'

With only ten paces between them, Glaucus broke into a charge. An awesome sight; Castus stood his ground, clenching his teeth as the huge man bore down on him. At the last moment he realised that the bodyguard was going to crash into him and try to wrestle him to the ground. He threw himself forward, flinging out his left hand to stop himself from tumbling over the side; the big man's club whirled over his head, and then Glaucus was right on top of him. Castus levered himself up, colliding with the other man's chest. For a few heartbeats they struggled together on the brink, trying to shove each other backwards. Castus felt his boots grating and sliding on the smooth stone. His sword was still in his right hand, but the blade was too long to get inside Glaucus's grip. The big man's heaving breath was loud in his ear.

Dropping to one knee, Castus hauled the bodyguard off balance. Glaucus stumbled, and for a moment Castus felt himself hanging over the void, clinging to the other man's body. He lost his grip on his sword, and heard it clink off the stone before it spun away into the blackness. Then he was rolling himself forward in a low crouch, onto the slabs of the walkway as Glaucus's momentum carried him tumbling into a face-down sprawl and a slide that almost flung him over the edge.

Castus was first on his feet. He kicked at the fallen man, but Glaucus lay heavy and inert, hugging the stone slab beneath him. There was a whirling sound, and Castus flung out his arms as the ropes and weights of the net snaked around him from the darkness. Staggering, he tore at the ropes. But when he tried to move, the net dragged at his feet and he felt himself pitching over sideways.

Helpless, his arms trapped, he saw the vast gulf rearing up at him. Below was only empty air and then the rocks and narrow seam of water. His feet slipped across the brink and he was falling, tumbling into nothing with the roar of the wind loud all around him.

For three heartbeats, he believed he was a dead man.

Then the ropes tightened suddenly around him, dragging and swinging him, and he was slammed hard against the rough stones of the aqueduct. Only then did he let out a cry.

Someone had caught the net from above. When he opened his eyes Castus saw that he was dangling, entangled, head down over the terrible drop.

'Aurelius Castus,' a voice said. He managed to twist his neck, and saw Flaccianus standing beneath one of the arches of the upper tier, leaning out with an expression of amusement. 'Aurelius Castus, you are charged with treasonous conspiracy against the emperor!'

'You're the traitor,' he managed to say, but the words came as a pained gasp. He felt the ropes creaking, straining. 'I'm loyal to Constantine Augustus.'

Flaccianus laughed. He was shaking his head.

'Constantine is dead,' he said. 'He fell in battle against the Franks. Maximian Augustus is emperor now!'

CHAPTER XIX

Greasy stone, iron chains, and the echo of dripping water in the dark.

The sound tormented him. His throat was parched and tight, and his head felt swollen. He could still taste the filthy sacking of the hood they had pulled over his head the night before. Was it only the night before? Castus had no way of telling; no light penetrated his cell. But he remembered a faint radiance from the airshafts in the vaulted chamber outside, when the jailer had last opened the cell door, and guessed that only half a day had passed since his capture.

Rolling over on the rough straw of his bed, he pressed his face to the stones of the cell wall, trying to lick some of the moisture that sweated from them. But the stones were just oily, sour with moss and old filth. Castus coughed, then spat, then slumped down again on his side.

His wrists were secured behind his back in iron shackles. His arms and shoulders ached, but his hands had grown numb, and when he flexed his upper body arrows of pain shot through his chest. But it was the thirst that bothered him most. Thirst, the growing pressure in his bladder, and that constant maddening drip of water from somewhere beyond the cell door.

They had taken him in a cart from the aqueduct. The hood had been over his head by then, and he had seen nothing of the journey, but from the distance and the noises that had penetrated the sacking and the haze of his pain he guessed that they had brought him back to Arelate.

The thought returned to him, a stab in his mind. Constantine was dead. Maximian was emperor. He had failed in his vows, and now he was a prisoner condemned for treason.

He could almost laugh at that: if he had conspired against Maximian, it had only been at the prompting of the notary Nigrinus, whose men had been responsible for trapping and capturing him. . . An elaborate deception, he thought. Perhaps too elaborate; something was missing from the picture. His mind turned, but only in one direction was there hope. If Brinno had evaded capture, if he had escaped and if he managed to get back to Treveris. . . But again he remembered: Constantine was dead. If Brinno reported what had happened, he would only be condemning himself.

No hope at all then. Castus grinned mirthlessly to himself. The pain in his arms and the constant thirst kept him from sleeping. Instead his mind turned again: he thought of Sabina, and wondered what she would be doing. Would she easily accept Maximian as her new master? And what of Fausta, a widow now: what was her part in this. . .? Castus suddenly remembered the sorcerer in the tomb outside Treveris. The letters of the next emperor's name revealed. *M. . . A. . . X. . .* Had it been a genuine divination, Maximian's accession foretold by the spirits? Or had the man been paid to sow the seeds of future loyalty?

The ceaseless whirl of questions lulled Castus eventually into a dull sleep.

He was woken by a crash as the jailer flung the cell door open. Weak daylight seeped in from the chamber outside, and Castus closed his eyes at once as the pain of his shackled arms exploded through his torso. The jailer came and stood over him. He was a small man with a perverted leer, but his arms were long and corded with muscle, and he wore a heavy military belt covered in ornaments: brooches and rings, keys and clasps. Taken from previous prisoners, Castus guessed. Prisoners who had no use for such things now.

The jailer's slave assistant, a youth with dirty blond hair and a bruised face, dragged Castus up into a kneeling position, and then the jailer amused himself by bringing a tin cup of water close to his mouth and then moving it away as he leaned forward to drink. Finally Castus managed to grip the rim of the cup between his teeth and suck the sour water down before the man could drag it from him. There was a crust of dry bread to follow; the jailer rammed it into Castus's mouth and left him to chew.

The door slammed shut and Castus was alone in the dark again. He rolled onto his side, then spat out the bread. It was drying his mouth, and tasted of ash. Hours seemed to pass, and as his eyes adjusted to the faint trace of light from beneath the door he stared at the walls of the cell, the low vaulted ceiling, the worn stone-slab floor, and saw no possibility of escape. He had lapsed into another stunned and dreamless sleep when the first scream woke him.

At first he thought it was the jailer beating his slave again. But the scream was followed by a second, a long drawn-out shriek that echoed and then died into racked sobs of agony. Castus struggled to his feet and stood staring at the door. His scalp prickled and crawled, and sweat ran down his back beneath his dirty unbelted tunic. The noise came again. The wrenching howl of a man in pain and terror. Castus was breathing hard through his nose. He felt panic rising in his chest, the overwhelming desire to get out, to flee whatever was causing that terrible agony.

Moments passed in long-held breaths. The screaming had stopped, and after a while Castus felt the ache in his legs and sank down with one shoulder against the wall. He had barely closed his eyes when the door slammed open.

'Big man,' the jailer said. 'On your feet.'

The blond slave entered the cell holding a trident; Castus wondered if it was the same weapon that the gladiator on the aqueduct had carried. The slave jabbed the points of the trident towards Castus's chest, then the jailer seized his arms and dragged him upright and out through the door.

Outside the cell was a long chamber with heavy brick vaulting overhead. Water seeped through the bricks to drip and puddle on the stone floor, and a pair of torches in wall brackets threw ugly angled shadows. With the trident jabbing his back and the jailer tugging at his arm, Castus stumbled on through a series of low arches and interconnecting rooms. He saw iron-barred doors in the torchlight, dark openings in the bricks. Now that he was moving, he was more conscious than ever of his swollen bladder; the possibility that he might have to piss, and it would be taken as a sign of fear, was all the more humiliating.

A sharp turn to the right, then another to the left, and Castus was shoved forward into a much larger chamber, the far end lost in smoky gloom. Squat pillars ran down the centre, with arches above, and the low vaulted ceiling seemed to compress the shadows. The chamber stank of hot iron, burnt flesh and blood.

'Ah, there you are,' a voice said.

Castus recoiled, and felt the trident prick his back. Nigrinus paced towards him from between the pillars, smiling.

'I hope they've been treating you appropriately down here,' the notary said. 'I did send food, but of course jailers have a habit of taking the best stuff for themselves. . .'

Castus glanced to his side, but the jailer had vanished. The trident was gone too. For a moment he thought he was alone with the notary, but then a movement at the far side of the room drew his eye and he saw the four men sitting together in the corner. They looked like labourers, gathered around a low table with their midday meal, but Castus could make out the burn scars on their arms, the dark stains on their sleeveless tunics. They were quaestionarii. Professional torturers.

There were others, too, in the chamber. Men moved from the darkness: a couple of guards in military cloaks, their faces without expression. Castus sensed a movement to his right and turned to see three more figures enter the room, bending their heads beneath the low brick arch. The newcomers also wore cloaks, but they secured them with brooches of gold and gemstones, and their tunics were richly patterned and embroidered. The first was Scorpianus, the Praetorian tribune. After him came an older man who wore an expression of mild surprise: Castus had seen him dining with Maximian, and knew he was one of the local provincial governors. The third figure was the eunuch, Gorgonius.

'Domini,' Nigrinus said. 'Welcome to the Stygian depths! I was just about to show this prisoner some of the more intriguing items kept down here.'

Gorgonius smiled and made a gesture for the notary to continue. The older man beside him was lifting the hem of his cloak to cover his nose and mouth, but the tribune Scorpianus was gazing about himself with frank interest.

'If you'll step this way please,' Nigrinus said. Castus remained standing, until the two cloaked guards moved up behind him and shoved at his shoulder. Then he paced heavily after the notary, the guards and the three distinguished visitors following behind.

'You see here, on this rack,' Nigrinus said, gesturing, 'the simple implements called *claws*. As you'll notice, they are razor sharp. These are used to rake down the flanks of the subject's body, ripping the flesh and muscle away from the bones beneath. . . It's said that they can rip a man's soul from his body too. . . Beside them here are the *hooks*. This one – if you look closely – is shaped to cut in beneath the ribs. The subject can be lifted from his feet using these chains here, and made to hang suspended on the hooks for a considerable period. . . These need cleaning, as you can see. . .'

He paced on down one side of the room, through the puddles of firelight, gesturing to right and left as he spoke. Rather like, Castus thought, a wealthy man guiding visitors through his house, pointing out the fine marbles and the wall paintings.

'These things upon the table are really very crude. As you see, a simple lash of nine cords, but the cords are tied with knucklebones and potsherds. When the subject is bound to that post over there, one of these lashes can strip the flesh from his back with surprising speed. . . Careful of that bucket. It's full of salt water. . .'

Castus paced steadily, conscious only of the twisting knot of pain between his shoulder blades and deep in his bowels, and the hatred he felt for Nigrinus. A hate so extreme it was almost sweet, almost pleasurable. He listened only vaguely to the man's thin droning voice, and paid no attention to the guards behind him or the guests trailing after them.

'Ah, now this is more interesting,' Nigrinus said, and turned to address his audience. He had led them in a half-circle, down the length of the chamber and back up the other side, and now they were standing beneath a hanging lamp in the open area at the far end. Castus blinked his eyes back into focus. The thing standing in the middle of the floor looked strangely familiar, but so out of place that for a moment he could not understand what he was looking at.

'This device we call the *catapult*,' Nigrinus said with a slight smirk. 'You military men will recognise it, no doubt, a standard army artillery piece, although the torsion arms are set rather differently, and this flat board here covers the channel where the bolt would normally lie. . .'

Castus stared at the device. He felt a deep revulsion crawling in his stomach. Scorpianus the tribune was bending across it, studying it with interest.

'You can surely imagine how it works,' Nigrinus went on. 'The subject is made to lie on his back on the board here, with his legs secured to the frame at the bottom and his wrists fastened to the two arms of the catapult, which are winched back against the pressure of the torsion drums. When we pull this lever here, the catapult is released, and the subject is dragged violently up by the recoil. In most cases, his arms and legs are dislocated at once. He then hangs here, suspended on his stretched tendons. . .'

The eunuch sucked a sharp hiss between his teeth, but he was still smiling. Scorpianus nodded in appreciation. Castus felt cold sweat coursing down his body, and weakening nausea filling his stomach.

'Our quaestionarii are quite adept at probing the tendons with these blades and spikes here,' Nigrinus continued. 'Although I'm told that the greatest pain is experienced when the tension is relaxed and the body of the subject allowed to fall. Some men are able to withstand three or even four sessions on the catapult. Though none can take more.'

'Perhaps we could have a demonstration?' Scorpianus said, straightening up and jutting his heavy jaw at Castus. 'Maybe the prisoner here?'

Castus glared back at him. How many times had he stood guard as Scorpianus reclined at dinner? How many times had he saluted as the tribune passed him in the corridors of the palace? He flexed his shoulders, and felt the shackles bite into his wrists.

'Sadly, the prisoner is a soldier,' Nigrinus explained. 'A member of the Corps of Protectores, in fact. An *honestior*. So he is legally immune from torture. . . except in cases of treason, of course. Although we do have reason to believe that treason may have been committed. . .'

'You would know about that,' Castus said. But the words came out as a choked snarl. Gorgonius stared at him in bemusement, as if he had just heard a dog speak.

'Yes, perhaps we *could* try you on the catapult,' Nigrinus said, perching himself casually on the bed of the machine. 'We could see how long you last. Such a brawny pair of shoulders – how long would it take those muscles to rip, do you think?'

'What do you want, you bastard?'

They understood him that time. But the three guests were not looking at Castus, but at Nigrinus.

'Well,' the notary said, 'I could demand the names of your fellow conspirators. But as it happens I already have those. Your friends Sallustius and the other one, the young Frank, gave me all I needed.'

Castus felt cold despair plummet through him. The man was bluffing, he must be. . . Sallustius was surely captured, but Brinno too? The notary tightened his mouth to hide a grin.

'So as it is, all I require from you is your oath of allegiance to the true emperor, Maximian Augustus. And, of course, your renunciation of the false oath you swore to the usurper Constantine, now deceased.'

'You won't get either.'

'No? Then our friend Scorpianus will get his wish after all. But think, first. To what do you owe your greatest loyalty?'

'To the emperor.'

'And what is the emperor?' Nigrinus said, still sitting on the torture machine. He made a casual rhetorical gesture. 'Is the emperor not a personification of Rome? Of the harmony between gods and men, the divine order of the universe? So you could better say that your loyalty is to that divine order: to the empire, and to the sacred majesty of Rome.'

Castus exhaled slowly. He dragged his arms against the bind of the shackles, as if he might break the chains that linked them; the effort made his neck swell.

'I see you are not considering this calmly and clearly!' Nigrinus said. The three dignitaries were observing him still, the eunuch with unfeigned amusement, the older civilian with bafflement and Scorpianus with an air of vague boredom.

'Constantine,' Nigrinus went on, 'was committed to a war with Maxentius. Everyone knew it. A huge and costly war, which would have left the armies of the west depleted and exhausted, easy prey to our rivals in the east. Such a war would have weakened the empire, weakened Rome, thrown us back into the bloody chaos of our fathers' and grandfathers' age.'

He paused for a moment, as if recalling some sorrowful memory. It was a performance, Castus realised. But for whose benefit? Certainly not his own. All Castus wanted to do was kill everyone in the room.

'But now,' Nigrinus said, brightening, 'we have a new emperor, a man united to Maxentius by paternal love which no sordid quarrel can extinguish! And with the united armies of the western empire under their command, they can sweep away their corrupt rivals in the east, banish our enemies from the frontiers and unite the Roman world under their divine rule.

So, you see, the demise of the usurper Constantine was a very good thing. Even the gods applaud it, I'm sure. And I myself have worked tirelessly for nearly two years to bring about this fortunate revolution!'

Castus felt his mind grow still and cold. The massive brick vaults overhead pressed downwards, and the faces of the three watching men seemed to blur and warp. Clenching his jaw, Castus forced himself to focus. He understood what was happening now. He would not be tortured, not yet.

'Go and fuck yourself,' he said. Scorpianus laughed.

They took him back to his cell, and the jailer pushed him as he crossed the threshold, so he stumbled and fell hard onto the stone floor. He knew at once he was not alone.

'Brother, is that you?'

With the door closed the blackness was a solid mass, filling the small chamber. Castus crawled to the wall and slumped against it. He flinched as he heard the movements of a body close to him.

'Brinno?'

Then the young Frank was crouched beside him; their arms were still shackled, but they pressed their shoulders together. 'I thought they'd killed you, brother,' Brinno said.

'Likewise. How far did you get from the aqueduct?'

'Hardly any distance. They were already waiting in the trees. When I looked back, I saw you fighting. How many of them did you kill?'

'Only three or four, I think.'

'Heh! That's good enough. Keep killing three or four, and soon they'll all be dead.'

'Victor died. And they've got Sallustius too.'

He heard Brinno make a spitting sound. 'Sallustius betrayed us,' the Frank said.

'I think I guessed that,' Castus said quietly. 'I didn't want to think about it.'

For a while they sat in silence, crouched against the wall. Then, haltingly, they began to fill in the details of what had happened to them. Their experiences were much the same. Castus told Brinno about the torture chamber, and Nigrinus's strange speech of loyalty to Maximian.

'I knew he was a snake,' Brinno said. 'You can kill him, if I can kill that bastard Flaccianus.'

Castus laughed, and it was a good feeling, even if it made the muscles in his arms ache again.

'There's something else I have to tell you,' Brinno said, a short while later. 'That slave boy, the jailer's assistant. He's Frankish. I heard him talking. He's of the Tubantes, I think.'

'So?' Castus had often wondered about his friend's attitude to the large numbers of his countrymen in slavery. Brinno had never appeared to give it much thought.

'The Tubantes are vassals of the Salii, my people.'

Castus nodded slowly, beginning to comprehend. Brinno said no more, but his silence told Castus everything he needed to know.

It must have been three hours later when they heard the rattle of the jailer's key in the lock. The door clashed open, spilling hot torchlight over the dirty stone floor, and the jailer swaggered into the cell carrying a water pot and a wooden tray of bread. The slave came in behind him, angling his trident down at the prisoners.

'Dinnertime! You first, barbarian,' the jailer said, nudging

Brinno with the toe of his boot. 'Up on your knees, or I'll pour this lot over your head.'

The Frankish slave had his trident pointed at Castus, who squatted with his back against the wall. Brinno was lying sprawled on the straw on the far side of the cell.

'Up, I said. I'm not feeding you myself. . . I don't bend over for any man!'

Without moving, Brinno began to speak. The words were fast and guttural, Germanic; Castus paid no attention to them, but watched the slave. At once the youth gave a start and glanced at Brinno.

'Quiet!' the jailer snarled. He dropped the tray of bread and pulled a cane from his belt. Castus saw the slave take a step back into the corner of the cell, his mouth open, and the points of the trident swung upwards. It was all he needed.

With one heave of his leg muscles he launched himself up, dipping his head and squaring his shoulders. The jailer only had time to notice the movement before Castus slammed into the man's chest, knocking him off his feet and driving him back against the far wall. He let out a shout of pain. Castus drew his head back and then jabbed forward, his brow thudding against the bridge of the man's nose. Another crunching headbutt, fast and hard, and the jailer's skull smacked back against the wall. His legs folded beneath him and he collapsed to the floor.

Brinno was still talking, giving orders in his own language to the slave. A note of command in his voice that Castus had never heard before. Reeling from the shocks to his skull – the jailer's head was almost as hard as his own – Castus slumped against the side of the doorframe and waited while the slave fished the keys from the fallen man's belt and unlocked their shackles. Castus gasped as the agony of release roared through his shoulders and back.

Flexing his arms, clenching his fists, he paced out through the cell door into the vaulted chamber. Nobody else in sight. Water jug on the table, but that could wait. Light-headed with relief, he lifted his tunic, pulled aside his loincloth and pissed a foaming torrent against the wall.

'Merciful gods,' he said. 'I needed that.'

Lifting the water jug from the table, he tipped it back and drank deeply. Brinno came out of the cell holding the trident. There was a short knife on the table and Castus armed himself with that.

'What about the slave?' Brinno said. 'We can't let him go. It'll look like he helped us escape.'

Castus went to the cell doorway and looked inside. The young slave was crouching on the floor beside the body of the jailer. Castus thought at first that he was trying to help his master; then he saw him clasp the man's throat with his hands and begin to press down. . .

'Leave him in there.' He closed the door and turned the key in the lock. 'He's got enough bruises already to look like we overpowered him.'

Brinno drained the last of the water jug and hurled it aside. He hefted the trident. 'Let's get out of this filthy place,' he said.

Slow and cautious, keeping together, they moved through the maze of underground rooms. Beyond the chamber of the prison cells there were no lamps or torches burning, but bands of faint greyish light fell from the small apertures up near the roof. Whether it was moonlight or dusk Castus could not tell, but when their eyes adjusted it was enough for them to make out the space around them.

'What did you tell him?' Castus said. 'The slave back there?'

'Heh!' Brinno replied. 'I told him the spirits of our ancestors are watching us always. I told him they are angry with those who submit to be ruled by evil men. But they love those who take avenging justice into their hands.'

'He did that, right enough.'

They slid around a corner into a low room, and Castus recognised the archway that led through to the torture chamber. Not that way. Tracing their steps back, they found another cell with a doorway knocked through the back wall. Edging through the opening, Castus with his knife bared and Brinno gripping the trident, they entered a long chamber that stretched away into darkness to their right. Squat pillars raised a line of arches down the middle, and to either side were stacked bales and crates, with ranks of huge amphorae standing upright like bloated corpses in the faint light from the airshafts.

'Where are we, do you think?' Brinno whispered.

'Don't know. Under the forum maybe, or the curia. But there must be steps out of here. . .'

Scuffing their feet, careful not to trip on anything in the gloom, they moved down the clear aisle of the huge storage vault.

'Stop,' Brinno hissed, grabbing Castus by the arm. 'Somebody's there.'

Sure enough, when Castus looked up he could see the light of a moving oil lamp, weaving like a firefly. He crouched, ready with the knife, and as he glanced to his right he saw a dark opening, little more than a crack in the wall, the shape of steps just visible within.

'There. . .'

Brinno went first, angling the long trident into the gap. The steps rose steeply, and soon they were in complete darkness. Castus backed slowly upwards, one hand on the slimy stones of the wall. Then there was a turning, and Brinno stopped, cursing.

'A gate – locked, I think.'

Castus pushed past him, reaching out to grip the iron bars. He ran his hand down and felt heavy chain links, and the rough metal of a rusted lock. Shoving against the bars, he felt no give at all. The gate had not been opened in years.

Light rose up the narrow stairway. Sounds of scuffing footsteps from below. One man, moving slowly.

Pushing back past Brinno, Castus leaped down the steps to the turning, then down the lower flight. The man was already at the opening from the storage chamber; Castus rushed him from the dark stairway, ramming him back off his feet. The lamp arced from the man's hand and cracked on the stone floor, the oil smothering the wick.

Castus dropped to one knee. He seized the man by the hair and dragged his head up, pointing the knife down at his face. In the faint light he made out the features of his captive. *Thanks to all the gods. . .*

'Kill him now!' Brinno cried, stamping down from the stairway with his trident aimed at the prisoner.

'I can understand your unhappiness. . .' Nigrinus said. Castus had his knee on his chest, and was still gripping his hair in his fist.

'Heh! He understands our unhappiness! *Kill him!*'

'Let me speak first, I beg you.'

Castus twisted his fist, and felt hair rip from the notary's scalp. 'Ten more words, then you die.'

Nigrinus rolled his eyes to one side, thinking fast. His mouth barely moved as he spoke.

'*I have. . . saved your. . . lives. . . you pair. . . of brainless. . . imbeciles.*'

Brinno let out a grunt, leaning closer with his trident. 'Kill him! No – make him show us the way out, and *then* kill him!'

'What a tempting offer,' the notary said.

Castus reversed his knife, and cracked the pommel against the man's head. Nigrinus flinched and hissed through his teeth.

'Say what you mean,' Castus told him.

'Maximian's people planned to have you murdered in your beds last night. I needed to get you out of the city and far away, so I could take you into my custody. They believe I'm part of their conspiracy, but I needed to prove my allegiance. . . What better way than breaking the oaths of Constantine's most loyal men? That performance in the torture room was for their benefit, of course. . .'

'But the villa,' Brinno said, 'the aqueduct – that was real. It was no game. Victor died!'

'Of course it was real – it had to be! I hadn't anticipated that you would defend yourselves so robustly, though. As it was, you cost me a dozen expensive gladiators and several members of the imperial courier service. Delphius in particular was a very effective agent. . .'

'And you couldn't have just told us all this beforehand?' Castus felt his mind swinging between pained belief and outraged denial.

'Excuse me,' Nigrinus said, grinning, 'but I didn't rate your abilities as actors. Far more convincing if the anger was real, no? And I couldn't risk you giving anything away – I mean, you might *actually* have been put to torture, and then what?'

Castus exhaled heavily, then eased his weight off the notary's chest and released his hair. Nigrinus let out a sob of relief, apparently involuntary. Then he sat up and brushed his hair into place with his fingers.

'You knew about Constantine's death too?' Brinno said.

He had not lowered the trident. 'Did you plan that as well?'

'Constantine isn't dead, you barbarian oaf! Gorgonius sent killers to Treveris, but they failed, I don't know how. So now – understand this, and please stop waving that trident at me – now the emperor needs us alive! Maximian and his supporters think I'm one of them, but I can't work alone. I need muscle. I need men I can trust, men Constantine trusts. You'll have to do, in the circumstances.'

'And how can we trust you?'

'When you get out of this place, look above the main gate of the city. You'll see the heads of two of your fellow Protectors decorating spikes there. The other two agreed to shift their loyalties to Maximian. As did your friend Sallustius: Maximian bought his allegiance months ago. And besides, if you can't trust me, whom do you have left? Or would you rather have your heads on spikes too?'

Castus looked at Brinno, who slowly lowered the trident. The notary was sitting on the ground between them, massaging his chest with stiff fingers.

'Swear upon the gods that this is the truth,' Castus said, raising the knife again.

'I swear upon the gods that this is the truth,' Nigrinus said, in the tone of a man with little belief in either.

'If he's wrong. . .' Brinno said. 'May the gods help us!'

'If he's wrong,' Castus replied, 'I think we're beyond their help.'

'Maximianus Augustus! Eternal Augustus! The gods preserve you for us! Your salvation is our salvation!'

Again and again the massed acclamation rang out from the crowds packing the stands of the circus, all the people of Arelate on their feet, all of them saluting, all of them repeating the ritual formulas as the crowd-leaders raised their batons.

'Maximianus Augustus! Eternal Augustus! The gods send you to us! The gods grant you triumph!'

Noon sun turned the swept sand of the racecourse into a glaring yellow plain. Trumpets sounded from the balustrades above the starting gates, and from the blue shade of the arches below the procession marched forth.

At its head came the new military commanders of Maximian's army: Scorpianus, dressed in silvered cuirass and peacock-plumed helmet in his new role as Praetorian Prefect, and beside him Gaudentius, the former commander of the Alpine force, now holding the rank of *comes rei militaris*, Companion in Military Affairs. Behind them the prefects of the legions from Spain, the centurions of the Praetorian Cohort and the tribunes of the legionary and auxilia detachments that Gaudentius had led down from Cularo.

Behind the officers, marching in glittering array with their standards proudly adorned with images of the newly restored emperor, came the troops. First the Praetorians, then the troops from Spain: four thousand men of Legion VI Hispana Maximiana and Legion VII Gemina Maximiana. After them were the mixed detachments from the Rhine army, with their small cavalry force. To the cheers of the crowd, they marched down the length of the circus, around the curve at the far end and back up the course to form in their units before the imperial podium that overlooked the finish line.

Eight thousand men, Castus thought. They made a fine sight, worthy of a better emperor. He knew that the soldiers had already been paid their acclamation donatives: a gold piece and two pounds of silver per man. He wondered how much was left now of the hoard taken from the mint at Lugdunum. But the soldiers looked happy, as rich men often do.

Castus was standing before the lowest tier of the seating, facing out over the assembled troops with his back to the imperial podium. The altar constructed on the sand below was still smoking; the priests from the sacred fraternities of Arelate were still gathering the meat of the sacrificial animals. On the seats just behind Castus, the city councillors and the provincial governors were sitting together, all of them now pledged to Maximian's cause. No mention had been made of the emperor's son, Maxentius.

The new emperor himself sat high in the podium, red faced and impassive. *Eternal Augustus*, Castus thought to himself: that was the message of the new regime. Maximian had never abdicated with Diocletian: that had been a mere administrative error; he had been emperor all along, the Senior Augustus, entitled to rule over the entire empire. . . The citizens of Arelate seemed impressed anyway. But they had already benefited from the golden rays of the emperor's favour.

Castus had seen Fausta seated some distance to her father's right, dressed now in muted clothes befitting her supposed widowed status. Somewhere among those gathered around her would be Sabina, but Castus did not have time to look. Besides, he did not want to see her, did not want her to see him. It was shameful enough just having to appear in public.

Sallustius was standing four paces to his left. He had tried to apologise to Castus and Brinno already. He had been born in Rome, he had told them, he had family there. He wanted to return to his home city one day, and not with a hostile army. Brinno had just turned away in disgust. But Castus tried to forgive the man, or at least feign forgiveness. Were they not all feigning loyalty, after all?

Only the day before he had gone dutifully to the shrines of Jupiter, Isis and Sol Invictus and given sacrifice, as he had promised, for having escaped alive from the aqueduct. Perhaps, he thought, it would have been easier to have died, like Victor. But another part of him felt that his escape had been an illusion: in his soul he was still perched on that high and veering precipice, still trying to pace that narrow path above a vast and yawning void.

Horns sounded from the military array, and the delegates of the troops began to step forward and take their oaths. When all had spoken, it was the turn of the Protectores. Castus had already sworn in private, of course. This was the public display of loyalty to the new regime. In his mind was the closing phrase of the vow he had taken to Constantine in the audience hall of Treveris. The terrible penalties of disloyalty.

. . . *I impose a curse upon myself encompassing the destruction and total extinction of my body, soul, life, children, and my entire family, so neither earth nor sea may receive their bodies nor bear fruit for them. . .*

Turning towards the podium, towards the glowering figure of Maximian, Castus raised his hand in salute and joined his voice to the others in crying out the oath.

May the gods forgive me. May the true emperor forgive me.

But the words in his head were drowned out by the ringing cheers of the crowd.

PART FOUR

CHAPTER XX

'By the fucking almighty balls of Jove, why is he still *alive*?' Maximian's roar echoed through the audience chamber and out to the corridor. Standing guard beside the open doors, Castus resisted the urge to turn and glance back into the room. The new emperor had been drinking since just after lunch; it was dusk now. Castus had seen Maximian drunk often enough, but had never witnessed him so angry. The news of Constantine's rapid advance southward from the Rhine had arrived only hours before.

'Didn't I tell you to see to it?' he yelled. 'Why did I make you Praetorian Prefect, Scorpianus, if you couldn't even manage that? You were supposed to send men to kill him, not warn him! How hard is it?'

On the far side of the door, Sallustius stood motionless. When he glanced across at him, Castus saw the face of his former friend creased with embarrassed anguish. Scorpianus was speaking now, his measured tones tight with discomfort.

'Most Sacred Augustus,' the Praetorian Prefect said, 'I assure you that the men we sent were the very best. They were apprehended on the road – some traitor must have given warning. . . But they will give nothing away, even under the fiercest torture. . .'

A sudden ringing crash: Maximian had either thrown his cup at the wall or kicked over a table. Castus could hear his snarls of outrage, his stamping strides as he paced from one side of the room to the other.

'So now,' Maximian said in a low growl, 'my bastard son-in-law is marching against me. He dares! He dares march against the *Man Like Hercules*! That horse-faced fraud. I never liked him, Scorpianus. He has no sense of fucking humour.'

Castus heard the prefect making sounds of assent. There were several others in the audience hall, but they were sensibly keeping quiet.

'And to think,' Maximian went on, 'I made his father everything he was! I raised him up, his father Constantius, with my own hand, do you know that?'

'Yes, your divinity,' Scorpianus replied.

'Appointed him my prefect, then my Caesar. . . And this is how his son repays me, can you credit it? Where are the gods? Where is justice?'

'I don't know, your divinity.'

For a while they fell silent, and Castus strained to hear what was happening. He kept his head motionless, staring across the corridor at the darkening windows above the courtyard. A chair grunted on the marble floor, then Maximian spoke again.

'Haven't we got people in his retinue? I am the Senior Augustus, the *Maximum* Augustus, of the entire Roman Empire, and if I want somebody to die they are *dead*!'

'Quite right, emperor,' Scorpianus told him crisply. 'We have many agents, as you know. One of them will see to him before long. . .'

'Or maybe one of *his* will see to *me*, eh?' Maximian broke in. 'Half my people are traitors anyway – betrayed one emperor, could betray another. . .'

'Oh, no, divinity. Your troops and officers are devoted to your cause. . .'

But the emperor's mood had clearly shifted. There was another silence, and then Maximian spoke again in an imploring voice.

'I never asked to fight Constantine!' he cried. 'The gods know I did not! I would have ruled by his side. He could have been my subordinate, my Caesar, as his father was before him. I could even have loved him, as a son-in-law. But no!'

'Sacred Augustus, the gods have decreed your rule. . .'

'Shut up!' the emperor shouted, and Castus could almost see Scorpianus flinch. The shout died away in echoes.

'Surrounded by traitors,' Maximian said. 'My daughter's no better – I told her what to do! I told her to wave those huge tits of hers around a bit more. He'd soon have given up that dry old stick Minervina then, and we'd have an heir to cement the union! But, no, she'd rather sulk and pout and stuff her face, the pig. . .'

Silence from Scorpianus, and the others in the room. Castus was not surprised; they had learned by now that it was never wise to agree too strongly with Maximian's outbursts. The emperor had an unnervingly acute memory.

'Send those two guards in here!' he demanded suddenly. Castus tensed, and caught Sallustius doing the same. A moment later, Scorpianus stepped through the doors and gestured to both of them.

They followed him back into the audience chamber. Maximian was slumped on a carved wooden chair set upon the low dais in the centre. Only ten days had passed since he had been acclaimed Augustus once more, but he seemed to have aged years. His face was flushed and pouched, his hair and bristling beard run through with grey, and the hands that gripped the arms of the chair were corded with veins. Shards of shattered glass and pottery on the floor showed the

evidence of the emperor's rage. The two Protectores stamped
to a halt at a respectful distance, saluted, and dropped to kneel
before him.

'Am I your emperor?' Maximian growled.

'Yes, dominus,' both men said in unison. Castus kept his
eyes locked on the tiled floor, but he could sense the emperor
looming over him.

'Yes? So if I ordered you to go and kill Constantine, you'd
do it?'

A pause. Castus felt the blood rushing to his head. The
prospect was dizzying – terrible and enticing at the same time.
Escape from Maximian's court – but then what? Would he even
be believed if he tried to report the truth?

Maximian was still waiting for an answer. Scorpianus bent
closer, spoke under his breath.

'What?' the emperor said, frowning. 'Oh, maybe not, then.
It seems even my own guards are not to be trusted!'

'Your divinity, that wasn't what I meant. . . We have other
agents, more versatile. . .'

'*Versatile!*' Maximian spat the word. 'Send that bastard
Constantine to me and we'll fight it out, man to man! Then
we'll see who the gods favour. . .'

Castus slowly eased out a breath. There was another man
speaking now, and it took a moment for Castus to recognise
the surprised-looking civilian who had visited the torture room
with Scorpianus and the eunuch. He recalled his name: Aelius
Macrobius, the governor of the Viennensis diocese.

'Our latest reports, most sacred emperor,' the man said, his
voice smoothly urbane, 'suggest that Constantine is moving
south with only a small contingent of men, no more than three
or four thousand. He has been obliged to leave the bulk of his
army on the Rhine, to guard against the barbarians. Also, he

has no siege engines and only a limited supply train – his men are already on half-rations.'

'Really?' Maximian said with renewed enthusiasm. 'No engines? Four thousand men?' He began to laugh, smacking his fist into his palm. 'Then the gods truly are on my side, at last! Once my son sends his four legions and two thousand *clibanarii* across the Alps, we'll smash Constantine easily! We'll smear his little army all over the plains of the Rhodanus!'

'It also seems, dominus,' Macrobius went on, with the faint smile of a man who knows his news is good, 'that Ulpius Caesianus, the governor of Raetia Prima, has now declared for Maxentius. Thus cutting all land communication between Constantine's territories and those of his erstwhile ally Licinius on the Danube.'

'Even better!' Maximian declared. He jumped up from his seat, letting his gold-embroidered purple robe slide heavily from his shoulders. 'Once he finishes off the rebellion in Africa, Maxentius can use Raetia as a bridgehead across the Alps to strike at Licinius's western flank, while I deal with Constantine here in Gaul. By winter we'll be masters of half the world!'

Castus was still kneeling on the floor, trying not to glance up at the emperor. Maximian was pacing fiercely again, fists clasped behind his back. Scorpianus made a quick gesture, then pointed sharply at the door. Rising, the two Protectores gave another salute, but the emperor ignored them as they backed silently out of the room.

Night had fallen by the time Castus made his way back towards his quarters. A southern night: the air felt warm and soft, and every lamp along the portico was hazed with a nimbus of tiny wings. The steady chirrup of insects came from the gardens. He was still turning over Macrobius's news, still trying to determine how much of it might be true, and what it might mean. As he stepped through the passage from the garden portico and entered the darker enclosed courtyard beyond, he was too distracted at first to notice the figure waiting between the pillars of the colonnade.

'Domina,' he said quietly as she approached him. There were others with her, a pair of slaves, a maid, a eunuch bodyguard, but they hung back at a discreet distance.

'What happened today?' Sabina asked him, drawing very close. Castus felt himself enfolded in her scent, her presence; but she was scared too, and he could sense it. The imperial household was a place of spies, and it was dangerous to be seen talking with anyone.

'You heard him, the emperor?'

'I think half of Arelate heard him. What was he so angry about?'

Briefly he filled in the details of the afternoon's and evening's news: the rapid approach of Constantine, the size of his army, Maximian's swoops from rage to triumphant hubris. Sabina took his arm.

'Then he'll fight?' They were walking together, around the turning of the pillared portico into the deeper shadow.

'He says so.'

'But what do you think?'

Castus frowned, only now beginning to consider some of the things he had heard. 'Constantine has no siege engines,' he said. 'I think after a while Maximian might remember that.'

'But that makes no difference! The walls of Arelate are falling down – an army could just walk straight in through the breaches!'

'Maybe they could here. But there are cities in Gaul with stronger walls.'

He felt Sabina shudder. She drew the shawl tighter at her neck. 'Is there any news of the fighting in Africa?' she asked.

'None,' Castus told her. He remembered that her husband was there, supporting the rebel Domitius Alexander.

For a few more paces they walked in silence. Her attendants had dropped out of sight and hearing now. Then Sabina drew him to a halt, and took his hand.

'Is it true that they tortured you?'

Castus shrugged. 'They thought about it.'

She appeared confused. 'So. . . you genuinely have gone over to Maximian?'

Uncertainty crawled up Castus's spine; was this a ruse to gauge his loyalty? Were they being observed even now? He had grown used to being watched, guarded, distrusted.

'Have you?' he asked in return, and caught her smile in the darkness.

'This is not the best time for such questions, I suppose,' she said quietly.

She pressed herself quickly against him, rising to kiss his lips, then stepped away. For a few heartbeats he gripped her hand, not letting her retreat.

'We all do what we must,' he said, 'to survive.'

Then he released her, and she walked away into the shadows without another word.

Five days later, Castus stood on the deck of the liburnian galley *Aurata* as it rowed slowly downriver towards the sea. On the raised stern platform, Maximian Augustus sat blearily beneath a purple and gold canopy, staring with dull and reddened eyes at the flat marshy land beyond the riverbanks. He was not retreating; this was not flight. Instead it was a strategic relocation.

Behind him the citizens of Arelate waited nervously within their crumbled walls for the arrival of Constantine. Their city, the first to acclaim the new emperor, was stripped of troops now. Their civic leaders had either deserted their posts or gone south down the river with Maximian. The soldiers that had been camped around the city were gone too, marching across the flat stony wastelands to the south-east, heading for the city of Massilia on the coast.

Massilia, with its strong walls and seaport, was to be Maximian's new imperial capital. Arelate would be left to make the best of things. There had been no cheering, no shouts of loyalty and acclaim, as the emperor had made his departure in the grey of dawn. Those citizens who had stirred from their homes had lined the riverbank and watched with blank expressions as the imperial retinue swept from the palace into the waiting boats, the big *Aurata* and the troopships and smaller galleys that followed in her wake.

Now the sun was high over the flatlands of the Rhodanus delta. Flights of waterbirds skimmed the lagoons, and flamingos stood balancing on one leg in the shallows. The double-banked oars of the *Aurata* beat slow and steady, pulling with the current, and around noon the flotilla passed from the river into the straight channel of the Canal of Marius, which would carry them free of the silted branches of the treacherous delta and out to the open sea.

Brinno was sitting perched above the oar box, watching the rowers with open curiosity. 'I never see one like this before,' he said to Castus. 'The oars. . . *so*.' He raised two flat hands, one above the other. 'In my country, all the rowers sit together, pull together.'

'It's a bireme,' Castus told him. 'Out in the east you see triremes – three banks of oars.'

Brinno raised his eyebrows, clearly perplexed as to how this might work. But then his eyes clouded and he leaned closer.

'*We could kill him now*,' he said in an undertone. Castus felt his shoulders tighten, but waited a few breaths before turning slowly to look back towards the platform at the stern. 'It is our duty,' Brinno added.

How easy it would be. Only a few attendants stood or sat around Maximian: the eunuch Gorgonius, Scorpianus, Macrobius and half a dozen secretaries and slaves. Besides Scorpianus, only the four Praetorians standing along the break of the platform were armed. A rush towards the stern and the job would be done. And, along with the emperor, both he and Brinno would be dead.

So many times over the last month, since his false pledge of allegiance, Castus had tormented himself with plots and plans. He could escape and flee to join Constantine; he could make some wild attack on the usurper. Each time he had held himself back, thinking that the time was not right – it would be a mistake. Each time he had cursed himself for a coward.

At least nobody now believed the fable about Constantine's death. All knew that the emperor was marching south against Maximian at great speed. Already he was at Lugdunum; in four days he would reach Arelate. He was falling like a thunderbolt out of the north, with the hardest veterans of the Rhine legions behind him, an army that grew larger with every successive report.

'We need to wait,' Castus told Brinno, whispering between his teeth. 'Wait for Massilia – things will be decided then.'

He heard Brinno smack his lips in frustration. There were seagulls whirling and crying above them now, and the air smelled of brine.

'Decided how?' the young barbarian hissed. 'And if not by us – then *who*?'

'I don't know, brother,' Castus told him, unable to meet his eye. 'I don't know.'

The *Aurata* and her flotilla of smaller vessels left the mouth of the canal that afternoon, and a fine westerly breeze carried them across the bay before sundown, to anchor in the lee of the small barren islands off Massilia. The night was calm and clear, the stars very bright, and as the sun rose the oarsmen backed water and turned the head of the ship towards the narrow inlet of the harbour mouth.

Standing beneath the high gilded prow, Castus watched the city appear out of the sun-haze of dawn. To either side was a rocky coastline, grey crags dusted with the grey-green of olive groves and wild trees. With the sun glaring off the water, Castus could see little of the city at first. Then he made out the wall that circled it on the seaward side, a massive fortification rising from the naked rock, with squat square towers every few hundred paces. As the *Aurata* pulled closer, it appeared that the wall entirely closed the city, cutting it off from the sea; then, as the ship turned, Castus made out the narrow neck of the harbour, clinched between the fortified headland and the rough slopes on the far side.

The galley pulled in through the neck, and the harbour opened before her. An expanse of enclosed water, glimmering pale blue in the early sun, half of it filled with moored vessels. Beyond the forest of masts and yards, the city rose in a broad arc around the northward side of the harbour, clustered houses climbing the hills in terraces. At the summit of each of the hills was a temple, the pillars and pediments gleaming white and gold in the morning sun.

It was a magnificent sight, the air so clear and clean that Castus felt he could see every detail of the city in perfect focus. For a few moments he forgot the grim mission that had brought him here, and gloried in the view of the city before him across the water.

But then, as the *Aurata* crawled the last distance between the moored ships in the harbour, Castus made out the squalor of the docks, the stone quays slippery with fish guts, the jetties of rotting black timber, the wrack of rubbish and half-decayed wreckage in the mud at the water's edge, and the mass of people spilling down through the gates in the harbour wall and between the chaotic assemblage of warehouses and taverns along the dockside. Horns were blaring from the temples on the hills, and the gathering crowd was already cheering, waving palm branches, crying out its acclamations. The people of Massilia, like those of Arelate before them, had been instructed on how to greet their new master.

Maximian stood up on the stern platform of the galley, beneath a flapping purple pennant. Castus stared at him, bemused for a moment. The emperor appeared different. His face had been whitened with some kind of paste, his cheeks rouged, his beard and hair dyed jet-black. Standing stiffly in his heavy embroidered robe and his jewelled imperial tiara, Maximian resembled a painted statue. Jupiter, maybe, or Hercules himself.

The oars backed water, bringing the *Aurata* smoothly round to the wide stone quay at the western end of the docks. Slaves wearing flowered wreaths lowered a gangway down to the galley's deck, and on the quay twenty young maidens of the city were drawn up in lines carrying baskets of flowers. As Maximian made his way with slow and stately tread up the gangway and along the jetty, the girls cried out praises and scattered the flowers before him. Music of pipes and tambourines eddied through the noise of the cheering.

At the head of the quay, across an open paved area, the grandees of Massilia were assembled to greet the emperor: the curator of the city, with decurions of the city council, the *flamines* and augurs of the temples and the imperial cults. All of them dressed in their heavy white wool togas, their rich silk and linen tunics, their plushly embroidered cloaks. As Maximian approached, all of them knelt on the greasy cobbles and performed their adoration.

Castus came up the gangway after the imperial party, with Brinno at his side. He tried to keep his expression blank, tried not to stare too critically at all the outpourings of loyal devotion. What was wrong with these people? How much had they been paid? How much had they been threatened?

He saw Fausta and her retinue disembarking from one of the smaller galleys at the next jetty. Constantine's wife had given up her pretence of mourning, and wore the full splendour of her wealth once more. Castus watched her as she moved to join her father; what were her loyalties now?

'*Maximian Augustus! Eternal Augustus! Greatest of emperors! May the gods grant you eternal life! May the gods grant you eternal rule!*'

On and on it went, until Castus felt the massed voices drumming in his skull. He scanned the crowd, trying to read the faces of individuals, but saw nothing. All looked as blank and bemused as he felt. Maximian stood in the cleared area at the top of the quay, motionless as a statue with his retinue around him.

Now there was one voice, rising clear above the rest. The cheering and the chanted acclamations died away, and the voice carried onwards. A panegyric of praise, of course. The orator was a plump-faced man dressed all in wine-red, and he sketched florid gestures in the air as he spoke.

'. . . *lover of your country, lover of the true gods, O greatest of emperors, you bring glory to our city by your Sacred Presence! All civil strife is banished, all traitors and impious followers of outlaw sects slink away before the dawn of your arrival! Maximian Augustus, the city cries aloud with one voice in praise and in ardent gratitude that you have chosen this place to commence once more your Divine Rule and given us this opportunity to once again adore your Sacred Features. . .*'

Just as Castus felt his ears growing numb, he noticed a stir running through the crowd at his back. Turning, he made out another voice, shouting from a short distance away, a harsh angry yell rising above the hushed noise of the crowd. Beside him was the low stone platform of a dockside crane: Castus shoved aside a couple of lounging labourers and clambered up onto it, peering back over the throng towards the line of warehouses that fronted the harbour wall.

'. . . Brothers and sisters, you see before you the emissary of the devil! A persecutor, despised by God! A man who has shed the blood of innocents, the blood of the faithful!'

The speaker was an older man, powerfully built but plainly dressed, with a bald head and flaring grey beard. He was standing on the back of a cart drawn up outside the warehouses, and the crowd was thick around him. As he spoke his words gained in power and volume, drowning out the honeyed phrases of the orator.

'Once more he comes amongst us, brethren, in the guise of an emperor, but he is the devil's shadow! I call upon you – cast him out! Reject this usurper, this persecutor, this enemy of God!'

'Who's he?' Castus said to a slack-mouthed youth sitting on the crane.

'That's Oresius, the head priest of the Christians,' the youth said, and spat. '*Bishop*, they call him. He almost managed to get his head lopped off the last time Maximian was in power here. Reckon he wants to be one of their *martyrs*, eh?'

Already the crowd was splitting apart, a solid wedge of Praetorians with locked shields driving a path towards the man on the cart. Another man was calling out to the Christian priest: a well-dressed citizen, wearing the insignia of a city magistrate.

'Cease this disturbance!' the magistrate shouted. 'For the good of the city, Oresius, I beg you – stop this criminal madness!'

'Madness?' the grey-bearded man yelled back. Veins were standing out in his neck, and he seized the front of his tunic as if he would tear it from his body. 'Who are you, Trigetius, to speak of crime and madness? There is no madness for those who know the love of God! For those who have Christ *there is no crime*!'

The crowd around the cart was shoving back against the phalanx of Praetorians. Some of them pelted missiles: rotten vegetables and kicked-up cobblestones spattered and rattled off the shields. Castus saw men knocked to the ground, scuffles breaking out. Bodies were swirling around the platform of the crane as the mass of onlookers tried to back away from the confrontation. A scream from just below him, and Castus saw a gang of sailors in greasy smocks shoving a woman between them as she tried to carry her child clear of the riot.

Jumping down from the platform, he threw his arms out straight before him and forced the bodies aside. The first sailor he caught by the neck, then kicked his legs from under him. The second went down with a fist in the face; the third saw the way of things and made his escape. Castus took a moment to catch his breath, then scooped up the woman and her child and lifted them up onto the crane platform.

By the time he clambered up after them, it was over. The Christian priest had raised his arms and stepped off the cart, surrendering himself to the centurion of the Praetorian detachment. The shields closed around him, and he was led away.

'With any luck,' the youth on the crane said with lazy relish, 'they'll throw him to the lions!'

CHAPTER XXI

Out beyond the city walls, men were working in the late-afternoon sun. Thousands of them, slaves and conscripted civilians labouring alongside legionaries stripped to their tunics. In the lengthening shade of the wall itself they were clearing out the defensive ditch, digging up the mass of rubbish and debris that had filled it over centuries of peace. In the open ground on the far side of the ditch there were gangs tearing down the clusters of huts and low houses that had sprung up outside the fortifications. Far away, past the grey dust clouds rising from the demolished buildings, more men were hacking down the olive groves on the nearer slopes. An entire harvest ruined, only to deny the enemy wood and shade. But there was nothing the people of Massilia could do about the destruction: they were under military rule now, and Maximian had ordered that everything must be sacrificed to strengthen the city for a siege. The work had been going on for five days, but could not last much longer. Constantine had paused at Arelate, but was advancing once more.

'All this,' Brinno said, 'for one man.'

Castus, standing beside him on the ramparts, nodded slowly. 'Two men,' he said.

They were both speaking quietly; following only a few paces behind them on the rampart walk were four soldiers of the Praetorian cohort. Officially they were supposed to be 'military servants' for the two Protectores, but their glowering watchful expressions showed plainly that they were intended as guards. Despite their lower rank, Castus did not doubt that the Praetorians had secret orders to report any treasonous words or actions to their superiors, and prevent any attempts to escape or sabotage the defensive works. He recognised at least two of them from the group that had surrounded him and Urbicus between the wagons at Lugdunum.

But the Praetorians could not stop Castus and Brinno from surveying the walls; as Protectores, they were supposed to be the emperor's own loyal bodyguards, after all. Castus was no engineer, but he had a clear eye for the military possibilities of any location, and during his tour of the ramparts and gates with Brinno he had made sure to remember all that he saw. Now, standing on the walkway of the wall that descended towards the Rome Gate, he had a panoramic view over the whole sweep of the city as it curved around the northern shore of the harbour.

Massilia was built upon a wide hilly promontory, with the streets rising in tiers from the docks up to the temple-crowned summits. On the nearest hill, Castus could see the huge structure of the temple of Ephesian Artemis glowing in the afternoon sun. That, and the temple of Apollo on the next summit, formed the ancient acropolis of the city. Any troops breaking through the walls would have to battle their way up to those temples through a warren of streets; any defender keen on fighting to the last could hold either of them as a citadel. But that was a desperate thought. Castus had never experienced a true street battle, but he knew it was always a bloody business.

On the landward side of the promontory the old walls were strong, and even stronger now that Maximian had ordered them repaired. Massilia had only been assaulted once, hundreds of years before, but on that occasion it had held out against the great Julius Caesar. Or so Castus had learned in the imperial council that morning. Sallustius had told him later that the city had surrendered to Caesar in the end, but only after six months of siege. There were no catapults or other engines left in the city to fight off attackers, but with several thousand men to hold the ramparts, and plenty of archers among them, Massilia's defences would be tough to break.

Only on the harbour side were the walls less formidable. Several gates had been knocked through them to give access to the docks, and the city merchants had built their warehouses and emporia higher than the wall tops, with overhanging attics and gantries to winch goods directly up from the wharfs. But anyone attacking on that side would have to cross the harbour itself, through the mass of anchored vessels, and Castus doubted that Constantine had either the boats or the manpower to attempt such an assault.

Surveying the scene, he frowned and shook his head.

Brinno leaned into the embrasure between the crenellations of the rampart, spitting noisily out into the cleared ditch twenty feet below. Castus had caught the twitch of his friend's expression, and leaned into the embrasure beside him.

'*What do we do?*' Brinno hissed.

Castus had no answer.

'We should have killed him on the boat!' Behind them they could hear the scrape of the Praetorians' boots on the paving of the walkway. 'We could still do it. . .'

'Couldn't get close enough,' Castus said under his breath. Both men were speaking through tightened lips, gazing out through the embrasure at the sun-drenched landscape beyond the walls. It was approaching late September now, but the heat of full summer still endured, and the air was humid with the scent of the sea.

'Then what. . .? We start a riot, a revolt in the city? What?'

One of the Praetorians leaned heavily against the wall beside Castus, clearing his throat. Castus nudged Brinno with his elbow, and the pair of them straightened up.

'Wait for a chance,' Castus whispered as they moved on. 'Hope we know it when we see it. . .'

He heard Brinno's choke of frustration.

A warm breeze lifted over the ramparts, loaded with dust and the smell of smoke from the burning debris of buildings. On the other side of the wall, the city side, more smoke was rising from the workshops just inside the Rome Gate as the blacksmiths laboured to prepare their quotas of spear- and javelin heads, helmets and mail. From high on the wall, Castus could see the white placards set up in the street, the bold red letters proclaiming the penalty of death for anyone failing to do their duty to Maximian Augustus.

In truth, Castus knew that this was about more than just Maximian's ambitions for rule. Maximian was like an actor, an old and worn-out actor, dragged back onto the stage to play his most famous role once more. He had been a capable military leader once, a ferocious and determined commander, a true emperor. Perhaps he could be again, but there were others around him who drove events now. Gorgonius, Scorpianus. Perhaps, behind them, Maxentius. It did not matter: men would die on both sides, and never know why.

He had seen Maximian at the council that morning, along with the members of his new imperial consistorium. They had all gathered in the apsed dining hall of the grand mansion on the hillside above the theatre, which Maximian had taken over as his palace. The house was the finest in the city, and had formerly belonged to Plotius Diadumenus, the curator of Massilia and head of the council. Diadumenus did not appear to mind being evicted; he had been promoted to governor of the Viennensis diocese for his pains. Now he stood with the rest of the assembled dignitaries – the military chiefs Scorpianus and Gaudentius, Macrobius the new Master of the Records, the eunuch Gorgonius, now promoted to Superintendent of the Sacred Bedchamber. . .

Castus had stood at the side of the imperial podium, scanning the faces of these men, the closest supporters of the new emperor. If they were anxious, they were careful not to let it show. There were nearly a score of new Protectores too, former centurions of the Praetorians and the Spanish legions, keeping a close and forbidding watch over the members of the assembly. Among their number, Castus recognised his old adversary Urbicus. The scarred veteran met his stare and held it for a moment, sneering with open contempt.

Maximian himself had sat, immobile and silent, on his throne of state while Scorpianus read in his iron voice the proclamations of the day. News had arrived by fast ship from Carthage: the troops of Maxentius had crushed the rebellion in Africa and executed the rebel usurper Domitius Alexander. Now Maxentius would be free to send men and supplies to support his father in Massilia. Cheers and renewed acclamations echoed off the marble walls, but Castus thought only of Sabina. Her husband had been one of Alexander's officials: what had become of him? Did she already know?

There had been other news, but it had not been proclaimed to the council. Instead it had filtered through the city, passed between the soldiers and the civilians. Castus heard it from Brinno. Nearly half the troops ordered to march from Arelate to join Maximian in Massilia had failed to arrive. At first it seemed they had mistaken their route, but the truth soon became clear. Led by their centurions, they had torn the images of Maximian from their standards and diverted their march to Aquae Sextiae, either to keep out of the conflict or turn themselves over to Constantine. Most of the deserters were from the Rhine legion detachments, eager not to have to fight their own comrades. But some had been men from the Spanish legions. The news had run through the city and the palace like a slow current, mixing anxious dread and hopeful possibility. Anything could happen; nothing was certain.

Pacing on down the rampart walkway towards the Rome Gate, Castus stared out once more at the activity beyond the walls. Gangs of men were dragging carts of rubble and debris from the demolished buildings back towards the fortifications, and building a new wall just outside the line of the ditches. It was rough work, no more than a straggling mound of stone, but it would further impede anyone trying to bring up ladders or siege towers to the ramparts.

Castus looked up at the hazy horizon. Somewhere out there was Constantine and his army, getting closer with every passing day. Then another sound reached him, a cry of laughter from among the buildings on the city side of the wall. Stepping across the walkway, Castus looked down into a dirty shadowed yard between the clustered houses and workshops. Children were playing there, boys and girls in ragged tunics running back and forth. They had built their own little wall across the yard, a low pile of stones and broken rubble, and separated into two opposing gangs. Waving sticks, they called out to each other in thin high voices: 'I'm Constantine! I'm Maximian! I'm the true emperor!'

Castus smiled to himself. Then he stepped away from the edge of the wall, in case one of the Praetorians approached and heard what the children were saying – could they be punished for it? But his smile remained as he walked on down the steps towards the gate.

That's all we are, he thought to himself. *Children playing at war.*

Until the killing begins.

Passing back through the city as evening fell, the two Praetorians still dogging his steps, Castus could read the strain of the approaching siege on every face. The broad main street that followed the curve of the harbour between the gates and the agora was still crowded; several of the shops and emporia on either side were still open for business, but many more had heavy wooden shutters firmly bolted across their doors. The majority of the crowd were soldiers, and the few civilians had a harried, uncertain look. From the narrow alleys to the left the sounds of boisterous laughter came from the cheaper taverns and drinking shops along the harbour wall and the dockside. The troops were enjoying their new billets, even if most of them did not know whether the citizens of Massilia were friends or enemies.

As he walked, scanning his surroundings carefully but appearing unconcerned, Castus noticed a small boy weaving along the street to his right, keeping parallel with him. There were plenty of street children in Massilia, just as in every other town and city of the empire, but this boy appeared to have more of a purpose, and was clearly following Castus in particular. Slowing his steps, Castus veered to the right, pretending an interest in the open doors of a silversmith's shop. He glanced at the boy, who nodded to him and sidled closer. The two Praetorians were still strolling in the middle of the street.

'Somebody wants to talk to you,' the boy said, in a tight whisper. Clearly he had been paid as a messenger.

Castus gave him a shrug. 'Who?'

The boy was keeping his eyes on the two soldiers, not looking at Castus at all. 'Somebody who sees better in the dark. That's what he said.'

Castus walked on a few steps, the boy keeping pace with him.

'Wait for me on the corner over there, by the bakery,' he said from the corner of his mouth. When he looked again the boy was gone.

The two Praetorians had noticed Castus slowing down; now he walked back to join them in the middle of the street. He knew their names – Glyco and Ursus – but found it hard to tell them apart. Both were squat, muscular, dull-eyed men.

'I have to go somewhere,' he told them.

They stared back at him, impassive. 'Then we're coming with you,' Glyco said. 'That's our orders.'

Castus feigned a smile, and tried to look crafty. 'I'm going to find a woman,' he said. 'You planning to follow me there too?'

The two soldiers glanced at each other, blank-faced.

Castus reached into his belt pouch and brought out a pair of silver pieces. 'Here,' he said, 'you've done well for the day. Why not go and find something for yourselves?'

Both men frowned heavily, contemplating.

'I suppose that sounds right,' Ursus said.

'We could do that,' said Glyco.

The coins vanished into their fists, and the two soldiers marched off together leaving Castus in the middle of the street.

He waited a moment, watching them, then cut across the street to the bakery. It was open at the front, with a selection of half-stale loaves and savoury pastries set out on a table. A crowd of soldiers and civilians gathered on the corner, and it was easy for Castus to slip between them. He had taken to wearing an old military cloak while he was away from the emperor's household, instead of his distinctive white one, and it allowed him to blend easily into the throng. The boy was waiting at the mouth of the alley at the far side; he beckoned quickly, then turned and set off down the alley towards the docks.

Castus had barely considered what the notary might want with him. He had not spoken to the man since the night he and Brinno had escaped from the cells, although he had seen him often enough hanging around the margins of the emperor's retinue. But he remembered all too well what had happened the last time he had followed one of Nigrinus's schemes. As he marched after the boy, he eased the sword slightly from his scabbard and kept his hand upon the pommel.

The alley was narrow and stank of fish and decaying rubbish. Stepping to either side of the gutter that ran down the middle, Castus turned the corner at the bottom and saw the boy dodging out through one of the low arches in the harbour wall. Three bored soldiers on guard, but they weren't keeping a close watch on anyone leaving, and gave Castus only the slightest scrutiny as he passed them.

Beyond the arch the street led between the crumbling brickwork of a pair of warehouses built against the wall, then out onto the open quayside. For a moment Castus paused to look across the water at the mass of anchored shipping in the harbour, the masts and rigging black and spidery against the evening sky. Then he glanced to his right and saw the boy waving to him from along the quayside. The warehouses here were fronted by wine shops and eating houses, sailors and off-duty soldiers crowding the benches outside. The cobbles were slick and greasy underfoot.

Castus followed the boy up the quay and saw him stop

before the open front of one of the taverns towards the end of the row. A man stepped out onto the quay, glanced at Castus and then tossed a coin; the boy caught it and darted away. It was Flaccianus, Castus realised as he approached. And, stepping from the tavern behind him, the hulking bodyguard Glaucus.

For a moment Castus stood still, his palm closing around the hilt of the sword beneath his cloak. Flaccianus gave him a quick nod and a smile, jerked his thumb towards the interior of the tavern, then turned and moved away down the quay with his bodyguard swaggering after him.

Castus took a long deep breath, his senses alert for danger. The tavern looked innocuous: to the side of the entrance was a smoking griddle, strips of fish blackening over the glowing charcoal. The word 'TRITON' was painted on the cracked plaster above the wide doorway, and a crude black and white mosaic covering the threshold showed a plump sea god cramming his mouth with fish. Castus moved closer, into the spit and smoke of the grill, and stared into the dark throat of the tavern. There were figures hunched over tables in the gloom. A last quick glance up and down the quayside, and Castus stepped inside.

Once his eyes had adjusted he found Nigrinus quickly enough; he was only man sitting by himself, at a small round table in a booth off the main room. On the table was a jug of wine, three clay cups and a wooden platter of food.

'Grilled squid,' the notary said, gesturing to the platter as Castus sat down. 'Try some. They cook it with a lot of spice here. Flaccianus did not care for it.'

'I don't care much for him,' Castus said. 'Or his friends.'

'Ah, yes,' Nigrinus said. 'Your last meeting with them was rather unfortunate. We must aim to avoid any further such misunderstandings.'

Castus tightened his jaw and exhaled slowly through his nose. *No*, he thought, *I won't forgive you that easily. I won't forgive you at all*. He poured himself a cup of wine, concentrating on keeping his hand steady and not letting his anger show.

'You wanted me for something?' he said.

'I do,' the notary replied. The casual tone had drained from his voice now. When Castus glanced up he saw that the man's face, usually so bland and inscrutable, was lined and hollowed by fatigue. He felt a pang of satisfaction, although he knew it was not a good sign.

'You've been surveying the walls, the defences,' Nigrinus said quietly. Castus nodded. No surprise that the notary had been informed of his activities. 'What do you think?' Nigrinus asked. 'Would they stand a siege?'

Castus sipped the thin sour wine, then peered around the room behind him. Darkness cloaked them, and the noise of the men talking around the fish-grill covered their conversation. Nobody was close enough to hear what they were saying.

'Probably,' he said. 'The walls are sound, the gates too. There are men enough to man the ramparts. There are no engines, no ballistae, but Constantine doesn't have any either.'

Nigrinus nodded. 'And the troops, do they seem loyal to. . . *our friend*?'

'Hard to say. They've been paid, they've got good billets, and they're in a strong position. No reason they shouldn't hold it. I hear Constantine's men are already on half-rations.'

'Naturally, I hear the same,' Nigrinus said with a creased grimace. 'I'm not interested in what you've *heard*, soldier. I want to know what you've *seen*. Could the city be taken by assault?'

'Of course it could,' Castus told him, refusing to rise to the goad. 'But it would be hard. Far better to blockade the place and wait for treachery from within.'

Nigrinus narrowed his lips, opened his mouth and closed it again. His thinking face, Castus guessed. He felt a knot of irritation twist in his gut.

'What are you planning?' he hissed, leaning closer over the table. 'Tell me now. . . If you want me to kill him. . .'

'No!' the notary exclaimed, raising a finger. 'Nothing like that! And you must restrain your barbarian friend too. . . No, if anything of that sort occurred it would seem an act of private revenge, or the deed of a madman. Only the rightful emperor can judge, only he can pass sentence. This must be *seen* to happen, do you understand?'

Oh yes, Castus thought as he sat back from the table. He understood very well what the notary was saying. He had the brief sickening intuition that this too had been planned, this too was part of the game.

'Then what?' he said. 'We just wait?'

'Not for too long. The enemy has agents in Constantine's camp. If they sense it could be accomplished, they will murder him. Then Maximian will be the only man with imperial authority. . .'

'Infernal gods,' Castus said under his breath. 'You *know* this?'

'I believe it. Retreating this far south was not entirely accidental. Constantine is far from his base, far from the bulk of his army and the provinces most loyal to him. Here we are closer to Italy, and to Maxentius. . . If the emperor was struck down by somebody close to him. . .'

'But it was you who warned him. You sent him the message, and that was how he was able to march south so soon.'

'Not I,' the notary said. 'Since I left Treveris I've had no contact with the imperial staff. I confess I have no idea how Constantine managed to act so quickly. Perhaps indeed the gods send him messages in dreams. . . But he is in danger here all the same.'

Castus nodded. 'Then whatever we do has to happen soon,' he said.

'I've been working, these past days,' the notary said. 'Probing. Trying to determine who among the usurper's people is weakest, who might betray him. So far I have discovered little. But when I do – and be certain I will – then I may need you to act. Are you ready?'

'Always.' A thought struck Castus. He glanced around the smoky tavern again, then looked back at the notary. 'What about the emperor's wife, Fausta? Is she loyal to her father?'

He caught Nigrinus's brief flicker of a smile. 'Perhaps you might know more about that than I?' the notary said. For the first time he appeared genuinely amused.

'That was you, then, last autumn? Your plan?'

'Oh, come!' Nigrinus said, feigning an expression of pique. 'Surely you don't think I could have arranged anything as crude, as. . . sordid? Why would I?'

'But you knew about it.'

'I discovered traces of it, afterwards. I believe Gorgonius was behind it. You may kill him, by all means, if you get a chance. As for the nobilissima femina: she is a woman, and young. Barely more than a child. I doubt she has wits enough to rebel against her father. And if she did, what could she accomplish?'

Maybe so, Castus thought. A sense of hopeless despair rose through him. Truly they were all at the mercy of the gods. He drank more wine.

'The most important thing, for now, is that you hold yourself in readiness, and resist the urge to make any rash attempts of your own,' the notary said. 'Things are most delicately balanced. Some clumsy gesture could do more harm than good. . .'

Castus glanced at him quickly over the rim of his cup. The notary seemed almost to be talking in his sleep, or to himself.

'Excuse me a moment,' Nigrinus said, rubbing the heel of his palm across his eyes. 'I will not be long.'

He got up, circling the table, and paced quickly through a door at the back of the room. Castus remained seated, sipping wine, but turned his body so he could watch both doors. Laughter came from the crowd around the griddle, and beyond them Castus could see the deep blue of evening darkening into night. He ate a little of the grilled squid on the platter. Then he got up and followed Nigrinus.

The doorway led to a short narrow passage, then a second door into an open yard. There was a harsh briny stink of rotting rubbish and old fish. Castus stood braced in the doorway, staring around the yard. Two men suddenly lurched through a low opening to the right. Their filthy leather aprons and grey tunics marked them out as municipal slaves, and they were lugging stained wooden buckets.

'Mind yourself, citizen,' one of them said, and Castus stepped back as the smell of stewing urine hit him. The opening led to the tavern lavatory, and the slaves were collecting the urine for the city fulleries. They stumbled out though a gate in the far wall of the yard, and Castus saw them tipping the brimming buckets into a tub in the alley beyond. Then they lifted the tub on poles between them and moved away down the lane out of sight.

Stepping to the right, Castus glanced into the lavatory. Flies whirled up from the wooden toilet holes. Back into the yard, he leaned from the rear gate and looked in both directions along the alley. But Nigrinus was gone.

* * *

The night was warm, and the air felt greasy with the breath of the sea as Castus passed back through the gate in the harbour wall and up the narrow alleys to the main street of Massilia. Still plenty of people about, mainly soldiers and dock labourers who had been working on the fortifications all day and were now enjoying their few hours of leisure; raucous laughter came from the bars on the alley corners, and from a distant side street came the noise of an argument breaking into violence. But still no sign of Nigrinus. Castus scanned the passing faces, but the notary seemed to have vanished. Let him go, he thought. The man had delivered his message, and there was nothing more to say.

As he walked, Castus thought over the conversation that had just passed. However much he detested Nigrinus, he had been relying on the notary having some scheme or devious plan to turns events around. Quite clearly he did not, or not yet at least. Perhaps his probing and plotting would get a result in time, but time, from what he had said, was in short supply.

Along the street to the west the crowds thinned, and by the time Castus emerged into the agora the city around him seemed almost deserted. The broad open expanse of paving was empty in the yellow moonlight, only a few figures moving under the colonnades. Massilia had been a Greek city once, and still preserved the Greek names of her civic spaces, but the agora resembled the *fora* of any number of Roman provincial towns. Castus crossed quickly, heading for the stepped path that led up from the back of the curia, the meeting hall of the city council, and around the side of the theatre to the large house that Maximian was using as his palace. As he moved from the darkness of the agora colonnade into the narrow cobbled street at the side of the curia, he paused suddenly and stared into the shadows ahead.

For a moment he wondered what he was looking at, but then the low shape hunched at the side of the street shifted and Castus saw that it was a small group of people, all of them in dark cloaks, sitting or kneeling at the base of the curia wall. They might have been beggars, or homeless refugees from the countryside, but all of them seemed to be facing inwards, towards the wall itself. The streets around him were almost silent, and Castus was sure that he could hear a muffled whispering coming from the group. He would need to pass them to reach the steps up to the palace; they did not appear threatening, but the whispering and the uncanniness of their huddling posture made him wary. He loosened the sword in his scabbard once more, then walked slowly towards them.

At the sound of his steps on the cobbles one of the figures sat up and turned to look at him. He got a brief glimpse of a face beneath the hood of a cloak: a girl, or a young woman. Somebody spoke, low and quick, and at once the strange gathering broke up. Castus stopped and waited, his hand on the hilt of his sword, as the five figures scrambled from their kneeling position against the wall and hurried up the street away from him without glancing back.

When they were out of sight he paced quickly across the street to the point where they had been crouching. Now he could see the low square opening in the stones of the wall: an airshaft, or perhaps a window into a chamber in the basement of the curia building. As he got closer and stooped down he saw the iron bars closing the opening. All around it the stone was scratched with words. Castus squinted, trying to make out the shapes of the letters in the dark and string together their meaning. It did not take him long.

DEATH TO THE HATERS OF THE GODS said one scrawl. *CHRISTIANS TO THE LIONS.*

As he glanced down at the barred window again, Castus saw a movement from the darkness inside. A face rose from the gloom, thin and hard as a mask, beneath the white curve of a bald head. The face stared back at him from a moment, then sank once more into the black shadow of the prison.

Oresius, Castus remembered. The priest of the Christians. And those huddled figures kneeling at the window, whispering to him: were they his followers? Castus suppressed a superstitious shudder. Why did Christians always seem drawn to dark places and secret rituals? But then he remembered the magical ceremony in the necropolis of Treveris. Christians were not the only people attracted by shadows.

Standing back from the wall and squaring his shoulders, he turned to continue on up the street towards the stepped path and the palace. Before he could move, he heard the sound of a shout echoing from the streets behind him, the clatter of hooves on cobbles. A rider was crossing the forum, heading for the theatre and the longer curving road up to the palace, and as he rode he was crying out to the citizens in the forum colonnades.

Castus ran the few paces back down the street towards the forum. By the time he reached the colonnade the rider had already gone, galloping hard towards the palace. But his words seemed to hang in the air; Castus had heard them clearly enough, and knew what they meant.

Constantine was here. His scouts had been sighted outside the walls.

The siege was about to begin.

CHAPTER XXII

The sun had not yet broken the eastern horizon when Castus threw open the shutters of his sleeping chamber on the upper floor of Maximian's palace. Leaning from the window, breathing in the cool air of the departing night, he looked down the slope over the pale curving wall of the theatre and saw the massed roofs of the city coming into definition, grey against deeper grey as the light grew. The slopes of the surrounding hills were still covered by sea mist, and the harbour was a vague expanse of white, with the masts and rigging of the anchored ships standing up from it like the stumps of a dead forest.

In the chamber behind him a slave was moving silently, setting out the basin of cold water and the platter of bread, cheese and onion. Stepping back from the window, Castus waved the slave away. He dipped his head over the basin, dashing water up into his face, then straightened again, gasping. Standing in the centre of the room, dressed only in his loincloth, he stretched his back and knitted his fingers at the nape of his neck, flexing the muscles of heavy shoulders. He breathed in deeply. The next few hours would be terrible; the next few days could be worse.

In the anteroom outside he dressed quickly: tunic, boots and breeches, then the padded linen vest and the cuirass of silvered scale armour. Brinno came from his own room, and the two Protectores checked the straps and lacing on each other's armour before putting on their belts. Neither spoke. Brinno wore an expression of sour and savage discomfort. Armed and equipped, helmets beneath their arms, they walked together down the steps and through the cool shadows of the courtyard behind the kitchens, then out onto the broad front portico of the palace.

The imperial retinue was already assembling. On the paved area between the portico and the upper wall of the theatre, fifty men of the horse guards stood beside their mounts. Along the portico were gathered the commanders of the military units and the ministers of state, all the members of the consistorium in their stiff court garments. Castus was surprised to see a group of women at the margin of the group: Fausta, dressed in a heavy cloak that looked like a shroud, and Sabina among the others at her back. He took up his position below the steps of the portico. Scorpianus, the Praetorian Prefect, marched from the house. To the east the sun was just breaking the horizon, washing the portico with golden light as a voice rang out from the doorway.

'Our Lord and Emperor Marcus Aurelius Valerius Maximianus, *Herculius, Pius, Felix*, Unconquered Augustus!'

Maximian walked from the house into the blaze of sunlight, and the assembly sank to their knees before him, their acclamations blending into a vast rush of sound.

'*Maximianus Augustus! Eternal Augustus! The gods preserve you for us! Your salvation is our salvation!*'

When Castus looked up he saw the emperor standing above him. No longer did Maximian resemble a wine-sodden old actor, no more a harried and desperate figure. Now, with the sunlight gleaming off his gilded breastplate and greaves, his golden helmet in the form of an eagle, crested with tall feathers, his gold-embroidered purple cape and tunic, he looked entirely like an emperor.

Descending the steps slowly, with ponderous gravity, Maximian paced between the ranks of the horse guard. A four-wheeled open carriage, decked with laurels and drawn by six white horses, was waiting for him at the top of the road that curved down to the forum. Maximian climbed aboard, standing stiffly, not making the slightest gesture to acknowledge the salutes and cries of his people. Then the entourage formed up into a column, the horses moved forward, and the emperor began his progress through the city.

Below the theatre the city was still in shadow, but the eaves of the houses and the pediments of the larger buildings around the agora blazed gold above the procession as it turned into the wide main street. Castus, marching beside the emperor's carriage, saw that few civilians were showing themselves. Except for the knots of soldiers at the intersections, grey-faced, red-eyed and unshaven, the city seemed deserted by its citizens. The procession moved in near silence along the main street, Maximian standing motionless on the carriage, one hand resting on his sword hilt, gazing ahead of him.

At last the arches of the Rome Gate rose before them. The carriage drew to a halt and the emperor climbed down, waiting a moment for his guards and ministers to form around him, then throwing back his cloak and striding to the entranceway and the steps that led up to the ramparts. Castus followed the throng as they clattered up the narrow stairway. He was feeling almost breathless; the morning was already growing hot, and the air felt still and clammy as a warm damp rag pressed against his face.

The stairs turned, then climbed again and brought them out into the open sunlight of the walkway above the gates as the

309

horns blared from the towers on either side. Blinking, Castus shuffled between the other men, trying to take up a position far to the rear of the group. He noticed Scorpianus peering at him. The Praetorian Prefect gave a quick smile, shook his head, and gestured for Castus to move forward and join the men flanking the emperor. Sallustius moved aside to give him room.

Low sun almost eclipsed the landscape outside the gates. In the still air the purple banners hung limp from their poles.

At first Castus could see only the dust cloud raised by the approaching riders, a haze of gold as it rose into the rays of the sun. Then, as he stared, he made out the small group of horsemen. Unlike the men gathered above the gate, none of them wore armour; they were dressed quite deliberately in civilian garb, the clothing of peace. They drew nearer, and Castus recognised Probinus, Constantine's prefect, riding in the lead. And in the small group behind him rode Constantine himself, dressed in a white tunic and purple cloak. Castus felt a surge of sickening dizziness. In the bright light of day he was exposed before the eyes of the rightful emperor. His treachery was clear for all to see. Stand straight, he told himself. Head up, chest out. Helmet beneath one arm, thumb hooked in his belt. There was no point in trying to hide now.

The group around Constantine halted and Probinus rode on alone. As the dust cloud faded, Castus could see the troops gathered further along the road. Cavalry guards, their spears winking in the dawn sun. Beyond them, on the sloping ground so recently cleared of olive groves, the infantry were assembled, blocks of men appearing from the haze, lines of shields emerging from grey shadow. Squinting, Castus tried to estimate their number. Six thousand, maybe? They outnumbered the defenders, but not by so much. He tried to pick out the individual shields, identify the legions. He saw the black shields of I Minervia, the bright green of XXII Primigenia. No sign of VI Victrix's winged victory emblem, and Castus was glad of that. The thought of Diogenes, Modestus and Rogatianus throwing themselves into the assault on the city was painful.

Glancing to one side and then the other, Castus saw Maximian's soldiers gathered at the ramparts of the walls and towers, their armour shining and their banners bright. They crowded the battlements, formidable in number.

Probinus had approached to within bowshot of the walls, and drawn to a halt.

'Maximian!' he cried, raising himself in the saddle. 'In the name of the emperor Constantine Augustus I call on you to open the gates of this city and surrender yourself to the Sacred Clemency!'

All eyes turned, just briefly, to Maximian. The golden figure remained motionless, only the feathers of his helmet crest stirring slightly.

'Maximian!' the prefect called out again. 'I beg you, cease this impious rebellion! Spare the lives of your soldiers and supporters. . . Spare this city from the violence of assault! In the name of the emperor I promise that you and your people will be treated with respect and forgiveness!'

'*Emperor?*' Maximian shouted. His voice boomed out from the walls. 'There is no emperor here but me! I am supreme ruler, and eternal Augustus. I, who stood beside the mighty Diocletian at the head of the Roman state!'

'In the name of Constantine Augustus,' the prefect called out as his horse champed and tossed its mane, 'I beg you to reconsider your actions. This rebellion is unbecoming to you, who have won such glory in the past! You have been honoured and given wealth and high status – what more do you desire? You have been seduced by the lying words of traitors. . .' He broke off, raising his hand to his face as if he were wiping away tears.

'Who talks to me of treachery?' Maximian cried. 'You, Probinus? I raised you myself, promoted you – and this is your gratitude? Half the men standing with me now gave their oath to Constantine! Some of his most loyal officers, even his Protectores. All have now returned to their true allegiance!'

Castus winced at the rush of shame twisting through him. When he opened his eyes, Probinus was staring directly at him. Worse, the emperor Constantine was staring up at him as well. It was a trick of the light, he thought. . . but, no, that was why they had been brought here, he and Brinno and Sallustius. Maximian wanted everyone to see that he had broken the oaths of Constantine's own closest bodyguards.

Maximian stepped up onto the wall, standing between the merlons of the rampart so every man in the opposing army could see him clearly. A single archer, Castus thought, a single ballista and all of this could end now. . .

'If Constantine wants to talk to me he can come and do it!' Maximian shouted, raising his fist and jutting his black beard. 'Let him prostrate himself in the dust and beg for my forgiveness! He calls himself an emperor? He dares to oppose me? He is *not even a man*!'

Probinus stared up at the golden figure poised above him. The purple banners stirred slightly, wrapping around their poles.

'Two years,' Maximian shouted, loud enough that every man on the wall could hear him, loud enough that his voice would carry to the front ranks of the opposing army. 'Two years since that man married my daughter! And she is *still a virgin*!'

A sound of several thousand men drawing breath at once. Castus swallowed hard, feeling his guts clench. A yelp of laughter came from one of the soldiers on the ramparts.

'How can he be an emperor,' Maximian called, jutting out his finger to point at his son-in-law, 'if he cannot even fuck his own wife like a man?'

Probinus was already turning his horse. The men around Constantine were beginning to turn as well, but the emperor himself remained still, staring up at the figure standing on the ramparts. His face looked hard and white with fury. Then he tugged sharply on the reins and galloped back towards his own lines. The mocking jeers of Maximian's soldiers followed him as he retreated.

'Well,' Sallustius muttered under his breath, 'that went excellently!'

Another dawn. Three days and three nights had passed since the conference at the gate, and the noose had steadily tightened around the city of Massilia. Now, Castus knew, they would see the first assault against the walls. Standing at the parapet of the third tower north of the Rome Gate, he stared eastwards at the dark horizon. The sky above was washed with delicate colour, and the morning star was clear and bright. Lucifer, the light-bringer, herald of the sun.

What am I doing here? He had asked himself that too many times. What trick of fate had led him to be standing on the wrong side of the coming battle? Often he had contemplated making an escape from the city – it would have been easy enough to slip from the palace by night, or to scramble down from the wall and make a run across the no man's land between the lines. But he had hung back, hoping somehow that he might find a way to make a difference. Nothing had presented itself, and now the dawn of the assault had come.

Officially he was in command of this section of wall. Brinno

313

had been stationed further to the north-west, near the Valley Gate. In truth, neither had any real authority; behind Castus on the roof of the tower were his two Praetorian minders, Glyco and Ursus, wrapped in their cloaks, stamping away the chill of morning. He was still under suspicion, his loyalties in doubt. The constant presence of the two soldiers had become familiar to Castus now, but he knew that they were growing restless in their duty. The prospect of an impending fight did not seem to excite them either.

'They'll come today, you think?' Glyco said.

'Yes,' Castus told him. 'They'll come soon, while the sun's still low in our faces. Spoil the aim of the archers.'

And now the sun appeared, sudden on the horizon like a burning coal upon the black hills. A few moments more, and the crests of the wall ramparts were lit with orange light. Castus felt the warmth on his face.

'*Unconquered Sun*,' he muttered, bowing his head and touching his brow in salute. '*Lord of Daybreak, your light between us and evil. . .*'

Despite his misgivings, he felt the gathering energy in his blood, the prospect of battle. Already he could hear the sound of the trumpets.

Squinting into the low glare, Castus made out the troops beginning to muster on the dusty denuded hillside on the far side of valley. Light caught their helmets and speartips, and the glitter of their mail; their banners stirred in the warm breeze. They were forming up in attack columns; too distant for Castus to accurately guess their numbers, but it was clear that this would be the main assault. Further to the left the walls stood on a slope, the ground falling away more steeply into the valley. But the Rome Gate faced a level strip of ground where the valley opened towards the silted-up inlet of an old dock

314

basin just outside the walls. Once across that, the attackers could either assault the gate itself or move northwards along the line of the wall and find enough level ground to prop their ladders below the rampart. The ditch, and the low rubble wall outside it, would slow them, but it looked a feeble enough defence from where Castus was standing.

Dust rose as the attack columns moved forward and halted once more to dress their lines. He heard the massed shouts drifting across the valley, '*Ready. . . Ready. . . READY!*' The traditional chorus, so familiar to him. He would have given anything to have been among their number now.

'Let's get down there,' he said, motioning to the two Praetorians, then he dropped through the trapdoor into the chamber below. A section of Mauretanian archers were stationed here, under the command of an optio from the Seventh Legion. All of them straightened up as Castus came down the ladder, giving their salutes.

'Dominus!' the optio said, his Latin thick with the accent of Spain. 'Looks like they're really coming this time!'

Castus could only nod. Three slot windows faced out over the valley, and two archers stood ready at each one. Beside each man lay a thick sheaf of arrows. Castus shifted one of the archers aside and peered out trough the slot. The sun was higher now, the dust had settled, and he could see the assault parties forming into testudo, their shields locked around them. At the heart of each block were the men carrying the scaling ladders; no doubt behind them were the archers and slingers who would try and drive the defenders back from the ramparts.

From the open door of the chamber, Castus looked down the short flight of steps to the rampart walkway. All the way to the Rome Gate men stood ready, their armour burning in the sunlight. Every few paces there were heavy baskets filled with stones and rubble gathered from the demolished buildings outside the walls. A crude weapon, but effective. Braced in the doorway, Castus surveyed the defenders. Most of the men came from VII Gemina Maximiana, one of the two Spanish legions, with a few auxilia and Praetorians among them. Some had the smooth olive complexions of recent recruits; others were scarred and sunburnt veterans of the Mauretanian war. But they looked capable, soldierly. For one guilty moment Castus felt glad that he was among the defenders and not in the assault parties who would have to face them.

Strangely, several of the Spanish soldiers were wearing old-style cuirasses of segmented plate armour. Castus had seen a few rusting sets in a storeroom in one of the fortresses on the Danube years before, but as far as he knew all the other legions of Rome had abandoned the armour back in the days of their grandfathers. It gave the men of the Seventh an antique appearance, like figures from the frieze of a triumphal arch come to life.

Now a stir ran through the defenders on the rampart, and when he looked to his left Castus saw the assault columns break into motion, four of them moving towards the Rome Gate and the section of wall to the north of it. They came on slow and steady, keeping to their rigid testudo formations. Their discipline was impressive. As they marched they kicked up plumes of dust, which rose into the low sun and cloaked the advance in a golden fog. Along the walls, archers strung their bows and slingers began to whip their slings in low circles.

A cry came from somewhere near the gate, picked up and echoed all along the wall. The defenders threw up their arms, raising spears and javelins, and let out a great shout.

'*Maximianus Augustus! Eternal Emperor!*'

Three times they cried, then every man battered his shield rim and the noise reverberated across the valley towards the advancing enemy.

Leaning from the door of the tower, Castus stared at the columns as they approached the wall. His throat was tight, and his breath came in short stabs. Sweat was rolling down his back. He realised that he was digging his fingertips into the stone of the wall beside him. For the first time he allowed himself to wonder what he would do if the attackers reached the ramparts. He would fight – he would have to, or die in the melee. But those advancing men were his brothers, his comrades. He could see their shields now: I Flavia Gallicana in the lead. Some of those men would have fought at his side in the riverbank battle against the Bructeri. Behind them came XXII Primigenia and I Minervia. All legions he knew, men he knew.

And yet, when he glanced along the wall he was willing the archers to watch their aim, look for their marks, make every arrow count. Without even thinking, he had drawn his sword. The logic of battle was carrying him now, and his blood was hot and quick with anticipation.

The advancing columns had passed the brick heaps that marked effective archery range. Down on the rampart, a centurion of the Seventh raised his stick, then let it fall. At once bows bent all along the wall, and the slingers began to whirl their slings higher. A heartbeat, held in tension, and the first volley was released.

Arrows and shot flickered from the rampart; some fell short, but most struck the advancing shield-blocks with a loud percussive thud and rattle. The assault columns let out a great roar, amplified under the roofs of shields, and broke into a charge, trying to close the gap to the walls. Another volley of arrows – now each charging testudo bristled with black shafts. Castus was holding his breath, wide-eyed.

An arrow flicked past his face and hit the tower wall, striking sparks off the stone. Down on the rampart below him two men dropped to the walkway, struck down by slingshot. Moving up behind the assault columns, the opposing archers and slingers had begun to return the missile barrage. Edging up from his crouch, Castus heard the strum of bows from the tower chamber behind him. Then a scream, echoing from the doorway; he glanced back and saw one of the Mauretanian archers fall sprawling with an arrow in his neck. Blood pulsed from the wound, and his heels battered the flagstone floor.

Outside, the sudden charge of the assault columns had carried them across the open ground and almost up to the fortifications. Now they had to negotiate the low rubble wall and the deep ditch. Castus saw the front rank of the leading column falter as one of their men was hit and went down in the dust. The shields broke apart, men stumbling out of formation and cascading down the outer slope of the ditch. At once arrows were flicking between them as hundreds of archers on the rampart aimed down into the shattered testudo. Another man fell, then half a dozen in a heartbeat. The rest spilled forward, hefting their ladders overhead as they swarmed down into the gulley of the ditch and piled up towards the wall, yelling.

A party of archers had climbed to the tower rampart and were shooting down directly into the mass of the attackers. Castus leaned from the doorway again and looked up, just as one of them was struck by a slingshot and toppled forward over the wall. The body fell, a brief dark blur trailing red.

'Aim for the enemy archers and slingers!' Castus yelled into the chamber behind him. 'The ladder-men are below the wall, you can't hit them – aim for the archers and slingers!'

He saw Glyco staring back at him, a smudge of blood across his forehead.

The assault columns had broken formation now, the attackers clambering up out of the ditch in groups of three or four, holding their shields above their heads. Several of those down at the Rome Gate had pickaxes and crowbars, while others carried burning fire-pots to try and burn the gates. Javelins darted at them from the ramparts.

Already the first of the ladders was rising towards the wall close to where Castus was standing, a knot of men below sheltering their comrades with their shields as they wrestled the wooden lattice up into position. Two more ladders swayed up only a score of paces away. Hardly had they touched the stones when the first of the attackers was scrambling up the rungs with his shield above his head. Up on the rampart walk, the defenders were dragging one of the heavy baskets of stones and rubble and lifting it to the parapet.

Castus stared in grim fascination as the basket was manoeuvred across the ledge of the wall and began to tip. The men below were climbing fast, but not fast enough. A rush and a crash, and the weight of rubble cascaded down, knocking them screaming from the toppling ladder in a torrent of dust.

Another ladder cracked into position against the wall, and immediately it was creaking under the weight of armoured men. The defenders on the walkway bunched and crouched; this time they were lifting a single great stone between them. It looked to Castus like a column drum. Pulling his helmet laces tighter, he leaned out over the parapet, gazing down at the men hauling themselves with savage determination up the ladder. Above them the great stone was in position, the defenders shunting it across the ledge of the wall until it tilted and fell.

319

The plunging stone struck the leading man, crushing his skull and bursting his torso, then crashed straight down through the rungs of the ladder, shattering it. Broken bodies fell into the wreckage, clogging the ditch below.

Arrows jarred off the rampart parapet, and Castus pulled his head back quickly. The archers below the wall had learned to concentrate their shots towards the tops of the ladders, driving the defenders back and giving the climbers time to scale higher. All along the rampart walk there were bodies sprawled, writhing, limbs struck with arrows, heads broken by slingshot. There were six ladders against the wall now, and the climbers were pushing higher.

'Out the way,' somebody said, and a man shoved through the tower doorway. After him came the second Praetorian, Glyco.

'You just planning to *watch*, dominus?' Glyco said, glancing back at Castus with a disgusted sneer. Then he jogged down the steps to the walkway after Ursus. Castus drew a deep breath, wanting to shout after them. But what could he say? His perceptions seemed to have slowed, and everything around him shone with a bright glaze. The air was fogged with dust, whirling in the sunlight.

Something was happening on the wall, a strange pause that for a moment Castus could not understand. He leaned out again, and his breath caught.

The leading climbers had reached the tops of the ladders, but they were still a good six feet below the parapet. The ladders were too short. Castus stared, incredulous. Could they really have miscalculated the height of the walls so badly? The men at the top of each ladder were trapped by those coming up behind them, and already the defenders on the ramparts had regained the offensive, stretching out over the walls to fling stones and javelins directly down into their faces. Bodies began falling. One of the ladders tipped sideways, men cascading off it with wild screams.

Still the climbers pushed upwards. The men at the top were struggling onto the shoulders of their comrades below and stretching their hands up to try and grab at the stone parapet. Castus could see their faces, straining and sweat-drenched. He could hear them crying out, their voices maddened, cracking. Another ladder toppled, leaving a single man still dangling on the parapet until the defenders above speared him and he fell.

Down below, the base of the wall was boiling with men, the injured and dead tumbled together, shields discarded in the wreckage of ladders, blood flowing in streams down the dusty slope. Up above, one heaving knot of men had managed to struggle up from their ladder and scramble onto the wall parapet. A few desperate moments of combat on the walkway, push of spears and flicker of blades. Castus saw Glyco reeling back, clutching his bloodied face. One of the attackers stood up on the wall, raising his sword as if in triumph; the next moment a javelin struck him between the ribs and he toppled stiffly backwards, his mouth open in a silent scream.

Then it was over. The last of the ladder parties had been battered away from the parapet, and the attackers that remained alive were falling back from the wall, crouched beneath their raised shields.

Castus heard the horns blowing from the far slope of the valley. It was the recall; the attack had failed. The shattered remnants of the assault columns were scattering back down the slope at the run, many of them dragging their injured comrades between them. For a few long moments there was a strange stillness and quiet. Leaning against the wall parapet, dry-mouthed and dazed, Castus stared into the sunlit dust cloud at Constantine's retreating soldiers. His fists were clenched, knuckles grinding against the stone, and his heart was beating fast.

Then the first cheers came from the defenders down at the Rome Gate, and in moments the ramparts were ringing with the cries of victory.

CHAPTER XXIII

'Visitor for you, dominus,' the slave said, and motioned towards the door of the bedchamber.

Castus paused only briefly to frown and clear his throat. 'Bring water,' he told the slave. Whoever this visitor was, they could wait.

Removing his belts, he ripped open the lacing of his armour and dragged the heavy scale cuirass from his body. His tunic was drenched with sweat and clinging to his torso. His skin and hair were caked with dust, and his throat was dry. He had eaten nothing since dawn, and drunk only a few cups of stale water.

All day he had been on the ramparts, enduring the heat of the sun and the slaughterhouse stink of clotting blood from the mangled corpses piled at the base of the wall, waiting for a second assault that had never come. At noon Constantine's troops had pulled back to their encampment on the hill, but still the defenders on the city wall had remained in their positions as their dead and wounded were removed, and the debris swept from the walkways. Only when the sun had begun to sink over the sea to the west had the order come to stand down.

Castus wondered whether Brinno had returned yet from his position near the Valley Gate. That section of wall had not been attacked, as far as he knew. He had a strong desire to drink wine.

The slave returned with a jug and basin. Stripping off his stinking tunic, Castus bent over the basin and plunged his face into the water. Then he tipped his head back and drank from the jug, swigging heavily. The feel of the water coursing down his body was blissful. Scrubbing a towel over his neck and shoulders, he picked up his scabbarded sword and went through into the bedchamber.

His visitor stood in the centre of the room with his back turned, as if he were studying the blank plaster of the far wall. Hearing Castus enter, he turned.

'What do you want, eunuch?' Castus said.

Serapion smiled, that same softly bland smile that Castus had come to distrust so much. Whose side was he on now?

'I come with a summons, once again,' Serapion said. 'Although I promise you that there will be no unpleasant surprises this time, for either of us.'

Castus flung the towel down on the narrow bed. He went to the trunk, found a clean tunic and put it on. 'No surprises?' he asked as he buckled his belt.

'No *unpleasant* ones, I said. Have you lost your two Praetorian shadows?'

'One of them got his face split open and the other caught an arrow through his wrist. So far nobody's suggested I find replacements.'

'Good. Then come.'

The eunuch stepped past Castus, keeping his distance, and paced silently out of the room. Castus paused only to sling the sword baldric over his shoulder before following.

The house that Maximian had commandeered as his palace had two wings on the upper storey, one above the kitchens and baths and the other, more spacious, above the private apartments. The two wings were connected only by a broad rear portico that looked out over the sea. Leading Castus from the anteroom outside the bedchamber, Serapion passed along a narrow corridor and out onto the portico. A cool salt breeze blew between the pillars, and the view was a wide expanse of perfect blue, sea and sky blending in the radiance of evening.

'I will leave you here,' the eunuch said, stepping aside and gesturing for Castus to continue along the portico. At the far end was a vestibule, with a marble bench set against the wall facing the sea. On the bench a woman sat with a deep blue shawl covering her head and shoulders.

Castus advanced cautiously down the portico. The vestibule at the end had no other entrances; it was a quiet and private place. He halted a few paces from the woman. Without looking up, she gestured to the bench beside her.

'Be seated,' she said.

He paused a moment, then took the last few steps and eased himself down beside her.

'Nobilissima,' he said quietly. She pushed the shawl back from her face and he saw the thick necklace of pearls at her throat, the hanging earrings of gold and lapis. Those deep-lidded eyes, giving nothing away. He was trying to breathe slowly, but his mind was whirling. He remembered the garden house of the Villa Herculis. Surely she did too – but did she remember him?

'The domina Domitia Sabina believes that you are to be trusted,' Fausta said.

'I'm glad of that.' His words sounded crude, almost a grunt.

'So – are you?' She turned her head to look at him for the first time, the earrings swinging. Her face was round and her lips full and petulant. Her eyes were cool, searching.

'That depends, nobilissima.' He had spoken more harshly than he intended, and saw her expression shift slightly as she registered the discourtesy.

'My apologies,' he said, but his voice still grated. 'I've just spent the day watching hundreds of my brother-soldiers being smashed to pulp in front of my eyes. I'm in no mood for subtlety.'

'I'm asking about your loyalties,' she said.

Castus sat back against the wall and stared out at the sea. Gulls wheeled and cried, dark against the evening sky. Why had he been brought here? It made no sense, unless. . . He decided to take the risk.

'My loyalties are to Constantine Augustus, and always have been,' he said. 'He's my emperor, for better or worse.'

He noticed her slight nod. She had turned to look at the sea again. Such a peaceful scene in the soft autumn light, Castus thought; nobody would imagine that a hard and bloody battle had raged all day not a mile from this place. He could see the low rocky islands off the harbour mouth, dark silhouettes in the sea. There were ships moving between them, a pair of single-decked galleys and a merchant vessel.

'Those are Constantine's ships,' Fausta said. 'He captured the islands this morning – did you know that?'

'No,' Castus replied, startled. Maximian had been careful to clear anything larger than a rowing skiff from the harbours of the Rhodanus.

'My husband sent riders east along the coast to Telo Martius and Forum Julii,' Fausta said. 'They returned with ships from those ports, and now they have the harbour blockaded.'

So Maximian could not leave, Castus thought. And his son Maxentius – if he ever did send aid or reinforcements – would have to fight his way in.

'I've had to play along with my father's plans,' Fausta went on. 'Or the plans of his advisors, I should say. Even if the performance was repugnant to me.'

'As have we all, nobilissima,' Castus said grimly. He wondered if she was referring to the night in the garden house too. The implication was hardly flattering.

'When I discovered what he intended, during our journey to Arelate, I immediately sent a message to my husband, warning him to march south as soon as possible.'

'You did?' So that was how Constantine had been able to move so quickly, Castus realised. Fausta had betrayed her own father.

'I wanted to stop this before it grew into something monstrous,' she said. 'But I was too late. However, here we are.'

'Here we are,' Castus repeated quietly. For a short while they sat in silence, and he wondered if she was waiting for him to speak.

'It seems we must choose sides,' she said. 'We wait for the gods to advise us, but they do not. So it's up to us. I have chosen my husband over my father and brother. Perhaps a selfish choice, impious, but I leave it for others to condemn me.'

Castus gazed at her as she spoke, marvelling at the calm assurance in her voice and manner. She was not yet seventeen years old; her face was still plump with adolescence: where had she gained this sense of poise? Already she understood power. And many people, Castus thought, had underestimated her. Himself included.

'I need your assistance,' she said. 'I have done all I can, but somehow this siege needs to end. You must find a way to surrender the city to my husband, as soon as possible.'

Before the traitor in Constantine's camp knifes him in his tent, Castus thought. Did Fausta know about that too?

'Surrender the city,' he said. 'You think it's that easy?'

'I don't know!' she exclaimed, and for the first time he saw a crack in her cool façade. 'But somebody must do something soon – start a mutiny, an uprising of the people, anything. . . You are the kind of man, I believe, that other men might follow. . .'

'Not to their deaths, domina,' Castus said.

'Then you must find men who are not afraid of death!'

She had half turned towards him on the bench as she spoke. Castus noticed that she was breathing quickly, and the colour had risen in her cheeks. Beneath her apparent calm she was in turmoil. He had a sudden vivid memory of the night in the garden house: the feel of her body naked beneath him, that drowning desire, and then the fear that had followed. His throat tightened, and without intending it he met her eye. Was she thinking of the same thing?

'You know,' she said quickly, turning back to stare at the sea, 'that the domina Sabina is a widow now?'

'I guessed she might be.' Castus looked down at his hands. His right knuckle was grazed and spotted with dried blood.

'Her husband was executed by my brother's troops in Africa,' Fausta went on, her tone deliberately light and airy, casual-sounding. 'In fact, her father had been arrested earlier for his rebel sympathies, and apparently he too has been put to death. Her mother died years ago, so now she is alone in the world, and has nothing.'

'Nothing?'

'Oh, she has some property in her own name, but it's in Rome, of course. My husband is her legal guardian now, her paterfamilias.' She paused for a moment, to let this information sink in. 'If you assist him in his victory,' she went on in that same lightly casual tone, 'he would certainly consider giving her to you.'

Castus stifled a snort of disbelief. '*Giving* her to me?' he said. 'For what?'

'For whatever you please,' Fausta said with a slight shrug. 'Marry her, or keep her as a whore.'

Staring away down the portico, Castus tried to remain still and not shift himself away from the girl beside him. How had she become such a strange and heartless creature? He waited for the shock of anger to pass.

'You don't care about people very much, do you?' he said slowly.

'People have never cared much about me.' She had pulled the shawl back to cover her face. He reminded himself that she was only a girl, barely more than a child. And she was well out of her depth here.

'I think a lot of people have cared about you, nobilissima,' Castus said. Just not in a very positive way, he thought.

She hunched forward, rounding her shoulders. A moment later he heard her sniff. Her shoulders were shaking slightly beneath the shawl.

'All my life,' she said, and he heard the tears in her voice, 'I have been treated as livestock. By my family. By those around me. I forget, sometimes, what it is to speak to a human being.'

Castus reached out, instinctively, then caught himself. *This is the emperor's wife. You have already dishonoured her.* Then she too reached out, clasping his thick fingers in both her hands. When she looked back at him he saw the wetness on her cheeks.

'That night at the villa,' she said, her voice choked. 'I knew it was you. Of course I remember. . . Just for a moment I pretended it was truly me that you wanted. Not her. I'd never been wanted like that, never. It was good to pretend. Shameful, but good. I forgive you for what you did. You must forgive me too.'

'Nobilissima,' Castus said, deeply uncomfortable, but moved. She tightened her grip on his hand. Her palms were soft and damp, her fingers stiff with rings.

'Will you help me?' she asked. 'If you do, my husband will honour you, I'm sure. But I would be grateful to you always.'

'I'll do what I can,' he said.

She released his hand, drawing a deep and shuddering breath. Castus stood up smartly, stepping away from her. The sky above the sea was glowing pink and gold now, the sun almost gone. He was about to make his salute and leave when a thought struck him.

'Back in Treveris,' he said. 'I saw you in the necropolis one night. A magical ritual. Astrampsychus of Cunaxa.'

She stared up at him, her eyes once more cool and deep-hooded. She smiled and shrugged. 'Yes, I was there,' she said. 'I wanted to employ the sorcerer to place a curse upon my husband's concubine.' Her voice sounded childlike, almost playful.

'On Minervina? How?'

'They can do these things. They make a doll, about that big. . .' Her jewelled fingers described a shape in the air. 'And they stick it with pins and nails, and summon demons to enact the same injuries on their victim.'

Castus fought down a shiver of unease. The thought of such things made his scalp creep. 'And you did this?'

'Oh, yes,' she said, smiling slowly. 'Although I don't know if it ever had any effect. Perhaps he wasn't a very good sorcerer?'

It was an easy matter to slip out of the palace once darkness had fallen. Less than an hour had passed since his conversation with Fausta on the portico, and Castus felt the fatigue in his limbs, the hunger eating at his strength. But the energy of action was propelling him. What he had in mind seemed desperate, and the plan only partially formed, but he knew he needed to act.

He could no longer wait for whatever devious schemes Nigrinus was hatching to bear fruit. To act: he fixed his mind on that, and forced himself to block out any further considerations. He wished he had been able to find Brinno before setting out. Then again, the young Frank might too easily have seen the absurd flaws in what he intended. Perhaps it was better just to fling himself out into the night alone.

Slipping through the side door from the kitchen court, Castus dashed across the darkened portico and dropped down into the bushes on the far side. He pushed through them, emerging into the grove of tall pines above the theatre. The city was spread below him, the rooftops merging into a smoky grey terrain. Fires still burned outside the temples on the hilltops, but the towers along the city perimeter were in darkness. Castus waited for a moment, crouched in the trees, watching and listening. The resin smell of the pines was strong around him, mingling with the briny scent of the sea; he heard the gentle creak of the trees, the rasp of crickets, the roll and hiss of the waves from the shoreline to his left. He moved off again.

Scrambling down the slope, he reached the stepped path that led from the front portico of the palace around the upper curve of the theatre to the rear of the curia building and the agora below. There were no sentries on watch here; since the siege had commenced, all the guards had been placed on the walls or in the palace itself.

With his army cloak wrapped around him, the hood pulled up to cover his face and the hem concealing his sword, Castus hoped he could pass for an ordinary soldier returning to his billet. The sound of his boots was loud as he jogged down the steps, kicking at loose stones. A dog barked from the houses just below him, and he tensed for the cry of challenge. None came, and he moved on.

He was trying to remember the exact time that he had passed this way before. Surely the hour was about right? So much now rested on chance, or on the will of the gods. Castus fought the temptation to pray: later for that. He would need plenty more divine assistance yet, if his half-made plan were to succeed.

Dropping down around the curve of the theatre wall, he descended the last few steps and turned the corner into the narrow paved alley that ran along the side of the curia. His pulse jumped as he looked along the alley, but there were no figures crouching at the low barred grille of the prison cell. He forced himself to move slowly, walking casually through the deep shadow and past the cell window. When he glanced down, he saw nothing in the darkness behind the bars. At the end of the alley he paused beside the entrance to the forum colonnade. Drawing back into the corner between a pillar and the wall, he pulled his cloak around him and sank down onto his haunches.

And now, he told himself, I wait. He had brought a chunk of sausage and a flask of watered wine with him, expecting that the night would be long. Squatting against the wall, staring into the darkness at the cell window, he ate and drank and tried not to think about what he was doing.

Fausta's words came back to him. *You must find men who are not afraid of death.* It occurred to him that he had no idea whether the Christian priest was still imprisoned beneath the curia. Perhaps he had been moved to a different cell? Perhaps he had already been executed, or even released? Castus knew almost nothing about the Christian cult either; he had always found the idea of it distasteful. The only Christian he had ever known was the imperial agent, Strabo, who had been murdered by the Picts in Britain. Strabo at least had been a brave man. But there had been plenty of them in the palace at Treveris,

332

and they seemed to spend most of their time muttering prayers and gazing at the ceilings. From what Castus had heard, they denied the existence of the gods, and believed the world was ruled by the ghost of a dead Jew. Surely an insane concept. Until a few years ago the cult had been outlawed; Constantine and Maxentius had recently legalised it, but Maximian had persecuted it savagely in his day. Who could say what the loyalties of these Christians of Massilia might be. . .?

A pair of soldiers came down the street, swaggering and unsteady, passing a heavy wine jug between them. Their hobnailed boots crunched and grated on the cobbles. One slipped, and the other caught him, barking a laugh. How easy it would be to join them, Castus thought. How easy it would be to forget all this, surrender to fate and let things happen as they would. Let the gods decide.

But then he remembered what Fausta had said about Sabina. Despite his anger at the time, the possibility was dizzying. Could that really happen? He had always regarded Sabina as far above him, both socially and in terms of wealth and expectation. Would she ever consent to be his wife? The idea seemed fantastical, absurd. But so much was absurd now. He shook his head. Pointless to even think about it.

Chewing on the last chunk of the tough sausage, he refocused his eyes on the prison window. He could almost trick himself into thinking that shapes were gathered there in the gloom at the base of the wall. But when he blinked there was nothing. He had been a fool, he told himself. Nobody would come. He was wasting the little precious time that remained.

He had almost slipped into a dispirited doze when a figure stepped past him from the forum colonnade, so close that Castus could smell the vague aroma of grilled fish and damp wool. Jolting back into the corner, out of sight, he watched as a second figure followed, and then a third. All of them were dressed in dark cloaks, pulled up to cover their heads, and one carried a basket. Silently they crossed the narrow street and moved along the curia wall, before sinking to a huddle before the cell window.

For a long time Castus watched them as they crouched, apparently immobile. He tried to stay calm and breathe slowly but his mind was rioting. As he listened, he could make out the sound of a whispered conversation, or perhaps some kind of chant. He concentrated on staying still, not making any noise or motion that would draw their attention. The muscles of his calves ached, and his fists were tightly clenched. At last, when he could hardly bear to wait any longer, the little knot of figures broke apart. The three shapes straightened, and once more ghosted back the way they had come. Castus held his breath as they passed, waited a few heartbeats, then eased himself upright and followed.

It was not difficult to keep to the shadows; the city was closed up after nightfall now, only the military patrols and a few scared citizens out on the streets. Here and there lamps burned in wall niches, casting the brick corners of houses, the carved stone of fountains and pediments, the masonry pillars of doorways into stark relief. It was more difficult to stay silent; the three cloaked figures moved with no sound at all, and Castus was very conscious of the noise of his boots on the cobbles.

Tracing around the margins of the agora, the three figures passed into the grid of narrow streets to the north. They were moving fast, not pausing to speak, and Castus guessed this was a journey they had made several times. Around a corner, down another alley crossed by heavy brick arches: he lost them for a moment but caught the flicker of movement from a gateway in the wall of a looming apartment block. Again he followed, feeling his way in total blackness through a covered passage that stank of drains and old cooking oil, before emerging into an enclosed courtyard.

Lamplight shone faintly from windows high in the surrounding buildings, and the open space between them was criss-crossed with washing lines. Castus stood blinking, waiting for his eyes to adjust. Shapes emerged from the dark: a well with a pump; a colonnade of low brick arches. The sound of somebody weeping came from one of apartments overhead; the barking of a dog and a baby's distant wail carried on the night air. Drawing his cloak tighter around him, Castus peered into the shadows around the margins of the courtyard, alert for any sign of movement. He had lost them, he thought; somehow they had melted into the warren of the city. Then he saw the shape of a cloaked figure pass briefly across a patch of lighted wall, and immediately he was moving again.

A stairway led from the courtyard to the upper storey. Stumbling, reaching out to grab at the wall, Castus took the steps two at a time. He heard the sound of a door closing, the click of the latch. At the top of the steps was a corridor, with a lamp burning in a wall bracket. Marching to the end of the corridor, Castus came to a halt before a heavy wooden door studded with iron nails. He gripped the hilt of his sword and took a deep breath. Then he banged on the wood.

For a while there was no reply. Just as Castus was raising his fist to bang on the door again, he heard the rattle of a chain and the crack of a bolt being drawn back. The door opened a crack. Staring over the chain was an old man with one staring eye and one puckered socket. The single eye narrowed into a squint.

'The hour is late, soldier,' the old man said. Warm lamplight came from the chamber behind him.

'Who is it, Polyphemus?' a woman's voice called.

Castus threw back his cloak and drew himself up to his full height.

'My name is Aurelius Castus,' he said, loud enough for anyone in the next room to hear him. 'I am a Protector of the Sacred Bodyguard, and I need to talk to you about your priest.'

The single eye blinked, then widened. The door swung closed, and through the heavy studded wood Castus heard voices in rapid debate. Then the chain rattled again, and the door creaked wide open.

'Welcome,' the doorman said.

CHAPTER XXIV

He had made a mistake. So he thought as the one-eyed slave led him through the dim passage and into the lighted chambers beyond. Castus had been expecting a cramped apartment, a huddle of desperate-looking conspirators. Instead, he found himself in a suite of high-ceilinged rooms, opening onto a wide portico and a garden courtyard. He had entered through the back door, the slaves' entrance, he realised; this was no humble dwelling, but the residence of a wealthy citizen.

There were about a dozen people gathered in the main chamber, sitting or reclining on dining couches, and Castus stood before them in his parade-ground posture and recited the short speech he had been rehearsing in his mind. As he spoke, stumbling over the words, he scanned the faces of his listeners. One was a heavy-jowled middle-aged woman in a flowing embroidered tunic, another a tall and vigorous-looking man with a balding head and a sombre expression; then there was an older man with a fleecy white beard. These three were richly dressed, the others around them less so, but all appeared to be equals here. When Castus had finished speaking they gazed at him for a moment in silence, then turned to look at each other. This is a mistake, he thought again. I've come to the wrong place. These are the wrong people.

'You want us to aid you in surrendering our city to a besieging force?' the white-bearded man said at last. 'To take up arms – with our *followers*, as you put it – against the soldiers of Maximian and help you seize the city gate and hold it until Constantine's troops can enter?'

'That's right,' Castus said. The burning oil lamps made the room hot. He was perspiring freely. The older man was frowning into his beard, shaking his head.

'Let us think clearly, Arcadius,' the tall, sombre-faced man said. 'This is. . . an unusual situation after all. . .'

'We have known worse,' the heavy-jowled lady broke in. 'The struggles of the rulers of the earth are not our struggles.'

'Sister, we must listen to what the soldier says,' the tall man insisted. 'If we do not act, Maximian will win this fight. Our dear Bishop Oresius will be executed, and quite possibly the persecution will begin once more. If there is anything that we can do to avoid that. . .'

'But not by force of arms!' the elder man, Arcadius, broke in. 'That is not our way! Bloodshed is forbidden to us – scripture clearly states this. Did not Our Lord take the sword from Peter in the garden? We fight against the beast through our prayers, not with our hands. . .'

For a moment it seemed as if everyone was about to speak at once. Castus felt his heart shrinking in his chest. How could he ever have imagined that this plan would work? Now a fourth man was on his feet – Castus noticed the dark cloak piled beside him on the couch.

'Brothers and sisters!' the new speaker cried. 'When I spoke with our bishop less than an hour ago, he said that he had received a message from the Lord. He said that God would send us a sign. . . And now this soldier appears. I ask you, is that not a sign?'

338

'A sign from somewhere, Fortunatus,' Arcadius mumbled into his beard. 'Perhaps not from heaven. . .'

Sudden uproar, everyone's voice raised. Castus ground his teeth, rocking on his heels. From the corner of his eye he could see through the doors of connecting rooms: figures were moving, other people talking and departing. How many were in this house? For the first time he realised the full danger of his position. It would only take one person to send a message out, and his treason would be reported. At any moment he could hear the hammering on the doors, the tramp of the soldiers forcing their way into the house. But the assembled people seemed oblivious, lost in their debate.

'Nation must not take up arms against nation!' the white-bearded man was crying, 'Nor will they train for war!'

'But think of Gideon, of David – mighty warriors! Were they not loved by God?'

'As the blessed Cyprianus says, the hand that has held the sword shall not receive communion. . .!'

'. . . But Jesus told his disciples to sell their cloaks and buy swords! Surely it is right to wage war if the ultimate cause is just, brother? Through persecution we have been made strong – why would the Lord give us that strength if we are not to use it?'

'The Lord gave our rulers the sword to execute his wrath against the wrongdoer!'

'. . . But scripture tells us to love our enemies and pray for those who persecute us, so that we may be children of Our Father in heaven. . .'

'QUIET!'

Castus's drill-field bellow instantly silenced the room, echoing through the connecting chambers. The gathering turned to stare at him, open-mouthed. Now that he had their

339

attention, he felt his mouth dry. He had never been accustomed to speaking to civilians, especially in mixed groups. But he had staked everything on this one gamble, and he had only moments to make it work.

'I remind you of the threat faced by your city,' he said, keeping his tone harsh, commanding. 'If there's another assault and the troops break through the wall, they will plunder and they will sack. That's the custom of war. But outside the wall is Constantine, the rightful emperor. He has favoured your sect, and ended the persecution against you. Allow him into the city and you limit the violence, and win his gratitude. Allow Maximian to win, and your priest dies.'

He paused a moment to let his words sink in. The people on the couches looked at each other again, pondering, uncertain.

'I'm not asking you all to take up arms,' Castus went on, trying for a more civil tone. 'All I need is a crowd, to make a diversion, and a few people willing to lend some muscle. It won't be easy, but with your help we could win. But I need you to be united, and to decide soon.'

Merciful gods, he thought as he stared back at them. How had he come to stake everything on the goodwill of a bunch of quarrelling religious extremists? The plump lady in the embroidered tunic drew herself up to address him.

'You cannot give us orders,' she said. 'This is not your house.'

'I'm not ordering you, domina. . .' Castus was trying hard not to grind his teeth in frustration.

'Brothers and sisters,' the tall, sombre-faced man said, getting to his feet and raising his hands. 'Authority in our congregation rests entirely with the blessed Bishop Oresius. He alone can decree what we all should do. But surely, in his absence, individuals among us can decide how the spirit guides them?' He shot a glance at the white-bearded man.

340

'May I remind you that you are only a deacon, Nazarius,' the plump woman said. 'Not even one of our Elders. We must summon others of our congregation to discuss this before we make any rash decisions.'

The tall man, Nazarius, nodded and sat down again. Now the assembled people drew together, speaking in hushed voices. An old woman approached Castus and took his arm. She had a kindly face, and a wild straggle of grey hair.

'Please sit and rest yourself,' she said with a cracked smile, gesturing to a chair beside the wall. 'The discussion may take some time!'

Castus nodded, mute, and dropped down heavily onto the chair.

'I am Epaphra,' the old woman said. 'You must forgive my brethren. Many of us lived through the persecution six years ago. We are not inclined to trust soldiers, or greet them warmly!'

'Fair enough,' Castus said. Now he was seated he could feel the fatigue soaking through him. His blood was still rushing with energy, and his limbs ached with it, but he had not slept since well before dawn and the day had been long and hard. He wanted to slump forward and put his head in his hands, but dared not show his weakness. The old woman, Epaphra, placed a tray of food and a cup of wine on the low table beside him.

'Eat, drink,' she said, still smiling.

Castus looked warily at the food. He had heard that Christians refused to eat the food of normal people; was there something abnormal about their own food? Was it somehow. . . *funny*?

'Don't worry,' Epaphra said, widening her eyes. 'It's just bread and oil, cheese and olives. . . not polluted!'

Shrugging, still not entirely convinced, Castus sipped the wine and picked at the bread and cheese. He heard the thud of a door from deeper inside the house, and the sound of voices. Newcomers were arriving, pacing quickly into the main chamber to join the assembly in their muttered debate. At the third or fourth arrival Castus sat up sharply, reaching for his sword. The stocky well-dressed man in the doorway was the magistrate who had tried to shout down the bishop during the demonstration on the quayside. Had they been betrayed so soon?

'Don't worry,' Epaphra said, placing a dry hand on his arm. 'That is Brother Trigetius. He is on the city council, one of the aediles. But he is also a reader of our congregation. You can trust him.'

'How many followers does your priest have?'

'Oh, our congregation numbers nearly a thousand citizens and another thousand again slaves and foreigners,' the old woman said. 'Not including catechumens.'

Two thousand? Castus felt a stir of hope in his heart. But it sounded incredible – surely one in ten of Massilia's inhabitants were not Christians? Then again, if men like Trigetius were among them, they were certainly diverse in their opinions.

'Where's your altar?' he asked, glancing around the room. 'Where do you. . . do your rituals?'

'Oh, no!' Epaphra cried, amused. 'This is not our *ecclesia*! Our congregation gathers in the Basilica of Saint Victor. . . This is the home of Antonia Sosibiana, whom you see there.' She pointed towards the plump jowly woman. 'We meet here to receive word of our blessed Oresius,' she went on, her expression growing sad.

Castus nodded, then drank more wine. It was strong, and helped him to focus his thoughts. By the sound of it, the debate was also gathering focus now. About time, he thought. It must be approaching midnight already. Every now and again the attention of the room shifted to him; he felt the collective gaze upon him, like a heat on his face.

Then, at last, the hushed conversation died away into silence, and Castus stood up as Nazarius, the tall man they had called a deacon, approached him. His head reeled briefly from the wine.

'It has been decided,' Nazarius said, and half turned to also address the people behind him. 'Although we cannot act as a congregation, any who wish can join you in this. . . attempt. There are others, sympathetic to our cause although not of our faith, who may also agree to assist.'

Castus nodded. He could see several members of the assembly shaking their heads, their eyes downcast. The white-bearded Arcadius and Trigetius the magistrate were among them. Those two could be dangerous, he thought.

'So, tell us what you propose,' Nazarius said.

'Tomorrow night,' Castus began, squaring his shoulders and hooking his thumbs into his belt, 'an hour before dawn, have your people assemble near the Sea Gate. There's a public portico, about a bowshot down the street . . .'

'The portico of the coppersmiths,' somebody said.

'Assemble there, and the watchers at the gate won't see you. But try to be unobtrusive.'

'Several of our congregation have houses near there,' Nazarius said. 'We can go to them in daylight tomorrow, and spend the night in prayer and vigil.'

'If you want. Any that own weapons can bring them, whether they mean to use them or not. I'll meet you there, and tell you what to do.'

Nazarius swallowed visibly, nervous, and glanced back at the assembly for confirmation. There were a few nods, some mutters of agreement.

'One more thing,' Castus broke in. 'I need somebody – a volunteer – to go over the walls tonight and warn the emperor of our plans, so he can have a strong force waiting to enter the city when the gates are opened. I'd go myself, but whoever leaves won't be able to get back in. . .'

He paused, shifting his gaze from one face to the next. Nobody met his eye. Nazarius was staring at the floor, his face reddening. The white-bearded Arcadius wore a smile of quiet satisfaction.

'I'll go,' a voice said from the back of the room.

It was a boy, Castus thought at first as the figure stood up from one of the rear couches. Then he saw that the figure was female, a girl of about fifteen, plainly dressed, with an oval face and very wide eyes. He recognised her; she had been one of the group gathered at the cell window that first evening he had seen them there.

'Sit down, Luciana,' Arcadius said angrily. 'This is no business for a child!'

'No!' Nazarius cried. 'No, the spirit has moved her. . . And is it not fitting that the holiest virgin among us should undertake this most dangerous of duties?'

Fantastic, Castus thought grimly as the girl moved forward between the couches. Her face was glowing, wide open, and she appeared slightly breathless. It was a look that Castus had only seen before on the faces of men in the moments before battle.

'This is Annia Luciana,' Nazarius told him. 'She is a ward of the Bishop Oresius, and came to us six years ago from Carthage. Her family were destroyed in the persecution there.'

'The beast raged most ferociously in Africa!' said Epaphra.

'You're really ready to do this?' Castus asked her. He already knew the answer.

'With all my heart,' the girl said, smiling widely.

* * *

Nazarius led them through to a side chamber and left them there. Castus had requested a private talk with the girl, but the lady of the house, the plump Antonia Sosibiana, insisted on being present. Stifling his annoyance – what did they think he would do? – Castus sat down on a stool facing the girl.

'Listen,' he told her. 'I need to give you instructions, and I need you to remember them exactly.'

Luciana nodded with a look of grave determination.

'I'm going to take you to the wall and make sure you get across, but once you're outside you're on your own. You need to get to the emperor's encampment as fast as you can. Don't speak to anyone except a centurion or a tribune. Can you recognise them?'

'I think so.'

'Good. Tell them you have a message for the emperor – only for him. Don't give the message to anyone but Constantine himself or his prefect, Probinus. Understand?'

'Yes,' the girl said. She was beginning to blush now, her eyes shining.

'I'm going to tell you the message. If I write it down, it might fall into enemy hands. . .' Not that I could write it anyway, Castus thought. But then he remembered the torture chamber at Arelate: the hooks and chains, the scourging whip, the fearsome catapult. He tried not to think of this blushing girl being subjected to that.

'The message is this: tomorrow night, an hour before dawn, I will open the Sea Gate and hold it until Constantine's men can enter the city. There must be a strong force waiting ready in concealment near the gate, ready to advance at my signal. I will fire the beacon above the gate as a sign to show that it's ours. Once inside the city there must be no sack, no looting. Got that? Repeat it.'

'Sea Gate, an hour before dawn. Force waiting ready. You'll fire the beacon above the gate as a sign, no looting,' the girl said, and nodded.

'Good. Another thing – we'll need a watchword and a response.' He thought for a moment. 'Right – the watchword is *Sol Invictus*, and the response is *Lord of Daybreak*. Repeat that for me.'

The girl blinked and bit her lip. 'I cannot,' she said.

'What?'

'I cannot. . . It's a blasphemy.'

Castus looked away, then scrubbed his fingers across his scalp. For a moment he considered inventing some lewd or obscene alternative.

'All right. . . the watchword is *Constantine Augustus*, and the response is. . . *Ever Victorious*. Can you manage that?'

'*Constantine Augustus*. . . *Ever Victorious*!'

'Good.' Castus turned to the woman, Sosibiana, who had sat through the exchange with a look of vague disapproval.

'But wait,' the girl said, concerned. Castus looked back at her. 'How will they know the message is genuine?' she asked. 'Why should they believe me?'

Castus frowned heavily. He had not even considered that. Sosibiana raised an eyebrow at him. *Think*. . .

'Here,' he said, and reached into the pouch sewn into his broad military belt. He brought out a thin vellum scroll, crumpled and almost flattened now.

'This is an imperial codicil,' he told the girl, 'appointing me to the Corps of Protectores. It was given to me by the hand of the emperor himself. Show this to anyone who questions you, and they'll know you've been sent by me.'

Luciana took the codicil and held it in both hands with an expression of reverence. 'The emperor,' she said quietly.

'And all I need now,' Castus said, turning again to Sosibiana, 'is a thirty-foot length of strong rope.'

The cocks were crowing in the city as they made their way through the dark streets, and by the time the first faint blush of light was in the eastern sky they were crouching together beneath a wooden lean-to, within sight of the wall.

It had not been an easy journey. Luciana had led the way, moving fast and silently through back yards and alleys, but several times they had been forced to stop and conceal themselves as patrols or gangs of drunken soldiers passed. At one point they had watched from the shadows as four legionaries kicked and beat a civilian at the door of his house, demanding to know where he had hidden his store of wine. Castus had taken a step towards them, his anger flaring, but Luciana stopped him with a hand on his arm. She was right, he knew; whatever protection he could offer would never be enough.

The Sea Gate stood at the furthest western end of the land walls, only a few hundred paces before the city fortifications angled southward to follow the shoreline. It was the smallest of the city's three gates, and the only one without a deep ditch beyond it; the ground outside was too low and sandy for excavation, and the defenders had contented themselves with digging up the causeway that carried the road up to the gates. Castus had determined all this days before, during his tour of the walls with Brinno. But now, staring at it, the gate appeared formidable enough. Sixteen men in the garrison, more or less, with probably another four in each of the towers along the wall to either side. The idea of trying to take and hold it with only a rabble of poorly armed civilians, most of them with a moral disgust for violence, seemed like the wildest madness.

But the plan had been desperate from the start, and it was too late to give up now. Squatting against the mossy brick wall at the back of the lean-to, Castus tried to remain alert. Gods, he was tired. Every time he closed his eyes he felt sleep massing in his head. The girl beside him seemed entirely awake, her eyes gleaming in the dark.

'You're very brave,' he muttered. 'Volunteering for this.'

'Maximian killed my parents,' she replied. 'Or his governors did. When you were talking back there. . . I agreed with all you said. I would do anything to defeat him.'

'Even so,' Castus said, shrugging. He felt the ache in his shoulders. 'Listen,' he went on. 'When you get outside the walls, you have to be careful, understand? Some of the men out there. . . well, they aren't good men.'

'I know what you mean,' the girl told him. 'But I'll be all right.' She looked up at Castus and whispered, 'The Lord Jesus Christ will be my shield and my guide!'

Castus just grunted. He was watching the wall, trying to make out the movements of the sentries. There were two of them, each pacing a slow and weary route between the towers. They crossed in the middle, and for a short space of time both of them were walking away, before they reached the towers and turned back again.

'See the steps there?' he whispered, pointing. 'As soon as the guards cross, we have to get to them, quick as we can. We go up to the walkway, and you climb over the parapet. I'll lower you down on the rope and then drop it after you. Then you *run*, understand?'

He saw her nod in the darkness. Then he took the rope and looped it loosely around her body, beneath her arms.

'Why are you doing this?' she asked as he secured the rope in a firm knot over her chest. 'I mean, why you out of all the soldiers in the city?'

Castus bunched his forehead. 'It's my job.'

He coiled the rest of the rope and slung it across her shoulder; once she was over the other side she could slip easily out of the noose.

'You're a good man, aren't you?' she said, and he paused in his work and gazed at her. He remembered the last time a woman had told him that: Marcellina, the envoy's daughter, back in Eboracum many years before. He just grunted again, checking the knot.

'I'll pray for you,' she said, with sudden passion in her voice. 'And I'll pray that one day your heart is opened to the love of God.'

'If you like,' Castus said, sitting back against the mossy bricks. He peered into the dark, trying to pick out the moving shapes of the sentries on the wall.

'Get ready,' he said. He eased himself into a crouch, and then stood. Luciana took his hand and pulled herself up beside him.

The two sentries met in the middle of the walkway, and for a few maddening heartbeats they seemed to pause. Castus heard the sounds of their voices, a snatch of laughter. Then they were moving apart again. He waited, counting their steps.

'*Go!*'

Luciana grabbed his hand again and they ran together, bolting from the shelter and across the strip of dusty open ground to the black shadow of the wall. Castus reached the steps first, climbed the first few and then turned to seize the girl and lift her. Raising her over his head, his muscles burning, he sat her on the walkway and then scrambled up after her as she crossed to the wall parapet.

A quick glance back along the wall: the two sentries were still moving away, oblivious. But the light seemed to have grown suddenly, and the land outside the wall was no longer lost in night's blackness.

Luciana jumped up onto the parapet, sitting between two of the merlons, then slid herself across and dropped her legs down on the far side. Castus took the rope, wrapping the end of it around his waist and uncoiling the rest onto the walkway beneath him. He took the girl by the shoulders.

'The gods guide you,' he whispered.

As he spoke he realised his mistake, but he saw her smile. She leaned and kissed him quickly on the forehead. Then she dropped, clinging to the edge of the parapet until he pulled the rope taut and took her weight.

He drew in a deep breath and held it, leaning back from the wall, forcing himself to pay the rope out gradually through his palms and not let the girl drop too fast. A rattle of loose stones came from somewhere below, and Castus clenched his teeth tight.

A shout from his left, and the sound of running feet. Castus bunched his shoulders, fighting the urge to let go of the rope. Suddenly he felt it slacken in his grip, and threw himself forward into the embrasure. The ground below the wall was a dense tangle of grey and black, but he caught the darting shadow of the girl as she ran for the open ground, and hurled the rope down after her.

'Who's there?' came the voice from the walkway. 'Identify yourself!'

'*Strength of Hercules!*' Castus said loudly, glad he remembered the night's watchword.

The sentry moved closer, his shield raised and his spear levelled. Castus stood away from the parapet, flicking his cloak back to show the markings on his tunic.

'Somebody went over the wall?' the sentry said in a thick Spanish accent.

'Just a girl,' Castus said, forcing himself to grin. 'I tried to grab her, but she got away. . .'

The sentry relaxed his guard and grounded his shield with a thud. 'Slippery as eels, these young ones!' he said, and Castus noticed the gaps in his teeth as he smiled. 'I guess one of those bastards out there'll be enjoying her before long, eh?'

'Maybe, brother,' Castus said, and gave an entirely genuine yawn. When he glanced out over the walls he could see no sign of Luciana. Cold remorse plunged through him suddenly: had he sent her out there to her death? Her god would protect her, she had said. *May mine protect her too.*

Stumbling, weary beyond thought, he climbed back up the stepped path towards the palace. No sun yet, only a misty grey half-light, the world still lost in monochrome. As he climbed, Castus pressed the heel of his hand against his forehead. He needed to stay awake, stay sharp. Given the choice, he would not return to the palace at all, but he needed to find Brinno and tell him about the plan. Needed, perhaps, to find Nigrinus too; however much he detested the notary and his assistants, he wanted to enlist all the men he could for the following night. But his throat was dry and his body felt racked, and all he wanted to do was lie down for a few hours and rest.

When he reached the top of the path he crouched and dodged to his right, through the pine grove and the dry scrub to the service wing of the palace. Silently he moved across the portico and into the quiet gloom of the kitchen courtyard. Passing through it, he climbed on up the steps; he would find Brinno in his room, then perhaps allow himself a few hours' sleep. . .

The shout startled him, echoing through the antechamber, and then a flare of lamplight burst whirling spots across his vision. He was turning, already drawing the sword from his scabbard, but strong hands seized his wrists and suddenly there were men all around him rushing from the reeling shadows.

'We've got him!' somebody cried, shouting into Castus's ear. He was trying to fight but his body was slow with fatigue and everything seemed to be happening very fast. He heard a roar, and realised that it was the sound of his own voice. Twisting, he flexed his right arm and managed to throw off the man who was gripping him on that side; then a fist punched hard into his sternum and drove the air from his lungs.

Cold steel at his throat. Another blade pressing into his back. He was down on his knees, choking breath, with men grappling him on both sides. Blinking, he brought the room back into focus.

Flaccianus was standing before him, with the burly ex-wrestler Glaucus leering over his shoulder. The men around him wore military uniforms and belts.

'What are you doing?' Castus managed to say. 'Get Nigrinus. . . get your master. I need to speak to him.'

'I'm sure you do,' Flaccianus said with a greasy smile. Then his expression soured. 'Julius Nigrinus has been arrested for treason against the emperor Maximian. As one of his confederates, you too are accused.'

Castus gaped at him, his brow knitting. Then he began to understand.

'Personally,' Flaccianus said, stepping closer to breathe into Castus's face, 'I've had about enough of Nigrinus's treacherous little schemes. As for you. . .'

He drew his head back, then spat. Castus turned his face away, and felt saliva spray his cheek.

'Sometimes you just have to choose whose side you're really on, don't you!'

CHAPTER XXV

Gripping the bars, Castus hauled himself up to the narrow slot window at the top of the wall and peered out. If he twisted his head against his shoulder he could just make out the line of the sea-wall fortifications, and a narrow strip of rocky shoreline. Gulls were wheeling and screaming, and the sky had an unnatural yellowish tint. He released his grip and let himself drop, landing on his toes.

The noise of the gulls had been tormenting him all day; they sounded so much like human voices crying in agony. Pacing back across the floor he slumped onto the broken dining couch that served as his bed. It was the only piece of furniture in the room. Aside from the couch and a few empty amphorae near the door, the chamber was empty, a bare stone-floored storage room with rough-plastered walls and a heavy wooden door. There was a jug of water and a crust of bread beside the door, a latrine pot in the opposite corner. Castus guessed he was in the basement of the palace, below the kitchens or the baths. The yellow light through the barred window threw distorted stripes on the wall above him.

It must be evening now, he thought. He had been imprisoned for most of a day. At first he had slept, plunging down into unconsciousness, dejected beyond all hope. But he had woken in a fury, jumping up to pound at the door, haul at the window bars, kick and punch at the walls until the plaster fractured to bare brick. It was no use: the door was solid, the walls thick, and the window would barely be wide enough to get his head through, even without the heavy iron bars. Slumped back on the couch, he had clasped his head in his hands, digging his fingers into his scalp in an agony of frustration and remorse. Not only had he allowed himself to be captured, but he had doomed all those who had agreed to help him. Had they already been arrested? Were they too in some prison cell, awaiting death? But he had failed not only the civilians: the troops that Constantine would send to wait outside the gate could easily be deceived by a false signal and lured to a slaughter. Then there was the brave girl that had carried his message: she could be executed as a traitor.

Fighting his way back from despair, Castus forced himself to think clearly. Flaccianus had ordered his capture and confinement. Perhaps it was only because of his meetings with Nigrinus? Perhaps the imperial agent and his new masters had not yet discovered anything more? That at least was a hope. But still, if he remained in this cell the plan had failed before it had even begun.

From outside came a low sustained roll of thunder. The light had faded to a dull brownish orange now, dipping into a stormy autumnal twilight, and soon afterwards the first heavy drops of rain spattered between the window bars. Lightning flashed, splitting the room in sudden illumination. Castus stood and stared up at the window, into the dark rush of the rain. Anger of the gods, he thought, and hunched as a shiver ran through him.

The storm gathered force as night fell, passing right over the city. In his cell Castus lay on the broken couch staring at the low ceiling and counting the spaces between thunder roll and lightning flash. The air felt heavy and damp, charged with fierce energy. Time passed, the storm moved further away but the rain continued, and the steady hiss and splash of the water falling outside the window lulled Castus into a fitful sleep.

He awoke to a rattle from the door and the sound of harsh voices. Lamplight spilled into the room, and he reached for a sword that was not there. Then there were figures in the doorway, a low guttural laugh, and the door thudded closed once more. Castus was on his feet, facing the dark-draped figure that stood just inside the cell door. He could smell the lingering trace of perfume: musk and saffron.

'Sabina?'

She came towards him, throwing the shawl back from her face, and just then a distant flash of lightning lit the room in harsh blue-white. Castus saw her face thinned by fatigue, the darkness under her eyes. She was plainly dressed, in widow's attire. Then the blackness closed around them again, and she fell into his arms.

'I bribed the guards to let me come,' she said, quickly and quietly. 'I gave them an *argenteus* each, and a flask of wine between them.'

'Good to know how much I'm worth!'

'No, listen,' she said, pulling back from him slightly. 'It wasn't just wine in the flask. . .'

'Poison?'

'A sleeping draught, that's all, but a powerful one. Serapion gave it to me. He'll wait until the drug takes effect and then come and unlock the door from the outside.'

Castus stared at her, speechless for a moment, the last shreds of sleep whirling from his mind. This was no dream. . . Hope, sudden and powerful, rushed through him. Sabina gripped his arms, urging him towards the couch.

'We have to wait,' she said. 'Don't do anything to draw their attention. . .'

She was right, of course. Castus took a deep breath and tried to calm himself. But the thought of escape was a spur at his nerves. They sat together on the couch, silent for a moment as they listened to the rain slackening from a rush to a steady drip. Faint wet moonlight shone across the room.

'Well,' Sabina said. 'We do meet in some unusual places.'

Castus was intensely aware of her presence beside him; for the first time in many months they were truly alone together. He remembered what Fausta had told him, and the bizarre offer of marriage she had made.

'I'm sorry to hear about your loss,' he said, feeling the clumsiness of his words as he spoke. 'Your husband and father.'

'Thank you,' she said, and drew a long shuddering breath. In the faint light Castus saw her shoulders rise. She let out a sigh, and it turned into a sob.

'It was a shame about Flavianus,' she said, her voice breaking. 'But I expected it, I confess. My father, though. . . I didn't even know he'd been arrested.' She covered her face with a shaking hand, and Castus sat beside her feeling heavy and awkward, not knowing what to say or do.

'He was a senator of Rome,' she said through her tears, 'and the Praetorians just butchered him like an animal.' She turned to Castus suddenly, clasping his shoulders, and in the faint rainy light her face was washed with anger and grief.

'He'll be avenged though, won't he?' she said. 'Constantine will march on Rome and slaughter Maxentius and all his supporters. . . And you'll help him! Promise me you'll help him!'

'I promise,' Castus said, feeling the words like something thick on his tongue.

She threw herself forward again, embracing him fiercely. For a moment they clung together, and then fell back onto the couch. Distant thunder boomed across the city, and far-off lightning flickered through the window slot. Castus felt himself plunging down into her embrace, lost in the sensation of her body, the perfume that surrounded him, the taste of her mouth.

'Wait,' he said, breaking away from her and glancing towards the door. 'Wait.'

His heart was beating quickly, his body felt full of blood and his mind glazed with desire, but he needed to stay ready for the moment of escape. He could not afford to lose himself now. Sabina was nodding, scrambling up to kneel on the couch and pulling her shawl back around her shoulders. They sat again, silent, both breathing hard.

'Your hands are bleeding,' she said.

'I was trying to punch my way out of here earlier.'

He heard her laugh quietly, then she gently massaged the grazes on his knuckles and the roughened welts on his palms.

'I've never known anyone with hands like yours,' she said in a whisper. Her thumb traced circles on his skin, and he could tell that she was shivering, nervous. 'I don't have anything now,' she went on, her words hesitant. 'All my family property in Rome has been seized, and I. . .' Her voice caught and she sniffed back tears. 'I have some jewellery, some clothes I could sell. . .'

'You don't have to do that.'

'But what I mean is. . . if you want me, I can be yours. I can love you and be your wife. . . I can't offer much in return. . .'

'Stop,' Castus said. He raised his hand, lifted her head and ran his calloused thumb across her cheek. He wanted to believe her, wanted to believe in her offer of love, but he was not fooled. She wanted him for the protection he offered, for the chance of revenge against those who had attacked her family. He wanted her too, for herself. But he barely knew her, and he was all too aware that she knew nothing of him.

Sabina leaned forward again and kissed him slowly on the lips. She sat back, and he saw her smiling. It was almost enough to convince him that her words were genuine.

A noise came from the next room, through the thick wooden door. A choking gasp, a muffled cry. Castus was up off the couch at once.

'Get back against the wall,' he told Sabina.

He barely had time to cross the room before the lock shuddered and the door banged open. Light slashed the room, cut by the crooked shadow of a soldier holding a knife in one hand, a flask in the other.

'What's *this*, bitch?' the soldier cried, and hurled the flask at Sabina. 'Trying to poison us?'

Castus turned fast, snatching up one of the empty amphorae from the corner. The soldier took a step into the room, Sabina screamed, and Castus raised the heavy clay jug and then brought it smashing down across the back of the soldier's head. The man dropped.

'Stay there!' Castus called to Sabina. Then he was out of the room.

He blinked, squinted: a white-walled chamber in lamplight, one man on his hand and knees, retching. Another slumped over a table. A third soldier rising from the table with a snarling cry, a naked sword in his hand.

A heartbeat to think about going back for the fallen knife. No time. The soldier was already lurching across the room, sword raised. Castus swept his arm down and seized a fallen stool, whirling it up into both hands. Somebody was hammering at a door, yelling. The man came on with the sword, but he was sick, weakened. He slashed wide, and Castus easily parried the blow with the stool.

Stepping in fast, he swung at the soldier; the stool cracked into the man's head and sent him reeling back across the room. The sword dropped from his hand and clattered onto the floor, and Castus snatched it up before it stopped spinning. Two long strides and he was across the room; one short savage hack at the man's neck and he buckled and fell.

The retching soldier was trying to get up, groping a sword from his scabbard. Castus stepped over him, dragged his head up by the hair and pulled the blade across his throat. The body jolted and then collapsed, blood spouting across the flagstone floor.

Stairs to the right, and the sound of footsteps descending. A barred door to the left, shuddering as someone threw themselves against it. Castus turned towards the stairs, dropping into a braced crouch, his blood-streaked blade held low. The lamplight throbbed with the rhythm of his breathing, and he felt the energy of killing racing through his body.

'I see I've come too late,' the eunuch said, stepping from the stairway into the light. His expression shifted only slightly as he took in the sprawled bodies, the spreading spill of blood.

'The domina's in there,' Castus told him, flicking the sword towards the cell door. 'Get her out of here. Get her to Fausta's chambers and keep her there. Bar the doors and don't let anyone in until this is over. Understand?'

He caught the eunuch's curt nod as he turned to the door at the far side of the room. Another crash from the far side, and a muffled shout. Stepping across the bodies, Castus readied his sword and then kicked away the locking bar. At once the door burst open, and Brinno stood squinting in the lamplight.

'Brother!' Brinno grinned and threw his arms around Castus in a fierce embrace. He had a bruise on his forehead, dried blood on his tunic, and one of his teeth was missing: he had not been taken without resistance. 'Heh!' he said, and gave a low whistle as he gazed at the scene in the room. 'Trust you to kill every bastard in the place. . .'

'This one's still alive,' Castus said. The man slumped at the table groaned and shifted. He was not a threat. Looking back at the bodies on the floor, Castus felt a brief clutch of remorse. These were Roman soldiers, men like himself, men who had taken their oath and done their duty. But there was no time for those thoughts now.

They took weapons and swordbelts from the fallen men, arming themselves quickly and in silence. From the next room Castus could hear the eunuch talking quietly to Sabina, telling her what they had to do. Four cloaks hung on pegs; Castus took one and threw another to Brinno. The only way out was the stairs; the two men took a moment to draw breath and compose themselves, adjusting their belts and pulling the cloaks around their shoulders, then Brinno nodded to Castus and they began to climb.

Wet night air from above, and the taste of rain and lightning. The stairs brought them up to a narrow muddy yard at the back of the baths complex. Castus paused for a moment, gazing up at the night sky: Polaris was bright, the Bear hidden by cloud, but the moon rode near full and low to the west, over the sea ramparts. There were a good few hours of the night left yet.

Quickly, as they paced through the yard and across the kitchen court beyond, Castus told Brinno about his plan for the taking of the Sea Gate. The young Frank listened, bemused.

'This idea,' he said. 'You were drinking when you thought of it?'

'I don't remember. Seems a long time ago now.'

They were moving carefully, trying to keep to the deeper shadows, but as they emerged onto the side portico Castus heard the first cry of challenge, then a shout of alarm. He slapped Brinno on the shoulder and they leaped together from the portico and began to run.

Armed men were coming up the stepped path that descended towards the agora. Castus cut to the right, down the slope from the pine grove and through an open gateway into the theatre. Crescent tiers of stone seating stepped into the hillside dropped towards the harbour. Brinno was right behind him, and without a pause they were leaping recklessly down the tiers, arms flung out for balance, their boots skating on the treacherous rain-slick marble.

Castus felt only the plunging energy of escape, the violent motion of his blood propelling him. The speed of their descent was dizzying; within moments the two men were racing across the marble floor of the *orchestra* and out through the side exit. Still running, they crossed the expanse of open ground between the theatre and the lower end of the agora. Now Castus began to feel the pain burning in his side, his lungs pressing tight against the base of his throat; he did not know how much further he could run.

Ahead stretched the mazes of the silent city, the black dripping streets emptied by the curfew. Brinno was turning to run towards the agora, but Castus caught his arm and dragged him onwards, into the network of alleys along the harbour wall and the docks. The last thing he wanted was to draw the pursuers towards the Sea Gate. At the corner of the first building he halted, the breath heaving from his chest, and looked back. There were men spilling from the theatre, others clambering down the stepped path to the right and a group of horsemen descending the road that curved from the front of the palace.

'Remember the aqueduct?' Brinno said, grinning wildly.

Castus nodded. This time they had a better chance. But this time, he knew, capture would mean a certain death.

They split up, Brinno taking an alley that climbed towards the main street and the hill of the acropolis. Castus flung one more glance back at the pursuers, sucked in a deep burning breath, then ran straight on down the narrow thoroughfare towards the docks. The sound of his hammering footsteps echoed off the shuttered façades of the shops and warehouses. At the corner he pulled to a halt, threw himself against the wall and stared back along the street.

The pursuit was still on; he could see six men with spears and military cloaks, and a few more carrying staves and wearing plain drab clothing: men of the city militia hastily raised by Maximian to keep order and enforce the curfew. Someone was shouting to bring torches and search the alleyways, and Castus recognised the voice of Flaccianus. From somewhere behind him he could hear singing, drunken laughter: the city was emptied of its citizens, but there were still plenty of soldiers on the streets.

Slower now and heavier of step as fatigue ached through him, Castus jogged through a transverse alley into the next street. It appeared deserted, with just the sound of water flowing in the gutters and dripping from the eaves to break the silence of the closed city. He paused to get his bearings, meaning to double back around to the agora and throw off the chase, but as he did so a figure stepped from another alleyway a short distance ahead. The man had his back turned, but before Castus could move he looked over his shoulder and saw him. It was Glaucus, the big ex-wrestler. For a moment they stared at each other, then the bodyguard let out a bellow and dropped into a running charge.

There would be other men behind him at any moment, Castus knew. He had already drawn his sword, but if he tried to fight now he would be surrounded. He turned again, his cloak whipping, and threw himself into a narrower alley across the street, little more than a gap between the houses. Slippery stuff underfoot; he collided with first one wall and then another before he was through and into a walled courtyard half piled with festering rubbish. Doors to his left, one with a blanket pulled across it and a light burning somewhere within. He could jump the wall, he thought, scramble across; but already he could hear the big man piling down the alley after him.

Trapped, Castus took two long steps and struck at the bodyguard as he emerged from the dark mouth of the alley. Glaucus yelled, raising his heavy club in both hands, and the blade hit the wood with a chopping blow. Heaving his arm back, Castus steadied himself for a second strike, but Glaucus had already whirled the club up and brought it smashing down onto Castus's right shoulder. Pain exploded through his torso, his arm went numb, and Castus lost his grip on the sword. The club was broken and the giant tossed it aside; open-handed, the two men circled. In the faint light Glaucus's great slab of a face was twisted into a grin, his lips curled back from his small crooked teeth. The man was a trained wrestler, Castus remembered.

Two steps back, then another step. Then Glaucus let out a grunt and surged forward, swinging his fist; Castus leaped away from him and collided with the wall of the building behind him. Glaucus was fast on his feet, and had a long reach; already he was aiming another reaping blow. Castus dodged at the last moment and the bodyguard's fist slammed into the bricks. Driving his arm up, Castus punched the man in the sternum, but Glaucus appeared unaffected. The lighted doorway was next to him, and Castus dragged himself around the doorpost, sweeping the hanging curtain aside.

He was in a narrow plastered corridor with a cell at the far end. An oil lamp burned in a niche near the ceiling. In the shock of the lamp glow Castus saw a bed in the cell, piled with rucked blankets, a blonde woman with a pink and white painted face and big pale breasts, a naked fat man kneeling over her, turning with an expression of shocked dismay. . . The vision lasted less than a heartbeat, then Glaucus came roaring through the doorway and slammed him against the wall.

Thick fingers closed around his throat. His body was pinned to the wall, the bodyguard's full weight pressed against him. Castus had seldom met another man who could beat him in a fight, but the ex-wrestler seemed to be built of solid muscle and heavy fat. Fighting for breath, he hardened his neck, but he could feel the unbreakable grip tightening steadily. From the corner of his eye he could see the prostitute kneeling on the bed, her mouth wide open in a scream, her client pressed back into the corner in terror. Glaucus's face was very close to his own, lips drawn back, and with every hissing exhalation Castus could smell the sour garlic on his breath. His right arm was trapped against his body; he managed to get his left arm free, but his attacker's grip was too fierce to break. Something shattered against the far wall: the prostitute was flinging things at them, screaming, '*Get out! Get out!*'

Reaching up and to his left, Castus felt the edge of the niche cut into the wall. He twisted his hand, then flinched as the flame of the lamp scalded his fingers. The grip on his neck was not slackening; he could feel his windpipe constricting, his consciousness shrinking to a single struggling point. Twisting his hand again, his fingers found the clay bowl of the lamp. He flicked it closer, into his grip, ignoring the flame dancing around his fingertips. Then it was in his grasp, his palm cupping the bowl, and he brought his arm down and pressed the burning lamp against the side of Glaucus's head.

The big man flinched; then he roared as the flame touched his ear. He released his grip, but before he could pull himself away Castus swung the lamp hard against his skull. The clay shattered and the flame snuffed out; black smoke whirled in the confined space, and the corridor was filled with the stink of singed hair as Castus stabbed the shards of broken pottery into the bodyguard's head.

Glaucus was reeling, clutching his bleeding ear and letting out a high keening shriek. Planting his back firmly against the wall, Castus kicked. His boot caught the man in the gut. Thrashing, Glaucus ripped the blanket down from the doorway and toppled out into the blackness of the yard, and Castus was right behind him.

In the trampled mud, moonlight gleamed faintly along the blade of his fallen sword. He snatched up the weapon; Glaucus was still staggering, shaking his head and shoulders like an angry bull, and Castus swung first one chopping blow and then another at the back of his head. The bodyguard grunted, dropped to his knees and then slumped forward in the dirt. Castus raised the sword and hacked down a third time. Bone cracked, and he smelled fresh blood in the darkness.

Stepping back slowly towards the alleyway, breathing hard, he kept his eyes on the fallen man, almost expecting him to get up again. His neck felt stripped raw. From the doorway of the prostitute's room came a steady gasping sob, and the sound of a man muttering prayers to Juno the Preserver.

A shadow moved behind him, and Castus levelled his sword as he turned. Flaccianus was in the mouth of the alley, shrinking back towards the darkness as he took in the scene in the yard. He fled, his sharp cry echoing down the alley's narrow culvert. Castus was at his heels; he saw the bar of blue moonlight at the end of the alley, Flaccianus's running form silhouetted against it. Then a dark lumbering shape blocked the exit. There was a shout, the sound of a heavy object dropping to the cobblestones, and Castus emerged from the alley to see Flaccianus sprawled over a large wooden tub lying in the street. Two figures in stained tunics were shuffling anxiously away along the wall. Castus had barely glanced at them before the rank stink from the tub struck him: stale urine, collected from the city's latrines.

Flaccianus tried to stand, and the side of the tub slipped beneath him, slopping foul liquid. He was trying to say something as he rolled onto his back, his mouth gaping.

'Spare me. . . I have money!'

'I want nothing you've got,' Castus said.

He stepped across the fallen body, raised the sword in both hands, then stabbed it down.

Blood spread in a lake across the cobbles as he walked away.

His left hand was stinging with burns, his torso felt pummelled and his legs were almost locked with fatigue, but already he could feel the reserves of strength building inside him. At the far end of the street he could make out the crenellated towers of the Sea Gate, solid black against the deep blue sky. It was nearly an hour until dawn; he had escaped; he had thrown off his pursuers and arrived on time. Now only the most difficult and dangerous part of the strategy lay before him. He could hear the voices as he jogged the last distance up the street towards the portico of the coppersmiths.

'That's him. . . He's here. . .'

Figures were moving in the deep shadow behind the pillars of the portico. Brinno appeared at his side, clapping Castus on the shoulder, bolting out questions. Was he injured? Was he being following? Castus shook his head as he stumbled the last few steps into the shelter of the portico and sank down against one of the pillars. Somebody passed him a waterskin and he drank deeply.

'But, brother,' Brinno said in a harsh whisper, 'where's your army? Is this all?'

Castus blinked into the gloom, then felt cold despair stab his chest. There were only a handful of men crouched along the far wall, less than a dozen; half of them looked like slaves, most of the rest barely older than boys. Nazarius, his face more than usually sombre, was kneeling beside him.

'I'm sorry, my friend,' the Christian said. 'There were more, but they. . . Fear took them. And some of my brothers-in-Christ sought to persuade others against coming. . .'

Castus shook his head. He should have known.

'But I am here, and Fortunatus, his son, three of his slaves. . . and there are more scattered around. They didn't know if you would come. . .'

For a moment Castus let the wave of angry despair roll over him. He let his head drop back against the pillar and closed his eyes. Perhaps it was not too late; perhaps he could send another message telling the troops outside that the plan had failed. . .

But Brinno was nudging him. When Castus turned to look he saw men gathering from the shadows of the surrounding buildings, slipping from alleys and doorways, converging slowly on the dark shelter of the portico. There were many of them, and at first he snatched at the hilt of his sword, thinking himself surrounded by some silent army. But as the figures took form from the darkness he saw they were civilians, citizens, dressed in the rough tunics and breeches of labourers and craftsmen. Another figure crouched beside him, thickset and dressed in a heavy apron.

'Hermius, of the leatherworkers' *collegium*,' the man said, seizing Castus by the hand. 'I've got ten of my boys with me. If you'll lead us against the soldiers, we're with you.'

All around him now there were milling bodies, packing into the portico with a steady subdued whisper. Most were men, a few women among them; some had their faces blackened, and many carried weapons: staves, knives, adzes, a few hunting spears. Castus counted a score, then double that, and more of them gathering in the shadows along the street. A third man greeted him, then a fourth.

'Nicephor, of the Lacydon stevedores' collegium. There are twelve with me. We're sick of the siege, and sick of Maximian. Command us, and we're your men.'

'Virianus, collegium of the agora marble-cutters. Six men with me.'

'I'm Ofilia,' said a woman with curling black hair and a broad, handsome face. 'I'm just a whore, and I'm on my own, but I'll help if I can.'

Nazarius was shaking, his nerves clearly on edge. 'All day I've been spreading the word through the city,' he explained. 'There are. . . channels, outside our congregation. People I could trust. I hope I did the right thing.'

'You did,' Castus told him. 'You did.' But even as he spoke he felt the icy breath of fate up the back of his neck. The risk had been terrible.

The sound of whispering was growing now, the shuffle and scrape of many people packed together, strangers, maybe rivals or enemies, all united in a common purpose. For a moment Castus almost felt he could weep. He tightened his jaw. The joy of relief was flooding through him, and a fresh and fierce determination. It would happen now. They would do this.

'Your bishop would be proud of you,' he told Nazarius.

'I'm not sure. . . It depends what you want us to do.'

The leaders of the collegia, the trade guilds and workers' collectives were gathering around Castus now, kneeling and crouching, waiting for his instructions.

Brinno stepped back into the portico. 'Whatever you're planning, do it quickly,' he said. 'There's light in the sky already.'

Castus raised himself up against the pillar. Until this moment, he had possessed only the haziest idea of what might happen next. His plan had carried him this far, but the last stage of it had been a blank. Peering at the faces of the men around him, he willed himself to think quickly, clearly. Willed the gods to aid him. He cleared his throat.

Then, even as the idea formed in his mind, he began to tell them what he needed them to do.

CHAPTER XXVI

As the first sounds of tumult rose from the streets behind them, the sentries on the towers of the Sea Gate turned and stared back over the inner ramparts, across the space of open ground within the walls and into the darkened city beyond. A warm clammy breeze was gusting in from the sea, and for a few moments the sounds were indistinct. Then, as the noise rose in volume, it became clearer: angry shouting, the clatter of staves on cobblestones, the stamp of feet.

Crouching in the shelter of a broken cart beside the last of the buildings, Castus watched the sentries silhouetted against the growing light in the sky. The sound at his back gathered rapidly, the shouts rising to a roar, echoing along the shuttered street. The boldest among the citizens had been first to raise the clamour, but the others were joining in now, shrugging off their fear. Flung stones rattled across the street, sticks clashed off the brick pillars of the portico. A woman was screaming, her arms raised to the sky. It sounded real, and Castus could see that the guards in the gate towers were taking notice.

Brinno was beside him, both men tensed and ready to spring as soon as Castus gave the word. How far was it to the gates? Between one and two hundred paces of open ground, Castus reckoned, the paved road running right up to the double arches. He tried to recall everything that he had seen during his

370

inspection of the walls days before: there were inner and outer gates, both firmly closed and barred from the inside, with a vaulted passage running between them and a chamber above. Flanking towers, four storeys high beneath the flat rampart roofs. The only entrances to the towers were inside the tunnel between the gates; with the doors sealed the gatehouse became a fortress, able to withstand attacks both from outside the walls and from the city itself. Without knowing the watchword for the night, there was no way that he and Brinno would get in. This ruse, this desperate stratagem, was their only hope.

Light flared in one of the upper windows of the tower as a lamp moved through the chambers. *Come on*, Castus hissed, *come on*. . . He was braced, ready, leaning on his naked sword. The feel of the worn bone grip was a reassurance. He ran his thumb down the blade: it was dull, and notched from the fight with Glaucus. His shoulder still ached from the blow of the bodyguard's club, and when he breathed deeply he felt the flare of pain in his ribs. Beside him, Brinno looked even more battered, but the lean young barbarian wore a fierce grin. He was poised like an athlete at the start of a race.

There would be archers in the towers. Castus had warned Nazarius and others that once they moved they had to keep running, not make themselves an easy target. The archers would be shooting blindly into darkness, but some of their arrows were bound to find a mark. Behind him now Castus could hear the shouts swelling in a chant. '*Massilia*. . . *Massilia*. . .' He nodded to himself, his jaw set. These people were about to throw themselves into deadly danger, but not for him. Not for Constantine or for Rome, but for themselves, and for their city.

Come on. . . A sliver of light showed beneath the gates. There were men in the vaulted passage between the arches now, others peering from the slot windows of the upper chambers and

leaning from the tower battlements. A few moments more. . .
Castus held himself back, but his heart was racing and sweat
was tiding down his back. Fear uncoiled in his belly.

'Ready?' he said to Brinno. The young Frank's savage grin
did not falter.

'*Ready!*'

Reaching back, Castus swung his arm and heard the men
crowding the portico give a yell. Brinno was already on his
feet, and Castus bolted after him, the two of them swerving
out from behind the cart and racing together towards the gates
as the noise of the crowd swelled behind them.

'Open the gates!' Castus yelled as he ran. 'The city's rising!
Open, in the name of the gods!'

He snatched a glance over his shoulder and saw the first of
the mob spilling between the houses at the top of the street,
a mass of running men brandishing staves and knives, stones
and raised fists. A broken brick smashed against the cobbles
just ahead of him.

'Save us!' Brinno screamed. 'Help us!'

Come on. . . Castus stared at the gates ahead, the doors
still firmly closed. A hundred paces left, then fifty. The sound
of his boots on the paved road was loud in his ears. Archers
were shooting down from the towers now: behind him Castus
heard a scream of pain. He glanced back again, and his boot
slid from beneath him. The world swung, and then he was
down on his back, sliding on the wet stones. For a moment
fear gripped him: the pursuing crowd was nearly on top of
him, their screams of rage so loud he could almost believe
they genuinely wanted to kill him. Then he was up again,
getting his legs beneath him and running, staggering, towards
the gate.

Open up. . . come on. . .! Brinno had turned to raise his

sword at the mob. A grate and a crash as the locking bar was raised, then the gate on the left creaked open. Castus let out a shout of gratitude.

There were three soldiers in the spill of light from the gate tunnel, an optio and two of the men from the towers. Helmets, but no armour, and their shields bore the blue and white blazon of VI Hispana Maximiana. The same numeral as Castus's old legion. They were Roman soldiers; they were his brothers. But now they were his enemies.

Brinno rushed up beside him and together they sprinted the last stretch, the optio gesturing wildly from the open gate. Stones clattered against the wall and the arches; then Castus was shoving himself between the shields with the sword still in his hand. Brinno was right behind them, and they staggered beneath the arch, into the damp stone smell of the vaulted tunnel. Already the optio was shouting for his men to close and bar the gate behind them.

Gods forgive me. Without drawing breath Castus turned on his heel, levelled his sword and punched it up into the optio's unguarded flank. The man stiffened, flinging out his arm to grab at the wall before his legs crumpled beneath him. One of the other soldiers was already down, Brinno's blade slicing him across the chest.

Screams echoed beneath the high stone vault as Castus wrenched his sword from the body of the fallen optio and swung it at the man wrestling with the bar of the gate. The soldier managed to get his shield up, and Castus's blade glanced off the curved surface and swung wide, the metal singing. Castus steadied himself on his back foot. With his free hand he grabbed at the shield rim and dragged it down; then he reversed his sword and punched the pommel into the soldier's face. As the body collapsed to the ground he could hear the gates heaving wide, the mob raising a furious cheer as it surged through the archway.

One soldier remained, backing away along the tunnel with stark terror in his eyes. Wild shadows reeled in the lamplight, and Castus saw the grille of heavy iron-studded beams blocking the passage between the gates. The last soldier threw down his spear and shield, pressing himself back against the bars of the portcullis with his hands raised.

But now the mob was filling the confined tunnel, their shouts deafening. Castus snatched up a fallen shield, flung a last pitying glance at the surrendering soldier as the bodies closed around him, then pushed his way through the milling crowd to the low doorway that led into the tower. Brinno was lost somewhere behind him, but there was no time to pause now. Every moment counted.

Through the doorway into a dark, dank-smelling vestibule. Narrow steps rose steeply to the right. Castus lifted the shield above him and began to climb. There were others coming up behind him, their whoops and yells ringing. An arrow darted from above, jarring off the wall and raising a trail of sparks. Castus lowered his head behind the shield rim and charged on upwards, roaring.

Another arrow as he neared the top, shot at close range, the iron head punching through the leather and wood of the shield to jut a hand's-span short of his face. Stumbling on the stairs, shoving himself away from the walls, Castus stormed up the last few steps before the archer could draw again. Throwing his shoulder into the hollow of the shield he leaped, slamming into the archer's body and knocking him off his feet. Castus angled his sword to strike, and the fallen man snatched wildly, his hand closing around the blade. Castus pulled back his arm, the sword shearing off the archer's fingers. Then he was through the next doorway and into the tower chamber, heaving the shield around his body to defend himself.

Not fast enough. A spear darted in from his unguarded right. Castus arched his back and sucked breath, feeling the speartip jolt off his belt, slice a searing line across his flank and catch in the bunched folds of his tunic. He slashed, the flat of his blade sliding up the spearshaft to strike the attacker's arm. The man dropped his weapon and fell back.

A moment to breathe. The mob on the steps behind him was hanging back, and in the low-ceilinged chamber of the tower Castus saw three men – no, four – arrayed against him, and a fifth still trying to crawl up from his bedroll as he groped for his sword. Bad odds. But he had a shield and they did not. He was in a cold fighting frenzy, and they were still stunned and confused, uncertain what was happening. He threw himself forward into the chamber, bellowing.

Punching with the rim of his shield, Castus struck one man across the chest and knocked him down. His opponents had spears and knives, better for fighting in close quarters than Castus's dull, notched broadsword. But he stamped forward, hearing the noise of his own yell echoing back at him, and saw the terror in their eyes. One dodged in fast, striking upward with a knife, and Castus stabbed straight and hard and felt his blade pierce the man through the shoulder. He kicked, the man went down, and then a blast of air rushed into the chamber. The two other two soldiers had thrown open the door to the rampart walkway and bolted out into the night.

'*You!*' Castus screamed, pointing his blade down at the panicking man on the bedroll. The soldier's sword fell from his hand. '*Who's the emperor?*'

'Uh,' the soldier said, his mouth working. 'Constantine?'

'Secure the prisoners!' Castus shouted to the civilians packing the doorway. The man he had knocked down with his shield was crawling away across the floor, feebly raising his hand. 'And get that outer door shut and barred!'

The press of bodies parted to let him through. Castus's ears were ringing, and the first waves of pain were rising from the spear-gash in his side. He could feel blood coursing hot and wet down his hip and left leg, but the energy of battle was carrying him now and he ignored the pain. What hour was it? With any luck the sentries would already have fired the beacon on the ramparts, a summons for help but also the signal to Constantine's troops outside. But first the portcullis that barred the gate tunnel would need to be raised.

Past the stairs and through the next door, Castus saw the narrow chamber above the gates. Windows to both sides, and the massive drum and windlass of the portcullis filling half the space, cables reaching up and over the roof beams. He froze in the doorway, panic flaring in his head. There was a soldier in the chamber, one of the sentries from the ramparts, and he was raising his sword to chop through the cables.

'Stop him!' The shout rushed from his throat, and a heartbeat later he was leaping forward. He was too slow; the blade would fall. . . Then the soldier jerked upwards, his back arched, and he let out at strangled cry. The sword fell ringing from his grip and he toppled sideways with a javelin jutting from his spine.

Brinno was grinning from the far door.

'Good thing I'm faster than you, brother!'

In all the chambers of the gatehouse, men were dying. Castus stepped over a sprawling body, and recognised Hermius the leatherworker. Blood was spattered on the whitewashed walls, looking black in the lamplight. In the chamber above the gates, Nazarius and half a dozen other men were heaving at the windlass bars, bringing the cables taut and the heavy portcullis grunting upwards. Most of the surviving soldiers were trying to surrender now, but the mob seethed around them, implacable. Castus saw a woman – the black-haired prostitute Ofilia – lashing a kneeling soldier over the head with a heavy stick.

'Spare them if they surrender!' he cried. He turned and grabbed somebody by the shoulder, surprised to find it was a boy of about thirteen. 'Get down to the tunnel,' he told the boy, 'and make sure somebody opens the outer gates, as soon as the portcullis is raised. Understand?'

The boy nodded and darted away down the stairs.

A shriek came from overhead, then a clatter. A gang of civilians had pushed up the next flight to the upper chamber and the ramparts; as they fell back Castus saw their leader speared and bleeding. They took him by the ankles and dragged him down, his skull knocking on the steps.

'Out of the way,' he said, and the crowd shrank back against the walls to let him through. Getting his shield up in front of him, Castus clambered over the bleeding man and stamped up the steps, his body primed for the first attack. He had almost reached the top when a spear came stabbing down at him, thudding loud against the shield boards. Castus angled his blade out from below the shield and pushed on upwards, almost tripping on the narrow steps. The spearman struck again, and the force of the impact almost sent Castus staggering off his feet. But then he was up, bursting from the steps into the upper chamber of the tower, two soldiers falling back before him.

'Surrender!' Castus yelled, but his opponents were already lunging at him again. He smacked the spear away with his sword, then rolled himself into a low crouch with his shield lifted, sweeping a horizontal cut that chopped the spearman's legs from under him. The man toppled, screaming, as the second soldier's swinging blow thundered onto Castus's shield. Castus flinched from the impact, then straightened and hurled the shield towards his opponent. It collided with the man's body, and before he could regain his balance Castus had closed the space between them and stabbed the blade of his sword up under his ribs. The soldier choked blood, fell against Castus, and was dead before his body folded to the floor.

Up the last flight of steps, no more than a wooden ladder this time, and Castus dragged himself up onto the flat roof of the tower. Not yet sunrise. Sagging against the rampart wall, he heaved air into his lungs. His legs felt numb, and the wound in his side was throbbing, pain shooting up into his left armpit. When he looked back he saw that he had left a trail of blood behind him. The land to the north was still hazy in the pre-dawn darkness. No sign of approaching troops. No movement at all. From the city Castus could hear cries of alarm and the brassy blare of horns.

Brinno raised his head from the ladder. 'Brother – the beacon hasn't been fired yet.'

Castus shoved himself away from the wall and jogged back to the ladder, following Brinno down to the walkway above the gates.

The beacon had not been fired, he discovered, because the stack of straw and tinder in the iron basket had been soaked by the night's rain and not replaced. Beneath it, under cover, the clay lamp still burned, but that small flame alone would not be enough to send a clear signal.

'Get down to the chamber below,' Castus ordered, not even sure who was listening. 'Bring bedding, straw mattresses, anything else dry that'll burn.'

He sank down to sit beside the crenellated wall. Brinno knelt beside him, calling for water as he pulled the folds of bloody tunic cloth away from his wound.

Castus closed his eyes, feeling the rapid ebb of his strength. Still no sound from the dark land outside the walls. Soon the city troops would muster to retake the gates; the civilian mob could never stand against them. Keeping his eyes closed, gritting his teeth, Castus remained seated as Brinno washed the wound in his side. Then somebody was binding it – the prostitute Ofilia, he noticed. No trace now of the killing frenzy that had possessed her only moments before. Quick and deft, she bound clean linen around his torso, padding it over the wound and tying it tight. Castus thanked her with a grunt, then pulled himself up against the wall. His guts burned, but he could stand, and when he raised his arms he felt only the dullest ache.

The iron basket of the beacon was piled with blankets and dry straw now. Brinno lifted the lamp from beneath it, then, shading the flame carefully with his palm against the damp gusting breeze, brought the fire to the heap of tinder. Straw crackled, smoke twisted, and then the flame burst upwards. A cheer came from the people thronging the tower doorways.

Fire-warmth lit his face for a moment, then Castus turned and stared out into the darkness beyond the gateway. Still nothing, no sound of marching boots, no shouted order to advance. He eased himself down again, sitting against the rampart. Had the message even got through? Above him, he could see Brinno on the top of the tower, standing on the rampart with a bow in his hand. As Castus watched, the Frank aimed and shot, then shot again. He was picking off the men advancing along the wall walkway below.

Then, just at the edge of hearing, Castus made out a familiar sound. He hauled himself up, gripping the merlons and staring into the grey gloom. The steady crunch of hobnailed boots, marching fast. Then, with a wave of euphoric relief that almost made him shout, Castus heard the voices of the centurions as they urged their men on. He could see them now, a tight column of infantry advancing at the jog up the road that led to the gates. He saw the standards swaying above them as they flowed across the breach dug in the causeway, the curling tail of a draco streaming in the sea breeze. Then he made out their shields: the winged Victory emblem of the Sixth, his old legion.

'*Constantine Augustus!*' came the shout from the head of the column.

Castus raised his sword, the flame from the beacon fire flashing off the blade, and shouted hoarsely into the morning mist.

'*Ever Victorious! Ever Victorious!*'

CHAPTER XXVII

The vaulted passage between the gates stank of blood and filth, and was thunderous with the noise of men. Castus emerged from the doorway to the stairs and saw shields and helmets and armoured bodies packed close in the torchlight. Six spears were immediately levelled at his face.

'Weapons *down*!' their centurion cried. 'Let him through!'

Beneath the helmet rim and nasal guard were the dark features of Rogatianus. The African pushed through his men and threw an arm around Castus's shoulders, punching him lightly on the chest.

'Good to see you, brother!'

'Good to see the Sixth in the vanguard again,' Castus said. He was shouting – everyone was shouting.

'We didn't volunteer. Somebody thought we might be the only ones to recognise you!'

'Buggers in the other legions might have taken you for the enemy and killed you.' Castus recognised Modestus, and grabbed him by the hand.

'They might have tried,' he said.

Now Rogatianus was re-forming his men in the tunnel before the inner gateway, throwing out a screen of skirmishers to watch the approaches from the city. Castus stood swaying, drinking in the scene. The noise, the faces, the shouts of command: they were music to him. Music and wine. All pain was gone from his body, and he felt strong, ready for anything.

The troops behind him parted, and a squat man in a gilded breastplate and gem-studded helmet came striding between them. It took Castus a moment to recognise his chief, Hierocles, Primicerius of the Corps of Protectores. Two tribunes of the horse guards followed him.

'Dominus!' Castus shouted, saluting.

Hierocles acknowledged the salute with a brief nod. 'What do you know of the forces arrayed against us?' he snapped.

'Dominus, there are men in the towers along the wall to either side. We've seen nothing from the city so far, but Maximian has his reserves garrisoned around the temple of Apollo on the heights to the east of here, and half a cohort of Praetorians at the palace above the western docks. If they heard the alarm they should be moving against us already.'

'Very good,' the primicerius said. He was glancing down; the bandage wrapping Castus's torso was already spotted with blood. 'Are you fit to fight?' he asked.

Castus squared his jaw and nodded.

'Then fall in behind me. I may need you to guide us once we're into the streets.' He turned to the troops massing in the tunnel, his cry echoing under the stone vaults. 'Centurions: battle formation! And somebody get this rabble of civilians out of the way. . .'

They moved out in a tight column, light infantry of the auxilia screening their flanks. First came the men of the Sixth, then a cohort of Legion I Minervia. Despite Hierocles' order, the civilians moved forward too, flowing along either side of the advancing column. Castus saw Nazarius run out of the throng.

'Praise be to God,' the deacon cried, taking Castus by the hand. Tears were flowing down his face. 'Praise be to God!'

'Praise be to *us*,' Castus told him.

The column had advanced only two blocks down the narrow street towards the agora when the enemy appeared before them. A solid wall of shields, Praetorians and men of the Spanish legions, blocked the street ahead. Castus heard the horns blowing, and the Constantinian column broke at once into an attack charge. Boots clattered on the cobbles, a couple of men slipped and fell, then the leading wedge of the column smashed into the wall of Maximian's men and the din of colliding shields volleyed along the street.

At once men were screaming, spears lashing and stabbing. The enemy line gave a little, staggering back under the weight of the Constantinian charge, then the Spanish centurions yelled and soldiers bellowed a cheer, locking their boots to the cobbles and shoving back against the pressure of their attackers. Flung darts whirled in the air above them. Beside him, Castus saw Brinno calmly lofting arrows over the battle lines into the rear ranks of the enemy.

'Heh!' his friend cried as he reached for another arrow. 'I'd forgotten how much fun it is to kill men with this thing!'

Craning up from his position near the back of the fight, Castus saw the solid mass of Maximian's men beginning to push forward. Spears clashed together. Swords swung, battering against the shields of the opposing line. Slowly, slowly, the momentum of the Constantinian charge was being turned, men in the front ranks falling.

Then a ripple went through the enemy formation. Looking up, Castus saw people scrambling across the roofs of buildings on either side of the street, pelting tiles down into the massed soldiers beneath them. Others appeared at the upper windows, hurling bricks. A cauldron tipped from a window ledge, dropping a steaming torrent of boiling water onto the frenzied men below. The advance of Maximian's troops faltered as panic spread from their rear. Then their line broke, and a wedge of Constantine's legionaries surged forward through the breach, driving the enemy before it.

Noise of horses behind him, hooves clattering on the paved street, and Castus looked back as a troop of armoured cavalrymen from the Schola Scutariorum came riding down from the Sea Gate. But the battle here was done. Everywhere the enemy soldiers were casting aside their weapons, fleeing into the alleys or surrendering. Castus saw the men of the Spanish legions ripping the images of Maximian from their standards and throwing them down. They were dropping their shields, emblazoned with his name, and stamping and spitting on them. He noticed with surprise that it was growing light. The faces of the soldiers were distinct now, and the blood pooled in the street looked violently red.

'We have to get to the palace,' he said, taking Brinno by the arm.

'Why? The battle's here. . .'

'The emperor's wife is there.' Even as he spoke Castus saw the terrible images appearing to him. Not only was Fausta in the palace, but Sabina too. If Maximian decided to fight – worse, if he chose to die – he could take both of them to Hades with him. Castus pictured the halls painted with blood, a slaughterhouse. He broke into a run, and Brinno came after him.

Down the street towards the agora they shoved through the last of the civilian mob and the surrendering soldiers, and then they were on their own. The fight seemed to have swirled through this district and then ebbed away eastwards, leaving a wrack of fallen weapons, and occasionally fallen men too. Most of the dead were soldiers; clearly the citizens of Massilia had been taking their revenge. Castus drew his sword as he ran.

384

A section of cavalry came cantering past as they entered the agora, then a scattered unit of soldiers moving at the jog. Whether they were Constantine's men or Maximian's it was impossible to tell. But at the far end of the agora Castus could make out the shields of the Praetorians in the gathering daylight, and they were holding a steady line as they retreated towards the quays below the theatre.

He halted, gasping, and clung to a pillar. The wound in his side was like a burning coal lodged in his flesh, and clammy sweat was running down his face. A tide of pain rose through his body, and for a moment he thought he would vomit. Then it passed. Brinno gave him a questioning look, and Castus nodded and heaved himself away from the pillar again.

There were more soldiers advancing around them now, legionaries of I Minervia and XXII Primigenia, with a horde of Germanic auxilia in support. They moved steadily across the agora in a skirmishing line, but the Praetorians were falling back fast and were not about to make a stand. Castus snatched up a fallen shield and shoved himself forward between the skirmishers, Brinno at his shoulder. They had reached the far end of the agora, moving through the colonnades and into the wide area of open ground between the theatre and the sea, and now they could make out the little column of troops and fugitives descending the slope from Maximian's palace towards the gateway of the western docks. The sun was just up to the east, and the scene was flooded with a golden morning light.

'There he is!' Brinno cried, pointing. Castus stared, and picked out the figure in the purple robe, hedged by soldiers on all sides as he paced quickly towards the dock gateway. In the sunlight everything appeared very clear, very bright. A moment later Castus saw a red parasol raised above the hurrying column, an open litter being carried beneath it by four slaves. In the litter was Fausta, and behind it, on foot, was Sabina.

The soldiers raised a great snarling cheer as they too caught sight of the usurper. They surged forward, but the Praetorians had formed into a solid wall, shields locked, protecting an open avenue between Maximian and the dock gateway. Some of Constantine's men still had their javelins and darts; they hurled them at the enemy formation, but most fell short. There seemed to be no officers among them, nobody to give the order.

'For Constantine!' Castus yelled, raising his sword so all along the line could see him. 'For Constantine! After me!'

He kicked himself forward into a charge, directly across the open ground towards the Praetorian line. Bellowing as he ran, he felt agony filling his torso and feared he would stumble and fall. But the Constantinian troops were surging forward after him, raising their own ragged cheer, and even before he had covered half the distance Castus could see the Praetorians beginning to fall back. Then their line collapsed, men fleeing to either side, and he was through.

Maximian had already passed the gateway into the docks. Fausta's litter followed behind him, and then the usurper's bodyguard peeled aside and re-formed to block the gate behind their master and ensure his escape.

Castus slowed as he drew closer. The men in the gateway formed a solid barrier. A soldier ran up beside him and hurled his javelin, and Castus saw one of the defenders fall. Brinno shot one arrow, then shot a second. Within moments all the advancing troops had begun to add their own missiles to the barrage, and the men packed in the gateway could only crouch behind their battered shields and wait to die.

Their resistance did not last long. Once half of them had fallen wounded or dead the rest broke and scattered away along the quayside behind them. Castus drew breath, ready to charge forward again. Then he saw the last defender, still standing in the open gateway.

'Sallustius!' he cried. 'Surrender! It's over. . .'

But Sallustius, sword in hand, clad in his silvered scale cuirass, just shook his head and raised his shield. Something flickered past Castus's ear; Sallustius took one staggering step back, then dropped his shield and grasped at the arrow jutting from his neck. He staggered again, then fell.

'He was a traitor,' Brinno said, shrugging grimly.

Castus paused only briefly to gaze down at the dying body of his former comrade; two soldiers pushed past him, and then he was running after them through the gateway onto the quay.

The sunlight was dazzling off the calm water of the harbour, gulls wheeled and screamed overhead, and a light twelve-oared galley was moving away from the quayside with Maximian's purple-clad bulk seated at the stern. From the far end of the quay came the clash of sudden combat, screams of pain; the last men of the usurper's bodyguard were gathered in a tight knot around the landing steps, still holding their positions even as their emperor was deserting them. The two soldiers that had passed Castus only moments before were already down, dying on the worn stones of the quay.

Slowing to a walk, Castus approached the group of men around the steps. He held his sword low, but kept his shield up. Behind him he could hear the mass of other soldiers gathering at his back. He kept walking, drawing closer.

'Throw down your weapons!' he cried hoarsely. 'Your emperor has fled!'

The knot of bodyguards drew tighter, closing their shields. Then a gap opened between them and a single figure stepped forth into the glare of sunlight. His scarred face looked like creased leather, and his mouth was twisted into a mirthless smile.

'So we meet on the battlefield at last!' Urbicus said, raising his sword.

Castus halted, only a few long strides between them. For over a year he had waited for this confrontation, but his body was flowing with pain, his limbs were heavy with fatigue. Urbicus was no callow soldier; he was a true warrior, a veteran of twenty years and more in the legions. In his eyes was the cold fury of certain death.

'We don't need to do this,' Castus heard himself say. 'It's over.'

'Over for him maybe,' Urbicus replied, making the slightest gesture towards the departing boat. 'For us? I don't think so. I'm bound for Hades, it seems. But I'm sending you down there before me.'

Maximian's other bodyguards were drawing back, closing ranks again. Castus kept his eyes on his opponent, but could sense the soldiers massing behind him. Both sides watched their champions: this would be a single combat, a bout of gladiators. Urbicus swung his shield up as he edged closer, already in a fighting stance with his blade levelled.

Castus focused on the man before him, trying to still the thunder of blood in his head and clear his mind of everything but his adversary. The morning sun was bright; death lay on every side. From the deepest well of his body he dredged up the last reserves of strength, of speed.

In silence they circled, edging and feinting, their boots scraping on the stone paving, and the troops gathered all around them were silent too, breathless as they watched.

Urbicus lunged suddenly, his blade darting out. Castus took the strike on his shield and turned it, but the older man kept up the attack. Another blow hammered down, then two more in quick succession. Castus kept his shoulder hunched into the hollow of his shield, absorbing the force of the attack, waiting for the other man to tire. But he was being driven back almost to the brink of the quayside. He pushed forward, stabbing with his blade and punching out with the boss of his shield; Urbicus dodged clear, then swung a high chopping blow. Castus got his shield up, realising a moment too late that it was a feint. The other man's blade skimmed around the rim of his shield and swung in low and hard. Pain ripped through Castus's body as the flat of the sword slammed into his flank, where the bloodstain on his tunic clearly showed the wound beneath. Crying out, he saw Urbicus snarl in triumph, then punch forward with his shield.

The blow caught Castus off balance, and his left leg gave beneath him. Toppling, he caught himself on one knee as his shield fell from his grip. Urbicus was already sweeping his sword up, then bringing it arcing down. Castus raised his blade just in time, gripping the hilt with both hands as he parried the blow. Steel clashed and shrieked in the sunlight as the blades ground together.

For a moment they struggled, weapons locked. Castus heard the screams of the gulls around them, the shouts of the watching soldiers suddenly loud in his ears. From somewhere in the pit of his chest he found a last surge of energy; roaring, he pushed himself upwards. Urbicus staggered back, his sword already wheeling to strike again, but Castus was on his feet now and drove forward into the attack. With a ragged yell he struck two-handed, his blade hacking shards from the other man's shield rim.

One blow, and then another. He saw fierce anger in the eyes of his enemy. Urbicus was gathering his strength, but for a few heartbeats he could only retreat under Castus's assault. A third blow, slashed backhand across the face of Urbicus's shield, then Castus grabbed at the shield rim with his left hand and pulled, hauling the other man's arm and body around with it.

His sword was already drawn back; with all the power of his arm he drove it forward, stabbing into the open flank of his enemy. The blade bit deep, and Urbicus screamed.

Muscles burning, Castus dragged his sword back again and lifted it, wheeling the blade in the air before hacking it down into the hard flesh and tendons of Urbicus's neck.

Blood sprayed from the wound, brilliant in the sunlight. For a moment Castus saw Urbicus gazing back at him, his eyes wide with shock at the blow that had half severed his head. Then the man's legs folded beneath him and the body dropped to the smooth stones of the quay.

Heaving breath, Castus sank to one knee in the spreading lake of blood. He grounded his sword before him and leaned on it, fearing he would lose consciousness at any moment. Around him, Constantine's men were advancing again, but the remnants of the bodyguard gathered around the landing steps were throwing down their weapons now. Several of them covered their haggard faces as they began to weep, but most just slumped to the ground, too weary to care if they lived or died.

Turning his head, Castus gazed across the sunlit water at Maximian's departing galley. There were others packed into the boat: he could see the eunuch Gorgonius, and Fausta and her ladies, Sabina doubtless among them. Then he raised his eyes from the galley and looked towards the harbour mouth. Edging in beneath the bastions of the sea fortifications, oars beating in time, were two double-banked liburnians. The galleys' decks were packed with troops, and both had heavy ballistae mounted in the bows, aimed down at Maximian's fragile craft.

The two ships slowed as they entered the harbour. Raising a palm to shade his eyes, Castus watched as Maximian stood up in the stern of his own vessel. The oarsmen ceased moving, and the motion of the light galley slackened as it turned slowly with the tide. A man in a linen cuirass was calling orders across the water from the bigger of the two liburnians, but Maximian paid him no attention.

Slowly, with careful dignity, the usurper slipped the gold-embroidered purple robe from his shoulders, lifted it and folded it. Then he raised his arms and cast the folded robe into the waters of the harbour.

'Will they let us take a bath and change our clothes before we meet the emperor?' Brinno asked. He was licking the blistered fingers of his shooting hand. Ofilia was trailing behind him, a smile on her broad, tanned face.

Castus shrugged, snorting. All three of them were bloodied and filthy, but the whole city of Massilia looked racked and battered. Soldiers were staggering everywhere, most of them drunk, but many of the citizens appeared drunk too. Maximian was beaten, the battle was over and soon the emperor Constantine would make his triumphal entrance into the city. Surely that was cause enough for happiness?

Stepping through the shade of the colonnades, Castus looked out over the agora. After the night's rain the morning was fresh and the sky cloudless, and all across the open space there were soldiers and civilians mingled together, cheering and laughing. Castus had not seen the prisoners being brought ashore after Maximian's surrender. He had seen nothing of Fausta, or Sabina. Even Hierocles had disappeared immediately after the surrender to take possession of the former palace.

In the corner of the agora a gang of soldiers was running, yelling with laughter. They were from one of the Spanish legions, Castus noticed as he heard their accents. As they ran they were kicking something between them; a heavy ball it looked like. Their game moved closer, and one kick sent the dark object spinning between the colonnade pillars to land with a dull thud near Castus's feet. It was a severed head, beaten and almost black with dirt and blood. Leaning closer, he could not for a moment make out the broken and swollen features. Then he recognised the big stubbled chin of Scorpianus, Maximian's prefect. He stepped away from the head, and two of the soldiers ran up and booted it back out into the agora again.

Leaning back against a pillar, Castus stared up into the wide brilliant blue of the sky. He was starving, he realised, and very tired. The crowd in the agora had started chanting again, and their voices echoed along the colonnades. Castus closed his eyes and listened.

'*Constantine Augustus! Ever Victorious!*' they were chanting. '*Constantine! Constantine! Constantine. . .!*'

CHAPTER XXVIII

The prisoners were led out into the evening sunlight with their hands bound behind them. They were barefoot, but still wore their richly embroidered tunics. There were four of them, the only men of Maximian's inner circle who had not managed to flee the city or take their own lives before capture. Perhaps, Nigrinus wondered, they had hoped for mercy? Perhaps they had trusted too much in the Sacred Clemency of the emperor Constantine?

Gorgonius was brought out first, the chief eunuch's heavy jowled face pale grey and quivering. Behind him was the army commander, Gaudentius, stiff-necked with either pride or fear, Nigrinus could not tell. After them Macrobius, blinking his watery eyes, and Diadumenus. The former curator of Massilia looked especially woeful; this building had once been his house, before Maximian had claimed it as his palace.

Maximian himself, their former master, would not be joining them. He alone had been granted mercy by his son-in-law. Nigrinus had seen the old man, his tunic ripped at the neck in shame, kneel before the emperor's horse and plead forgiveness. And forgiveness had been given, of course. Even Constantine, it seemed, could not order the death of a man who had been one of the two supreme emperors of the world, a man who had stood beside the gods.

Now the prisoners were being made to kneel, each man forced to his knees with a rough hand at the back of his neck. The execution party was formed of eight tough-looking horse-guard troopers of the Schola Scutariorum. They would be paid a good bonus for this duty, and were going about it in a brisk efficient manner.

Nigrinus was standing with the other spectators, a gathering of military officers and civilian dignitaries, in the shade of the portico that circled the courtyard. He tried to keep his eyes on the condemned men and their executioners, although he was aware, despite his play-acting in the torture dungeon beneath Arelate, that he was still not inured to the sight of bloodshed. He had no pity for the men. Only hours before he had been released from a prison cell himself, perhaps the same one that had later held Gorgonius and his comrades. He had been lucky. Being found in captivity had preserved his life; that, and the information he had already been able to give about the usurper's court and military affairs, and his connections with his son in Italy.

But Nigrinus knew how close he had come to disaster. A different throw of the dice, and he could be kneeling with the prisoners in the courtyard. Still, he felt a sour sense of disappointment. Flaccianus's sudden treachery had robbed Nigrinus of the chance to arrange the surrender of the city to Constantine. In the end, of course, the citizens themselves had done it, led by a few renegade soldiers. All his months of slow steady planning had come to nothing. Or, Nigrinus thought, almost nothing. He had escaped with his life when he could so easily have lost it; now only one brutish soldier still knew the depth and extent of Nigrinus's deceptions. He wondered if he should rid himself of Aurelius Castus. It could certainly be done. But, then, the soldier's unwitting dalliance with the emperor's wife was still a secret. That was a weapon that Nigrinus could use against him, if in his stupidity he ever dared to mention what he knew.

Down in the courtyard the optio of the execution party was swinging his long cruel blade. One of the prisoners – the civilian, Macrobius – retched and spat on the gravel. Nigrinus felt the pulse jumping in his neck. There was a flutter deep in his stomach, a sensation of combined repulsion and excitement. It was, he was embarrassed to note, almost a sexual feeling. He had a strong desire to wash his hands.

The sword flashed up, then dropped, and Nigrinus closed his eyes at the last moment. A sharp exhalation came from the spectators in the colonnade, and when Nigrinus looked again he saw the eunuch's body sagging sideways, his severed head lying in a spreading lake of blood. Now the soldier moved on to Gaudentius. A swish and a thump, and the second head fell. Nigrinus forced himself to keep watching. It was fascinating, he decided. Swish, thump. Macrobius died, then Diadumenus. Four bodies slumped like sacks of grain. Four heads lying on the bloody gravel.

'It must please you to see this,' a voice said. Nigrinus turned, startled, and found Probinus standing beside him. The Praetorian Prefect rocked back on his heels, pursing his lips.

'Justice enacted is always a pleasure, dominus,' Nigrinus said.

'Indeed.'

But now another figure was approaching along the colonnade. Nigrinus bowed his head and saluted his chief, Aurelius Zeno, Primicerius of the Corps of Notaries. Zeno bobbed his shaved skull in response, giving Nigrinus a sideways smile.

'I'm glad to see you free once more!' he declared. 'I look forward to hearing a full report of all you learned after infiltrating the usurper's court. A very full and *confidential* report, of course!'

Nigrinus bowed his head again, inhaling slowly as his chief turned to walk away. There was a pressure in his chest. He lifted his head and addressed the Praetorian Prefect.

'Unfortunately, dominus,' he said, 'the most highly placed member of Maximian's treasonous conspiracy has yet to be brought to justice.'

The prefect gazed at him, raising an eyebrow.

'Oh? His name?'

'His name, dominus. . .' Nigrinus felt his mouth grow suddenly tight and dry. He swallowed, then raised his voice slightly. 'His name is Aurelius Zeno.'

The chief of the Corps of Notaries stopped mid-pace. He began to turn, began to smile, but a look of sick panic was flickering in his eyes. 'Surely you don't think. . .' he began to say.

'He was organising the murder of our emperor Constantine,' Nigrinus declared. 'He intended to strike on the third day of the siege. I have documentary proof.'

Zeno let out a low groaning cry and turned sharply, beginning to run towards the far end of the colonnade, his shoes skidding and slipping on the smooth marble floor. But Probinus raised his arm, calling an order, and two guardsmen appeared to block the fugitive's way, hands on the hilts of their swords.

Turning again, Zeno glanced quickly into the courtyard: the slumped corpses, the pooling blood, the executioners standing ready. He was breathing hard, biting his lips. Then, with one motion, he drew a short dagger from his belt, reversed the blade and plunged it into his sternum. He fell forward onto his knees, then collapsed onto the polished floor as the guards closed around him.

'Interesting,' said Probinus with a sniff. 'How did you know?'

'Nearly a year ago,' Nigrinus told him, 'Aurelius Zeno ordered me to investigate the correspondence of Maximian's intimates.' He was shaking as he spoke, but his voice was steady. Just for a moment, he had felt death's black wing brush against him.

'Zeno intended,' he went on, 'that I should report to him if I found anything suspicious. It was an insurance policy, I believe. If I found evidence of treason, he would know that his communications network had been compromised. And I would be signing my own death warrant, of course. However, he did not know that I was also investigating his own correspondence.'

'How very. . . *thorough*,' the prefect said. He stiffened his shoulders and drew away from Nigrinus slightly.

'Yes. And when I discovered in one particular concealed message a reference to Zeno himself, I realised the nature of the game. Instead of reporting it, I travelled south and pretended to Maximian's people that I was Zeno's intimate and fellow conspirator. They accepted me amongst them, and I was able to fully examine all their correspondence from then on.'

'Ingenious,' Probinus said with something like a sneer. He took another step away from the notary. 'It occurs to me,' he said, 'that there now exists a vacancy at the head of your department.'

'I suppose there does.'

Probinus sniffed again. 'Perhaps you will be hearing from us shortly, then,' he said.

Nigrinus glanced away to hide his blush of pleasure. He tried to form the correct words, the phrases of polite gratitude that protocol demanded. But the prefect was already striding away from him with his hands clasped behind his back.

All the other officials gathered under the colonnade also seemed to have moved away from Nigrinus, and he stood alone, gazing down into the courtyard.

It matters nothing, he thought. Soon they will have cause to hate me more. Soon they will have cause to fear me. His thin lips tightened into a smile. The rich metallic stink of fresh blood was in the air, and it no longer made him feel queasy. No, he thought; it smells very much like triumph.

CHAPTER XXIX

'What I don't understand,' Brinno whispered, 'is why they didn't just kill him? In my country, if a man rises up against his king his head ends up on a spike and that's it.'

'This isn't the same,' Castus told him. 'Maximian was an emperor. One of the supreme emperors. Constantine couldn't just execute him, could he? It would look bad.'

'Don't see why not. . .' Brinno muttered to himself, unconvinced.

Castus too had very mixed feelings. Even after all the treachery, all the killing, even after his own life had been in peril, he could not fully condemn Maximian for what he had done. Still less could he hate the man. For most of his military life Castus had saluted the former emperor's image, given sacrifice for his welfare, sworn oaths of loyalty to his name. Along with his old colleague Diocletian, Maximian was like a god on earth. Even now, when he was just a beaten old man shambling along like a prisoner in the emperor's retinue, he possessed the last gleam of that undying glory.

It was near midnight, and the two Protectores were standing together at the balustrade of a balcony that circled the small enclosed garden of the old residency on the riverbank in Arelate. Behind them was the door to the emperor's apartments. The night was cold and clear, with an edge of the approaching winter in the air, and the garden below them a maze of grey and black under the moon.

Constantine had moved his court to Arelate only days after the end of the siege. He had left Massilia in a blaze of victorious glory, the citizens lining the streets from the agora to the Rome Gate and spreading flower blossoms before the emperor's carriage. Riding with the imperial retinue, Castus had noticed the Christian bishop, Oresius, raising his hands to the emperor in some sort of salute or benediction. Beside him, sombre as always, stood the deacon Nazarius, and almost hidden between them was Luciana. Gazing down from horseback, Castus had saluted the girl as he rode by; for a moment he saw her waving back at him, then the crowd shifted and she was lost from view once more.

Nearly a month had passed since then. Everything had returned to peace, officially at least. But much remained uncertain, much unspoken.

'They didn't even reward us for what we did,' Brinno said, breathing the words. 'I mean to say! We captured the city, didn't we? They should have given us a purse of coins, or another golden torque each. . . Or at least made us into tribunes!'

'You know the story,' Castus said, frowning, barely moving his lips. 'It was the loyal citizens of Massilia who opened the gates, out of love for their true emperor.'

Brinno gave a snort of disgust.

But so much else about Maximian's uprising had been officially forgotten now. It had been a brief moment of madness, soon suppressed. One of the Spanish legions, VI Hispana Maximiana, had been disbanded and the men absorbed by VII Gemina, the sister unit. Maximian's Praetorian Cohort had been similarly broken up. Aside from that, and a brief spate of private executions, the whole matter had been consigned to the past. Needless to say, Castus had heard nothing of Fausta's offer of marriage to Sabina.

Fausta had been keeping herself and her household secluded. She was not entirely in disgrace, but neither was she wholly trusted at court. Before she was even reunited with her husband, she had learned of the recent sickness of Constantine's lover Minervina. A mysterious fever had taken her, and for days she had been close to death. Only the fervent and ceaseless prayers of a group of Christian priests had preserved her life. When Castus had last seen Fausta, her face had been shadowed by guilt.

Castus wondered if he would get a chance to speak with Sabina again. Perhaps she would avoid him, now that the danger had passed and she no longer needed his help. Perhaps, he thought, that was the best thing.

Brinno nudged his arm, breaking the thread of his thoughts. A figure was approaching along the darkened balcony, a man dressed in a white sleeping-tunic with a cloth girdle. Castus straightened, gripping the hilt of his sword. He opened his mouth to call the challenge, but his words died.

'Fellow soldiers,' Maximian said. He was barefoot, his hair and beard wild and grey in the moonlight. His slow dragging pace gave him the appearance of a sleepwalker, and his voice was slurred. 'Fellow soldiers, you must let me pass. I must speak to the emperor, my son-in-law. I have had a dream, a very important dream, and I must tell him about it. . .'

Castus stepped quickly to one side, blocking the door to Constantine's apartments. Brinno stood solidly at his shoulder. 'We're sorry, dominus,' he said.

'Let him pass.' The voice carried along the balcony, and both Protectores turned to see Hierocles, their primicerius, pacing quickly up behind them.

'Dominus,' Hierocles said to the old man, bowing his head briefly. 'Forgive these soldiers. You may go where you please.'

Castus looked at Brinno, who shrugged.

Hierocles stepped between them. 'Move aside for the former Augustus,' he said. 'That's an order.'

Squaring his shoulders, Castus took two steps to his right. Brinno moved aside likewise, and Maximian, ghostly in his long white tunic, passed between them and into the imperial apartments.

'Dominus,' Castus said between his teeth. 'What's going on?'

'We should at least have searched him!' Brinno hissed.

'Quiet,' the primicerius said curtly. 'Be quiet and wait.'

For a long while they heard nothing. Hierocles cleared his throat with a wet cough.

Then, from deeper inside the building, a single cry.

'Follow me,' Hierocles ordered, striding through the door. 'Draw your swords!'

They marched along the dark corridor and across the mosaic floor of an antechamber. The slaves and eunuchs who usually waited there, attending the emperor, were gone. Then Hierocles swept aside a curtain covering the far doorway and they were stepping into Constantine's own bedchamber. A lamp burning on the side table lit the scene: the body huddled on the sleeping couch between the parted purple drapes; the damask sheet punctured in several places, blood spreading across the fabric. Beside the bed, Maximian stood with a knife in his hand, his head thrown back.

'I've killed him,' the old man said, and turned to the men in the doorway. 'I've killed him!' he shouted, his eyes gaining focus in the wavering lamplight. 'I've killed Constantine! I am the only emperor now. Kneel before me.'

Castus stared at the bloody corpse on the bed. His throat was locked, his neck muscles stiffening, and the badly healed wound in his side flared with pain. He tightened his grip on his sword, fearing it would fall from his hand. He heard Hierocles exhale slowly. Then a door opened at the far side of the chamber.

First Probinus, the Praetorian Prefect, stepped into the room. After him came two more Protectores, also armed. Then came Constantine, hard-faced and staring, wrapped in a dark robe.

It was Brinno who stepped forward. He grasped the end of the bedsheet and dragged it back. The corpse lay on its side, naked and bleeding from several wounds. Reaching out with a grimace, Brinno shoved the body, rolling it onto its back. Castus knew the features at once. It was the eunuch, Serapion.

'You are all witnesses!' Probinus cried, raising his hand to point at Maximian. 'This man has attempted to murder the emperor!'

The knife fell from Maximian's hand. He staggered back, slumping against the wall, and let himself slide slowly down onto his haunches. His head dropped forward into his cupped palms.

'The emperor's wife warned us of her father's insanity,' Hierocles told Castus quietly. 'But, of course, we could do nothing until he acted. Her eunuch volunteered to take the emperor's place. A good death, for one of his kind.'

Castus found he could still not speak. He felt rooted, the strength drained from his limbs. Serapion had surely not volunteered to die. Had he been told that Maximian would be apprehended before he struck the killing blow? Had Fausta herself known? Castus had never trusted the eunuch, or liked him, but as he stared at the corpse on the bed he felt a strange sympathy for him. *I am just as human as you*, Serapion had told him once. *We are both slaves...*

The two Protectores flanking the emperor had moved to seize Maximian and draw him to his feet. He hung between them, limp as a corpse.

'Go to the prisoner's room before dawn,' Hierocles murmured, leaning closer to Castus. 'Make sure he does the honourable thing. If necessary, help him to do it. But he must never see daylight again. Understood?'

'We will do what we are ordered. . .' Castus said, reciting the customary soldier's oath. But the words clogged his mouth and tasted like ash.

A lamp was burning in a niche outside the room. Castus stood for a moment staring at the boards of the door. Then he raised his fist, knocked, and shoved the door open.

Maximian was sitting on the edge of the couch, still wearing his blood-spattered white tunic. The room was dark, and Castus carried the lamp through from outside and set it on the varnished wooden chest beside the door.

'You've come to kill me, then,' the former Augustus said. 'They've sent you to be my executioner.'

Castus wanted to deny it, but he could not. He stood at attention, thumbs hooked into his belt. Maximian was not even looking at him, barely even registering his presence. He looked old and wild, but there was still strength in the man.

'They think you can do it?' he said, his voice rasping and catching. He lifted a hand and tugged at his beard. 'They think you can kill me, the *Man like Hercules*?'

He twisted on the couch, staring at Castus. 'You CANNOT!' he shouted.

'I'm sorry, dominus. I have my orders.'

'I. . . am. . . your. . . *EMPEROR*!'

Then, just as sudden as the burst of rage, the spirit seemed to ebb from Maximian. He sagged on the edge of the couch. 'You know, when I ruled the world,' he said in a musing voice, 'my colleague Diocletian warned me against pride. Only the gods direct our fate, he told me. We ourselves are just pieces in their game. You should remember that. . .'

'Dominus,' Castus managed to say. 'I can give you a sword if you need one.'

'A sword?' Maximian said, staring at him with vacant eyes. 'A sword? Don't insult me. I know what must be done. Leave me alone to do it.'

Turning on his heel, Castus strode from the room and closed the door behind him. In darkness he stood and waited. The light beneath the door shifted, and a short while later something clattered to the floor. Castus stood still, feet braced, hardly daring to breathe. Then he went back into the room.

The body turned slowly in the lamplight, the grey calloused feet hanging bare beneath the hem of the loose tunic, the kicked stool lying on its side beneath. Castus found it hard to look up. When he did he saw the girdle tied tight around the corpse's neck, looped over the roof beam above. The face of his former emperor was already swollen and distorted by death. He stepped outside again, closed the door, and let his forehead drop against the wall.

Constantine was sitting in one of the upper dining chambers, with a brazier of hot coals pulled up beside him. He had his back to the door, and did not move as Castus entered the chamber behind him. Three stamping strides across the floor, and Castus dropped to kneel, facing the emperor's chair.

'Tell the Augustus what you've told us,' Probinus said quietly.

'Most Sacred Augustus!' Castus declared. 'The former emperor Maximian. . . has taken his own life.'

Constantine raised a hand, one finger pointing upwards. 'He has lived,' he said.

The faint cold breeze from the windows stirred the long drapes. Castus could see only the back of the emperor's head, the line of his jaw. Probinus made a sound in his throat, and he saluted quickly and got to his feet again.

'What did he say?' Constantine asked before Castus could retreat. 'When he came to my room, what did he say he wanted?'

Castus glanced at the prefect, who gave a quick nod.

'He said, Augustus, that he'd had a dream. He didn't say what it was.'

In the moonlight from the windows Castus saw a muscle twitching in the emperor's cheek. 'Shame,' Constantine said. He paused for a long moment, warming the palm of his hand over the brazier. 'Most people have dreams,' he said. 'But only the dreams of great men are sent by the gods. Was my father-in-law a great man?'

'He was an emperor,' Castus said quickly. He caught Probinus's warning hiss.

'For months now,' Constantine went on, 'I have been waiting for a sign. A dream, a portent, a vision. . . Anything to tell me that my actions are just, that the gods commend me. Or any god, in fact. I wait for a sign and I receive nothing.'

He raised his hand again, stirring the air with loose fingers. 'You have done well, Protector Aurelius Castus,' he announced in a brisk tone. 'Your loyalty is proven, and you shall be rewarded.'

Then the prefect gestured, and Castus bowed once more and paced backwards out of the room.

* * *

They were smashing the statues of Maximian as the imperial retinue left Arelate. Castus watched the hammers swinging, the painted images shattering to lumps of rubble and dust. It pained him: most of the statues showed Maximian in a filial embrace with his former colleague Diocletian, and Diocletian's images were being destroyed along with them. Surely that was sacrilege, Castus thought. Whatever Maximian himself had done, the great Diocletian was above all criticism, his fame and glory immaculate.

But everything was changing now. Even sacred things could be smashed to ruin. Maximian was dead by his own hand. Constantine was rid of his troublesome father-in-law with all his honour intact, and nobody could say he had acted improperly. Maxentius would declare his dead father to be a god, and the battle lines would be drawn. It all seemed simple now. But Castus remembered what the old emperor had told him before he died. *Just pieces in their game.* He tried not to dwell on these thoughts.

It had been a hurried departure from Arelate. Only two days after the death of Maximian word had come from the army commanders on the Rhine that the Franks had again crossed the river and were plundering the provinces of northern Gaul. Constantine had assembled his force quickly and marched north at once, riding grim-faced and ferocious with his bodyguard around him. By the following morning they had reached Arausio, and the news met them that the Franks had retreated once more. They had fled before the terror of the emperor's name, or so the despatch claimed.

The barbarian threat was gone, but the journey north continued, back towards Treveris. The pace was slower now, allowing the baggage train to catch up with the vanguard, and Fausta and her household had followed with it. Somewhere in that moving column of carriages and wagons, Castus knew, was Sabina. And soon, only a few months from now on the first auspicious day in early spring, they would be married.

Before the sudden departure from Arelate, one of the imperial eunuchs had come to him with a message, which he was pleased to read out. The emperor Flavius Constantinus Augustus – *et cetera et cetera*, the eunuch had said, smiling – is happy to receive the request of the distinguished Aurelius Castus, Ducenarius of Protectores, that he become engaged to the imperial ward Valeria Domitia Sabina, Clarissima.

Castus was baffled at first, then apprehensive. He had not spoken to Sabina herself since that night in the prison cell in Massilia. He had barely seen her. He sensed the knotting of a net of obligation, a snare to drag him deeper into the wiles of the imperial court. But then the joy of it rose through his fears. That night, he had given grateful sacrifice to all the gods.

There was no great ceremony to their betrothal, no banquet or exchange of lavish gifts. In the audience hall of the residency in Arelate they had stood together before Baebius Priscus, the emperor's Quaestor and legal advisor, while a notary drew up a codicil of engagement. Sabina had appeared subdued, her face lowered beneath her veil. She was still in the drab costume of widowhood; the marriage would not be contracted until the official ten-month mourning period for her former husband had elapsed. Once their promises were exchanged and the formalities completed, Castus slipped the iron ring of betrothal onto her finger. He felt crude and coarse, and was aware of his heavy gnarled hands on her soft skin. But then he felt the gentle pressure of her touch, and through the thin gauze of the veil he saw the smile in her eyes. The memory of that smile had warmed him ever since.

Perhaps it had been genuine. Perhaps they would know happiness together. But always the shadow crept at the back of his mind, and he thought he heard a dry rasping voice whispering sly words. I am a simple man, he told himself. I am a soldier. Nobody can ask any more of me than that.

As they travelled north they met the change of season, and the weather turned chill and grey. A few days from Treveris the imperial retinue turned off the main road and branched away to the west. The emperor wished to visit the famous sanctuary of the great god Apollo, to give thanks for the retreat of the Franks and his own recent survival of the plot against his life. It was a cold day, the skies silvery with cloud as the imperial cavalcade passed between low wooded hills. Castus looked around for Brinno; his friend had ridden back down the column an hour before and had not yet returned. There would be a celebration that evening at Apollo's sanctuary. Perhaps – he allowed himself a smile at the thought – Sabina might even consent to set aside her mourning, just for one night, and come to his bed. . .

There was a cry from further along the road. Horses backed and shied as the column pulled to a sudden halt. Hand on his sword hilt, Castus stared at the woods to either side, then forward along the line of march.

'Apollo!' a man shouted. It was Probinus, the prefect. 'The god is with us!'

Castus peered around him, bemused. All along the column men were staring into the sky. Several dismounted and knelt beside the road. Then Castus saw the emperor climbing down from his horse and kneeling beside them.

'The Unconquered Sun!' one of the officials of the retinue cried, and threw up his arms in salute. *Unconquered Sun, Lord of Heaven, Light against Darkness. . .*

Looking into the sky, Castus saw only a bright point of light between the clouds. When he squinted, it seemed to expand and spread. 'What did you see?' he asked the rider beside him.

'A sign from heaven!' the man replied, wide-eyed. 'A blessing upon our emperor. . .'

Twisting in the saddle, Castus stared back down the line of the column. Then a great shout rose from the people behind him, and light flooded suddenly from the sky. The carriages and carts, the horses and riders, the ranks of soldiers were illuminated in a glowing burst of sun.

All of them were shining like gods.

AUTHOR'S NOTE

The strange and dramatic events that led to the death of the former emperor Maximian are described by several ancient sources; characteristically, none of them quite agree on what happened.

The bare facts are clear. Maximian – 'an unnatural parent and a perfidious father-in-law', as the Christian writer Lactantius calls him – rebelled against Constantine and proclaimed himself emperor, probably at Arles (ancient Arelate), but was later defeated or surrendered at Marseille (Massilia). Beyond that, accounts vary and the exact sequence and motivation of events remains cloudy. Perhaps out of confusion, perhaps out of political expediency, our sources often prefer to gloss over many of the details.

In this novel, I've attempted to make the best sense of these conflicting stories, stitching together the shreds of evidence and supposition to create something like a coherent narrative. I've tried to use all the material from the sources wherever possible: an oration given shortly after the event (*Panegyrici Latini VI*) describes Constantine's march south and the subsequent siege of Marseille, for example, but remains deliberately vague about what happened next. We must rely on Lactantius for the story of Maximian's final nocturnal assassination attempt; it might seem far-fetched, but he was resident at the imperial court only

411

a decade after the event, and his information may have come from palace insiders, or from rumours otherwise suppressed.

Almost all of the sources mention Fausta's role in warning Constantine of her father's treachery. Fausta remains one of the most intriguing, and perhaps the most inscrutable, figures in the story. Even her age is the subject of debate, with some historians estimating that she may have been as young as seven or eight when she was married. However, her part in defeating Maximian's schemes suggests, I think, that she was a young adult capable of making her own decisions and not a child, and so I have chosen to accept the more traditional view that she was in her later teens at the time.

Constantine's concubine (or former wife) Minervina disappears from the historical record shortly before his marriage to Fausta. Most scholars have assumed that she died, but I think it not unlikely that Minervina remained in the background and continued to play a part in the emperor's life; Constantine's mother Helena experienced much the same relegation shortly after his birth. Fausta, meanwhile, was dogged by allegations of adultery in later years, although there is no suggestion in our sources of any suspicion at this early date.

The imperial panegyrics provide our only evidence for the campaigns that Constantine conducted against the Frankish Bructeri, and the spectacular public execution of the two barbarians kings in the amphitheatre at Trier. More importantly, at least for later historians, one of these speeches also describes the apparition of the sun god that Constantine allegedly saw in the sky during his march north from Marseille. This vision gained added prominence when it was reinterpreted by Christian writers – Constantine is best known, after all, for seeing things in the sky – but nobody today is quite sure of what it might have been. A mirage, a hallucination, or just a convenient fiction? Perhaps, as A. H. M. Jones first suggested in 1963, it was the light effect known as a solar halo? The caution in my own description perhaps reflects the confusion of observers at the time. . .

Anyone wishing to read more deeply into the tangled events of the period will find a wealth of recent scholarship, although much of it, for obvious reasons, remains somewhat opaque on the matter of Maximian's revolt. Recent titles by David Potter, Raymond Van Dam, Paul Stephenson, Timothy Barnes and Jonathan Bardill offer a rewarding spectrum of opinions.

The imperial court of the early fourth century was, appropriately enough, somewhat Byzantine, although it had yet to acquire the truly baffling complexity that would fully justify that name. Like so much at the time, it was a blend of earlier and later practice. In this novel I have tried to find a middle ground, and avoid too much confusing nomenclature where possible. Christopher Kelly's *Ruling the Later Roman Empire* (2009) provides a good modern study, while Anthony Spawford's *The Court and Court Society in Ancient Monarchies* (2007) has some usefully concise chapters on the subject. What I have called the Corps of Protectores (*schola protectorum*, or *protectores divini lateris* – literally the 'guardians of the sacred flank') developed steadily from a select group of senior officers in the mid third century to something like an officer-training cadre in the mid fourth; my portrayal here is necessarily speculative, but I hope captures something of the feel of the elite bodyguard unit the Protectores appear to have become by the age of Constantine.

H. C. Teitler's *Notarii and Exceptores* (1985) collects what little is known of the organisation and activities of the imperial notaries of the period; they were probably not in reality the sinister inquisitors of popular imagination, but certainly included some unsavoury characters in their ranks.

There is a surprisingly small amount of literature on eunuchs in the ancient world, bearing in mind how influential many of them were to become in the fourth century and later. The methods for 'making' them mentioned by Sallustius in this novel are based on those described in a seventh-century Greek medical treatise by Paul of Aegina.

One of the pleasures of researching this story was the opportunity to visit many of the locations involved. Constantine's great audience hall still stands in Trier (ancient Treveris), and with the massive ruin of the nearby baths gives a good impression of the scale and grandeur of the imperial palace complex that once covered the surrounding area. In France, the great aqueduct of the Pont du Gard is one of the most iconic structures of the Roman age. The ruins of a Gallo-Roman villa lie beneath the nearby chateau of Saint-Privat, but little is known of its date or appearance. The underground *cryptoporticus* of the ancient forum of Arelate can still be visited in modern Arles, although earlier in the Roman era it was probably not the dungeon-like place it appears today.

In the same city, the amphitheatre and parts of the theatre still stand, as do the remains of the fourth-century baths beside the river, and the Musée Départemental Arles Antique displays a fascinating selection of local finds and some very elegant models of the city in its ancient heyday. The Musée d'Histoire de Marseille holds a similar selection of objects from ancient Massilia, and while actual Roman traces in the city are scarce, the Panier district of the old town to the north of the harbour preserves something of the shape of the ancient city. All these sites are fully described in Simon E. Cleary's *The Roman West, AD 200–500: an Archaeological Study* (2013).

Perhaps surprisingly, as this novel largely concerns the activities of the imperial court, I drew much inspiration from

Robert Knapp's *Invisible Romans* (2011), a book about the lives of the ordinary people of the empire: slaves and gladiators, soldiers and prostitutes. Knapp also writes about the role of magic in everyday life; for more about the more supernatural aspects of Roman belief, Georg Luck's *Arcana Mundi: Magic and the Occult in the Greek and Roman Worlds* (2006) provides one of the best surveys.

Writing is often a solitary business, but a finished novel is not a solo production. Once again, I thank my agent, Will Francis, at Janklow & Nesbit, and my editor Rosie de Courcy, together with the rest of the publication team at Head of Zeus, for their invaluable support. My thanks also to Michael King Macdona for his help with Latin translations, to Ross Cowan for the ongoing discussion on late-Roman rank structures, and to Professor Raymond Van Dam for sharing his views on the original name of Flavia Maxima Fausta. Any mistakes and misapprehensions remain my own!

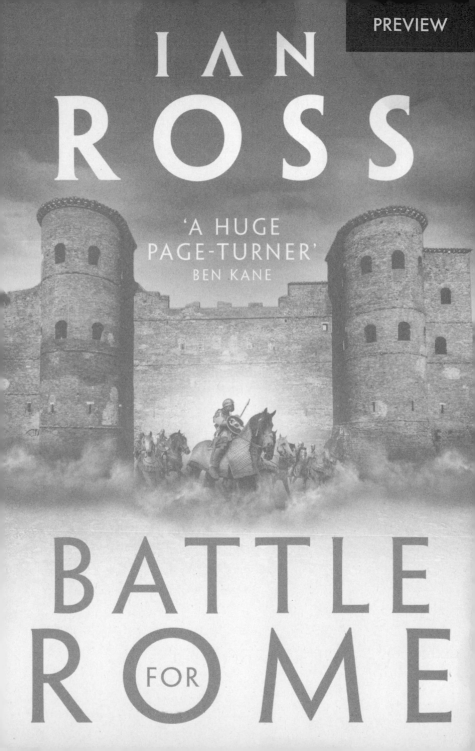

PROLOGUE

Agri Decumates, Germania, December AD *311*

The nine men were riding hard, bursting the silence of the winter forest. All trace of the road was gone, and they navigated only by the pale gleam of the sun through the weave of black branches overhead. Five hours the chase had lasted, and still they did not know who was pursuing them.

Up the slope between the trees, the riders crossed the bare summit of the ridge and plunged down the far side, into a narrower valley thick with dark pines. They had only ridden a short distance when the two remaining guides hauled on their reins and drew to a halt. One of them, the taller man with the red-dyed hair, raised himself in the saddle to peer between the trees, then called back. His breath plumed white in the frigid air.

'They are ahead of us.'

'How is that possible?' the tribune, Ulpianus, said. He had been wounded in the morning attack, speared in the gut with a javelin, and his face was grey from loss of blood.

'The valley goes like this,' the guide told him, sketching a wide arc with his right arm. 'They went around, I think.'

Ulpianus hissed between clenched teeth: 'Find out who they are.'

The two tribesmen slipped from their saddles and began to edge down the hillside. The cries of the pursuit had fallen away now, and the slow silence of the forest was ominous. Pines groaned in the icy breeze.

'Castus,' the tribune said, wincing back over his shoulder. 'To me.'

The rider behind him nudged his mount forward. He was a big man, with a thick neck and the ugly broken profile of a boxer. Like the others, he wore Germanic costume, and he had let his hair and beard grow out in a scrub of yellowish bristles. But the broadsword belted at his side and the gold torque at his collar marked him as a Roman soldier.

'They have us surrounded,' the tribune said. He sat hunched in the saddle, and the linen that bound his stomach was soaked through with blood. His strength was ebbing fast. 'If we have to fight, take the package in my saddlebag and break through. Alone if necessary.'

Aurelius Castus twisted the reins between his fists, exhaled slowly. 'I think we can make it if we stay together,' he said. 'I'm not leaving you, dominus.'

Ulpianus glanced at him. 'As a Protector of the Sacred Bodyguard, you're sworn to obey your commanding officer's every order!' He drew his lips back in a pained smile. 'However, I expected you might say that… We all have our duty.'

'*We will do what we are ordered…*' Castus replied, his throat tightening as he spoke the first words of the traditional soldier's oath.

Turning in the saddle, leather creaking beneath him, he looked back at the surviving members of the group. The attackers had hit their camp in the hour before dawn, howling out of the darkness in a swift raid that had left three men dead and two more wounded. Castus knew that they could all have been slaughtered, half of them in their sleep, but the raiders had only wanted to determine their strength, their identity and their purpose. One of the guides had vanished too, captured or fled.

Two of those that remained – his friend Brinno and another man – were fellow members of the Corps of Protectores. Two more were mounted archers of the Equites Sagittarii: good soldiers, but close to exhaustion, and still shaken after the loss of their comrades. There was the single surviving slave, the tribune, and then the two guides up ahead. All them uncertain and confused.

Castus's hands were numb as they gripped the reins, and his face felt flayed and raw from the cold. A web of aches ran from his thighs up his spine and across his shoulders. The wind breathed ice across the back of his neck, and he tried not to shudder.

Six days had passed since they had left the imperial court at Treveris. Their mission was simple enough: they were to carry a sealed package to the court of the emperor Licinius, who ruled on the Danube. Only the tribune knew what the package contained, but whatever it was must be valuable to warrant sending such a strong despatch party through barbarian country in the dead of winter. In times of peace, they could have travelled south, around the headwaters of the Rhine and up through the province of Raetia. But the governor of upper Raetia had declared his allegiance to the usurper Maxentius, controller of Italy; now Maxentian patrols ranged freely through that territory. Whatever the dangers of the barbarians, the risk of the package falling into the hands of the usurper's men was far greater.

Castus eased back in his saddle, flexing his spine and his shoulders. He gazed at the forested hillsides around him. This wilderness between the Rhine and the Danube had once been part of the Roman Empire: the Agri Decumates, it was called.

Fifty years ago there had been farms in these valleys, roads and towns, settled villas. For the last three days Castus and his party had been following the line of the old fortifications, the overgrown ditch and collapsing palisades that had once marked the edge of civilisation, now just a dead-straight scar across a wild landscape.

This was Alamannic country, but the Alamanni were bound by treaties with Rome. Either their attackers that morning had decided to ignore the treaties, Castus thought, or they too were intruders in this land, and had no treaties to break.

He looked down the slope and saw the two guides clambering back up between the trees, returning from their brief reconnaissance.

'They wait for us, down in the valley,' the red-haired one said. 'They want to talk, looks like.'

'Who are they?' the tribune demanded.

'Burgundii,' said the other guide, and spat.

The guides were each from a different Alamannic tribe; the idea was, Castus supposed, that they distrusted each other more than they disliked Romans. With any luck, he thought, they hated the Burgundii even more.

'Castus,' Ulpianus said quietly. 'You and Brinno go down there with the guides. Find out everything you can.'

And make sure the guides don't betray us, Castus thought as he shook his reins.

They moved through the trees, leaning back in their saddles as the horses picked their way downhill into the valley. Castus was not a good horseman at the best of times; his mount was big, powerful, but it was also ill tempered and had a heavy gait. Ahead of him, Castus could see the two guides talking. They too seemed in a bad mood.

'What are they saying?' he asked Brinno, who rode just behind him. Brinno was a younger man than Castus, lean and sinewy; he was Frankish himself, a chieftain's son born in the barbarian lands near the mouth of the Rhine, but had lived in Treveris these last twelve years. The language of the Franks and the Alamanni was similar enough.

'The dark one wants to sell us to the Burgundii, I think,' Brinno said.

'And our red-haired friend?'

Brinno grinned, showing the gaps in his broken teeth. 'He wants to wait. Maybe we meet somebody who will pay better!'

Castus felt a knot of tension slip in his chest. Brinno was a good man to have at his side. They had trained together, and stood side by side in battle before. He trusted the young Frank as much as he had ever trusted another man. As much as he had ever trusted anybody.

The slope levelled, and they rode slowly out from the cover of the trees onto the open valley floor. A shallow stream flowed wide over a shingle bed, the water glinting with ice between the rocks. The air was so cold down here it hurt to breathe. Almost too cold for fear; Castus just wanted this to be over, and soon. He could see the moon, a perfect white half-circle low above the treetops; only an hour or two of daylight remained.

On the level ground at the far side of the stream the Burgundii were waiting. Four of them, sitting with careful idleness on their shaggy little horses. Castus glanced quickly right and left. As many again on either side, just within the trees. Beyond them the valley narrowed, with high spurs of rock showing between the pines. A bottleneck. He realised that their pursuers had been herding them to this exact spot. Reaching beneath his cloak, he tugged at his sword hilt, freeing the blade from the cold lock of the scabbard mouth.

Leaning forward over his saddle horns, Castus surveyed the enemy riders. They wore capes of animal pelts, and each man had a wolf's tail hanging from his shield. One had a red tunic, and his hair hung in neat braids – the chief, Castus guessed – but the others looked rough-edged and thick-bearded after many days of hard living. Their weapons were clean enough though, spears and broadswords, and the men had the look of fighters.

The two guides were talking, the Burgundii answering them in curt dismissive phrases. Castus heard Brinno sniff in disgust.

'How many do you count?' he said quietly, barely moving his lips.

'Four right there, four more up the slopes on each side,' Brinno replied.

Castus nodded. 'Twelve, and nine of us. Not bad odds.'

'You include the guides?'

'All right, seven of us.'

'One a wounded man who can hardly sit on a horse?'

'Six, then.'

'One a slave?'

'So, *five*... What are you saying?'

Brinno gave a slow shrug and widened his eyes. 'Nothing, brother. Only... if we go at them we have to go *hard*.'